D0786841

*by Barbara Rex*
Vacancy on India Street
Saints and Innocents
I Want to Be in Love Again
Ugly Girl

# Ugly Girl

# Ugly Girl

## Girl

### by Barbara Rex

W. W. Norton & Company
New York          London

Published simultaneously in Canada by George J. McLeod Limited, Toronto.

Printed in the United States of America.

Library of Congress Cataloging in Publication Data

Rex, Barbara.
  Ugly girl.

  I. Title.
PS3568.E8U33   1982      813'.54      81–22372
                                      AACR2

W. W. Norton & Company, Inc. 500 Fifth Avenue, New York, N.Y. 10110
W. W. Norton & Company Ltd. 37 Great Russell Street, London WC1B 3NU

1 2 3 4 5 6 7 8 9 0

ISBN 0-393-01582-3

*For*
*Louise Weyl Kirschbaum*
*with love and gratitude.*

# Ugly Girl

# Prelude

*Mr. and Mrs. Frederick Severn are seated in the breakfast room of their summer camp on Upper St. Regis Lake in the Adirondacks. The time is 1919.*

*Frederick Severn is tall, thin, still erect although in his middle seventies, with an impressive graying mustache which hangs, perfectly tended, to his chin. He has a long, rather austere esthetic face with small, very bright black eyes. His smile is wonderfully attractive and gay, also kind. Once well-known as an anthropologist, he is at present writing his fourth volume on the Western Indians. Anna Severn (neé Anna Cary, an eighteenth-century Philadelphia family) is blue-eyed, slender with thick white hair, of which she is exceedingly proud, and wears drawn back in a low knot. Five flat white curls are immaculately twisted onto her forehead. She is not a tall woman. Her manner is serious, even stern, her smile "gracious," except to her husband upon whom she smiles freely and often merrily. He is two years younger than she, a matter of concern to Anna.*

*Both Anna and Frederick Severn hold firmly to tradition and pride of family. Lord Frederick Severn (1566–1603) is said to have stood guard at Queen Elizabeth's door the night Lord Essex ran through the streets of London with a naked sword in his hand.*

*Anna has just finished reading aloud a poem she composed. The State of Pennsylvania recently declared her Poet Laureate, and she is immensely proud of the title. Although her poems speak mostly about nature and the sweet song of birds, there is nothing foolish about them nor sentimental. Mrs. Severn and her husband are talking about their ward, Eva:*

"*I never saw her uglier than she was this morning!*" *Anna Severn cries.* "*In that middy blouse and old khaki skirt and her hair straggling any which way . . . I couldn't look at her.*" *Anna twists a handkerchief in her hands. She and Frederick are seated on a low bench by the windows of the room, now filled with sunshine. Outside the windows is a magnificent stand of Norway pines. The ground is carpeted with pine needles. A faint whirr sounds as the wind brushes the trees. A very blue lake can be seen, and a curving shore line edges a thick forest. Far off a boathouse with a white railing is visible.*

*Frederick Severn folds the* Adirondack Times *into proper order. He is impatient to start work, but will not leave Anna while she is distressed, which happens more frequently now that Eva is growing up.*

"*When I was fifteen I knew how to dress. Eva seems to have no feeling for clothes.*" *Anna's blue eyes open wide, astonished.*

"*Does she have much choice?*" *Frederick asks. He puts* The Times *down neatly beside him.*

"*No, I suppose not.*"

*They are both admirably detached. They provide shelter, meals, clothing—when the chambermaid, Fanny, brings it to their attention—and music lessons, for Eva plays the violin. They owe the girl nothing, as they often remind themselves.*

"*She's had every advantage.*" *This has been said so often it falls into silence. No Severn, no Cary has ever been ugly. (To be unattractive seems almost a breach of taste.) Here is a girl with a large nose, long jaw, small eyes, bunchy mouth, straight limp black hair. . . . Fortunately her ankles are thin and her teeth straight. She has a slatlike body, unformed for her age. Eva constantly creates problems for Anna; in fact she is a problem. What are they to do with her?*

"*In a way Eva rather appeals to me, she seems so defenseless,*" *Frederick says, somewhat naughtily, knowing Anna's reaction. But his good humor is fading, for he is being kept from work on his Indians. He sees no point in their conversation, which they have all too frequently.*

"*Oh pooh, Frederick! She has no appeal.*" *Anna shoves her handkerchief, a paper one, down the V of her dress.*

"*She has nice manners. You've taught her, my dear.*" *He smiles rather*

( 10

*carefully at Anna.*

*"Well, yes. But she never was a biddable child. Fanny's had most of the managing."*

*As the conversation shows no sign of abating, Frederick decides to bring up an issue that bothers him. "Are you still set on this debutante business for Eva, my dear?"*

*Anna turns on him. "But it's all planned! We're giving a tea. The date has been down at Dreka's for ages." Anna and Frederick Severn live in Philadelphia during the winter, and Dreka's is the name of a stationer on Chestnut Street who for years has kept the one and only social calendar of debutante events. To be "down in Dreka's" assures the date for whatever function is to be given.*

*"I keep thinking of the Shanker girl," Frederick speaks gravely.*

*"Now really, Frederick! That has nothing to do with Eva."*

*Frederick answers harshly, for some reason driven by a fear that has lately fallen upon him. "Ida Shanker was a fat, unappealing girl who was forced by her father to 'come out.' She and her mother went to large parties together, sometimes sitting side by side on chairs. No one asked Ida to dance. Quite understandably, the girl became despondent and did away with herself. The reason I mention this," Frederick hurries on as he sees Anna preparing to interrupt him, "is because the psychological effect of being shunned by one's group—for instance in flocks of Canada geese—can indeed cause death. It is also my understanding that Mrs. Shanker still attends large parties, sitting and acting in much the same way as she did with her daughter."*

*"Well, one can't not ask her," Anna says, annoyed that such an unappealing and bothersome subject should be introduced.*

*There are times when Anna does not understand Frederick and when she suspects that those long lonely hours in the wickiups of the Shawnees have made him "different," perhaps even altered his values. Canada geese! (People said that poor Mrs. Shanker is off her head and sits talking as though Ida were right beside her.)*

*Frederick Severn has seldom taken an active part in Eva's upbringing, but once started he feels driven. "Eva might consider going to college." He pauses.*

*Anna says sharply, "We've done enough for Eva, Frederick. A small tea and a few dresses will cost far less than four years at college. And what is to become of Eva? She plays the violin rather nicely, but shows no great flair, just a pleasant talent." Anna looks around defiantly at her husband. "The solution for Eva is marriage. We will subject her to as many young men as possible, which is the reason for 'coming out,' as everyone knows. Surely one of them will take her. She is not without spirit."*

*The barb that has entered Frederick's conscience and forced him to speak, has done its work. The situation is really out of his hands. At least he has made his feelings known.*

*"David will look out for her." He senses immediate relief. David, his grandson, who lives with them, has always looked after Eva.*

*"David will be at Yale," Anna replies sharply. The idea of Eva's depending on David is intolerable.*

*"Back for the holidays," Frederick says naughtily. He sees Anna's color rise again and is pleased. He likes her animated. "Well, I must get to work," Frederick says, rising. He leans to kiss Anna. "Today I'm beginning on the battle for the Ohio Valley. I'm going to talk about Alexander McKee, the Shawnees' great friend." He knows he is speaking to empty air and doubts Anna has read any of his books. But it does not trouble him. He is a man of great determination, and—when younger—deep passion. He knows the Ohio Valley and has stood on many of its battlegrounds. A large portion of his life has been spent alone, on the plains of southwestern America, or earlier, in Peruvian swamps in search of Incan traces. As an anthropologist he is somewhat isolated from the usual run of Severn men, most of whom are either bankers or lawyers. He had married late and finds life with Anna extraordinarily satisfying. He has slipped into the old Philadelphia customs easily, almost as though the great Western distances, the brown craggy mountains had been the strange part of his life. In spite of his age he has a feeling of freshness which often takes an unexpected turn, like his attitude toward Eva, although he has no intention of assuming responsibility for her. His son Frederick once confided in him that Eva's mother had trapped him into marriage by the old "I'm pregnant" ploy. But Frederick Senior is kindly, and Eva's plight appeals to him, if only momentarily. Mainly his mind is fixed on the work he has laid out for today.*

*Anna gets swiftly to her feet. As Frederick opens the door she tells him that Eva is rowing over to Spitfire Lake to try to find the Framely girl. "The Framelys bought the old Frick camp that was falling to pieces."*

*"Ah, yes," Frederick says, closing the door behind him.*

*Left alone, Anna moves toward the breakfast table which is set at one end of the round room near the fireplace. She picks up a pint bottle from which she has carefully ladled cream by the spoonful during breakfast. Her family, the Carys, were well born but hard pressed for money and Anna is still given to little unnecessary economies.*

1 The recent nation-wide publicity about my husband Newlin Slatter (known as "The Master") and his relationship to me has proved so inaccurate, even false, that I am compelled to tell what actually happened, even though the account will be very personal and revealing, full of what Mama and Papa, my guardians Mr. and Mrs. Frederick Severn, would call "unnecessarily intimate details." These details will have to stand for I certainly do not want to give a lopsided, pared down account with half of what really happened left out. And anyway I have always been highly charged and cannot be expected to set down a few cool facts.

It is necessary to understand the early period of my life because my inexperience, naiveté, even *carelessness* are shown so vividly. And also I want to disprove completely the charge made by a certain reporter that I was "brought up in the lap of luxury," a "spoiled darling of the rich." This last charge is laughable. I was raised parsimoniously. No one could have yearned more passionately for a simple, unadorned life.

The catalyst for much that happened to all of us was Joyce Framely. I met her quite innocently. She was sitting on a rock in the middle of Spitfire Lake in the Adirondacks that first time I saw her. The date: July 10th, 1919, and I was fifteen.

She did not look like a catalyst in her black taffeta bathing suit and black stockings rolled below her knees, but she changed all our lives and she was even mixed up in the tragedy that descended upon me.

Her appearance that day struck me forcibly. Thick yellow hair rippled down her back, she had huge grayish eyes, a flawless skin, full cheeks, a cupid-bow mouth, unsmiling. Her manner was calm, self-possessed (calculating, if I had only been old enough to realize). She simply stared at me as I backed water in my rowboat.

Usually I avoided pretty girls. This one was beautiful, and for some reason drew me to her. She was just a touch overweight, I noticed. (I was "thin as a rail," according to Mama). She also had the most unfortunate "fronts"—as they were called—large and sticking out when every girl longed to be flat-chested.

In spite of her beauty and her "fronts" she fascinated me. The girls I knew giggled, or threw themselves about. This one seemed wholly poised, regarding me with interest. A new experience for me. I shipped oars and drifted toward the rock.

"Hello," I said rather carefully, reaching out to grab a tuft of grass growing from a crack, "I'm Eva Colby and I live at the Severn Camp."

She wasn't exactly smiling; she looked amused. Not amused at me, although I did have on my old khaki skirt and middy blouse. I must have looked about twelve. Meeting anyone for the first time makes me conscious of my really stringy black hair and long jaw, biggish nose, and of what Mama calls an "unformed" mouth. I try not to think of these drawbacks all the time, and surprisingly I could sense right away that they didn't mean a thing to this girl on the rock.

She said: "You live in the camp with the barn, don't you?"

"Well, it's not a barn *now*," I said. "It's a living room."

"Your grandmother is Anna Severn, the poetess." She seemed given to abrupt statements.

I did not stop to explain what my relationship was to "Mama"—as both my stepbrother David and I call her (with the accent on the last syllable). This girl wasn't exactly nosey, she just seemed interested, as though *I* were interesting. She wasn't thrown off by my looks, nor was I by hers, although usually a girl with a face like hers can put a kind of blackness over me.

"I'm Joyce Framely," she said, gathering up her hair onto the top of her head. She had the tiniest wrists I ever saw and small hands. She seemed perfectly oblivious of either her pluses or her minuses, because raising her arms revealed more of her unfortunate breasts. But she went right on, picking up the bone hairpins lying on the rock and fixing her hair.

"Would you like to see our camp?" she asked as she pulled on a brown rubber bathing cap. I said yes, and she started sliding off the rock, revealing very white, rather fat thighs.

Joyce was a poor swimmer, for she simply flopped into the lake and did a kind of breast stroke toward shore, white arms tumbling the water before her. Having had David spend hours teaching me to crawl, I was amused at this exhibition.

Everyone on St. Regis Lake (which was right alongside Spitfire Lake, and joined by a little waterway called a slough) wanted to know about the Framelys. They had bought the old Frick camp, in bad repair. Mama told Papa that although the Framelys came from Philadelphia, they were "no one we know." This usually ended the matter, but now all the "campers"—as they call themselves—were so glad to have someone buy the Frick place who were not "undesirables"—that they eagerly speculated about the Framelys. (David says the campers are so bigoted he won't go near the place.)

I was mad with curiosity about the Framely camp because everyone said that the Framelys were spending enormous sums of money fixing it up. I had no sooner tied my boat to a cleat on the dock than I realized this rumor was false. The Framelys seemed to have done nothing at all. The docks sagged into the water. There was a small boathouse with the roof falling off. As Joyce led the way up the path I saw the main house, a hideous two-storied affair, painted a kind of puce with green trim and a green asbestos roof. All the other camps around the lakes were built "simply" of polished logs, with lovely casement windows. Pebbled paths ran from cabin to cabin. There were flower boxes of blooming plants—usually petunias and geraniums—everything was unostentatious and expensive. At our camp, Mama even fussed about the arrangement of the pine needles. And the "barn," as Joyce called it, had been brought piecemeal from Connecticut because Papa admired the beautiful narrow gray boards dotted with lichen. Inside, the room always smelled of mildew, but Mama felt very proud of the barn, and it was there that she gave her poetry readings and I practiced my violin.

All the "campers" made a particular effort to maintain what they call the "spirit" of the place, "the simplicity." There were three small lakes and no roads into the camps; everyone had to come by private boat. (Later, a reporter said that this isolated enclave held the richest, most socially prominent people in the country, perhaps in the world.) It's true that the Vanderbilts brought over workmen from Japan to build their camp. The effect, Mama said, was in good taste and not at all ostentatious, the houses being green and white with little cupolas and spires that I thought adorable. Of course there was Mrs. Whitelaw Reid, whom everyone made a great fuss over, according to Mama. And the Ogden Reids, who ran some sort of newspaper, and various other people from New York like the Denbys and the Wainwrights. Then there was Mrs. Hutton, at the end of St. Regis Lake, who bought the old Marvin camp. She was the only camper who did not hold with the unwritten rules and was rumored to be having electricity installed. To the campers this was heresy and David said it broke the spirit of self-reliance so necessary to the rich and well-born. And Mama said that one of the charms of camp were the lanterns and the kerosene lamps. But Mrs. Hutton did not give a fig for "spirit" and was even rumored to be contemplating a new-fangled escalator or elevator that would waft guests from the lake to the main cabin, some distance upward, for her camp sat almost as high as ours. Mrs. Hutton was a Post of Post Toasties and played golf in a harem veil. She had been divorced and the campers felt she was to be avoided. "No one," according to Mama, "calls." (This threat of electricity occurred long before Mrs. Hutton became Mrs. Merryweather Post and had the Arthur Murray dancers flown in from New York one week and movies flown in the next and became madly popular with the campers.)

The setting of the lakes was thought to be idyllic. St. Regis mountain rose seemingly right out of its own lake high into the air. Even the less wealthy, of whom there were one or two, had a feeling of belonging. The men all joined the St. Regis Yacht Club and in the evening wore green coats (in place of tuxedos, but not "tails") made for them by Brooks Brothers. There were sailboat races for "Idems" only, and although gusts of wind blew fitfully on St. Regis Lake this only added to the sportiness. People entertained, sometimes quite formally. It took a team of servitors to run the camps, which had separate cabins, motorboats, as well as the sailboats. Paths must be raked and weeded, wicks trimmed, lanterns hung....The guides were considered "characters," most of them having lived in the region all their lives. Each camp had a head guide, usually with others under him. He was responsible for taking campers and their guests over the Seven-Carries and hoisted the beautiful rowboats (perhaps made by himself) through the woods on a special yoke, passing by small lakes where a bear's footprint had once been seen. Loons and ducks clattered from the ponds and many times deer leaped away. The Seven-Carries ended near Saranac Lake Inn, always a letdown, because total strangers rocked in chairs on the porch.

Although the Framely girl had not said much about herself, I knew about her family. Her father was a very successful broker, newly-rich, an unfortunate, pushy type, given to calling out "Hello, McAlpin" at The Landing (where the campers kept their cars and received their mail) after having only shaken hands with Mr. McAlpin once when their mail became mixed up. Mrs. Framely was rumored to be "sweet." Mama told Papa no one knew whether to call or not, but she thought she might.

The Framely camp, as I looked around, was a disaster. Besides the puce-colored house, there were three rickety platforms, on which spotted, mildewed tents had been erected. No raked paths led about; instead green-slatted boardwalks shot off in all directions. The woods were not properly cleared and dead firs stood here and there, unforgivable negligence to any camper. There were also red print curtains at the windows of the main cabin. They would simply be considered vulgar. Campers did not need curtains. They counted on complete privacy; they paid for isolation, privilege for the few born to it.

As I gazed about, and Joyce stood dripping on the boardwalk, a man came out of the main house. He was short and fat with gray hair, a thick moustache, and was frowning heavily. He wore light tan plus-fours and a rather loud, striped tie. He was smoking a cigar. "Hello, Joyce," he said, as though seeing her for the first time. His face cleared. "Who's your friend?"

Joyce introduced us, standing quite poised in her wet suit. To my surprise, Mr. Framely advanced, took the cigar out of his mouth and shook my hand. I curtsied awkwardly, for I was unused to such attention. Like Joyce he simply seemed to accept me.

"W-e-l-l," Mr. Framely said, putting his cigar back in his mouth and taking a puff, "what are you two young ladies up to?"

No one had ever called me a young lady before. But Joyce answered right back.

"We're taking out the *Katydid*."

"Watch yourself," Mr. Framely said, his face darkening, his good humor evaporated in an instant. "She's the only boat that runs in the whole damned place." And he struck off down the slatted walk towards the dock.

His change of mood was startling. When Papa disapproved of anything he went no further than to say, "I hardly think, my dear," etc. Wasn't Mr. Framely happy here? Should we take the boat in the face of his disapproval? And how was it possible Joyce could run a motorboat, anyway? Only Gordon was allowed to touch our launch. However, Joyce paid no attention, simply walked toward one of the tents. I followed as she climbed the steps of the platform. Even mildewed, the tent was heavenly, light and airy. I felt immediately part of the woods. Imagine sleeping outside, hearing an owl close by and all the night sounds! Open at the front and sides, the spotted canvas roof seemed winglike. At the back was a small room where Joyce dressed.

"I won't be a moment," she said. "Take a pew."

Being called a young lady by Mr. Framely and being asked to take a pew was all so totally new I felt a different person, of some importance. Joyce was treating me as an equal. Yet Joyce was beautiful. Beautiful girls usually ignored or made a fuss over me because of David.

I sat down slowly in a white wicker rocking chair. The only other furniture was a white bureau. My own room at camp was small and rather gloomy, but I had a kerosene lamp by my bed so I could read until Mr. Jaffrey, Mama's accompanist, called from his cabin—"douse the glim, kid."

"We'll take my boat, the *Katydid*," Joyce said from the back room. "It'll be fun."

"Are you allowed?" I could hardly believe her, after Mr. Framely's reaction.

"Of course. She's mine. Pop gave her to me by mistake. He thought the other two boats would run—but they're busted. He's half wild most of the time and wishes he'd never bought the camp. The only way he can get to the golf club is by water. He and Mother don't know anyone. They're both miserable.

This frankness was almost shocking. I waited a moment and then asked rather boldly, "What about you?"

"It's OK." She swung open the door of the little room and walked into the tent. I nearly gasped. She had really huge fronts. And she wore a kind of net brassiere so you could see everything. She was the most unselfconscious girl I had ever met. Of course I looked away as she pulled a blouse on over her head. "There aren't any boys around," she said, starting to button her skirt. "There's Snooty Canby—I call him 'Snooty' because he won't speak to me. He lives in the next cove and takes his boat out every day. That's why

I was on the rock. I thought he might stop." This seeming frankness, I was to learn, was typical of Joyce. I also found out she never told you the whole story, there was always some sly bit left out. For instance, we could have taken poor Mr. Framely over to his golf club. He must have expected to play; he was dressed for it. But Joyce never offered, and I suppose he was too proud to ask. So his day was spoiled for our silly pleasure.

She said, standing by the bureau, "You've got a brother, haven't you?"

"He's counselor at a boy's camp," I said. I did not want to talk about David.

Oh." She turned toward the mirror, started brushing her hair. Not exactly cooling off, but I fancied no longer so eager. I was quite used to this: girls "cultivated" me on account of David. But even so, I had an advantage of some kind in the Framely camp. I felt it, maybe because I was one of the campers, or perhaps because of Mama and Papa. Anyway, I meant to keep it and not turn back into the shy kid who had shipped oars while approaching the rock a moment ago out in the lake.

2    In quite a casual voice, I said, "I'm an orphan, you know." As soon as the words were out they sent a snock through me. I had never made this announcement before and saying the words seemed to worsen my situation.

Joyce turned right around, hairbrush in hand.

"An *orphan*? I've never known an orphan!" She stared at me, face flushed, as though a strange furry animal had come to sit in her rocking chair.

The effect on her and on me was unexpected. I had taken the

wrong way to try and maintain my position, for now I felt pitiable; worse, alien. So in order to lighten the situation, mostly for myself, I said, "David's not my real brother, he's a stepbrother." Then, with more spirit, "Mama and Papa aren't my real grandparents, either. They took me into the family out of the goodness of their hearts." I could hear the falseness in my voice. I was quoting David. He constantly reminded me of the day he and I walked into Mama's and Papa's house on DeLancey Place when I was only six and we were orphans. And how we were no sooner in the house than Mama had drawn David aside and told him that she and Papa were not going to keep me. She meant, take me into the family. I was going into a "very nice home" for orphans. Right then David said that if I went to a "home" he would go too. This story I can recite word for word because David is always reminding me, particularly if he wants a favor, or if Mama punishes me unfairly or is cold and unkind. "Rather be in a 'home?'" he'll say, raising one eyebrow in that new way he's practicing.

"David's your stepbrother?" Joyce was still staring at me.

"Both his father and my mother were married before," I said.

"Then your father died and so did David's mother. And his father and your mother were killed. I never heard such a story!"

I'd never told it in such a way. Her heartlessness made me silent. I had a feeling of exposure not experienced before. Of course all the girls in school knew I was an orphan, but no one ever spoke about it. I had an adorable picture of my mother with dark, curly hair and round brown eyes. My father had a long jaw, straight hair, large nose and squinty but intelligent black eyes. I once looked up "ugly" in Papa's big dictionary. "Offensive to sight," it said, and I slammed the book shut. I cannot believe I am offensive, but I know my appearance has added a certain fierceness to my character.

"Are any of you related at all?" Joyce asked as though amused.

"David is the grandson," I said stiffly. She apparently gave little thought to my feelings.

"Where's he go to college?" She turned back to the mirror.

( 23

"He's going to Yale. I'm at Miss Irwin's which is just down DeLancey Street in Philadelphia where we live in the winter."

"Really?" Joyce finished pinning up her hair, then turned to me. I must say with her frilly blouse and hair fixed in some complicated fashion she was very pretty and looked about nineteen.

"I hear David's terrific-looking." She gave a little confident smile.

"He's all right," I said. David was handsome as a god, blond, too. But I wasn't going to tell this to Joyce. Instead I told her he played on the football team, was crazy about track, and took swimming seriously. "You're no place with David if you can't swim." This didn't phase her.

"You're lucky to have a brother," Joyce said. "Being an only child is simply lousy." She disappeared into the back room.

Already she was thinking of David as my real brother. For that matter, David had convinced himself that I was his real sister. Which of course was the reason he could live in such close proximity and look after me. David and I swam together late at night when he was in camp. A defiant gesture. We swam naked. He had seen my bare back, my buttocks, even my breasts. As far as I knew, they meant nothing to him, or so he persuaded himself. He treated me like another boy, not waiting until I was ready to get out of the water; he got out when he chose, tying a towel around himself and beating it for the shack. I could find my way in the dark. Afterwards, when we huddled in blankets, we huddled separately.

David believed I was a complete innocent, which came close to the truth, but might also be responsible for the way he set himself so firmly. It might be that but for me David would not have created what I called his "island," his inviolate spot, a place where he was most himself, quite alone, and where no one touched. At this time he wouldn't tolerate being spoken to and shut himself in his room. David's need for isolation spread wide and deep, necessary to him.

Speaking of David's father made me think about him. A big,

powerful, attractive man with heavy hair and a thick moustache. I had not known him long. David adored his father. Then suddenly he was killed. So no doubt David felt an even more overpowering need to build inwardly for himself, where there was no risk of being hurt, and where he stood, a man.

I do not mean to imply that David was unsociable or strange. He never seemed like anyone else, but even so he was popular, as though other boys knew and admired his difference. Girls were silly about David, always asking me stupid questions and then giggling. He teased girls in his own special way; I'm sure he kissed them, although he never told. On the other hand he was prudish about me and said I was never even to let a boy hold my hand.

I had absolutely no premonition of David's savagery, which I was to experience later. I had seen his eyes glitter, noticed his uncaring smile. Of course I had felt the lash of his tongue. In teaching me to dance he would not let me rest. "You've got to build up endurance!" he'd cry, and put the record "Aint Misbehavin'" on again. I still can't hear that tune without feeling my legs ache.

I suppose David and I had a remarkable childhood. Sitting in Joyce's airy tent, I thought quite solemnly that there had never been a time when David had not known my need. He knew or sensed at an early age that he was the only one I could love. Because I had no real memory of my mother and never knew my father I sometimes could not endure the feeling of *no one*, and I would run to David, usually late at night, and get right into bed with him. He'd just grunt. But at least it was a body. When I got to be about fourteen David would not allow me inside the covers, but made me sit wrapped in a quilt at the foot of the bed and let me talk or cry. Very often he went to sleep, but I kept right on talking and usually crying, too.

I do not mean to underrate my gratitude for being given a home. At Mama's age it must have been difficult to bring up a child, and then not to have her pretty...with little charm of manner and feminine submissiveness. I played the violin and occasionally Mama listened to a new piece I was studying, but seldom commented. Papa, although kind, focused his attention either on Mama or his Indian book. Fanny, the housemaid, often saved me, for she let me sit on her lap and although she would tell me I was a "silly-boots," still she listened. I persuaded Miss Craven, my music teacher, to teach me an Irish jig. Then I brought my violin to Fanny's room and she actually jumped to her feet and jigged around the room, laughing.

How did people learn charm? Or was it necessary to be beautiful? David utterly charmed Mama. When he was only twelve and she reprimanded him he would stand looking straight at her and then say he was sorry, that he hadn't realized, that he wouldn't do it again. And she would throw her arms about him, sometimes in tears, as though she were at fault. Odd that I wasn't jealous. David never failed to come tell me he had made "everything" all right with Mama. "You've got to play it her way, Eva. You've got to learn how." But very little I did ever convinced Mama. She so seldom looked at me. She would look at my shoulder, or my collar, but almost never at my face.

When I once told David this he became livid. He reminded me of the "home" again. Asked why I didn't realize how lucky I was going to a private school like Miss Irwin's. How typical of me to feel sorry for myself. David knew I adored him; in return I thought he tolerated me. But later, when that changed, then the whole world became strange and bitterly sharp, and I nearly perished.

Being Severns, Mama and Papa (and of course David, too) were Eighteenth-Century Philadelphians. Mama and Papa were great snobs, quite unconsciously. They only knew one kind of world. They saw the same people over and over. In the summer it was the Whitelaw Reids and the Vanderbilts and the Denbys, etc.; in the winter it was the Biddles, the Scotts, and the Ingersolls. Our house on DeLancey Place was high-ceilinged and had a formal front parlor with a pale blue rug and Mama's grand piano. Glass cabinets stood here and there filled with china objects. There was a vast mirror edged in scrolled gilt along one wall. Next to the living room came the dining room with a big, mahogany table and Hepplewhite chairs. The house was rather dark and had an air of emptiness, and yet the pale rug and low, blue-upholstered chairs, the vast mirror, piano, and fine black marble fireplace were all very handsome and rich-looking. I don't know that we were rich, because our meals were quite meager, but we never wanted for anything.

Mama was an intensely feminine woman, attractive even though white-haired and, to me, very old. She was proud of her slimness. In the evening, going to the opera, in her v-necked purple velvet with the diamond necklace, she was beautiful, and almost timeless.

David said no one wore "tails" the way Papa did, for he was tall, his figure spare and upright, his thin graying hair fluffed a little at the ends and his long moustache trimmed neatly. Papa had been quite famous as an anthropologist, worked in Peru with Julio Tello, whom he admired intensely. Papa had written three books. They stood in his study, bound in red. Papa did not often speak directly to me, or ask me a question. "School go all right?" was as close as he came. But I knew he was kind. When I was eight he had given me Prescott's *History of Mexico* to read, and when I told him regretfully that I could not understand it, he rather lost interest in my education.

Mama was so strict and proper that no one would even have guessed her past. I should never have known what happened if David had not told me. It seems that she was brought up strictly, watched over carefully. For although her family did not have much money, no name was more venerated in Philadelphia society than Cary. Mama had a happy girlhood, protected and loved, an only child. Then at sixteen, one day as she was going through the Academy of Fine Arts galleries she bumped (quite literally for they both were hurrying through a doorway) into Cecil Komitow, a student at the Academy. Mademoiselle—happening to be in another part of the exhibit—was not there to prevent the encounter, so young Anna

Cary and Cecil Komitow walked happily around the Hobbema collection, while he pointed out certain aspects of the paintings which she never would have noticed. The next day, aware that she was deceiving her family and gravely misbehaving, but intent, (for there is a deeply stubborn streak in Mama) she met Cecil Komitow again, getting rid of Mademoiselle by some strategy. This went on for a week. And at the end of that week Mama simply went off with Cecil Komitow. She lied about her age. They were married in Maryland.

When David told me this I could scarcely grasp what he said. Because Mama, in one of our rare conversations, had told me about her childhood, how happy she had been, how she loved her life, everything so ordered and in place. Never a word about her previous marriage. David said it was a fiasco. Cecil turned out to be coarse and a bad painter. Mama hardly allowed him to come near her, as David carefully put it. She longed to return to her safe girlhood. In disgust, Cecil left her, signed on a ship, a whaler, and was drowned off Tierra del Fuego. Mama returned home to complete forgiveness. The queer thing was, David said, that literally no one knew. Mademoiselle had been discharged before Mama ran away. The Carys told everyone that Mama was in Egypt with friends. As Mama only stayed with Cecil a matter of months, the entire deception succeeded. Mama had told David in deepest secrecy.

"She has a habit," David said, "of putting unpleasantnesses, as she calls them, into boxes, or slots. Like those food compartments at Horn and Hardart. She slams the little door. She can look in and see what's there, but does not have to touch. I bet there are things about Papa she can't stand. She hates hearing about the Shawnees. She puts all his work, and even the books, into those same compartments." I had an instant's vision of Mama standing alone on the tiled floor of the automat with all the little doors gleaming at her.

"I should think being so wrong about Mr. Komitow would make her more understanding," I said. "She's so impatient!"

"Not at all," David said. "She has no tolerance of what she calls 'misbehavior.' She has convinced herself Komitow mesmerized her, she was under a spell. I think her family made her see it that way. And I suppose other people's mistakes make her less tolerant because they remind her in some way of her own, which she has so carefully closed away."

The foremost characteristic of both Mama and Papa was their absolute self-assurance. The way they lived, their circle of friends, their carefully regulated social life—attendance at the Assembly, and Academy of Fine Arts opening, the opera, occasional appearance at Holy Trinity, all fitted into a recognizable family pattern. If something happened to threaten this pattern or assurance they withdrew from society temporarily, gathered themselves unobtrusively together, and acted. As for instance when David took to drinking and was found lying out on the front steps. Mama cancelled one of her "at homes"; she and Papa did not attend the Assembly. Then Mama hit upon the solution of paying Fanny a "little extra" to wait up for David and see him properly to bed. The idea of tackling David's drinking habits and delving into the reason behind them never entered their calculations. A weakness, Mama would term it.

Mama, being a poet, was regarded by the Duanes, Cadwaladers, etc., and later in the Adirondacks by the Vanderbilts and Whitelaw Reids, with awe. She seldom spoke about her work. Although she gave readings both at camp, in the one-time barn, and in he living room at DeLancey Place, she was always very professional about it. With her snowy hair, the row of curls, her sweeping dress, her beautiful voice, just a little tremulous but full of warmth, she was impressive. Tubby little Mr. Jaffrey accompanied her on the piano. Surprisingly, he did quite well. True, Mama might be eulogizing about birds and bees, as David said, but there was nothing mushy about it. David thought Mama a hard-shelled realist, and if the poems had a 19th-century tinge, they were also sinewy and occasionally epic. David said she was big on death and weak on love.

I did not find Mama an interesting person. I suppose she had too much power over me. As I said, she could not bring herself really to see me. Certainly I was not neglected, but not loved. With

David it was very different. Mama adored him, and he was the apple of Papa's eye, at least for quite a long time.

David, as I said, went out of his way to charm Mama. Even at the awful age of thirteen, wearing those terrible knickers and hideous, brown stockings, he would sit on the big sofa in the living room and tease Mama, saying things which no one else would dare.

The household on DeLancey Place consisted of Robert the butler, houseman, and chauffeur, a tall, melancholy, disagreeable colored man; Mrs. Mertz, the Swedish cook who would allow no one in her kitchen except Mama; and Fanny McConnell, who was my friend. Fanny was a short, black-haired Irish woman with huge violet eyes behind thick glasses. She was not exactly a loving person, being petrified of Mama, but, as I said, she listened. When I was only six, and had just arrived in the house and was so frightened, she took me into her arms.

Robert, the houseman, stayed home when we went to the Adirondacks because he could not swim and refused to put foot into a boat. At camp we had Mrs. Mertz (who wore a feather toque on the Albany Night Boat, which was part of our early trips), and Mr. and Mrs. Gordon. Mr. Gordon was our guide, taking care of the *Carafa*, our launch, and the two handmade Adirondack rowboats. Mrs. Gordon helped Fanny and did odd jobs. As I said, our camp stood on a high promontory with magnificent pines, carefully trimmed. Then there was the beautiful barn, and the dining room in a smaller round house with a sitting room attached. The kitchen led off this. There was a special cabin down by the dock for Papa and his books. Then, dotted through the trees were the ice house, and a house for Mr. and Mrs. Gordon, and quarters for Fanny and Mrs. Mertz. Almost in the center of all this was the beautiful tent in which Mama and Papa slept. It had been specially made and was oblong, pure white. It held two beds, a bureau, a dressing table for Mama, a closet, and a place to sit. It looked right out on the lake. I slept near the Main House, in a cabin by myself, shaded by hemlocks. Mr. Jaffrey, whom I loathed, had a cabin nearby. When

David was in camp he put up an old Sears Roebuck tent with a pole in the center and slept on pine boughs, hardening himself. David always said our camp was considered the handsomest on the lakes because of its high location and fine stand of trees. Just as Mama and Papa were considered the most distinguished "campers."

Joyce sauntered back into the tent. She had put on high-heeled patent leather shoes, thoroughly unsuitable, Mama would have said.

"You go to Irwin's don't you?" Joyce asked.

"Yes. It's right down the street." If I sounded a little stiff it was because no one ever called the school "Irwin's," it was "*Miss* Irwin's." And did Joyce imagine that she would automatically be taken into the "sets" because she happened to be pretty? Her prettiness would work against her, I told myself. "Everybody" was coming out. (When I thought of this I closed my eyes, or prayed.) "Who you were" counted at school. And who was Joyce Framely? Mama had never heard of her. I thought Mama ridiculous because she drew the lines so rigorously and would not accept anyone who lived in Wayne or Overbrook or Narberth. That I was a worse snob myself did not occur to me. I guarded my "position." Although I had friends in school—Nancy Prior, Debby O'Halloran, Mary Devlin—they were never going to be asked to the Saturday Evening, or debutante parties. As Eva Colby I was nobody. As Mr. and Mrs. Severn's "grandchild," I went every place.

In spite of being thoroughly "acceptable," I already knew the effect of my appearance. I had seen what could happen to me at the Friday Evening Dancing Class, where David could only go on holidays, being too old for the group. I was asked to dance just once: when Mrs. Duer, who ran the class, brought a boy up. The rest of the time I spent with the girls. Or I sat on a chair at the side of the floor, alone. Mrs. Duer did her best. But I vowed never to repeat that experience. So I only went to the holiday dances because David would be there. When we danced he would not tolerate a mis-step or stumble. I must be able to follow any step he invented. David laid down the rules. I must *never* get "stuck" with a boy, never dance round and round. "Just leave the guy when the music stops. Thank him and walk off. Go over to the other girls. I'll get you out as soon as I can."

I soon learned that "being popular" was deadly serious. What had I to go on? Here my mind went astray. As I watched Joyce fuss with her lovely soft hair, and although I knew she hadn't a chance at "Irwin's," yet suddenly I hated her beauty, her fairness, the great eyes, the beautiful mouth. Some sort of premonition ran through me (was she not bound to meed David?), and I sat very still.

Joyce, fortunately, was not one to notice other's moods, except as they affected her, so she did not see the alteration that came over me.

"We'll go down to Paul Smith's in the *Katydid*," she said as easily as though announcing a change in the weather. "There's sure to be dancing, and we can look through the windows. Maybe we'll be asked in."

*Paul Smith's*? I was strictly forbidden even to approach the place, let alone go in. Recently Al Jolson had been seen stepping out of a touring car. People from Lake Placid and Saranac came over to dance in the afternoon. The place was considered "fast." Mama said the hotel had gone downhill and she didn't know what old Paul Smith would think of it if he were alive. Occasionally, when guests arrived by train, Gordon was sent down in the *Carafa* to meet them.

Fortunately, Joyce changed her mind about Paul Smith's because the Framely guide, a strange-looking fellow with a red beard who slouched down the dock, said there was a log floating in the slough between Spitfire Lake and Lower St. Regis Lake where "poor Fels Baker" lived. The campers always called him "poor Fels" because he had a camp on Lower St. Regis Lake where none of the campers would be caught dead. We decided to go to The Landing for the mail instead.

Joyce's boat, the *Katydid*, had a white hull, a sharply pointed bow, a curved oak deck, a windshield, one gear, a starter button, and a gas gauge. We sat side by side on a wide leather-cushioned seat. The boat was good-sized and had another smaller seat in the stern. A large American flag dangled over the exhaust pipe. Joyce stuck the Framely flag (blue background with white stripes) into the socket on the bow. Every camper had his own flag, only flown when a member of the family was on board. It was tremendously heady to be out with another girl in a boat. Such a thing had never happened to me before. I must say Joyce's costume was astounding. She pulled her white, ruffled blouse off her shoulders so a lot of bare skin showed. Her skirt was slit to mid-calf and she still had on the high-heeled shoes. The whole effect looked ridiculous, but Joyce never knew how to dress.

At the Post Office dock Joyce made such a poor approach we had to be hauled in by the Reid's guide. The Landing consisted of a small wooden building, which was the Post Office, and a row of garages where the campers kept their cars. As Joyce and I were handed the mail for our camps, Joyce let out a squeal. "Look—I've got an invitation!" she cried. In an instant she had the envelope ripped open. Her voice shook as she said: "Eva—I've been asked to William Vanderbilt's twenty-first birthday party!"

I did not say anything. I had received the identical envelope but quickly hid it in my pocket. I would simply pretend I had not been asked. I was too young. This was a party for older girls, like Joyce. Although I knew none of this would work, it would put off my having to think about the evil day, a character weakness that has followed me all through life. Right now, however, my plan was spoiled by the wide-eyed Joyce, who cried, "You got one, too, Eva. I saw you stuff it in your pocket!"

# Prelude

*Anna and Frederick Severn are in their tent preparing for bed. The place is very cozy with rush mats on the canvas floor and three lanterns giving out a soft light. Anna is sitting before her dressing table twisting the five curls on her forehead into perfect circles, fastening each one with a hairpin. Eventually her head will be enveloped in a tulle scarf, which is worn for Papa's benefit. Anna has on a high-necked, long-sleeved, white lawn nightgown with hand embroidered ruffles. She pads comfortably about in an old pair of sneakers.*

*"No one thought of asking the Framely girl to young Vanderbilt's party," Anna says, "until I told the Denbys she's quite a beauty. I can't imagine what she sees in Eva."*

*"They're dancing," Frederick says. He is gingerly combing his moustache by the unsteady light of the lantern. Every few weeks he contemplates shaving the whole troublesome business off and tries to imagine his face first with no hair, then with a short moustache, and ends by realizing he is far more distinguished looking with than without. There is little Frederick misses about himself or others.*

*"Dancing?" Anna turns, still holding a curl to her forehead.*

*"Preparation for the Vanderbilt party." Frederick raises the lantern glass and blows out the flame.*

*"Oh." Anna resumes work with the hairpins; next the tulle scarf. Finished, she looks, Frederick regretfully thinks, like a Mother Superior. He*

( 35

goes toward his cot, flips back the covers. At his age life is supposed to be a serious business with the end in sight. He has taught himself to regard occasional yearnings as imbecilic. Anna's cover-up effect squelches any surge of imagination.

Anna says, "Eva at last has made a friend who can be useful." She slips out of her sneakers, shoving them under her cot. Both beds are hard, springless, and have a definite musty odor about them, carefully never mentioned.

Frederick knows better than to discourage any of Anna's ideas about Eva; better for Eva, that is. He does little enough for the child, but occasionally he is able to head off disaster.

"What do you mean, 'useful,' Anna?"

"The Framelys, I'm sure, are ambitious for the girl. Eva says they think of sending her to Miss Irwin's. I shall have to see what I can do about getting Joyce into the Saturday Evening. I shall hint that the Framelys consider giving a large dance, perhaps a ball, for both girls."

Frederick stands by the bureau stunned. "But Anna, you don't even know *the* Framelys!"

"I thought we might call on them next week," Anna slips down into the damp bed.

Faced with his own chilly bed and still vaguely irritated over the indecision regarding his moustache, Frederick speaks rather heatedly. He is also still haunted by the tragedy of the Shanker girl's shocking end. "For the last time, Anna—do give up this idea of bringing Eva 'out.' It's bound to be a disaster. And you run the risk of completely ruining her self-confidence, maybe for life."

"Don't be ridiculous, Frederick. The Shanker girl must have weighed close to two hundred pounds and had a bad skin."

But Frederick has graver news. "Did you know that David is thinking of leaving Yale?"

Anna lies quite still. "I don't belive it." She is suddenly hideously afraid.

"It's true, nevertheless. He's spoken to me."

"And you never said anything!" Her whole body surges with distress. She is also jealous.

*"David made me promise."*

Anna covers her face with her arms.

*"It makes sense, Anna."* Frederick speaks coldly, for he blames her. This is her doing, a foolishness that will have many repercussions. *"David is devoted to Eva. You've always known that. He regards her as his sister. He won't see her put through this debutante mill, ground to bits, without a move to rescue her. He intends to stay close by. He'll go to Temple."*

*"Temple!"* Mama cries. *"Oh, no!"*

*"The tuition is less."*

*"But that makes no difference!"*

*"To him, yes. He wants to get a job and pay for part of his tuition."*

*"But why, Frederick?"* She sits up in bed, appealing to him. *"What's happened?"*

She is crying openly in a heartbroken fashion, her speech interjected with sobs. Papa slowly walks over to her. He sits beside her, tries to put his arms around her.

*"Don't blame yourself, Anna. You've done what you thought was right."*

*"But any preparation I've made could have easily been stopped. If I'd had any notion that David would leave Yale..."* she is crying in a wild way, refusing Papa's arms, holding the sheet up to her face. She now rips off the tulle net. *"Oh, I can't stand it! Why didn't you tell me?"* Her blue eyes glare at him. He leaves her and stands in the center of the tent.

*"Unfortunately, Anna, it is not just a question of a few little preparations. You also reminded David that his father had died in debt, and that it was thanks to my generosity that he went to Yale."*

*"But I only wanted him to be grateful!"*

*"A feeling few of us enjoy."*

*"But you know how unstable Frederick was about money. You've often said it."*

*"But never to David."*

Silence. A sniffle. *"It's all too dreadful."*

*"Perhaps not. At any rate, we shall see more of David."*

*"I blame Eva for much of this."*

*Frederick turns. "You're quite wrong, Anna. The girl does not even know about it."*

*"He'd still be at Yale, except for her." There is malice in her tone.*

*As this speculation is a waste of time, Frederick does not answer but walks to the door of the tent. The flaps are tied back. A mosquito net hangs to the ground. He pulls this aside and steps out. The stars are extraordinarily bright and close, the night still, the air sharp. Down by the lake he hears Eva. She is late. She must have forced herself to take this swim, which she used to do with David every night. Frederick can imagine the iciness of the first plunge into the water, her fright at the dark. It is fortunate for Eva that Anna's hearing has become quite dulled in the last years. Frederick listens to Eva scrambling up the path, hears her door close. That idiot Jaffrey (Anna's piano accompanist) must have drunk himself to sleep again. Frederick is not necessarily a secretive man, but the happenings around the camp—if they do no harm—he keeps to himself. Such knowledge would upset his wife and, in the case of Jaffrey, lose her an excellent pianist. Frederick has witnessed in people very strange behavior of the sort Anna cannot imagine. Her innocence, the various customs of her closed, privileged world entrance Frederick, a never-ending wonder to him. He enjoys meeting the requirements of his long-neglected relations; it amuses him. On the whole he finds tradition and manners more attractive than the codes followed in the rougher camps near the Mexican border. He is a good-natured man, somewhat inflexible and lacking any real warmth of heart. For instance he feels sympathy and some responsibility for Eva, but he did not choose her as part of his family (David chose her); therefore she must take her chances. To himself Frederick admits that this new move of David's has completely surprised him. The boy's unruly, stubborn side appeared rather suddenly, and Frederick does not find it attractive. A maverick. A boy trying to be a man, flinging off dependence, much as he himself had done. Waiting table or working in the library of a second-rate college, according to Frederick, seems very low. David has shown no consideration for Anna. Having to tell her David's decision in such brutal fashion Frederick finds upsetting. He had no choice after receiving a private communication from David. Poor Anna, why did she never see the danger of raising those two children so closely? She insists on this foolishness of brother*

( 38

*and sister, which Frederick suspects is ignored by Eva but David relies on. David may go against Anna's wishes as far as college is concerned. But when it comes to looking out for Eva, Frederick feels fairly certain that David will also steer clear of her.*

3   The mail has been heavy. Finally, when the letters became obscene I stopped opening them. But in the beginning, newspaper clippings often were included. One particular favorite was a photograph of me doing a high kick, and the caption: "High-Stepping Society Girl One-Time Friend of Bill Vanderbilt." I met Bill Vanderbilt at his twenty-first birthday party and have never seen him since. The occasion was memorable, not because I actually shook the Vanderbilt hand, but because I had my first experience with Joyce: a warning I did not heed. In fifteen-year-old parlance, I told myself that Joyce was "mean." Whereas in reality she was showing an ambitious, ruthless, wholly self-centered side of her character that I was to come upon time and again in my life and never be willing to recognize, until at last I saw her whole.

One reason I did not sense danger in this instance (although "danger" may be too strong a word), was the naturalness and familiarity, not only of the setting, but Joyce's behavior. After squealing gleefully over the Vanderbilt invitation, she babbled on about the dress she would wear, taking more interest, per usual, in her own choice than in mine and deciding on a pink organdy with a big sash that "takes inches off my hips." I would wear my yellow organdy, I said, with ruffles around the skirt supposedly making me look taller. All this seemed quite normal.

And next my attention was taken up with teaching Joyce to dance. For we had no sooner moored the boat to the Framely dock, than Joyce went straight to the main cabin and started shuffling through her records.

"We've got to practice our dancing, Eva. The Vanderbilts are bound to have New York men. They'll know all the new steps.

New York men...I should not survive! Worse than the Friday Evening Dancing Class. I could not ask a New York man about his dog...maybe I'd be sick and not able to go. If I forced myself to stand around naked after swimming at night surely I'd get a cold. Mama hated colds. She'd send me to bed. None of this could I confide in Joyce. Instinct told me to say nothing. Then my predicament faded in the struggle to teach Joyce how to dance. She was a no-sense-of-rhythm type, lumpish and clumsy. If I had shown as little natural ability with David, he would have given me up. She knew none of the new steps. However, her recording of "In The Mornin', in the Evenin', Ain't We Got Fun?" had a sax solo that was neat. Or, as Joyce said, "the cat's pajamas." Joyce had a lot of dated slang that I hoped she would not use in front of those New York men.

I tried to teach Joyce some of the steps, holding her hands and making her watch my feet. It was while we were practicing that Mrs. Framely came into the room. I remember her so well standing in the doorway with her head lifted in a proud, little way she had. She was medium tall and slim; gray showed through her fine dark hair. She had small, very blue eyes, a thin straight mouth. She came forward smiling, and shook my hand. I curtsied. She seemed unlike either Joyce or Mr. Framely. Joyce burst out with the news of the Vanderbilt invitation. Mrs. Framely did not seem overimpressed. She laid her hand for an instant on my shoulder. "And now you're trying to teach Joyce the new steps."

I could not remember anyone having put a hand on my shoulder in quite a while. It seemed for a moment that she understood the entire situation, even my dread of the party.

"I'm pretty young for a party like the Vanderbilts', Mrs. Framely. Maybe I shouldn't go." I kept my eyes on her face, hopefully.

Here Joyce let out a scream. "Not go? You even told me you were going to wear your yellow organdy!" She threw herself onto the couch and kicked her legs. I could see she was very spoiled.

Mrs. Framely said seriously, "You might be sorry to miss it. Just think how you can boast afterwards." She smiled again at me. Then, as though solving the whole problem, she said, "You can leave early. I don't want Joyce to stay late."

This brought more screams from Joyce. Mrs. Framely seemed perfectly unconscious of Joyce's behavior. Of course if I had ever tried such an exhibition before Mama I would have been sent to my room, even though I was fifteen.

"You'll stay for lunch, won't you Eva?"

Mr. Framely came banging through the screen door evidently in high good humor. "Of course she'll stay for lunch! Stay for lunch!" he cried. "And afterwards I'll dance with both girls and give them a *real* treat."

To my surprise Joyce jumped up, ran over and kissed him. "That's my girl," he said, grinning. "She wants something," he winked at me.

"No, I don't," Joyce said in a rather whiney voice. "Mother says I have to leave the Vanderbilt party early. Now that's not fair, is it?"

"I don't think you should go at all!" Mr. Framely said, looking quite fiercely at her. "Who is this Vanderbilt fellow, anyway? He's got too much money for his own good." Mr. Framely, without even a glance at Joyce, slammed out of the door again.

I stayed for lunch and we had lamb chops and stuffed potatoes. The Framelys ate twice the amount we did. At camp Mama was always quite frugal and we usually had sandwiches for lunch. But at the Framelys we ate three courses with ice cream for dessert.

Mr. Framely talked steadily, whether anyone listened or not. He was dead set against Wilson and the United Nations. "Silliest damn-fool idea." Mrs. Framely told him please to be careful how he spoke. "Now this man Harding I've been hearing about seems like a good steady fellow." Mr. Framely managed to chew and speak all at the same time. "Keep the country normal. That's what we need with those Communists making trouble in our country and the Red

Army marching all over Russia."

Surprisingly Mrs. Framely took out against him, quoting an article she read in *Harper's Magazine*. "People are afraid of being thought radical if they hold opinions that differ from the Rotary Club or the American Legion. America is no longer a free country," she said, all this quite calmly, eating her potato, while Mr. Framely looked ready to explode. "Liberty is a thing of the past," she finished looking squarely at him.

It was that day at lunch when Mrs. Framely made her announcement about the boathouse. She intended to build one that would hold four boats and have a summerhouse on top. Mr. Framely stared at her, mouth ajar. "With the money I made in that little flier I took in asphalt," she said, quite positively.

"Why build a boathouse for a lot of boats that don't run?" Mr. Framely asked, looking blank, as though he could not believe what he heard.

"They'll run eventually, and that old shack we have now is a disgrace. I want someplace where I can entertain people for tea."

"Helen," Mr. Framely said, putting down his knife and fork, "there are many better ways to spend your money than putting it into this camp. And who's coming to tea?"

Mrs. Framely just gave a little smile and took a sip of water. Two days later there were men in camp tearing down the old boathouse and mending the dock. A big barge drew up with lumber piled onto it. The boathouse was built in record time. It seemed a matter of days and there was Mrs. Framely's new room, open on all sides, baskets filled with ferns, and furniture bought at Saranac Lake—brown wicker, and a rocker or two. Mr. Framely rarely went near the place, although he had to admit it was pretty. By now I was used to the Framely's and no longer jumped when Mr. Framely cursed, or blushed when Mrs. Framely got the names of the campers mixed up. Every afternoon Mrs. Framely sat out in her boathouse having tea. There she was, by herself, calmly sipping, quite content. I knew she loved the camp. She was tired of having Mr. Framely drag her all over the country so he could play golf. Joyce told me that since the Vanderbilt invitation her mother was sure people would start calling. She wanted a proper place to receive them.

Mrs. Framely treated me with special care. I often thought that my mother would have been just like Mrs. Framely, who always made a point of putting her arms around me, with a hug and a kiss. She often sat sewing while Joyce and I danced. (Sewing, I noticed with despair, on more red curtains.)

Finally I blurted out to Mama that I wished she would call on Mrs. Framely. To my surprise, she agreed. And the very next day, with Gordon at the helm of the *Carafa* (which steered at the side and had an exposed motor, but was made of solid mahogany), we started off. Papa held his Panama with one hand, Mama raised her black umbrella. She wore her best amethyst pin (and her white gloves with the fingers showing), her black shawl, and her newest black dress.

Of course neither Papa nor Mama looked up to date, but they had such an air, and their own style, and utter confidence. Other people might do differently; this was their way. I thought we all looked very special and smiled hopefully at Mama. But she glanced away, as usual, which always made me feel that my smile must be grotesque, although David assured me it was not. Ordinarily, when Mama did this I felt a little desolate, but today I didn't care. We were like a family, going somewhere together. And Mrs. Framely would hug and kiss me. (Oftentimes I put my arms right around her neck and hugged her back.)

When we came to the Framely camp I pointed out the new docks and the red geraniums to Mama. "Quite nice," Mama said, which augured well. Papa gave her his hand, and even helped me out. I tried not to be nervous, telling myself that surely Mr. Framely would not call out "Hello there, Severn!" to Papa, the way he had in that unfortunate encounter with Mr. McAlpin. Nothing of the sort happened. Mr. Framely came along the dock wearing a linen coat and quiet tie. He shook hands and bowed most formally to Mama, scarcely smiling, and told her how much he and Mrs. Framely enjoyed having "your charming granddaughter at Caudebec." "Caudebec," according to Mr. Framely, was the name of the camp, chosen because of an estate given to one of Mr. Framely's forebears by William the Conqueror.

Mr. Framely gave a manly handshake to Papa and then turned with almost a flourish as Mrs. Framely appeared. She looked just right in a tailored blouse and long skirt, almost young, and quite unselfconscious, simply glad to meet Mama and Papa, "because we have become so attached to Eva," she said.

Mrs. Framely led the way along the slatted walks to the new boat house. Papa took off his Panama again when Joyce appeared. I think she amused him. Not that they had much conversation, but he seemed to understand her better than I did, although I can't exactly say how.

Tea was an enormous success. Mama and Mrs. Framely talked at length about the Vanderbilt party, agreeing that Joyce and I must not stay after ten-thirty. Mama even asked Joyce to spend the night because our camp was nearer the Denby camp, but Mrs. Framely said Garrett, the guide, would go for Joyce. There was quite a little speculation about the fortune Bill Vanderbilt would come into. Mr. Framely saying it was over three million, but Papa objecting to more than two. Joyce sat in a rocker, silent for once. She appeared dazed by the visit. I could see Mr. Framely getting up his nerve to put a question, fiddling with his cigar, wriggling in his chair, finally saying that he thought it was a funny thing that parents were not asked to the Vanderbilt party. Although I knew that Papa and Mama had been invited, they never considered going. Mama leaned forward at once, and I liked her for it. "Oh, but Mr. Framely, this is a young people's party!" she said. It was nicely done and I looked gratefully at her. At once a sense of ease fell over all three Framelys; Joyce even crossed her legs, something Mama would never allow.

Only one thing marred the perfection of the party. As Mama was going down the path towards the boat she said softly to Mrs.

Framely, "No one has curtains at camp, Mrs. Framely. It's simply not one of our customs." She pressed poor Mrs. Framely's arm. I stood miserably on the boardwalk. Those curtains had been made by hand. I had seen Mrs. Framely stitching by the hour. What difference did it make if no one else had curtains! No one else had a puce-colored, two-storied house, either. I thought Mrs. Framely paled; I saw her blink her blue eyes, and look confused. But all she said was, "I see." And followed Mama down the walk.

When at last we were in our boat and going through the slough to St. Regis, I went right at Mama. "Why did you have to tell her, Mama? She made those curtains herself. She spent *hours* on them!" I was close to crying.

Mama snapped up her umbrella, although the sun had gone under. Then she turned to me and said in that patient voice I hate, "I am quite aware of the blow to Mrs. Framely's pride, Eva. I considered seriously before speaking. But Mrs. Denby is contemplating a call. I felt it only a kindness to keep the Framelys from being the laughing stock of the lakes." She pulled her scarf more closely around her thin shoulders. Why couldn't she let people be what they were? Why must everyone conform? And I thought with wicked glee that such tactics would not get by with David.

But then Mama said, "I had some difficulty arranging an invitation for Joyce Framely to the William Vanderbilt party. I heard she was quite a beauty. Unless I am much mistaken, Mrs. Framely is anxious to make a good impression, even with that boor of a husband."

I forgave Mama, and although I knew she did not like to be touched, I leaned over and pressed her gloved hand. She responded with a little smile, not looking at me.

"Framely's not so bad," Papa said in his slow way. "I sounded him out on investments, and I thought he made good sense. In fact, I'm going to write to the Guaranty tomorrow." This was most gratifying, even though as a retired anthropologist Papa was probably pretty naive about financial matters.

Joyce and I went right on practicing our dancing. We tried the dip—very popular, David had told me. We did side steps and Joyce even managed the spin with great effect, although I had to haul her around. One day Mr. Framely came back from Saranac Lake Village with three new records. He was sick and tired of "Love Nest" and "Ain't we Got Fun," and brought a new version of "Swanee," also "Avalon," and "Hard-Hearted Hannah," the last one not being particularly good for dancing, but evidently a favorite of Mr. Framely's. Besides liking to dance he also liked to sing and had a very true voice. One rainy day Joyce persuaded him to sing all ten verses of "Abdul A-Bul-Bul Amir," with Mrs. Framely joining in on the last verse—

> "And the name that she murmurs in vain
> as she weeps
> Is Ivan Pterovsky Skivar!"

Mr. Framely was a great talker with no one to talk to. I was amazed at his attitude toward Prohibition. He spoke openly of the bootlegger he used at Lake Clear Junction, and the possibilities of actually making gin. As Mama and Papa had even ceased serving wine, although there was plenty in the DeLancey Place cellar, Mr. Framely rather shocked me. Mrs. Framely was part Quaker. She told me about her cousins who still came to the house in their Quaker gray, "only the finest silk," she said, and laughed. Often at lunch Mr. Framely would go on about the Chicago Riots until Mrs. Framely simply told him to stop. "But it's a state of Civil War!" he cried.

One night at dinner I wanted to show off to Papa and said that I understood President Wilson was a poor benighted sick man with a lot of loony ideas. Papa sent me from the table.

Life was very confusing. Evidently Papa was big on Wilson and his peace plan, and the League of Nations. He said voters had associated Wilson with the war. And Chauncey Depew's speech had made a mockery of Wilson and his hopes for the League. "Guns will never be still. There will always be a war someplace," Papa said, sitting up quite straight and gazing down at the table.

Joyce made me her friend, which was amazing because even one year's difference in ages usually meant an unbridgeable gap. But Joyce treated me as an equal, which was so complimentary that it lulled any suspicions or awareness that I might have had. In her casual way she seemed goodnatured, also wonderfully sure of herself. She knew her own beauty, although at times overdid her appeal, as when meeting Snooty Canby in the Post Office at The Landing and saying, "*Hel*-lo..." just like Clara Bow. It was terribly embarrassing when Snooty did not answer or even turn around, but only waved his hand. Joyce said he couldn't have heard and was waving to someone else. But I noticed she didn't want to sit out on the rock and wait for him to go by in his motorboat any more. Of course, if there had been boys in the camps, I doubt if Joyce would have gone on many picnics with me. But it was an unusual summer, with few young people around. Mr. Framely blamed it on the war. "Upset everybody. No one can settle down. Look at Prohibition, think of the effect of the automobile, *True Confession* magazine, the movies!" I couldn't figure what all this had to do with there not being anyone my age or Joyce's on the lakes, but Mr. Framely had his face all screwed up and his moustache jutting out and I knew he meant what he said.

Although Joyce was overweight and somewhat lumpish I never ceased being conscious of her beauty. I watched the sun fall on her cheeks, showing her skin smooth and fair. (In her whole life she never had a pimple, she said, whereas I had a horrid one on my chin most of the summer.) Her color would flush and then recede, a few freckles appeared across her nose. I watched her thick blonde hair blow and shine in the wind, and the careless way she swept it back or plaited it. Her eyes had strange gray irises, edged in curling eyelashes. Even wearing her old brown bathing cap with water streaming down her face, her skin glowed and her small mouth stayed pink. There was no question of being jealous, exactly. I simply wondered how she could be so perfect. And because what I saw made such a wide gap between us I could watch her quite objectively. She was not in competition with me, but with herself.

I never understood Joyce, not when we were young. But then would I ever understand anyone beautiful? What have we in common? She cannot approximate my feelngs nor conceive what it is to be a kind of outsider. (David won't let me use the word "outcast.") Joyce's problems were solved by her beauty, so I felt. Her future assured, a simple matter of choice. And although she might throw a tantrum and cry, it was only to get her own way. I had a sense, even then, that she was headed steadily in one direction.

I could not come close to Joyce. She was too contained. Yes, and too self-centered. Although, as I said, the full impact of this did not strike me until years later. When I say Joyce made me her friend, I was her confidante, her admirer. Joyce was the one to whom things happened, the center of her family's attention, an only child, whereas every day, in one form or another, I fought for survival, wrestling over Kreutzer, hauling Mr. Jaffrey out of his hammock to practice a Bach Concerto, or avoiding Mama's displeasure (the hardest task), or keeping my spirits up. None of this Joyce understood; my struggles bored her. I once asked her what she thought of the way I did my hair. Would it be better short? "Oh, it looks all right," she said. So I never asked her again.

I cannot remember a time when I did not mind about my looks. I minded terribly. As I said, how I looked set the pattern of my whole life. And although this might not be the case today, or even in the 20s under different circumstances—for instance someone like Elsie Janis who made such a success in spite of not being a raving beauty—in the life that was laid out for me I was meant to be pretty. (A non-pretty girl needs special loving care.) In the social world what else counted but one's looks? And supposedly I was being prepared for this world. Easy to say that I should have stood out against it—but how? With what equipment? Better to be a salesgirl in Woolworth's basement than try to enter the highly competitive social world. *But is it?* I was competent on the violin, but hours and years away from being a professional. And how many women were admitted to orchestras, particularly at my age? My teacher, Miss Craven was far from being Jascha Brodsky or Frederick Hahn. My technique needed constant work; I had never studied theory. I cared passionately about the violin because it was mine. Had I played better I would have been able to pour out my anger, frustration, yearning, so I told myself, battling away through the interminable Kreutzer exercises or practicing long bows, or Schradieck's scale studies. Or I would be getting ready the slow movement of the second violin part of Bach's Concerto in D minor so if asked I could play with Mr. Thaddeus Riche, who sometimes came to camp. Occasionally Mr. Riche let me play on his instrument, which was heaven. Strangely, I was not nervous playing in front of people. When Miss Craven gave one of her pupil recitals at the Aeolian Hall, I liked getting up before an audience. Once I clamped down on my chin rest, then all my gritty determination rose and I usually played up to my own pitch.

Occasionally Mama asked me to play a short piece at one of her recitals, and then I would hound Mr. Jaffrey, making him accompany me. I suppose part of what I felt as I stood with my fiddle firm under my chin was that for once my looks did not count. I knew how to give a certain panache to my playing. I knew I was effective. The campers would come to me after a recital and actually shake my hand, and I stood right up and shook back.

The violin was more than compensation. I loved the fiddle for itself. And of course it was a tremendous advantage having old Jaffrey at camp and also in the DeLancey Place house because an instrumentalist, in fact any player, longs for the dual sound, the fitting in and matching with another instrument.

The piano was Jaffrey's sole asset. "Loathsome Jaffrey," David and I called him. Fat and lazy (an excellent, effortless pianist), short and bald, he oozed perspiration even in the barn, which was always cold. He was a permanent guest, accompanying Mama in her recitals, composing music for her poetry. The musician side of him was admirable; he gave me many tips when we played and even explained the music to me if he felt in a good mood. When he went swimming he wore dark blue flannel trunks that came to his white knees. Wisps of pale hair stuck out from the scooped neck of a jersey top. I used to pray I would never see him raise his arms.

Reciting poetry was a great trial to me. Each morning everyone in camp (except the maids and guide) knocked on the door of the dining room and said, "Manners maketh man." "Entrez!" Mama cried. One morning I came in, stood in the exact center of the room and said I would recite "Break of Day," by John Donne:

"Stay, O sweet, and do not rise;
The light that shines comes from thine eyes;
The day breaks not, it is my heart,
Because that you and I must part.
Stay or else my joys will die
And perish in their infancy."

After this recitation, Mama told that she wanted to look over my selections in the future. I recited the poem to Joyce and she had a good laugh and called me a goose and asked didn't I know *anything*. Which was quite right, for I didn't. I had a vague general idea, very vague. So Joyce, after we had docked at my favorite vacant camp, told me. She wasn't coarse, just specific. "You mean he sticks his thing in you and you have a baby?" I cried. "Well, there's more to it than that." And then Joyce was pretty vague herself, ending up with the advice that I'd better marry a nice, patient man and he'd show me. I must say I was silenced. All Fanny had told me, when I started to menstruate, was that this would keep me from having a baby. And certain things the girls at school giggled about. And then I thought of David's "thing," and I didn't feel so lost. Nothing could be wrong about David. No, I told Joyce I had never "experimented" as she suggested with other girls. "Gracious!" Joyce said, not quite looking at me. Had I no best friend? I said not really, although I liked a lot of the girls at school.

The conversation was memorable. And I found that at the end of the day I was rather puffed up, rather pleased with myself. Now there could be no more secrets from me—and giggling. When Joyce had asked me about other girls I had not told her that I "experimented" with myself. After all, no one need know about that. And anyway, all the time I was promising myself it would not happen again.

Now that I knew as much as everyone else, I found many occurrences that had puzzled me smoothed out. Dragonflies, for instance. And although I was totally unfamiliar with John Donne and had only happened upon him in a *Treasury of Great Poems* Mama had loaned me, yet now I read his poem with quite sudden understanding—as though *he* had initiated me into knowledge. And therefore, most fortunately (and really no thanks to Joyce), I associated sex—at first learning—with a young man's plea, and love.

Although Joyce told me the facts-of-life we did not confide in each other, there were no giggly whispered confidences such as I had with Debbie O'Halloran at school. I kept feeling that in some indefinable way in spite of her beauty we were in competition, or that I had some advantage she envied. Then one day she asked me about the Friday Evening Dancing Class. After I told her she said, "Oh, I thought it was a grown-up party," and turned her head away. She was jealous. She had not been invited to the Friday Evening. Now she faced the Saturday Evening Dancing Class and was not at all sure of being asked. I failed to understand why anyone wanted to go through that torture. But of course the dance would not be torture for Joyce.

In her way, Joyce was secretive, she rarely came out frankly. But her secretiveness was not like Mama's compartments, for Joyce seldom held grudges, whereas Mama was liable to bring out some past mistake whole and alive. Joyce had a kind of sublime, flowing confidence, enforced by a powerful will. The fact that all this might hide a deeprooted insecurity I was too young to consider, nor am I at all sure that it did.

When I use the word "outsider" about myself, I am exaggerating my situation. Because my teachers at school completely accepted me, and I had many good friends. In fact, I was popular at school. It was what I thought of as the "outside world" where I failed. Possibly my personality worked against me. I spoke abruptly, and I was not particularly feminine. (Helpless females have always enraged me.) I had no "line," although at times I could be quite funny.

Mama never really liked Joyce and took to calling her "your fat friend." But Papa was very attentive in what I thought a faintly ridiculous manner. Joyce received letters from boys, which she did not hesitate to read aloud although I found them horribly boring. She wore silver bracelets hung with "charms" that boys had given her—a little windmill, a canoe, a heart. Sometimes when she tallked about boys I thought her confidence covered her like a seamless skin.

From the day we got the Vanderbilt invitation we practiced dancing, cheeks plastered together, Joyce stumbling but determined. As a bribe she let me run the *Katydid*, and she went on picnics, which bored her.

I loved the picnics, and running the boat was tremendously exciting. I became expert and could make a landing anyplace. I worked over the *Katydid*, kept her polished, giving particular attention to the riding lights and the cleats, also the deck.

There was the day when Joyce announced she was going to be a writer. I remember exactly where it happened. At the Kingston's old camp. We were climbing up some rickety steps. *Oh, piffle!* I thought, and I jumped off the steps and went exploring.

I came upon another side of Joyce Framely, a frightening side. I should have stowed this insight away, to be remembered. But I am apt to take people as they seem at the moment, a fatal fault, David says. Joyce could be violent, a side I only saw once. That was the night she discovered Garrett, the guide, had taken the *Katydid* out.

She screamed across the living room table at her father, her face a queer purple color, and her mouth wide and ugly—I had never imagined such an exhibition. Garrett must be discharged at once! Mr. Framely rose to his feet and told her quite roughly to keep out of his business. She broke into violent tears. I sat appalled. Mrs. Framely went to her and tried to comfort her. But Joyce actually threw her off. Mrs. Framely said nothing, just walked quickly from the room. Then I ran out, and ran all the way back to camp. I never wanted to see anything like that again. Later Fanny said that Mr. Framely told Garrett to get out of camp that night. Where did he go? What happened to him? I never knew.

The next day you might have thought nothing had happened. Mr. Framely and Joyce were the best of friends. Only Mrs. Framely seemed a little silent, and I thought her particularly affectionate to me.

4 Even though Joyce and I danced all the time, I had managed to put the horror of the Vanderbilt party out of my mind. Yet, in spite of telling myself it couldn't really happen, there I was, in my yellow organdy with the ruffles ironed all wrong and Fanny telling me for the love of God to stand still.

"You've got even skinnier, and how am I to make the dress fit at all?" Fanny had put my hair up in rags the night before. Now ringlets jounced alongside my long jaw. As I looked down at my dress while Fanny pinned it, I had one of those horrible freezing moments where I suddenly wanted my mother so *badly*....My mother would have seen I had a decent dress, not this limp, too big sack with the ruffles all crushed. She would understand what I was *feeling*—and would have taken me in her arms, probably. But now if

I should cry, Mama would simply turn and leave the room. At least she was tying the sash about my waist, making a bow, and it *seemed* attentive.

"Do hold your shoulders back, Eva!" Mama said. After all, I was facing her friends. I could see her making up her mind. "The dress will do perfectly well. The length is just right. You certainly don't want your knees to show, I hope."

"You're a treat!" Fanny said, without conviction and getting up stiffly.

When they left I had the sense to brush out the jouncing curls. Frizzed, my hair was startling. How queer and gaunt my face looked! I had borrowed one of Joyce's lipsticks and intended applying it on the way to the party. The party was considered such an occasion that, instead of walking through the woods, I was to be transported in the *Carafa*. Papa had arranged it, I knew that. And now it was he who saved my pride again. "Why Eva," he said, as we both went down the path side by side towards the dock, "how very grown up you look. Quite a young lady!" And he held my elbow as we approached the steps.

There was a mist on the lakes which I feared would take the frizz out of my hair. How was I to talk to New York men? Joyce was going to talk about the time her father took her to the Plaza. Perhaps I could tell them about Al Jolson stepping out of his touring car at Paul Smith's.

Gordon overshot the Denby dock, but finally after reversing, we made it. At the last moment Mama had insisted I wear her gray crêpe de chine cape which hit me just above the ankles. I simply would not think about the effect. For by now I could feel the wet strands of hair sagging on my shoulders. I could imagine what was happening to the ruffles. But never mind...I had managed to smear on Joyce's lipstick. I was about to have an experience, as Mrs. Framely said. No matter what happened I was taking part in an event. I could not expect to talk to New York men about Al Jolson. I was a spectator, and I knew the role. As a spectator little was expected of you. I intended to hold to that idea.

The Denby's guide helped me out of the boat and I followed him up the dock.

I had imagined the Denby camp blazing with lights and guests moving through the trees to strains of music. But instead, everything was very still and very dark. Here and there a lantern had been nailed to a tree. Surely the Denbys—if not the Vanderbilts themselves—could have brightened up the place.

Ahead, windows of a cabin glowed. The guide opened the door and held it while I went through.

I entered into a blaze of light. The scene was so dazzling, so unexpected after the dark walk, that for an instant I stared. Lamps and candles shone from the walls, bejeweled women sat about, their arms and necks bared. They were dressed as for a ball. Mrs. Whitelaw Reid had three inches of diamonds around her neck. Others wore small crowns made of jewels. The men were in dress suits. I hardly recognized anyone except old Mr. McAlpin, who stood by himself in a corner drinking champagne. The women, for some reason, sat in wicker chairs; the men stood in front of them talking. Everyone seemed very animated. I stood in my yellow organdy and Mama's long gray cape. No one paid the slightest attention to me. I saw Mrs. Slade Wainwright, but she was busily talking to Mr. Denby. Was Joyce already surrounded by New York men? Then Mrs. Denby came toward me. "How nice to see you, Eva, here's someone to take your cloak." A maid appeared. To my dismay Mrs. Denby simply moved off.

Where was Joyce? Then I saw her and could not believe my eyes. She was sitting *on the floor* in a corner. I went right to her.

"Whatever are you doing, Joyce?"

"There aren't enough chairs. And there aren't any New York men. You might as well sit down. The food's all right."

A waiter handed me a plateful. Joyce looked suddenly up at me, her face flushing its queer maroon color. "Mother wouldn't let me put my hair up! She said it wasn't *proper.*" Joyce was nearly crying.

( 57

Of course, that was the difference! Her hair was down her back. She looked my age! A child with round cheeks and big, gray eyes and long, yellow hair in a pink organdy dress.

I could see she was deeply shaken, and this came out in a kind of careless, slapdash manner. She chewed her food with her mouth open. She sat sloppily on the floor with her dress hopelessly crushed. She must be bitterly disappointed about the New York men. (A feeling of delicious relief stole over me.)

Slowly I sat down on the floor, not caring about my ruffles. Joyce and I ate in silence. People chattered over at the side of the room. There was constant laughter. They all seemed to be sitting in a rosy nimbus, every woman beautiful, every man handsome.

"Where'd you get the cape," Joyce asked, chewing on the lobster and actually taking a piece of shell out of her mouth with her fingers. Before I could answer she said, "Watch it, here comes the aunt." She raised her face, giving her prettiest smile.

"I'm so sorry we've run out of chairs," Mrs. Denby stood tall and elegant.

Joyce and I started to scramble to our feet.

"No, don't get up!" she smiled briefly and moved off. Next came white-haired, handsome Mrs. Whitelaw Reid, who impressed Joyce stupendously. Again we were not allowed to rise. How were we getting on? Wasn't it all *fun?* she asked, nodding her white head over the diamond collar. We both nodded back. Wait until we had some ice cream, she said with a little wink, and walked on.

Occasionally one of the husbands would stop and chat, his eyes always on Joyce. But no one stayed long. It seemed that on one side was the party in its private light, and on the other were Joyce and me and the maids and waiters; spectators, enjoying a treat.

Joyce who was watching the older people, said sharply, "There's Bill Vanderbilt. They'll have to introduce us."

I looked quickly over. Handsomer than Gerald in *The Meadowbrook Girls*, only dark.

"Not bad," Joyce said. I thought her manner had coarsened. I was right, for after this evening she never again held the campers in awe. The wicker chairs, the fact there was no orchestra, no New York men, she never understood. She entirely missed the quality of the party. The campers, dressed in "full fig," were highly entertained by the wicker chairs, the big bare room. An orchestra, to the campers, would have been vulgar, the noise horrid. But to sit on faintly uncomfortable chairs and drink impeccable champagne was all part of the proper fun.

After dessert—meringues—Joyce and I decided to get up. Even Joyce looked a little frumpish with her sash in a string and the bow limp. My ruffles were flat in the back and stuck out in front. It was at this confused instant as I was trying to fix my dress that Bill Vanderbilt approached. It all happened in a second. There I was sticking out my hand (for once I did *not* curtsy) as Mrs. Denby introduced me to a dark-haired, excruciatingly good-looking man in tails. I had never seen anyone like him, so at ease, smiling at us. Not even David had this man's manner. Then I saw, standing quietly beside him two beautiful girls, the misses Baldwin, Mrs. Denby said. Famous New York beauties, I learned later. They were twins and dressed alike in low-belted pink and lavendar dresses with skirts that fell in points. They were bare-armed. Joyce and I wore sleeves to the elbow.

"We could dance," Bill Vanderbilt said. "There's a victrola in the playroom."

A few moments later I found myself stumbling along a path after Joyce, who was following the two girls and Bill. The cabin, when we got there, was quite large, a single room, painted green. Rocking chairs lined the walls. There was a large, empty fireplace. The floor slanted. A victrola stood on a round wicker table. Bill went over at once and started winding. The machine seemed much older than Joyce's and there were only three records, "Oh, Suzanna" and "Woodman, Woodman Spare That Tree," or whatever it was called, and a warped record you could hardly hear and Joyce and I didn't know anyway. Everything about the situation seemed to strike Bill and the Baldwin twins as uproarious; they laughed and laughed. It was all so strange, so totally unlike anything Joyce and I had imagined. We were onlookers, not with the party at all.

Bill Vanderbilt made no move toward us. He danced first with one twin and then the other. They would start at one side of the room and then—because of the slanting floor—find themselves on the other. This seemed endlessly entertaining. Joyce and I stood watching, and then finally sat on the rockers. It wasn't as trying for me as for Joyce because at fifteen you don't expect to be asked to join in.

But suddenly, after a few minutes, by mutual consent, without a word, Joyce and I rose to our feet. I took hold of Joyce, and we danced. We performed our dip to perfection; we whirled knee to knee and ended up on the down side of the room. There was no thought of impressing the others. They paid no attention to us, anyway. We danced for our own amusement.

As the third record bleated to an end, Bill took off the needle. "I'm awfully sorry," he said, as though addressing Joyce and me. "These are the only records we've got." His face reddened.

I heard Joyce say, "I've got lots of records." And then unbelievably—"I don't know the way through the woods, but Eva does."

What a nerve! How *could* Joyce suggest such a thing? Even though I did indeed know my way through the woods, how awful of Joyce to suggest I run an errand—and in front of the Baldwin twins!

Then Bill Vanderbilt came over to me. Tall, white-shirted, a smile on his handsome lips. I had never been this close to anyone like him in my life.

"*Would* you, Eva?" He remembered my name! "The guide will go with you. You're in the Severn camp, aren't you?" He knew where I came from! My entire attitude changed. Bill said with a kind of tenderness: "You're a wonderful sport!"

The roots on the path caught the heels of my pumps. The guide and I walked without speaking. He carried a large lantern. I don't know why we didn't speak. I think I was too intent on getting to the Framely's camp and back as soon as possible. My big worry was leaving Joyce. She had foisted this whole thing on me and I suddenly did not trust her. Now that Bill had noticed me, I wanted to be back in the same room, or rather I didn't much care for Joyce being there. At one point it occurred to me to wonder why I didn't ask Joyce to come along with me, or why she didn't offer. Yes, how *could* she let me go alone?

At last the guide and I arrived at the Framelys'. The light was on in the main house. As I came up the steps I could see Mr. Framely by the center table reading. As I entered, he stared at me. "Eva, what's wrong? What are you doing?" He asked this because without speaking I had gone over to the record table and was shuffling through the discs. "Where's Joyce? The party isn't over, is it?"

"Of course not," I said. I was looking for "Avalon" and not paying attention. I could afford to be impatient and even important. I took about ten records off the pile.

"What in God's name are you doing!" Mr. Framely came toward me.

I looked at him. He was delaying me. "I'm bringing records over to the party," I said.

"You mean the Vanderbilts don't have any victrola records?" It was too much for him. He glared at me.

"That's right," I said, "they don't."

"Oh, for God's sake!" If Mrs. Framely had been there he never would have sworn.

"They don't have enough chairs, either, and there aren't any New York men." Then I made up the kind of lie that Joyce was so good at. "Bill Vanderbilt didn't come because he couldn't leave the party."

Mr. Framely kept staring in a dazed way. "They don't have any records and there aren't enough chairs..." He would never understand these campers, never.

"Well, I must be off," I said, rather brusquely. "Bill sent a guide over with me." I couldn't resist it.

"He did?"

I left Mr. Framely standing in the middle of the room, still staring.

When I arrived at the Denbys' camp, everyone made a great fuss over me, even the Baldwin twins thanked me. Bill took the records saying I surely was a great little sport. He went right to the victrola and put on "I've Got A Ticket To Paradise." I stood waiting for him to ask me to dance. Suddenly I noticed Joyce. While I was gone she had put up her hair. She must have brought the pins with her! Then, as the music started, and while I watched, without a word, Bill Vanderbilt walked over and took Joyce in his arms.

# Prelude

*"I imagine the party went off very well," Frederick said. "Although it does seem strange to have Eva walking back to camp instead of waiting for Gordon and the* Carafa. *We must be sure the Denby's lantern is returned. Eva says it was hanging on a tree. Odd there were no guides about." He seems confused, although looking correct in his thin black coat, but sitting very straight.*

*He and Anna are in the breakfast room. Eva has appeared for breakfast, but did not recite poetry. She wears her old brown skirt and faded, checked shirt of David's. She seems uncommunicative about the party. Yes, Bill Vanderbilt is very handsome. Yes, the party evidently was a success. Mrs. McAlpin had spoken to her and so had Mrs. Whitelaw Reid. There weren't enough chairs. She had left the party early because the heel came off her shoe. She had chosen to walk through the woods because she knew the way, and anyhow Gordon had not arrived as yet.*

*"It's typical of Eva to lose the heel of a shoe, after we took the trouble to send her in the* Carafa, *Anna says. She is sewing and now bites off her thread after gnawing at it, rather than applying her usual method, which is to clip the thread neatly with a little pair of gold scissors. She is embroidering a doily that is to go under the cream bottle and she holds the work close to her eyes. She wears small unrimmed glasses. Her manner is not as warm as usual and she seems inattentive. David has chosen to tell Frederick that he is leaving Yale in his sophomore year and going to...she can hardly say it to her-*

( 63

self...*Temple, a place no one they know even mentions. She is not only furious at the boy but peeved that Frederick has been the confidante. David had often asked her opinion. Surely she should have been warned. Of course she never would have approved, seeing these matters in a different light than her husband. She had been so proud of David.* "My grandson at Yale..." *Who would boast of a grandson at Temple? With this on her mind she is in no humor to talk about Eva. But Frederick keeps on.*

"I really thought it a pity to send Eva to the party in that unfortunate dress. She should never attempt to wear yellow. And with those dreadful ruffles, I wonder she had the courage to step into the Denby camp!" *A flush appears on Frederick's sallow cheeks.*

"Now come, Frederick." *Anna looks angrily over her glasses.* "That's not fair. The dress was perfectly adequate."

*Pause. A knock sounds on the door.*

"Entrez!" *Anna calls without thinking.*

*Mrs. Paul Framely stands in the doorway. Both Frederick and Anna stare at her. Then Frederick rises and goes toward her. Can they offer her some coffee? He is at loss because of the unusual hour.*

*Mrs. Framely does not reply to his question but says:* "I've come to apologize for Joyce's unforgivable conduct last night. How she could have allowed Eva to walk through the woods to get *victrola* records—even though with a guide—I cannot understand. The least she could have done was to go with her."

*Stunned silence. Then Anna, grasping the situation, says easily,* "Dear Mrs. Framely, do not upset yourself. Eva is used to running errands and thought nothing of going to your camp. Why should she? I'm sure she was happy to perform the service."

*Mrs. Framely looks in bewilderment at Anna. She is correctly attired in hat, dress, and gloves, which seem to emphasize her astonished stare.* "But I think Eva was looking forward to the party!"

*This is such a non sequitur that Anna and Frederick simply smile.*

*Mrs. Framely, standing very straight in the doorway and with a certain dignity, apologizes for calling at this early hour, turns, and is out the door. Frederick is so taken aback that he makes no move to accompany her down to the dock, but watches her make her way over the pine needles, then run lightly (like a girl, he thinks) down the steps to her waiting boat. There is the grind of the engine starting, and she is gone.*

5 Joyce came to camp only once during the following week. Mrs. Framely was punishing her. I was relieved she stayed away. It would take a while before I could forget the triumphant look on her face as Bill Vanderbilt put his arm around her while the Baldwin twins and I stood along the wall, watching.

"But I couldn't *refuse*," she cried. She had come to apologize. Her big eyes widened so that the lashes curled against her lids. She still had her hair up. Showing off, I thought. For the first time I took note of her smug, flaunting air, and the swing of her too-large hips and her prim walk. "What did you expect?"

Well, there wasn't any answer, if she didn't know it.

"He'd have danced with you next, if you hadn't gone home. He told me so."

She was lying. I couldn't remember anyone lying directly to me before. Of course the girls in school told fibs. But here was a grown-up important lie. I thought that if Joyce would lie about this, she'd lie about anything.

"How'd you get home?"

"The guide gave me a lantern. He wanted to come with me but I wouldn't let him." Not for the world would I tell Joyce Framely how scared I had been. The guide told me to bear left when I came to the fork in the woods. ("It's only a step, miss. I'd go with you, only the older guests are leaving and I have to be on the dock.") I knew it wasn't far, as he said. But it seemed miles and with the path so unfamiliar in the dark, and my shoes slipping on the needles. What would happen to me if I were really lost? At this, my breath started to come in gasps and I was sobbing. Then suddenly I saw Mrs. Mertz's light shining from her cabin. I cried out loud with relief. And then I simply lay down on the ground, with my head in my arms and the lantern beside me.

Joyce knew what the woods were like in the dark. She said nothing more about my walking home. Our whole friendship was a joke, I thought. On me, so far.

I would not let her have it all her own way, and I looked straight at her and said, "You never should have let me go alone to get the records, Joyce. That was *mean* . . ."

"Well, you didn't have to go." She glanced away, played with a twig, twirling it in her little hands.

"You told them I'd go."

"You didn't *have* to," she repeated, looking bored.

"Oh, shut up!"

But now Joyce kept on: "You wanted to go for the records. You thought it would get you in with Bill."

She was shrewd, in her nasty way. It was the very reason I had gone off into the woods, only to realize what a jackass I'd made of myself.

"I suppose you're seeing him all the time," I said, rather sarcastically.

"Just this afternoon," she answered, with such complacency I could have hit her.

We left camp early that year. I'd only seen Joyce a few times. Their new guide had run the *Katydid* into that log in the slough and broken the cam shaft. So we couldn't have gone on picnics, anyway. Fortunately, before we left, I met Mrs. Framely at The Landing. She was just getting into their boat. I went right up to her. She kissed me.

"We haven't seen you in so long," she said.

"No. I'm sorry."

"I've missed you. So has Mr. Framely."

"I've missed both of you," I said. I looked carefully away from her. I remembered how soft and loving she had always been and how much it meant to me.

"We're leaving next week," I said.

She held out her hand, then put both arms around me. "This is goodbye, isn't it? But not really." She held me by my shoulders. The wind blew her hair about her face. "We'll see you in Philadelphia. We aren't far away."

I squeezed her hand. I really couldn't say any more. She was the kindest person I had ever known.

"Don't forget!" she cried, stepping into the boat and sitting down. Then she turned and waved her hand. The guide shot out of the slip in reverse, slammed the gear into forward. He'd ruin this boat, too, if he wasn't careful. So I thought of that instead of remembering my last glimpse of Mrs. Framely.

As the summer ended and I prepared for my senior year at school, I knew the time was fast approaching when I must make a serious effort to head off Mama's catastrophic plan. She and Papa expected to bring me "out," she said. They would give a formal tea for the occasion. They would also provide me with proper clothes. She herself had enjoyed a most successful debut. How this related to me I could not figure. (Mama had been presented at the Court of St. James. Was all this supposed to fit in with the one-time husband, poor Mr. Komitow?)

Touching one by one the five curls that lay so whitely on her forehead, Mama said that I would love the balls and dances and that if I just learned to carry myself properly, it would add inches to my height. I think my height was all she dared contemplate.

This conversation brought the situation sharply before me. I went directly to Papa. He was in his study off the dining room. A coal fire burned in the grate. I knew I interrupted him but that could not be helped. Clasping my hands carefully behind my back and standing stiffly, I said I understood my mother had left me some money.

Papa placed his pen on the silver tray.

"Your mother left you three thousand dollars," he said.

It seemed an enormous sum to me. Why hadn't I asked about it before?

"I would like to use that for college, Papa. I mean—I want to go to college."

"College?" He raised gray eyebrows. "That would hardly pay for a college education. To say nothing of your lack of preparation." When I started to interrupt he held up his hand. "The money will not be yours until you are twenty-one," he said.

I was dashed and did not know what to say, but held on, quite desperately.

"Papa, couldn't you loan me the money and let me pay you back?"

He folded his hands. "Eva, you baffle me. Your Mama and I are giving you a tea. The date is down at Dreka's. You know all this. Mama is quite set on the whole plan."

"But I could 'come out' and go to college too, Papa!"

"That scarcely solves the money problem, now does it?" He picked up his pen from the tray. "And I don't believe you would want to go against Mama, Eva. I'm sure not. Nor against me."

I said nothing. I turned and left the room. The disappointment was shocking. My last hope. Why had I let college go until so late? By the time I got my money I'd be too old to care. Now that there was no hope I realized what college could mean. A haven, with girls from all over, places like Utah. Pretty or not wouldn't matter. Everyone would be too serious to bother about a debut. Why had I not realized this? Would it have done any good? Mama's program was to be inexorably carried out, no matter at what cost to me. I had the feeling that from the moment they accepted me as a member of the family, the plan was made, a kind of package, expected by the society in which they moved. Perhaps if I had shown some outstanding brilliance in history, Papa might have reconsidered. But I had failed him with Prescott and been too concerned simply living in the household day by day to become engrossed in studies. For although

David's taunt: "Would you rather be in a Home?" put the stiffening in me, it also deeply increased my sense of insecurity. I could never be *sure*. Therefore getting by, not being conspicuous, holding my own was my aim.

All this may seem overstated, put in for effect. But it actually happened and is an answer to the charge made recently that I was dissipated, a flapper-type, superficial, even depraved in my "lust for a good time." It is also said that I do not even have a college degree. No one regrets that more than I. As it turned out, Papa was wholly inaccurate (and I think inexcusably careless), for my mother had made no stipulation as to when the money was to be mine, and I could have used it any time.

Three thousand dollars would not have paid for my college expenses, but Papa could have stood me the rest, as against a debut, no matter how cheaply done. It was odd that David did not come in on my side. Surely college must seem like a solution. I suppose it was because he regarded college girls as "grinds," girls who weren't popular and did not "have a good time."

Having a good time in the twenties was a way of life, which increased my apprehension and sense of isolation. Those families with money, social position, and even a moderately pretty daughter planned for this "good time" with hard-headed realism and with full understanding that a proper debut would cost a large amount of money, particularly if it included a ball. Work must be done well in advance, foresight masked in the usual phrases, saying that one's daughter was going to St. Timothy's (or even Foxcroft) because so many of her friends were there. Whereas the real reason might be to keep her out of possible circulation (so that her "freshness" did not wear off) and at her debut she would burst upon her expectant world. Or the girl was sent to Miss Irwin's, The Shipley School, or Springside. Attendance at these schools in the twenties meant that one kept largely with one's own kind. Recognition of likeness would help a girl pick a Proper Mate. In 1922 there still existed in Philadelphia much the same society that Mama had known. More license, certainly. Petting and even necking went on, but never openly, and if there was any hint of promiscuity, the ranks of Nice Girls closed inexorably. Life for the college boy was very different. But for a girl, purity was an enhancement, making a girl more valued and valuable.

Prohibition added a hectic note and something of an illicit flavor because boys carried flasks. But the "front" was ever soberly correct and formal. The "flapper," publicly "living it up," did not exist in decorous, social Philadelphia, or at least was not acceptable and never "included."

David said: "Why do you suddenly want to go to college? You're not much of a student."

He sounded like Papa.

"I'll change," I said.

"You haven't even taken college preparatory."

"I could tutor. Nancy Prior would help me."

"You should have thought of this last year."

"I didn't believe Mama would insist on my 'coming out.'"

"Of course you're 'coming out!' Why did I slave over your dancing? That's your trouble. You won't look ahead."

"David..." I stood quite still. We were in his room and he was dressing for a party. He had on his tuxedo coat. His face was set and hard, his eyes bright. His blond hair sprang thick and glossy from a perfect part. He seemed miles away.

"David," I said again, the words sticking, *"I can't do it."*

He turned. I saw the sharp wariness in his eyes. "You'll do it and you'll pull it off. You did quite well at the last Saturday Evening, although you were a mess with Ted Rickard."

"He wanted to tango!"

"You've got to follow anything."

I tried again. "I *can't* go to these big parties alone."

"There'll be a dinner dance first."

I didn't say anything. I just stood by the bureau, holding onto the edge of the mahogany top. At the Saturday Evening (supposedly a "dancing class"), David had shown off with me, doing a whole lot of fancy steps in a corner while a group of boys stood around watching us. David could do anything, get me anywhere. Without him I was simply lost. The popular girls at school already had boys come to call, as it was termed. These boys looked after them at parties, wanted to dance with them. I had nothing like that. A boy had never come to see me. David brought his friends in, but that didn't count. I must have a "line," David said. Once I asked a boy if he had a dog. My best ploy (which I couldn't use all the time) was suggesting we persuade the orchestra leader to play "Ain't Misbehavin'" which, though having painful memories for me, usually pleased the boys. David was there, watching. He brought boys up, or sent them to cut in. He managed, I never knew how. The Saturday Evening was a real party. Any girl who did not get asked might as well give up being a debutante. Joyce was there. (She had also been in the senior class at Miss Irwin's, to my surprise, and did not seem to mind being somewhat isolated. She went her own way.)

I had not done too badly at the Saturday Evening, as David said. But the whole day before I had been half sick. Why should I endure this night after night? As I stood by David's bureau I wondered why I was being forced against my will, and I thought that the reasons I had made up were not enough. I was being put through this torture hoping that I might find someone to marry. Why did they bother? I was going to marry David.

# Prelude

"Well, Frederick?"

"Well, Anna? I think you've pulled it off. Aren't you pleased?"

"I suppose so." Anna is unusually vague.

Frederick swerves from the subject. "I think you'll come to like Framely. Even though he's such a common fellow. I have a feeling she didn't approve. When the arrangements were being made she didn't come with him."

"Mrs. Framely is rather shy." There is a shade of tightness in Anna's voice. She has not failed to note Frederick's admiration.

"She does not strike me as being socially ambitious." He smiles rather tenderly.

Anna says coldly, "I always regretted being involved."

"But Anna!" Frederick is astonished. "You told me two years ago that the Framelys might do something for Eva. A dance, you hoped. Now you've arranged everything so marvelously. And you like managing such affairs, admit it." He is teasing her.

"These affairs took rather more than I bargained on. Getting Joyce into Miss Irwin's was not simple. And I nearly failed with those women who run the Saturday Evening Dancing Class. After all, the Framelys are nobody. Without me, Joyce would not have even been considered." Anna speaks almost churlishly and seems unlike herself, as though she has been forced to take her first step down (or perhaps her second if Komitow is counted).

# Ugly Girl

*She and Frederick are seated in the dining room at a large mahogany table. Ten badly polished Hepplewhite chairs line the walls. High windows overlook the alley and the back of the houses. A gray day with a cold light. In the evening when a dinner party is in progress, the heavy curtains of the room are pulled, the big candelabra lighted. A fine cloth spread over the lengthened table, Meissen plates gleam gold. Even the portrait of Mad Anthony Wayne, one of Anna's forebears, no longer appears shabby and in need of cleaning, but seems dashing and romantic, the cockade on his hat whitened, his uniform a deeper blue.*

Anna says in some distress, "Having the Framelys give this party, standing in the receiving line with Mr. Framely! . . . What will Marie and Geoffrey Van Ness think?"

"They'll be amsued, Anna." *He puts his hand over hers and gives it a little shake.* "Can't you see the amusing side? Here we are with this unfortunate child trying to bring her 'out,' when along comes Framely père who wants to wave a wand, give a dance, and ease the burden—for a price. So we're stuck. And we pay up."

Anna regards him sourly. "I'm the one who's been stuck, Frederick."

*He smiles with satisfaction.* "You've been brilliant."

*An answering smile curves her rather straight mouth.* "I suppose you could say so." *She reaches for a small silver bell, rings it. Robert, the butler, comes in.* "You can serve the dessert, Robert."

*He moves slowly, at his own pace. Tall and lugubrious, his black face is sullen. He picks up two plates at once, flaunting Anna's rule of one plate at a time. She notes his action and although she says nothing, the smile leaves her lips. Again she feels frustrated and manipulated. It will take time for her to become accustomed to the sensation.*

6 "Eva Colby," Bernard Cranby wrote in his syndicated column, "lived in the world of privilege. Her summers were spent in an exclusive mountain retreat where she had a fleet of motorboats at her disposal (did he mean the old *Carafa?*)) and whiled away the hours visiting the camps of the Vanderbilts or the Denbys. In the winters she inhabited a handsomely appointed mansion on exclusive DeLancey Place in Philadelphia. Eva Colby only knew the feel of satins and silks, the taste of champagne (smuggled illicitly into the cellars of the rich, socially elite). Dressed in a long gown, wrapped in furs, she walked down the marble steps of the DeLancey Place mansion into a purring motor car and was wafted to a ball where she danced until two in the morning. Real life passed Eva Colby by. She was totally unfitted for The Master's spartan existence. She flinched and fled."

There is hardly an accurate word in Cranby's article. We lived far from luxuriously, even food in Mama's house, or at camp, was barely adequate. Not so when Mama and Papa gave a dinner party, then the food was so plentiful Mrs. Mertz complained that Mama had bought enough guinea hen to feed all DeLancey Place.

As for wearing furs. I wore Mama's old chenille evening wrap and carried her black caracul muff. The "purring motor car" was a secondhand Packard with isinglass windows.

Champagne did not enter my life. At balls and dances there was spiked punch, tasting like stale lemonade, which I never drank. Mama and Papa gave their tea (small sandwiches and cakes). They invited about a hundred of their friends, with a few debutantes, carefully chosen. Silks and satins I knew. For Mama provided me with two evening dresses, one red, which David had picked out, the other lavendar, not wholly successful but favored by Mama. These preparations I endured with difficulty. Time went so fast. It seemed only a few weeks from the day I graduated to the moment I received the first cream-colored envelope, an invitation to a luncheon.

Today sociologists speak of the grave consequences to the individual who is denied access to the peer group. Ida Shanker, the fat pimply girl with whom no one would dance, had done away with herself. Because she wasn't popular? society asked. Surely there must have been another reason.

I was not fat and my skin had cleared up, but my face remained the same. Some of the dread that filled me showed the night I had dinner with David. It was early October, a warm night. Mama and Papa were out. David sat at the head of the table. I sat at the side. The long windows of the dining room stood open. We were in full view of the houses opposite. I watched a delivery boy come down the alley, push in a gate, and disappear.

"How was the lunch?" David asked.

"All right." It had not gone too badly. Some of the girls I knew from school, although of course they were in their own "set."

"Well, who was it given for?"

"Babs Clayton."

"She gets around." David picked up a chicken leg, bit into it. For some reason his table manners when he ate with me were disgusting, whereas with Mama and Papa he ate quite fastidiously. As he went on chewing and talking in a careless, slangy way, I watched him, and like a transparency superimposed on an original photograph I saw again what had been his fair handsomeness, the high color, his grave, attentive look that so quickly changed to fierceness. The reality at the table was someone thin, angular. David must have lost twenty pounds in a few weeks. The handsome blondness was still there, but now hawkish and hollow-cheeked with a beaky nose and an edgy manner, also accompanied by a peculiar smirk, although occasionally he would break into his former wide embracing smile. I knew he worked hard; the job at the Temple library was boring.

David said, "I want to tell you something, Eva." He gnawed on the joint of the bone. I knew I had a "lesson" coming. "You ought to see more of Joyce. The Framelys are being pretty wonderful to you."

He was referring to the dance for Joyce and me.

"I don't like Joyce."

David paid no attention. "Joyce knows her way around. Boys like her. She wants to be friends, but she says in school you went with pills like Debbie O'Halloran and Mary Devlin."

At that moment Robert's head appeared around the corner of the pantry door. "You want more chicken, David? I gotta small piece here." When Mama was home it was "Mr. David" and "Miss Eva." David said no. Robert started taking the dishes. "You could do with more flesh on you, David." Robert laughed, a raucous sound. "You losing all them good looks. Girls is going to notice pretty soon."

"That'll kill me!" David said, and Robert laughed again. David was always able to manage people. Even mean-hearted old Robert joked with him.

I said hotly, "I have a right to pick my own friends, David. And they're a lot nicer than Joyce Framely. Joyce is nothing but a laugh, really. "Biggie!" I said, half to myself.

"Is that what she's called?" David grinned. "Boy! Biggie— and how!"

I told him he was disgusting, but he just laughed. What was he doing listening to Joyce? I'd seen them dance awfully close at the Saturday Evening. I suppose Joyce must have "It." But couldn't David realize how shallow she was and self-centered? Some sort of hot honesty had left David. He was no longer serious, the word much used by everyone. We could not have a serious discussion.

"It's girls like Joyce and Babs Clayton you want to go around with. And let me tell you, popular girls are important." Here, to my horror he took out a package of cigarettes and struck a match.

"You're not allowed to smoke, David! What are you doing?"

"That's true of a lot of things," he said, not looking at me. There was something in the way he spoke that made me silent.

Tapping the ash from his cigarette, David said, half squinting at me, "Most girls would give their eyeteeth to be in your position."

In a world where only prettiness was acceptable? I said nothing.

David went on: "Why can't you realize you're coming out as my sister? Don't you see what that means, how it looks? There are lots of fellahs owe me favors. I got you through the dancing class days, didn't I?"

A favor...I couldn't comment. And yet I appreciated what he was doing and knew I should sink without him. But then a sudden suspicion went across my mind.

"David," I said, "Why did you leave Yale?"

He blew smoke in the air. I thought maybe he wouldn't answer. So far he had refused to tell me whenever I asked. But now he said quite simply, "I didn't want to be indebted to them."

"Them" always meant Mama and Papa. "But you never minded before."

"I found out my father had died in debt. Papa had to put out thousands of dollars." David glanced away. He had a strange intent look. Uncombed hair fell over his forehead. He was in his shirt sleeves, cuffs rolled sloppily.

"But that's got nothing to do with you!"

"It's a debt I should pay."

"David!"

He kept staring out the window. Dusk had fallen. A light appeared in the house opposite. "Yes, it is. I'm going to pay Papa back."

What did David feel about his father, a kind of sacredness? David had built Father into twice his size. Finding Father in debt must have been a terrible shock. So terrible he had never told me? Now he had changed colleges, lived at home and worked part-time at Temple University. Pay back a debt? It would take a lifetime. I didn't dare ask how much Father owed. Father was vitally necessary to David. My mother was vitally necessary to me. Naturally, you had to belong to someone.

"I mean to be rich some day." David seemed suddenly pleased with himself, gloom gone.

"Anthropologists aren't rich!" I said impatiently. David was always going to be an anthropologist, like Papa.

"I might go into business."

I paid no attention, which was a pity, because right there David set a clue and I should have picked him up and challenged him.

The Saunders dinner dance was the first big party of the winter and it nearly turned into a fiasco. David had to work late at the library. "You'll be all right for dinner," he said. "When the regular dancing starts I'll be there."

I did quite well at dinner. In between courses we danced and I showed Bill Osborne, who sat on my right, how to do the dip and sidestep. And when I told Lou Allen, on my left, a small, rather wasted-looking boy, that he must be on the Penn crew he was evidently pleased and started talking. We exchanged Red Grange stories. I laughed a lot and had as much to say as anyone. With my new shingle slicked forward into spit curls (Mama said shingled hair was hopelessly vulgar) and my lips painted cherry red (applied in the car going to the party), I looked very different than the other girls and quite dashing. Shingle, spit curls and lipstick were David's idea and they gave me confidence.

Just as Lou Allen and I were about to have a real conversation, dinner was over and the music stopped. Now I looked for David. But he wasn't in the room. Boys started to drift off. I saw Naomi Biddle and went towards her, but the music began again and suddenly I was standing on the edge of the floor alone. A stag line formed. Where was David? I stood for an instant and then fled to the Ladies Room.

"My God!" David cried, later that night when we were home, sitting on the edge of his bed, still in our evening clothes with the old blue quilt draped around us." You came out of the Ladies Room carrying that *book*. You even had your finger in the place where you'd stopped reading. Don't you know it is absolutely *fatal* for any of the girls to see you sitting there *reading?* They'll circulate it all over!"

"No one saw me reading but the attendant, David," I said tartly. "Whenever the door opened I hid the book. ·I'd brought it along in that big muff Mama made me carry. I was afraid I'd have a bad time. And I did! You weren't there. I couldn't believe it!" I would never tell him the agony I had gone through, nor the innumerable times I had pretended to fix my hair or wash my hands, or fasten a garter whenever girls came in. Sometimes the girls would stay gossiping, and I'd have to give up and go sit in the toilet cubicle. If this was to happen at parties I would never go to another. I had completely relied on David. He had told me not to worry, he'd be there.

"What happened to you?" I burst out at him, doubly angry because I must have sensed from the beginning he was unreliable or I would not have grabbed up Trollope's *Is He a Popenjoy?* and stuck it in my muff.

"Well," David said, somewhat reluctantly I felt, "Joyce was waiting for Bruce Williams. She was standing alone in the lobby. Bruce was supposed to be taking her across to the Ritz where a whole bunch of people were having a party in the grille." He said this quite earnestly, but I saw his face redden.

"Joyce!" I cried. "That's impossible. She can perfectly well take care of herself!" If Joyce was responsible for putting me through this agony and humiliation she could have her old dance and everything that went with it!

"Well, no she couldn't, Eva. She had to get across Broad Street and I didn't think she should do that alone.

"So you had to take Joyce to the Ritz. That didn't take very long." I was so furious I pulled the quilt away from him and around myself. The room was icy.

"No, it didn't." He was feeling his way, trying to figure out what had happened and make it presentable to me. "But you see this Williams guy wasn't at the Ritz, either. And Joyce didn't want to go into the grille by herself—"

I started to blurt out something but he stopped me. "Look Eva, I couldn't just leave her stranded. Have some sense!"

"So then what?" I kept my eyes right on him. I wanted the truth.

"There were a whole bunch of people at a table. They were older. Girls who maybe 'came out' two years ago. When they all got up to dance, naturally I dance with Joyce. "Not too bad," he said thoughtfully. He was so engrossed in his story he'd forgotten the point. And he went right on in this sort of dazed unreal voice, like someone reciting a lesson. "The men all had flasks, and I had this old battered leather one of my father's, so I could offer Joyce a drink."

Joyce drank! And David didn't seem to think a thing about it. He had told me never to take a drink from a boy's flask. It was an absolute rule. Why did he become so mesmerized? He was telling this story as though I didn't exist, whereas in fact I was going through torment.

"Joyce and the other girls kept telling me it was early. At a dinner dance the dinner went on forever.

"Well, I knew that was true. And I was right in the middle of a talk with this fellow from Graham Parson's about the bond market when suddenly Babs Clayton appeared. I knew she'd been at the Saunders' party. Dinner must be well over. I left. I didn't say good-bye or anything, I just went."

What was there to say? If Joyce's date hadn't arrived then could I blame her for holding on to David? No, but she was always making trouble for me.

Facing what had happened head on, I decided I better forget it. David would never understand how being so dependent on him affected me. And then there was the realization that David had this other life—gin in flasks...

David said, "You had a fine time the rest of the party, Evie. I was proud of you when those boys gathered around to watch you and Tom Shiver. That doesn't happen very often."

I turned and deliberately smiled at him. He had let me down and it was over. I had done well once I got out of the "Ladies." David had taught me just how to move my body and spent hours teaching me the newest steps. I knew I had pretty legs and managed to hold my skirt up a little as Tom Shiver and I did some fancy work. When the music stopped there were boys standing around watching and they clapped. Two of them flipped a coin for who was to dance with me next. So, for the rest of the evening, which wasn't long, I stayed in the same corner.

David had one final word and stood up to say it. "I really think you're started, Evie. But you'll have to watch this Tom Shiver. He's smooth. He may try something. Remember the same rules hold." David faced me, red-eyed. By now the quilt was on the floor. "Don't let anyone get away with *anything*."

"I won't," I said. I nearly told him that Joyce petted, but it seemed cheap, somehow.

David considered the list for the Framely party extremely important. This was going to be the party of the year, he said, with Paul Whiteman, spiked punch, and a waiter by every bowl to see no one drank too much. "We want it gay, but no brawl." Mr. Framely agreed. Whatever David planned, Joyce said, was sure to be all right. This nauseating remark I let pass. Joyce had made a point of coming to me after the Saunders' party and apologizing for keeping David. She said someone told her they had seen me in the Ladies Room. I had my answer ready and I let her have it. I had ripped a seam of my dress, I said, and the maid offered to fix it. "Was David late?" I asked, rather icily. "I don't think anyone noticed. The party was really the bees knees." Ordinarily I wouldn't have considered saying anything as dated, but I knew I made an impression on Joyce, who had the nerve to hint I was stuck in the "Ladies." I went on to tell her casually about the boys flipping a coin for a dance with me. I thought she turned a shade paler.

When David went over the list for the dance he said there were too many pills.

"They're Eva's friends," Joyce replied with memorable candor.

"They'll kill the party," David said, striking out the names of my friends. I felt bad because at school these girls had voted for me and almost made me class president. But they weren't 'coming out,' and they wouldn't have a good time. Anyway, David was adamant.

David and Mr. Framely seemed friendly. But Mrs. Framely was not nearly as easy with David as I expected. She rather stood her distance. Whenever David was in the Framely house a kind of tension built up. Mr. Framely questioned him closely about Temple and the future. David said he'd always wanted to be an anthropologist and he'd try for a scholarship to do graduate work at Penn.

"You look like a businessman to me." Mr. Framely puffed hard on his cigar. I remembered that night at dinner when David said he might go into business. Had it been Mr. Framely who put the idea into his head? I expected David to argue, but he just kept pushing a piece of apple pie around on his plate. I saw Joyce eyeing him. Mrs. Framely had a little fit of coughing and drank some water.

"Penn's got the best business school in the country," Mr. Framely said. He finished his coffee, flicked his fingers in the finger-bowl, and put his napkin down on the table, a signal that the meal was over.

7   The Framely dance was declared certain to be the best party of the year. Mama stood at the head of the receiving line magnificent in blue velvet, bowing graciously although knowing almost no one.

The whole party was intoxicating. A line formed behind me, boys kept cutting in. I danced a staid foxtrot in the middle of the floor instead of flinging myself around in a corner. There was no fear of being "stuck" with the same boy. Now I went from hand to hand. It was at the Framely party that I played the violin for the first time. I went right up on the stage with Paul Whiteman, stood in the beautiful cloth of gold dress Mrs. Framely had given me, tucked Mr. Whiteman's fiddle under my chin and played the obligato to "Smiles." Afterward everyone clapped. I was "popular." This was what other girls felt: no cares, all joy. I wanted the party to last forever but at three o'clock Mr. Framely told Mr. Whiteman the party was over. As the orchestra played "Goodnight Ladies" David came and and took me in his arms. We danced quietly, just his arms around me and my head on his shoulder.

Although the Framely party "established" me, I still had to "keep up." Much of the winter lay ahead. Fanny (grumbling) shortened my evening dresses. I took to smoking with a long cigarette holder, like the John Held girls. I had my hair cut in a shorter shingle because David said my head was a good shape. Slowly, slowly, the image of myself that had forever beset me started to fade. I became what I pretended, with a certain swagger that was pure pride.

After that first time David never failed me at a party. He was always there. He brushed up my "line," telling me new stories about football players, gossip about the coming Dempsey-Firpo fight, stories about Tilden, Helen Wills. He made me read about Tutankhamen's Tomb being raised at Luxor. He persuaded Papa to buy a radio. I didn't need coaching about art or books; they weren't subjects popular with the boys I knew, and anyway art and music rubbed off on me from Mama and Papa. I mustn't let myself get thought about as "bright," David said. Boys didn't like too much cleverness in a girl. But I ought to be ready to comment on most subjects, and I must have an opinion about Prohibition. He was against my discussing the Pig Woman and the Halls-Mills murder case. So I was the girl who could babble along on most subjects, who was always cheerful and full of pep, and who "danced like a streak." With my spit curls (now worn openly in spite of Mama), and my widened mouth and my cigarette and short skirts, pulled down sash, I was conspicuous, and it worked.

I had a whole group of "new friends," Liz Alexander, Naomi Biddle, Babs Clayton. I went to school with these girls but did not really know them. Now we saw each other at parties and occasionally went to a movie. (However, I still saw my real friends Mary Devlin, Nancy Prior, and Debbie O'Halloran, whenever possible.) Occasionally I asked Babs Clayton to lunch. She had rather big legs and a sharp way of speaking. Mama thought her amusing and said she never knew what that Clayton girl was going to come out with next.

David talked again to me about "not letting any of these fellahs get away with–uh–anything."

"Necking, you mean."

"You've got a rough tongue."

"I learned it from you."

"Well, unlearn it. Don't talk that way. You'll give a bad impression. You want to watch Tom Shiver."

I had already "allowed" Tom to kiss me. He was now fumbling for my breast. I was confused about all this because although I withdrew from Tom, with a severe reprimand, yet the plain fact was I enjoyed these tussles. Tom was very expert in his kisses and I didn't know *where* that would end. He now had taken not only to caressing my breast but reaching for my *knee*. I had jerked away, stung and resentful, although breathing quickly.

"There's no harm in it, Eva. You know how I feel about you."

"No, I don't."

Tom blushed. "Well, I come to call, don't I?"

"So do Stewy Frazer–and Arnold Buckley."

"I certainly hope you don't allow Frazer..."

There was no doubt about it. I had sex appeal, even "It." I was different. I could joke about Freud or Coué.

Stewy Frazer and Tom Shiver and Arnold Buckley, formed a nucleus. It was not enough to have men dance with you, they must also come to call, as David said. I was not to go out unchaperoned except to an afternoon movie (he was like Mama, with his rules). Tom Shiver, who had a Franklin car, took me for an occasional spin. This didn't happen very often because both Tom and I preferred dancing. Tom brought me a new recording of "Me and My Shadow," with a drum solo that was terrific.

I wondered if my success riled Joyce, because one day over the phone when we were talking about a party, she said, "You were quite a hit," and sounded mad.

"Come on!"

"It's all that dancing. I don't see how you keep it up. I should think you'd be exhausted."

She made it sound like basketball practice.

"No. It was fun. I never get enough."

"Your brother gave me quite a rush last night."

"He did." I cooled off. Had they sat out? I wouldn't ask.

"We sat out a couple of dances."

"David's a good dancer," I said.

"He told me why he gave up going to Yale."

I was silent.

"He wanted to be near you, he said. He felt you needed him."

All the fury left over from Bill Vanderbilt, through the Saunders party—right up to this shocking moment—rose in me. She was lying in her teeth. David never would have told her such a thing. And it wasn't *so*. And even if it were, what right had she to stick her nose in? *And taunt me...* "Yale" had been pencilled on the leaves of David's school books. He'd always been going to Yale. He went to Temple to save Papa money. He *couldn't* have given it all up for me. I wouldn't have it. I couldn't *endure* it. He couldn't have told her. Damn her soul!

"Of course he likes the department at Temple. . . ." Her satisfied voice went on. What a nasty little beast she was, with her blonde, fat face. How many times had she ruined things for me? *But not this time.*

I said, right at her, "David never told you that, Joyce."

"No. But he told Pop," she came back quickly. "And he and I talked about it the other night."

"Not about me, you didn't," I said, and hung up. Right in her pudding face. Then I rushed upstairs.

David was in his room, studying. I burst in. "David—you didn't give up going to Yale because you felt—" I stumbled—"because of me?...You couldn't!"

"Well, in a way." He seemed unsurprised and very matter-of fact. "I couldn't leave you alone. How would you get on at dances and stuff? If things go wrong, a girl can be affected for life." He didn't need to mention poor Ida Shanker. He was smoking, blowing the smoke out the open window. The room was freezing. He wore his overcoat. "There's my father's debt and I didn't want Papa spending money on an expensive college." He looked at me. He was quite serious and unemotional. "I like being home, frankly. It's fun. I like the parties. Liz Alexander has asked me to dinner at her house. And I'm 'rushing' Joyce, although she's got the craziest 'line'..." He grinned at me.

I suppose I'd known all along that part of his reason for leaving Yale had been for me. My "coming out" was that important to him. I must be like "other girls," he evidently told himself. Of course I appreciated the sacrifice, but I realized I did not feel grateful. David himself had toughened me. Gratitude was an emotion he would not tolerate. His act, I thought, bound us even closer together, but in a different way. A mature decision had been made. David was frank and objective about it, letting me into his confidence, being matter-of-fact. He paid me the compliment of believing I was old enough and tough enough to accept what he had done and not be "sloppy," as he would put it. At this I felt my eyes fill with tears and turned my head away.

## Ugly Girl

That night I was again in David's room. Dressed in my old blue wrapper. I watched him struggle with the studs in his stiff shirt as he tried not to "break" the starched front. It was at this time that David would give me advice or perhaps feed me a new "line." We were both going to the Cranshaw party in their big country house on the Main Line. A very small, spiffy affair, according to David.

As I sat cross-legged on David's bed I fell suddenly silent watching him push through a stud. He never would let me help him. Because it might mean touching him—which was never permitted? What did that mean? As the thought of touching him went through my mind I realized that I was scrutinizing David. I saw his strong neck as though my hand lay on it, his shoulders, the smoothness of his arms with a bulge of muscle as he exerted strength on the stud. David was in his underwear, now slipping into his shirt. The only man in the world who could manage to look attractive with shirt tails hanging. Although the sight was familiar, yet now I found it absorbing. I doubt if I had ever taken in his legs before, hairy as they were and strong, the thighs firm and quite beautiful. What lay above? As I thought this I had a sudden sense of suffocation, blood rushing through my body. I may have made a sound. For David raised his head and stared at me. And then suddenly, seeing my face, he tore off his shirt, stood for an instant in front of me. And then with a groan or cry he threw his arms around me in a kind of crushing embrace, rolled me over on the bed, lay beside me, and held me to him. He was trembling. I could feel his whole body shake. He did not kiss me, only pressed his cheek so hard against mine that I could have cried out. But I did nothing, only gripped him tightly. *It's David...it's David...* I kept repeating, and felt a kind of dislodgement inside myself and my arms go loose. In an instant he was off the bed. His back was turned to me. "Go get dressed, Eva. Go now."

I stood in my room by the window. *I was in love...* I steadied myself holding to the sill. For David loved me. All these years of never touching—I had always loved David. And then I thought: *and he has always loved me.* Forever there had been this love, this man—now mine. Surely mine...a moment ago he had trembled against me. And leapt away. Then told me to go. Surely he should have lain softly beside me, kissing me?...If all had been right.

At this the room seemed to bulge and contract. And I found myself on the floor and lay there quite still.

I don't believe I stayed long on the floor, because I remember getting up and sitting on the rocker. Somehow it seemed terribly important that I get dressed. I had had my bath and must put on my stocking belt and my bra and my slip and then walk over to the closet and get out my red dress, because David had picked it out for me.

I don't know why I felt doomed, but I did. I think I saw what would happen quite clearly. David would not allow himself to love me. I must be his sister. He had lain and trembled beside his sister. Forbidden. He clung to this myth, this handy invention of Mama's to keep him from me. Why? No answer. When David held himself rigid, nothing, no one, had any power over him. I had seen that rigidity all through our lives. He would act in some irrevocable way. He would do something. I could not think what. To him this household, our upbringing, was inviolate. He might go against Mama's and Papa's wishes, but never against their moral code. They had taken us in, and I suppose the only way it was possible for Mama to adopt me was by constant repetition that I was David's sister. So this created my life, too. David would tell himself that never would he destroy that fragility. I feared what he might do. I must try and think of some way to stop him. But what? How—when I did not even know his plan? He did not want to speak to me. And I seemed engulfed in a soft droopy feeling...impotent, when I should be acting. But wasn't it up to him—not to me? He knew me. He knew what had loosened my body on the bed—and he had leapt from it.

Not once did I think of my ineligibility, of the snobbism that ruled our lives. Or that I was nobody and that more was expected of David.

A knock on the door, Fanny's tap. I couldn't face her and said please come back later. With that the door swung wide. Fanny hurried in. "You're not even dressed!" Then seeing my face: "What's upset you?"

I said nothing. I was sitting on the chair and I rocked a little.

"Get up! Get up!" She tried to pull me to my feet. "You're wearing the lavender. Your grandmother is lending you her amethysts. That'll cheer you up!"

"I'll wear my red dress," I said, getting to my feet.

"But your grandmother—"

"Fanny..." I went up to her. Poor unfocused eyes, so kind. I pushed a hairpin back into place. "The gold shoes and that big gaudy necklace Tom Shiver gave me."

"She'll have a fit!" Fanny rushed to the closet.

The action I took was confused, partly rebellion, not so much a question of the lavender dress—impossible anyway—but the red, which even David felt was now a little too short. He should see me differently. I would not go blindly, obediently. He should not have his own way. There was something here...something harsh and strong...David must *feel* what had happened. Not only to himself, but to me. I must live. He must be mine and I his. (Had I made a terrible mistake when I walked out of his room?)

Now I loosened my brassiere. I had grown a little in front. Tom Shiver's necklace was big, red, and gold. I put on lipstick, fluffed out my hair, toned down the spit curls, added a pair of earrings I'd bought for a dollar. The sleek severity I had cultivated under David's regime was almost gone. Before I left the room I deliberately walked to the mirror and gave myself a rare, hard look. My nose no longer seemed utterly impossible. My cheeks had filled out. I thought my jaw line had "character." My forehead was always my best point— who cared? For the first time in my life I thought I'd *pass*.

David stood waiting in the hall. He held Papa's high silk hat in his hand and wore a white scarf. He glanced at me and his eyes glittered in the old hard way. He did not miss the necklace or the fluffed hair. But he said nothing. Maybe I would not have managed to leave the house so easily if Mama had been downstairs. As it was, Papa helped me into my coat.

"My dear," Papa said, "that extraordinary necklace you are wearing either came from Isfahan or perhaps Nepal."

"Tom Shiver gave it to me," I said.

"Really? I'm surprised Mama let you accept it." He opened the front door. It was snowing; huge white flakes lay on the steps. "Well, go along. And be sure to remember us to Helen and Louis."

"I will, sir," David said, and we were walking through the snow to the car. Robert held the Packard door. He actually wore his chauffeur's cap. I climbed in. David threw a robe over my lap, then deliberately closed the door and opened the front and got in beside Robert. As we drove out of town he worked the windshield wiper back and forth. I sat frozen in the back. There was no warmth in Mama's coat. But I was icy in myself and could not speak.

Robert did all the talking. He had some new story about Red Grange hauling so many pounds of ice last summer. David neither looked back at me nor spoke. As we drew into the country I sat watching the black branches and the snow patching over the side of the road, covering old weeds.

Robert said: "Hope you don't plan on staying late. It's a mean night."

We had arrived, and swept by the gate posts and up the white driveway. Every light blazed in the Cranshaw's house. Then Tom Shiver was beside me. "You're wearing my necklace!"

David disappeared. I spoke to Mr. and Mrs. Cranshaw who stood at the entrance of a large room, cleared for dancing. The orchestra was terrific, Tom said. But there were a great many old people. It was going to be a stiff party, I thought, although I did not really take in what was happening. I was glad to have Tom and Arnold Buckley. I asked Tom to take me through the rooms, but David wasn't there. Liz Alexander appeared in pearls and a silver

dress, ravishing. No David. I thought of asking Liz if she'd seen
him, but decided against it. Tom asked some of the men, but no one
had seen David.

Tom and Arnold took me to supper. Tom commented on my
hair, remarking that I really looked different. I was too preoccupied
to ask what he meant. Finally, around one, when the party was
starting to break up, David came through the front door. His hair
was sopping wet. So were his shoes, which were also muddy. I could
see his coat glisten. He looked awful with his hair dripping over his
pale face. He wore a strange expression, almost a grimace. Robert,
he said, not looking at me, was drunk in the kitchen. He, David,
would have to drive. He'd bring the car around to the door.

While Robert slept on the back seat, I sat in front, helping
David with the windshield wiper. The snow fell steadily. We kept
sliding off the road. I told David he was driving too fast. He
wouldn't answer. It was terribly cold.

I said finally, "Where were you?"

"I was at Joyce's."

"Joyce Framely?"

"Yes."

"You walked?"

"I did."

"But it's miles!"

"Yes."

"And back again?"

"As you see."

There was a long silence. I tried to think it all through, little
and big pieces. But I couldn't.

"Why?" I asked.

He said in a high-pitched voice, "Because I wanted to propose
to Joyce. And I did."

"You did?" The words came without thought.

"Yes. We're engaged."

"You can't do it, David."

"But I have."

# Prelude

*Frederick: "My dear, what do you think?"*

*Anna: "Unfortunately, David will marry her."*

*Frederick: "Is that so bad?"*

*Anna says, her voice sharp: "Surely he could have done better."*

*Frederick: "They're quite rich. I looked into it."*

*Anna, with a hopelessness that is new to her: "But they're* nobody.*"*
*Her voice trembles. "I don't know how I'm going to stand it."*

*Frederick, unobservant: "I can probably get Framely into the Ritten-*
*house Club. The Philadelphia is out of the question, of course. I suppose he*
*already belongs to the Racquet." They are sitting in the living room by the*
*coal fire. Anna has on her rimless spectacles because she is sewing. Seated in a*
*low, blue chair she looks ancient and is pale. She stares into space, hands*
*falling idle in her lap. "Joyce got him away from Eva."*

*Frederick, alarmed: "Now come, my dear!"*

*Anna: "Fanny tells me nothing has happened. He hasn't kissed her but*
*once, whereas Tom Shiver kisses her all the time."*

*For a moment Frederick is too stunned to speak. Then in a rather choked*
*voice he says he is glad that David is not guilty. The ridiculousness and*
*inefficacy of making Fanny an oracle, or even believing in her capability as a*
*spy, does not apparently occur to either of them. Nor does the implication—as*
*far as Anna is concerned—of incest, bother them. They have become adept at*
*changing points of view.*

*Anna sighs, then takes up her sewing. She is mending a small pillowcase.* "You don't suppose he got the Framely girl into trouble, do you? She's a loose kind of girl."

*Frederick:* "No, I don't. As a matter of fact, I hinted around and received my comeuppance." *He gives a strange, cracked laugh.* "David told me to my face, 'I haven't got her pregnant, if that's what you mean.'" *Frederick fingers the end of his moustache carefully.* "It was embarrassing, I can tell you."

*Anna:* "But a relief."

*Frederick:* "Yes, a relief."

*Anna:* "And he will go through with it." *She makes the statement.*

*Frederick:* "Oh yes. He's set on it."

*Anna:* "When I think of the Framelys..." *Her head starts to tremble..*

*Frederick:* "Little Mrs. Framely's not too bad."

*Anna:* "Perhaps not." *Pause. Anna suddenly twists the pillow case in her hands as though she has lost control.* "I blame Eva..."

*Surprisingly, Frederick is silent. Then quite simply:* "I wouldn't, my dear. I know she and David have an unusual relationship." *Frederick is quite aware that they have been through this discussion before but cannot resist saying,* "You let them have rooms on the same floor."

*This is an old accusation, and Anna ignores it.*

"I thought David wanted to be an anthropologist," *Frederick says sadly. He leans forward, clasping his hands between his knees.* "I had hopes. I think he did, too. Now he'll be in business school and eventually commercial paper!" *Frederick stares at his hands. Then he shrugs, an odd gesture for him.* "David hasn't even tried to hold out. I don't understand it. He contemplates taking money from Framely."

*Anna speaks carefully:* "Was he ever a student? He may not have had the capability. Maybe anthropology was more your idea than his."

*Frederick:* "Maybe so." *He gets to his feet, moves to the mantle, leans an arm along it.*

*Anna says, surprisingly:* "He doesn't have much character, *do you think?*"

*Frederick's face tightens, he appears shocked, then settles into it.* "Maybe not. *Although I'm surprised to hear you say such a thing. Of course his life and mine are very different. I never had all this folderol." He waves a hand. "Dances and parties, girls and liquor. I led a scholar's life. Also an explorer's."*

*Anna has smoothed out the pillowcase and now resumes her sewing. There is a short silence. Again laying down her work, Anna says in her deepest tone: "I feel he's been corrupted."*

*This idea does not shock Papa the way it might have a few moments earlier: "Ah, maybe so . . ."*

*A large piece of cannel coal in the fireplace breaks off suddenly, exposing a blood-red sliver. Frederick picks up the fire tongs, rearranges the coal neatly. He is fastidious in his movements.*

*Anna, not looking up from her sewing: "We must reach some decision about Eva."*

*Frederick appears uncomfortable: "You're hard on her, Anna."*

*Anna: "I don't think so. We've done everything for her. And we owe her nothing. I feel she has learned all too little from her experience in our household. She makes herself conspicuous at parties, I'm told."*

*Frederick says patiently: "What's your plan, my dear?"*

*Anna: "She simply won't go to the Adirondacks with us this summer."*

*Frederick: "Isn't that rather sudden?"*

*Anna: "No. I've been thinking about it for quite a while."*

*Frederick: "This will be a great shock to Eva. I don't think such a possibility has occurred to her."*

*Anna: "Probably not. But as we never adopted her she cannot really believe we would support her indefinitely."*

*Frederick makes one last try, an unfortunate one: "I find her rather engaging." He knows so little about Eva, this comment is all he can dredge up.*

*Anna: "I'm tired of her. Now that she is no longer a child we are two women in the house. Always unfortunate."*

*Frederick: "Perhaps someone will come along. Young Jim Rickard seems quite serious."*

*Anna: "Possibly."*

*Frederick walks to her, puts his hand over hers. This usually signifies the end of a discussion.*

*Anna looks up at him:* "I shan't tell her she has no choice but to marry. The idea will occur to her eventually. She's thoroughly untrained. We've brought her up to be idle."

*Frederick:* "I suppose we have." *Then, quite deliberately,* "Aren't we dining with the Claytons tomorrow evening?"

8 In telling the outcome of David's dramatic action, which changed the whole direction of my life, I believe I must tell all of it. (Even knowing I risk public speculation—and that there has been too much publicity already.) For if I leave anything out then the reasons behind the action will never be understood. No one will be exonerated; no one accused.

Mama, I thought, would never consent to "this crazy idea of David's," as I called it. For the reality, its actual occurrence, the possibility of David's being seriously involved was intolerable, therefore I did not believe it. Like his appearance at the Cranshaw party sopping wet, his insistence that he had walked to Joyce's house, and what had been said. None of this I believed. He simply could not have gone from me—to *Joyce?*

Everything he did that night was over-dramatized—his taunting silence in the car, forcing me to ask; his brutal answer.

Then my mind swiveled around and I told myself that just because Mama allowed Mr. Framely to give a party for Joyce and me, did not mean the Framelys could latch on to David....Latching on would never be allowed. (I still thought Mama's power was absolute.)

Mama did not like Joyce. Mama was ill at ease with her, spoke of Joyce's bad manners and lack of "respect." Mama considered the Framelys "rather underbred," and although I never knew clearly what this meant, I realized the accusation was fatal. Mama probably expected David to marry Liz Alexander. Of course the Framelys had money. I must remember this counted with Mama. But it was whom-you-were-related-to that laid down the lines.

At the time I did not ask myself how Mama would take the news that David was—for instance—marrying me. I know now that she would have been capable of turning us both out of the house.

I think the reason I did not speculate on this possibility was that I had *always* been going to marry David. I belonged to David and he to me, although I admitted the claim had weakened in the last year.

I refused to believe David would never face Mama or disappoint her. I knew David could be ruthless, even cruel. I put it down to David's having experienced some awful disappointment. Perhaps he never got over being an orphan, feeling abandoned. I know I was the only person David trusted. But where had he gone wrong, strayed?

I had opened myself to David. My whole being had been full of him...yes, and he full of me in that fierce clutch...how could I now be refused, shut out, *given up*? Whenever I thought of this I would go to my room, or stand a moment until the whirling sensation stopped.

On the day after David's announcement, I waited for Mama to confide "the worst." Nothing happened. Two days later she and Papa appeared dressed in their best clothes and drove away with Robert, who wore his chauffeur's cap. Next, Mrs. Framely came to call. Mama had the Lowndes silver out and her lace-edged napkins. When I came through the front door I saw them all sitting, like a stage set. Mrs. Framely glanced up. She would not be happy about this. (Where was Mr. Framely?) But if she came to the house, Mama and Papa had already been to call on her, then the plan was being considered. I leaned against the bannister and steadied myself by the rail.

"Mr. Severn," Mrs. Framely said in a high, unnatural voice, "I'm sure you are upset at this plan of my husband's. David wanted to be an anthropologist. I've heard him talk about going to New Guinea."

"There never was anything definite about it," Papa said. Pause. Then in an altered, rattley voice: "Evidently David wants to marry your daughter." The flippancy was shocking, so unlike Papa.

"But it should not be at the expense of his career." Mrs. Framely was fighting. Could she win, possibly? Had she arrived too late?

Mama said in a voice as false as Papa's, "I'm not sure David could tolerate the discipline required of a science. He will feel ever so much freer under your husband's guidance—and help," she added hastily.

Was Mrs. Framely up to it? Did the Framelys want a son-in-law who had no money and no prospects?

"Do have one of these cakes, Mrs. Framely."

Evidently this was the signal, for Papa said with false heartiness, "I really think the young people know what they want. We old folk must sit back and wish them well."

Was he out of his *mind*? He never in his life talked in such a fashion. He knew that David couldn't marry Joyce.

I turned and walked up the stairs. When I reached my room I went across to the window, looked out. It was dusk, light vanishing and dimness setting in. One tree, the maple, stripped of leaves, showed black glistening branches. Snow lay on the street. Here and there a gray pavement was visible where the snow had been swept away. I could feel again the cold car, see my hand against the windshield moving the wiper, David's profile sharp in the light, then dim, barely discernible. Had my entire existence, all my hopes begun that evening and ended only a few hours later? I turned, and lay full length on the bed.

A week went by. David was not in the house. I knew why he stayed away.

Joyce must soon realize that I stood in her path and was definitely part of the scene. She might try and work through David, fight off my influence, or perhaps attempt to beat me off herself. I expected the latter, knowing Joyce.

So I was not surprised a few days later when she phoned. "We haven't seen each other in ages," she oozed. "I'm in town. I'd love to stop by."

I would not welcome her. And although the thought of seeing her sickened and frightened me, yet in another way I was crazily eager. At last I was playing my part. I knew my position. I came first with David, no matter how confusing things were. He had walked to Joyce's house in all that snow and proposed to her. But he didn't mean it. He couldn't. Even Joyce's mother realized that. But when I remembered the scene between Mrs. Framely and Mama and Papa I felt iciness around my heart. For it was not so much the forces moving against me as forces moving without me.

Joyce, I saw at once, looked extremely smart. She had lost weight. She wore her hair coiled low on her head and tied with a face veil which put an attractive mesh over her big eyes. Her brown wool dress had gold buttons and was chic, expensive-looking, and for once not gathered over the hips. She wore beautiful brown suede gloves and a beaver coat which she threw carelessly on the hall bench. I reminded myself that after all she was only Joyce Framely who used to spit grape seeds over the side of the *Katydid* when we went on picnics in the Adirondacks.

For some reason I took her into the dining room. We sat at the table. She sat quietly, her smooth clear face expressionless. Her strange grayish eyes caught my gaze. She spoke right up.

"You don't like my being with David, do you?"

"Being with" was as vulgar an expression as "keeping company."

"Don't be ridiculous, Joyce."

"Well, you don't. I think you're jealous."

Childish. Typical Joyce.

"I didn't realize I had anything to be jealous about," I said. Not brilliant, but getting a lick in.

Joyce sat up, breasts to the fore. "Look here, Eva. I don't want to hurt you. But it's best to be straight about these things.

"What things?" I said, looking directly into her oyster-eyes.

"Since you want it like this," she said, "David and I intend getting married."

"Oh?"

"David is going into Pa's business."

I stared. "David hasn't even graduated from Temple."

"He's going to business school. Pa is giving us an allowance. It's all arranged."

The mention of money was real. A handout! He *couldn't*. Not David. Joyce had made a silly mistake, always wanting her own way. It infuriated me to see her so smug, so sure. I could let her know a hundred things about David she never dreamed of. I knew everything there was to know about David. Joyce Framely meant nothing to us. A nobody. Yet here she sat watching me, plucked eyebrows raised and a supercilious expression on her face.

I blurted out, "None of this will work, Joyce. David won't do it."

"I think he will."

"No, it won't work." How stupid to keep on repeating myself. Joyce smiled. She could sit so calmly—and play with our lives? Why didn't I shout at her that she was a ninny, a jackass, and that David loved me and always had...

What was it I must remember? What were the words? *"I wanted to propose to Joyce. And I did." "You did?" "Yes. We're engaged." "You can't do it David." "But I have."*

I felt my skin tighten, my throat ached. I would not let her see how I was affected. That's what she wanted, to see me cry, demeaned. She had always known about David and me. It was that damned sixth sense of hers...

I could not sit with her an instant longer. I got to my feet, walked over to the big high window. Across the alley a woman appeared in a lighted bay window. She was dressed in her slip. I could see her bare arms. Dark hair, thin. I watched her walk to a table, pick up a book, and sit down in a deep chair near the light.

What was she doing reading, in her slip, at four-thirty in the afternoon? Perhaps sensing that she was being watched, she rose, went to the window, pulled down the middle shade. I walked back to the table, sat down. David would take Mr. Framely's handout. In fact, it might be possible that David had sent Joyce to me, one way to reaffirm.

She picked up a lump of sugar from the bowl on the table, took a small bite. "Why do you and David keep up this pretense of being brother and sister?" she asked, crunching. "David has a real fixation." Fixation was the new word.

I simply could not answer and stared along the table, smeared, needing polish, Robert neglectful.

Joyce said, still half sucking on the lump of sugar, "You and I don't have to pretend, anyway."

"No. Of course not." What was she getting at?

"You know, Eva, I often wondered why you didn't rebel against all this..." She waved her hand at the room. "It's so stifling. You've always been such a good girl." She was smiling.

"Not particularly," I said, thinking of Tom Shiver with some satisfaction.

"But Mr. and Mrs. Severn are no relation to you."

"They brought me up." I held my whole body stiff. Rebel? Managing to survive from one day to the next took all my wile.

Joyce wiped her fingers on a tiny handkerchief. I watched her. Having her challenge my way of life for some reason strengthened the reality of what had happened. It drew the line between us. Composed, assured, she could wipe her hands or throw down her beaver coat on the bench with never a thought. She was rich, really rich. And utterly different. What made me think I could set myself against her or this "plan"? In a panic I suddenly saw that I was being isolated, left out, with everyone moving off. Could I bear to lose all contact with David?

I sat numbly watching her as she leaned across the table and in her tight decisive voice cut hope to shreds.

"David and I are going to be married in April." I heard her say. "And of course you've got to be maid of honor, Eva. We wouldn't want it any other way."

As I turned from the door after seeing Joyce out Mama faced me in the hall.

"Was that Joyce?"

"Yes, Mama."

"Why wasn't I told? I should very much like to have seen her."

"I didn't know you were home." A lie, but necessary.

Perhaps even in that dim light she saw the look on my face. Once I had shut the door on Joyce, then I could let go. She had caught me at it.

"What did she want?" Mama said.

"She wants me to be maid of honor." It was the easiest thing to say, and most on my mind.

"I hope you accepted." Mama came quite close to me and for once scanned my face.

"I didn't say yes or no."

Pause. Mama ceased looking at me and fastened her gaze on my left shoulder. She spoke very clearly: "I think you should understand one fact, Eva. You will gravely distress both Papa and me if you give way or exhibit any petty displeasure over David's marriage. We are delighted with his choice. And we want happy, smiling faces around us, not dour, envious ones. I cannot remember the precise quotation, but Samuel Johnson said that envy desires not so much its own happiness as another's misery. I would not want to think that of you."

"No, Mama." How often had I said it, or "Yes, Mama"? Was I simply a kind of stooge? The word rebel only had meaning now that David would not be with me. I could say the words, but I withered as I said them. Envy, misery? What in hell was Mama talking about? What did she know about the human heart? She wrote poetry about birds and bees—heroic, unlikely sagas.

I stood watching her walk up the stairs, her grip firm on the banister.

9     That afternoon David came home. I met him outside his room in the hall.

At sight of him words burst out of me. "What's got into you?" Fanny's phrase. "Taking a handout from the Framelys. You shock me."

"What's wrong with it?" He kept smiling, yet watching me. I knew I couldn't reach him. "I'll be working for old man Framely. He wants me to carry on his business. It all makes sense."

"And Joyce?"

"You never liked her."

He contemplated me, leaning against the wall. Did he think nothing of what had happened to us in his room. He was bound to forget it.... Slippery, he seemed slippery. His eyes shone. He seemed secretive, gone. When he spoke again his voice was odd, flat.

"Stay away, Eva. You can't understand and don't try. You're too young."

The meanest taunt of all! He not only refused to admit my feelings, now he told me I had no right to feel.

"This can't have been your plan all along."

"Maybe."

"You can't really say that."

"It's the plan now." Jaunty.

I went into my room and closed myself away from him.

As time went on I saw how wrong I had been about Mama's and Papa's reaction to Mr. Framely. He had become quite respectable. A conservative, an enthusiastic supporter of Harding, a member of the

Union League, and played golf at Merion. Whatever Mama and Papa felt about David's taking support from the Framelys was never mentioned. Mama now said David was marrying advantageously. "We're very pleased," I heard her tell two ladies who stopped in for tea.

No one asked my opinion. After that one talk with Mama my reaction was predictable. I was careful to say nothing, thinking that Papa would surely question my silence. Finally, I was forced to realize that my feelings had no bearing on the situation. I was not, after all, a recognized member of the family.

To this day I have difficulty believing that Joyce took David away from me. I think he walked away.

As the December days shortened we all seemed to be living at full speed. The month rushed by. We had Christmas dinner at the Framelys'. I thought Mrs. Framely did not look well. She said very little.

I still went to parties—like a child being amused. I was glad to go. Arnold and Tom may have sensed some difference in me for they treated me tenderly. (I no longer let Tom kiss me and this made him all the more eager.) Although some of my merriness had gone, yet I was the girl who had a smart comeback and danced "like a streak"...I found I had achieved something of a reputation. It was the "thing" to dance with me. Paul Whiteman often asked me to play and I'd run up on the stage, stand in front of the orchestra and play "I Can't Give You Anything But Love," or "Avalon," or "Mary." I'd play my heart out with Mr. Whiteman's fiddle in my hands and the big orchestra booming behind me.

I noticed a gradual change in my party-life. Whereas before I had been intent on making an impression, now I need not be nervous, or *as* nervous. I had enough confidence to know that boys liked being seen dancing with me. Now we could talk, not show off fancy steps all the time. David came to few parties, or if he came he danced with Joyce or maybe Liz Alexander. He never danced with me.

I did not so much grow up during those few months, as catch

up. I think I became the personality I had assumed under David's tutelage, only toned down, reflecting the inner change that so occupied me.

David was a stranger. I heard about him. Plans were afoot. My fury, desperation, ignominy must be packed down, out of sight. Fortunately I had been trained to control, not dissolve or show hurt. And fortunately, when a child, I had sat on the foot of David's bed and cried out my loneliness, anger, forlornness, even while he slept. Desperation and anger had not festered, repressed, to undo me years later. As the weeks advanced I knew that the least sign of feeling sorry for myself would be fatal. I was young for this wrestling, but as I had been brutally repulsed, retaliation called for like measures. I must do more than tolerate this union, I must accept it without loss of self-respect.

I would have difficulty in describing my character then or now, yet I took pride in my resilience, the tough muscles, and although I still came across soft spots, yet on the whole I kept upright and moved ahead.

I lived a strange loose life, without ties or purpose. No one touched me. Papa seemed even less available. There was no doubt he had aged. Whereas Mama went around putting a good face on the marriage.

It was after Christmas that I noticed a further change. During the times I was home for a meal, the Adirondack camp was apt to be discussed. For instance, the main living room needed a new roof. The *Carafa*'s engine wanted a thorough overhaul. Mama and Papa planned to leave for the Adirondacks in late June, and perhaps stay through September. Neither by glance or word was I included in any of this discussion or in any plan. It would have been natural for Mama to say that as we were staying later this year, I must not forget to bring extra sweaters. But when such a discussion took place she did not so much as turn her head in my direction. Lately, she hardly addressed me at all. I don't know when I realized what was happening, but quite suddenly I understood that I was not being included in their plans. Now that David was no longer part of their life, I would not be counted in. I had come with David, hand in hand.

When this revelation came to me I remember thinking I heard someone shrieking... I dreamed at night of being lost in strange cities, of losing my pocketbook, of not knowing the streets I walked. In the daytime I was unsure of my footing, stumbled against chairs in the living room, stumbled on the stairs. What could I do? What would become of me? When I yelled in my sleep I woke terrified and so cold I had to get up and put on my wrapper and then go back to bed again. My precarious foothold was gone. I no longer had a position in the household. I took to wondering if I had not always lived on borrowed time; even the furniture in my room did not belong to me, nothing in the house was mine. I literally shuddered away from the future. I could not even think about it. Plan? What sort of plan?

What terrified me even more severely was that outwardly nothing changed. The wedding took everyone's attention, even Fanny's. I was indeed to be maid of honor. When Mrs. Framely expressed the wish that I be Joyce's attendant I could not refuse. So now I went for fittings as though everything was quite normal. The bridesmaid's dress was a kind of pale mauve, rather like the Baldwin twins dresses at Bill Vanderbilt's birthday. My arms were bare, like theirs. I thought the dress hideous. The color made my hair mousy, my skin yellowish. I mentally accused Joyce of choosing a color I could not wear.

My sense of insecurity reached such an intolerable pitch that I found myself confiding in Fanny.

"Did they say anything to you about camp next summer?" I asked her. No need to explain who "they" were.

"Never a word. Except we're to take the blankets up again."

"I mean about me."

Fanny sat in a small rocker sewing. She held the work very close to her eyes, for although she wore thick rimless glasses, she could hardly see. She was turning down a hem, pale upper lip caught in her teeth, breathing heavily through her large nose. She looked up, recalling the question. "Well, what about you? Aren't you to go with us?"

"I don't think so."

"You always go to camp. What's the matter with you?" She raised the work again.

"It's different this year."

"You're imagining things."

"No."

"Because of the wedding?"

"Partly."

"That's foolishness. David'll be married and you'll come away for the summer."

"Mama hasn't *said* anything."

"Whatever would she say?"

"She always speaks about plans, Fanny. Look—she's already mentioned blankets to you."

"You've just got hold of a lot of silliness. You're too full of fancies."

We were in her small room at the top of the house. Low eaves came down on one side making Fanny's iron bedstead jut into the room. A light bulb on a cord hung from the center of the ceiling. On the bureau a plaster crucifix with blue loincloth leaned carelessly against the wall.

"Maybe you're right," I said uncertainly.

"You'd best marry," Fanny said, pulling a thread through her needle, and giving a sidewise smile.

"Oh, come on, Fanny!" The unexpectedness of it scared me.

"You've got fellows around." She picked up the dress again, an old one of Mama's. Of course I had wondered about marriage. But to *hear* the idea...

"You'll be asked," she said, pushing her needle through the thick hem. "There's that black-haired one, the new one."

"Jim Rickard."

"That one. Robert says he drives a fancy car."

"A Stutz," I said, without thinking. Soon after this I kissed her soft cheek and left.

Marriage....You had to be in love. This thought created such pain for me that I simply turned away. How would it be married to someone like Jim Rickard? I wondered what there was about him that unnerved me. He had started paying attention to me in a casual way. He seemed so much more worldly than anyone I knew and at the same time reserved, as though no one came really close to him. Or if close, it might be that when *in*, there would only be space. That was what I felt in him, space—rather hollow. He had his own meticulous ways, a special little leather folder with his initials on it to hold his car keys. An "older man," studying law. Jim asked me to his house for tea. I had met his mother. (She made me feel all bunchy lips and jaw, and I watched her eyes shift from my face.) His father was a darling, bumbling, big-stomached man, a doctor, puzzled by his elegant son—and his wife. Mrs. Rickard asked me rather pointed questions, referring to my mother—which no one ever did—saying she had been at the same school. And what were my plans for next year after I came out? The Junior League? She cocked an eyebrow, but her black eyes were quite still and not amused. On the instant I said I was looking up courses in sociology at Penn, a brilliant lie which impressed everyone. The whole idea seemed so lovely, such a perfect solution, that I let it float about until I half believed it myself. When I made the announcement, we were seated around a little table covered with an immaculate embroidered cloth. (Mama's cloths were apt to be rumpled and even stained.) Mrs. Rickard was meticulous. The silver had a high polish. The little cakes were just the right size; the lemon, paper thin. Mrs. Rickard, I sensed, was forever pursuing her son. She was super-conscious of him. Even while talking to her husband, if Jim tried to put down his napkin, she held out her hand for it.

How alike they were with their thin noses and their black, unrevealing eyes. I felt an uncomfortable closeness. They seemed falsely cheerful, too brightly smiling with no humor.

Mama spoke quite highly of the Rickards, saying they came from undistinguished but respectable stock. So I tried quite hard to consider Jim and like him. I had long since given up the idea that kissing must only be allowed if it led to marriage. Although I was not permissive, as I told myself. I never really petted, although I again allowed liberties to Tom Shiver because he was so persistent— and skillful. Jim Rickard was not expert, but not awkward, either. He seemed rather fierce, kissing me and then flinging away—which I enjoyed. I did seem to lead a rather complicated life with my beaux, each of whom had such a different attitude toward me, including fat Arnold Buckley.

It was Tom Shiver who brought Newlin Slatter one Sunday to call. Mama and Papa were out in the country at the Cranshaw's for lunch. On this particular Sunday Tom rolled back the rug, pulled the furniture around almost automatically. Then Tom and I danced, while Newly—as he was called—sat on the sofa. I noticed the way he kept peering around the room as though he could not believe his eyes. Once he got up and walked over to a little table and stared at the paperweights. Although I sensed the atmosphere of the house was new to him, he appeared curious, not awed. Now he sat on the couch with his thick hands clasped between his knees. "Calling" on a Sunday afternoon was an unusual experience.

When the record was over and Tom and I stopped dancing, Newly rose to his feet. "Another older man," I thought. He had a long nose, very round, rather protuberant eyes, a high forehead. His manner was alert and no-nonsense. It had taken him a time to get used to Mama's drawing room, he told me later. Now he had eased into the situation and when the record was over he went to my rack, picked out "Mary" and put it on. Light on his feet, I told myself, and positive. Taller than I was and a strong chunky body. Rather given to pumping the right arm, turning his head from side to side. And he talked. Tom and I never talked and neither did Jim. Dancing at home was serious. To Newly it was a chance to exchange ideas. I can't say exactly why he appealed to me—or if he really *did*—or if I was answering a call. His earnestness, which would not have drawn most girls, drew me. He regarded me as something fragile (a new experience). I was unlike anyone he had ever known. Mama's parlor impressed him. When she and Papa came in later, she greeted him frigidly, not knowing the name Slatter, not liking it, and not liking to see the rug turned back and the furniture moved. Did he live in the city? she asked, raising her veil. He worked at the Guaranty? Really. He lived in Radnor? That was on the Main Line near Wayne, wasn't it? According to Mama, "nobody" lived in Wayne.

"We were just about to put back the furniture," Tom said.

"And the rug," Mama reminded him. Turning to me: "I shall want you to do some addressing for me, Eva. If you will come upstairs."

"Yes, Mama."

All this, my obedience, her sternness, made a tremendous impression on Newlin Slatter. He had never seen anything like it. He could not imagine what my position was in the house. A different name, he knew that. Yet Tom spoke of me as the Severn's granddaughter. Newly never got over his awe and fear of Mama—which she encouraged, being more autocratic and outrageous in front of him than she was with anyone else.

Newlin came to call the following Wednesday, bringing a box of sad-looking white roses. ("Puts on airs," Mama said, when she saw them.)

Fanny loved Newly from the start. "Will you look at that!" she cried, gazing at the small shriveled buds, and smiling fondly.

10    One Sunday Newly asked me to tea with his mother. Right off, I liked Mrs. Slatter. There was no nonsense about her, she spoke her mind. She had dyed black hair,

a nose like Newly's, black, heavily made up eyes and a voice more cultivated than Mama's, with occasional moments of nasal naturalness. She played Mah Jong regularly three times a week. There was a card table on the sun porch set up with four racks. She talked rousingly about Al Smith, whom she evidently admired. This astounded me. A Catholic.

"So what?" Mrs. Slatter said, crossing her high-heeled shoes and showing her legs. She had tuned in KDKA on the radio and told us of a neighbor who had actually heard Havana. She and Newly talked about Prohibition as though some day repeal was possible.

"The Literary Digest Poll showed thirty-eight point six for Enforcement, forty point eight for Modification, and only twenty point six for Repeal," Mrs. Slatter said. I was impressed with her use of figures.

"They'll repeal it," Newly said. "With Henry Ford not allowing the workers to drink in their own homes, people are going to get tired of being told what to do. Now the government says no foreign ships are allowed to bring liquor within the three-mile limit. So Great Britain announces she won't permit her vessels to be searched." He gave his loose, easy laugh, smiling over at me. He had a way of including me that was entirely different from the boys I knew, as though he expected me to be interested. He made me feel twenty, at least. And important. I was astonished at his easy relationship with his mother, quite friendly.

Mrs. Slatter wore five gold bracelets (Mama would have said they were vulgar) and was not much of a housekeeper. I could not help but notice the newspapers and books lying on tables and chairs, even on the floor. A picture postcard had been stuck on a lampshade to prevent glare. The upholstered chairs looked old and tired with indentations where people had sat. Heavy, rose-colored curtains hung at the windows. A large rubber tree loomed up in one corner and in another there was a cage with two motionless, silent parakeets.

None of this went with Newly's personality, which was very

manly. Certainly not handsome with his long nose, high forehead, and protuberant eyes. When talking he seemed almost over-animated, his mouth moving in all manner of shapes. In repose his face was rather sad, all nose and disappointment. Years later this expression made many people believe he was meditating, or perhaps silently praying, and that there was something sacred in his solemnity. But usually he was only puzzled or had indigestion.

Newly spoke excitedly about the Klan. I had thought that grown men riding around in hoods was a joke. But Newly's face set and he flung out the words. "They killed a man in Louisiana." Pause. "They're out to get the Negroes. And they want to stir up Gentiles against Jews and Protestants against Catholics. Three thousand people in Plainfield, Illinois, joined the Klan only the other day. They're no joke." He looked quite fierce.

Mrs. Slatter, evidently wanting to ease the atmosphere, asked me if I'd read *Captain Blood*. "It's by Raphael Sabatini and it's good. Do you read Hergesheimer?"

"No, but I've read *So Big*," I said. "I loved it."

"Edna Ferber." Mrs. Slatter narrowed her eyes, the discussion evidently being extremely important. "Do you like the movies? I cried my eyes out at *Orphans of the Storm*."

Newly said, rather stuffily, I thought, "Eva's seen the *Chauve Souris* three times, Mother, and *The Bat* twice. That's what being a debutante means. You go to the theater."

"I know it, Newly. I wasn't in the dress business without learning about society debs. I dressed enough of them." She sat back, jerking her bracelets about. I could see she was a woman of intense feeling.

"Do you know Mrs. Meringo?" I asked, wanting her good humor to return.

"Sophie? Of course!" Mrs. Slatter batted her hand at me, smiling.

"She's making my bridesmaid's dress for a wedding I'm going to be in." Then I heard myself say, "It's David's wedding. David and I were brought up together, although he's really no relation." With his name the words had gushed out. I wanted to go on, tell more about him, but found I could not speak and sat looking at the buttons on my cuff.

"He's marrying Joyce Framely," Mrs. Slatter wiped her mouth carefully with a napkin. Both she and Newly must have sensed my wretchedness, for I sat very silently. After a moment Mrs. Slatter commented on my dress, black wool with jet buttons.

Other subjects were pursued, and the knot in my throat that had so surprised me, finally loosened and I joined the conversation.

Later Newly told me his parents were divorced. I had wondered about his father. To get a divorce, Newly said, took real courage in his mother's day. His father drank and couldn't hold a job, but had been a brilliant man who spoke Russian and Chinese. He had taught at Temple. "He believed in the occult," Newly said, turning rather pink. "He foretold the Great War and the German defeat and that Scott would reach the South Pole and that we'd fly in the air. All kinds of things. Whenever anything was lost he could usually give a hint where it might be. He was entertaining and I loved him until it became impossible to have any feeling for him at all."

I had never had anyone talk to me like this, or speak so frankly about his parents. The whole household was different and so was Newly. He knew nothing about the rules and customs I grew up with, and did not care. True, he was awed by Mama and Papa, regarding them as specimens. He never criticized them, except where their action and attitude concerned me. I think from the beginning he sensed my loneliness and fear. He always told me I looked smashing, that I had the clearest eyes he'd ever seen. He would comment shyly on my figure. I never told him how I felt about my looks. Only David knew that.

Newly and I fell into the habit of having tea with Mrs. Slatter on Sundays. And it was she who discovered my predicament.

"You'll be joining the work force next year, I imagine," she said, quite casually as she bit into a sandwich.

"Well, yes—yes I will." No one had spoken so directly to me. I could feel myself getting hot and knew I blushed. In our "set" no girl ever mentioned taking a job. The girls who went to college might think of careers, I supposed. But we debutantes were supposed to join the Junior League and "Work for Others," volunteers. Evidently I was to be in a different category. And as I was unable to fully acknowledge that Mama and Papa had withdrawn from me, I had not in any visible way accepted my real situation. Mama and Papa were leaving for camp in July. I kept telling myself July was a long way off, but then what? Sitting in Mrs. Slatter's living room my mind started to run around these realities. Why did I not speak to Mama? Why did she not speak to me? Somehow she had suspected me with David. (How much did she know?) This turned her against me.

So great was my concentration on my awful future—which it seemed I had never faced until this instant beside Mrs. Slatter's tea table—that I paid no attention when Mrs. Slatter asked me a question. Fortunately Newly, who had been leaning protectively toward me, answered. Mrs. Slatter had evidently spoken of my being a salesgirl.

"Eva may not want to sell clothes, Mother."

"Well, *I* began as a salesgirl," she said, smiling.

"Quite different." Newly was almost spluttering. "It's not the same at all. And Naomi Finch's shop is a rotten place to work."

"Oh, I don't know..." Mrs. Slatter folded her napkin. Evidently the question had something to do with a job for me at Naomi Finch's, considered Philadelphia's Bergdorf Goodman—small, very smart, very expensive.

"You're too short to model clothes," Mrs. Slatter patted my arm as though apologizing. Models were *pretty*...

In the car on the way home Newly said he thought I should study design. There was a real future in it. Not that I showed any talent or enthusiasm, but Newly evidently sensed my situation and perhaps even realized I was evading it.

"Look Eva, how about, uh, money? I mean is that a problem?" He stared ahead at the road, lips tight, his face tense.

"I've got three thousand dollars from my mother," I said.

Newly's face cleared. He smiled. "That's great, Eva. You can take up all sorts of things. Design, for instance. Go to school. Maybe get into the world of fashion."

"I don't know anything about design, Newly." I was discouraged enough anyway without being told I should try something I knew I couldn't do.

"You could learn. I bet you've got a real flair for it. You've got to *believe* you're a designer, and then *be* one." He was in dead earnest, speaking decisively and banging his hand on the wheel for emphasis. This was the first time I ever heard Newly go on about his believe-and-be theory, which he used later with such evident success. At the time I felt he was wholly unrealistic. It seemed impractical to spend what little money I inherited on a study for which I had no particular liking. And then I remembered that when I pled with Papa about college he had said I couldn't touch the money until I was twenty-one. When I told Newly, his face set and he was quiet.

I said: "I don't know what having a job means. Where am I to live? I don't see why anyone would take me on." I felt hollow, deserted, inept, and almost idiotic. What excuse was there for such inexperience? "I'm seventeen," I said, grabbing hold of something real, "and I've had very little formal education. I went to a 'finishing school'... If your mother could get me a job at Naomi Finch's maybe I'd be lucky."

The idea that Mrs. Slatter had made an extraordinarily generous offer, or that jobs with Naomi Finch were hard to come by, did not enter my head. I even failed to thank her. Yet she showed no irritation. She must have realized my sleek hair, makeup, long cigarette holder and animation were only a front. She also must have seen her son's interest in me. Wouldn't she have wondered what I had to offer?

Newly was my first real beau. He took me out every week. We went for long walks, plowing through snow in Fairmount Park. I could depend on Newly. Tom Shiver, Stewy Frazer, Arnold Buckley would "happen by" occasionally. But they never sent me flowers. And they would leave without asking to see me again. They gave me a good time at parties because they wanted to dance with me. And I knew what Tom wanted, which now embarrassed me. With Newly things seemed uncomplicated. In his shy way, I knew he liked me. And I liked him.

Until that day at his mother's tea table, I had been able to push the future away from me. But Mrs. Slatter's remark, about my joining the work force, carried it right into the room. A salesgirl? What would I be paid? Where would I live, also eat? Fear brought a kind of curtain rustling down, hiding every contour of Naomi Finch's shop on the corner of Locust and Sixteenth Street.

Newly must have spoken to his mother because she never mentioned Naomi Finch's shop again. He surprised me with his perception, For I had said very little on that ride home. Perhaps the fact that I questioned the only job offered, showed him how little I really understood my position. He let me sleep.

I don't know what held me back. General lack of self-confidence, fear of my looks in the outside world? I had learned a patter that took me around my own closed world. I had literally danced through it. Why didn't I go to Papa, ask him to lend me the money to take a typing course, or borrow against the money I would inherit? But I knew nothing of independent action, I had followed after David too long, if that's an excuse. Even the boys I knew (except Newly) were all in college, there was never any talk about jobs. And parties still went on; nothing changed, only the future, way off someplace.

On Sunday afternoons Mrs. Slatter was apt to read news from the *Public Ledger,* picked on purpose to discuss with Newly. I think she felt that the social news would be of special interest to me. We always ended with some tidbit, usually about Mrs. Stotesbury, a favorite of Mrs. Slatter's.

"I see where Governor Sproul says there is a fine spirit of cooperation among all Philadelphia agencies enlisted in the cause of a better city. 'No community has a better citizenry,' he says."

"It's nice to get a pat on the back from the Governor," Newly winked at me. Mrs. Slatter turned over a page. Newly and I were sitting on the lumpy couch. I often wondered why he did not hold my hand, but at his mother's he kept rigidly to himself.

"Bonwit's are having a sale." Mrs. Slatter looked over heavy horn-rimmed glasses at me. Newly ate another cake, remarking between bites that he questioned all these sales. Was the economy going into a slump? Mrs. Slatter said the sales were after-Christmas and nothing unusual. Newly liked to have his mother pick out bits from the paper, speculating on her choice, ready to argue with her. I was surprised he hadn't said more about Governor Sproul.

"Now here's something you'll like, Newly." Mrs. Slatter flipped back a page. "'British believe that Elihu Root's Proposals Pave the Way for the Abolition of the Undersea Boat.' That means the end of the submarine. Isn't that a darb?" Mrs. Slatter often used what she felt was the latest slang.

"Nerts," Newly said. "I betcha we're just starting to build our own little fleet of what they call 'Undersea Boats.'"

Mrs. Slatter now arrived at the amusement page, always a favorite. She liked being able to read about a play or movie I had not seen. "What about the photoplay *Disraeli* with George Arliss?" Raised eyebrows at me.

"I'm seeing that with Debbie O'Halloran tomorrow. She's a friend from school."

"That's nice. He's wonderful in the part, they say. *Declassé* with Ethel Barrymore is still playing. Here's a big interview with her."

"Mother, skip it," Newly spoke decidedly.

Mrs. Slatter rattled the paper. "I will, I will."

Newly's education was certainly superior to mine. He'd studied two years at Penn and then gone to Temple business school. But he had large gaps in literature, and the arts. He regarded my violin-playing with awe, and at one party when I had played with the orchestra he came up afterwards with his eyes full of tears. "You were the cutest little kid standing on that stage." As we danced he gave me a rare hug.

In the living room Mrs. Slatter was busy turning the pages of the paper. At last, triumphantly: "The American Committee for Devastated France will Send 500 Delegates On a 'Good-Will Ship' to review the devastated villages on the battlefields where Americans fought." She lowered the paper. "That shows we care."

"Sure we care," Newly said. "But when Wilson tried to build The League of Nations, and wanted Americans to take what he called world leadership, he lost popularity like shedding skin. The country's tired of reform and sick of responsibility. The war's too near. Sure, we'll help rebuild France and get hated for it. Normalcy is the watchword. Look what Harding said. I know it by heart: 'America's present need is not heroics but healing; not nostrums but normalcy; not revolutions but restoration; not surgery but se-renity.'" Newly laughed. "By golly, there's something lulling in it. Puts all your fears at rest. We're in a slump with department stores having sales, and automobiles slashing their prices, but as long as Harding is there we're OK."

He astonished me. No one I knew talked as he did. About world affairs, he was well-informed. When I said this, he laughed. "I work in Research at the bank. We've got to be on the ball and know what's happening."

It was now that Newly made the remark, since become famous. I remember what he said because he so evidently enjoyed himself, his face quite red and his manner rather pompous. "Now that Lindbergh has flown the Atlantic we will have general air traffic with planes carrying more than fifty people." His mother simply glanced politely at him, being used to his predictions. I remember smiling because he seemed so puffed up and pleased with himself. But this remark, which I told Bernard Cranby, has been taken as a further indication that Newly has occult powers. And of course later he foretold World War II, the atomic bomb, and the moon landing. At his mother's tea table that Sunday he seemed quite as usual, reaching forward to pour himself another cup of tea. He had a hearty appetite.

Newly finished his tea quickly, put the cup on the round table. "You better get to the society notes. I'm not allowed to bring Eva in after dark. I'll hear from Mrs. Severn." He winked at me.

What a comfort he was! And this room and the house, Mrs. Slatter, the gooey cinnamon buns she bought at Sautters. Everything, as President Harding said, had a consoling normalcy about it. You felt kindness in these people, none of the sharp bitter edges of Mama, or the negligence and indifference of Papa. And David was way off someplace, with Joyce, I was able to think, and let it *almost* glide over me. I smiled at Newly.

"Hasn't she got the cutest smile?" Newly said, and at last reached for my hand.

"Oh," Mrs. Slatter went on, "I see that Mrs. Edward Stotesbury is at Palm Beach, 'living quietly,' it says. She came down in her own private car, and Mr. Stotesbury is joining her later. Mr. and Mrs. Irénée DuPont are at the Everglades..." Her voice trailed off. She folded the paper. "It's been quite a gay week, hasn't it?" She nodded, satisfied that she had amused and informed both of us. Newly jumped up, pulled me to my feet.

"We must go."

I kissed Mrs. Slatter, thanked her. Newly hustled me into my coat. In a few moments we were rolling along Montgomery Avenue, headed for Philadelphia.

That winter the "Charleston" came in strong, and David wasn't around to teach me. So I turned on the victrola in the living room and practiced by myself when Mama and Papa were out. I became quite expert, could cross hands on my knees and even did a high kick at the end. (Bernard Cranby's article includes a picture of me in a low-waisted dress doing the kick.)

At parties, now that I was managing without David, my "line" became much sexier, I took to letting my dress fall off one shoulder. Yes, as I said, I petted and necked, not with everybody, but enough. I suppose my reputation suffered, but who was I to care? I had my way to make, and the party was not over.

11     I no longer challenged David, after that one confrontation. But I could barely suppress the distaste, the lumplike hate that spread in me as I watched him. I despised what he did and sneered at him as I saw the kind of person he was becoming. I'd have understood if David had been gruffly accepting, or even shown signs of triumphant glee—although this would have been a shock. But instead he seemed haughtily impatient, taking all the handouts as his due. He must have sensed my distaste for he constantly pecked at me. "Having fun?" he'd smirk, if we met in the downstairs hall as I was going to a party. "Who's this Slatter bird you're seeing so much of?" I told him to get out of my way and slammed the front door behind me.

But although I could be furious at David, I was very polite with the Framelys. I had made the choice, almost automatically, and the choice lay with them. I soon found out that David might put up with slamming doors, but Joyce wanted nothing but admiration. Undoubtedly she had sniffed around my relationship with David. She may have sensed that even now I would not let myself be wholly separated from him and therefore would not risk her disfavor.

I tamped down my feeling that he had made a fatally bad choice. (Or—equally important—that he should have made no choice at all. Or—almost invisible but burning hotly—that he should have chosen me.)

Although I was unable to face my own future, I faced what was happening to David straight on and showed nothing. Two-faced, it was a new exercise in deceit, and I worked on it.

I remember a scene one night at dinner: Mr. Framely became quite playful, tossing his head from side to side, throwing arch glances at Joyce and saying, "Wouldn't you like to know," as though she were ten years old. She played right back to him, suddenly jumping up and running around the table to kiss him.

"Oh, Pa!" she cried, "you've bought it—the one I liked!" Her pale eyes lighted. Her face took on the strange, reddish hue.

Mr. Framely gave a swipe at his moustache. "That's right! The one you liked. All yours—and David's," he added quickly.

Joyce went to David, putting her arms around his shoulders. "Pa's bought us a house," she said, awed. "It's red brick and it's in Rosemont, on Orchard Way."

"Convenient to the station," Mr. Framely put in. "You won't have to walk far to the Paoli Local."

Joyce was smart, I'll hand it to her. She saw David's scowl, eyebrows drawn together. Quickly she took his hand. "Pa won't do a *thing* unless you like it," she said. "Not a thing."

"I don't mean to stand in the way," David said, and glanced over furiously to me. He minded my hearing that he was being presented with a house. One that he had not even seen.

"You're not, darling," Joyce said, pulling out her chair and sitting down again, leaning toward him. "Maybe we shouldn't have done it so suddenly. But Pa and I were out driving—and there was the house with a 'For Sale' sign on it. Oh David—" now she pressed close to him. It was like a Mary Pickford movie without the curls. "You're going to love this house!" She was hard to resist for she spoke tenderly. (Later David showed me around the house as though he'd bought it himself, throwing open closet doors, taking me up to the maid's room, rather haughty and impatient.)

I was often at the Framelys' in Villa Nova. I doubt Joyce ever regarded me as a serious rival, only speculated. Put safely in place where I could do no harm, I was fun. Joyce had never made any real friends, so I was the only one who could share the wonders of her new world.

Joyce and David were to be married in the Bryn Mawr Presbyterian Church with aisles that ran slanting toward the altar like the spokes of a wheel, as Mama pointed out. The altar itself consisted of a highly varnished, wooden table. Above rose the pulpit. Joyce insisted on having the entire space behind the pulpit banked with flowers.

"I know Pa will let me do anything I want to the church, but Ma thinks I'm being ostentatious. She's so proper! You talk to her, Eva. You can persuade her."

My role: the go-between.... So I talked to Mrs. Framely. She was indeed quite a proper little person with a strong will and not at all intimidated by her husband or her daughter. She never seemed to notice my looks, except to tell me I was "very smart."

Mr. Framely apparently genuinely liked David. Not that he had the faintest understanding of his prospective son-in-law. But David's respectful attitude and careful politeness created in Mr. Framely's mind the feeling of intimacy. It was also true that the business firm of Framely & Brink, upon which Mr. Framely had expended much effort, would now remain in the family because of David. This gave Mr. Framely real satisfaction.

"I think David wanted to be an anthropologist like his grandfather," Mrs. Framely still worried the question. We were sitting on the sun porch, working over the guest list. "He'll soon be starting up-country."

I asked what she meant. She said that Mr. Framely did a large part of his business around Lancaster and York, and that David would sell commercial paper to the banks in those towns. "He'll be away from Joyce most of the week." She had a rather thin mouth and her lips seemed to close tightly. "It's not right," she said, as though she'd said it often.

Years later the scene came back to me, the green-topped card table, the brown wicker furniture, the big fern against the paned glass, and Mrs. Framely's straight, pressed-together lips.

The intricacies of David's actually being married I put from me. We were both, David and I, in some queer way, for some reason I would not examine, pretending to be other people. I never thought of the Framelys as corrupting me or David. They were, in some inexplicable way, simply there—as it were—for the taking, although I'm sure neither of us ever put the question to ourselves. I know I didn't, and in the beginning, neither did David. But then David allowed his whole life to be shifted about. Earlier he had hated taking a handout from Papa, his own grandfather. Yet Mr. Framely was giving him a house, furniture, an allowance, and perhaps even paying for the honeymoon in Bermuda. Would he eventually pay the debt David's father owed?

I think David found that once he became used to taking gifts he could accept money without flinching or protesting. Money was all around him. The Framelys were the most lavish, kind-hearted people in the world. Mr. Framely was enormously impressed, even awed, by the new connection with the Severns.

David may have persuaded himself that he had no right to refuse the "comforts" Joyce's father wanted to give her. David drifted into the situation, the first acceptance making the second easier. In return David would work hard for Mr. Framely, who so wanted him in the business. David thought he had a flair for finance. He would do his best. After all, he was giving up a lifelong desire to be a scientist. Not that I had ever believed David would long survive the desert country or the swamps about which Papa talked so affectionately. But for David Papa's experience was a reality to hold on to. I think there were certain structures in his life, absolutes, that he really never questioned. And when they gave way he was done for. When he had gripped me in his arms on the narrow bed, he was lost. So now, lost and dazed, he had wandered into a whole new territory that required new attitudes and behavior, but little moral effort. For David to let this happen was—in many ways—more easily understood than my own conduct. What did I give the Framelys in return for their generosity? I knew how a wedding invitation should be engraved; how to decorate the church; what Mrs. Framely should wear to the wedding (not the pink lace Joyce had picked out for her); the menu for the reception. I became interwoven in their lives. I don't mean to say I planned it, but I let it happen. And when the Framelys said they were going to Japan and the South Pacific next winter and wanted me to go with them I accepted with such a sense of relief I felt weak.

On the positive side, I told myself, was a growing interest in Newlin Slatter. Newly knew nothing about my feeling for David. He had not seen me with him. He apparently accepted the fact that David was marrying Joyce, and if he noted my perturbation that day at his mother's, he did not question it.

Every Saturday Newly and I walked in Fairmount Park. He had a surprisingly playful side and he wanted to amuse me. (Also, money was an important consideration.) In the Japanese Garden we found a long plank and made a bridge across the rather slimey water to the little island. We even trudged up the red temple stairs, surveyed the limited vista. It seemed an appropriate place to confide in him that the Framelys had asked me to go to Japan. Leaning against the railing, Newly regarded me. He was certainly not handsome. (I couldn't have borne being constantly with a handsome man. David's good looks now irritated and depressed me.) Newly's large nose was rather red. "It'll be damned dull, won't it?" he said.

At once I was furious. "Why do you say that? I *like* the Framelys."

"They're so old."

"No older than my own parents would have been."

He shrugged. "You like them. It's your choice." He turned and started down the stairs. At the bottom he waited for me. "So the

Framelys have solved the problem of what to do next winter. You won't be looking for a job."

"What's wrong with a trip?" I faced him, ready to have it out. Another sneer and I'd walk home!

But instead he said mildly, "Not a thing in the world." And then, "Come away from this place, Eva. It's cold." He swung down the path.

No one else challenged me. Mama simply said, "How very pleasant. I've never been to Japan." Papa mumbled something about the invitation being-uh-nice of the Framelys.

Newly and I covered Fairmount Park, mostly on foot and in galoshes. Newly was not only well-informed but carried a guide book. He particularly wanted me to see Lemon Hill. He had heard it was to be restored. "Once belonged to Robert Morris who helped finance the Revolution." Newly stood outside reading while the wind blew dried leaves around his feet. "And don't you forget it," he said, taking my arm. "A quiz comes after the tour."

Although we rode to the Park in Newly's old Maxwell, we walked for miles. I remember one milky day in February with the bare trees shaped gray and black against the white sky. Snow lay thinly on the ground with tufts of brown grass and weeds showing above the crust. Here and there a yellow leaf clung to a maple, brown clusters rattled on the oaks. And always the crows cawed in the trees, flapping away in front or far behind us. On the hill above the river few cars were on the road. We were alone with winter. And if at first the gray landscape seemed cold and forbidding, after a time we walked into the grayness and became part of the scene.

Newly felt I must see Mount Pleasant mansion. It was a lovely cheerful house standing high, with handsome brick trim around the corners.

Newly was more interested in the history of the houses we visited and wanted to talk about Benedict Arnold, who had once owned Mount Pleasant. "I might have been a Loyalist myself," Newly said, raising his eyebrows. "I'm not crazy about Jefferson and I don't believe Washington was such a fine fellow, either." He talked heresy, I said. All my forebears were fighters. Newly loved to hear about my family, perhaps he realized what pleasure it gave me to talk about them. I had no living relatives except Uncle Carter Bigelow in Pittsburgh. Other Colbys I had read about in a diary of my father's. The diary noted the purchase of a new ice box; my birth, and the discovery that Timothy Colby had been a surgeon on the S.S. *Constitution*, all of equal importance. Newly wanted me to tell him everything I remembered about my mother and gazed intently at the picture of her sitting on a small stone bench, a wasp-waisted woman in a striped dress. I thought my mother very pretty. As I said, I looked like my father with his long nose and jaw and his mouth.... But I didn't tell Newly all this.

"Your ignorance of the environs of your native city appalls me," Newly said. "Surely you have been to Strawberry Mansion?" We often walked by the Barge Clubs, while Newly spouted more information. He sometimes made rather paunchy jokes, but was serious about our "project" for the day, which made it fun. As we came to know each other, I suppose he sensed my inward soreness, no doubt drew conclusions from my silence about David and my seldom mentioning Joyce. I was quiet and he let me be. He never demanded my attention; apparently consideration and unselfishness were natural to him. Once, when I slipped on the plank of wood in the Japanese Garden, Newly grabbed and held me. "You all right?" He dropped his arms. Of course I realized that in his own way he was "giving me a rush" and that he must find me attractive. "You have the snootiest face," he'd say. "Such a regal air." And he would mince ahead of me, holding out his overcoat with his lips bunched up in a way that made me lean against a tree and laugh. As I said, he complimented me on my figure, my hair, and made remarks about my eyes ("they go from gray to almost black") and my "pretty mouth." No one had ever even considered my mouth, which I felt was my most unfortunate feature. The main favor Newly did, as I said, was to make me forget my looks. (If pretty women are supposed to be self-conscious, they are nothing compared to an ugly woman. Although ugly is a word I almost never use.)

Newly was older than either Jim Rickard or Tom Shiver. Tom would have tried to neck behind every vault in Laurel Hill Cemetery. Newly was of marriageable age. I liked him better than any man I knew. I was not in love with him, an impossibility because of David. I might never fall in love. I don't mean I yearned after David. It was, as I said, a childish feeling that I belonged to him and that, in a sense, I loaned myself out. How could I tell about the future and Newly? What were my real feelings about him? Would the question come up? I knew it would. Did this mean marriage? I told myself that it undoubtedly did. Newly was gathering me to him, in his own way. Seeing him every weekend I was allowing myself to be "gathered." I made a conscious effort to think objectively.

Marrying Newly would mean stepping into a very different life. Mama would say I was marrying out of my class. What did that mean and who cared? I would lead a plain life. I liked the idea; it seemed to fit my circumstance.

I remember that when this thought entered my mind I was standing by the bureau in my room, gazing absently at my reflection. There must have been something different in the moment because it seemed as though the flesh on my face dissolved and I saw my cheekbones, the long bones of my jaw. Here was the structure: the face of an orphan ... a girl with neither father nor mother. An orphan who might be in a "home," but for David. Or working a sewing machine in a sweatshop. Mama and Papa had given me shelter, even without love. Now, inexorably, they were shutting me out. Why had I never brought myself to the point of seeing who and what I was and the fragility of my situation? Was I now looking at myself and where I stood because help lay at hand? At this I remember gripping the edge of the bureau—*saved*.

Now I must go over in my mind the many qualities I loved in Newly. I knew his honesty and goodness. He would take care of me. I need not live in fear. He showed interest in my family and brought them alive. He valued my opinion. Most important, he could support me. He was six years older than I was. Life, I must realize, with Newly might be somewhat unadorned and intellectually a little bleak. But I had lived in an intellectual atmosphere for years, unshared, joyless. I was not afraid of the unadorned life, I welcomed it. Harsh, rough-edged, the thought came into my mind: how many offers of marriage would there be? Quickly I told myself I would never marry Newly for this reason; nevertheless, the thought remained.

All February the debutante life went on. I saw *The Bat* again. I passed sandwiches at teas, went to luncheons, and danced at night. The whole business became an endurance test.

"Whatever's happened to your hair?" Fanny asked one night when she was helping me dress. "And you're too thin. Your dress is hanging on you."

"Oh, don't fuss, Fanny!"

"Short-tempered, too," Fanny said, as she hooked me up the back.

Silence. Then she said, "Whatever is David doing with that Joyce Framely? Pudding-face, Robert calls her. And the airs!" Fanny sucked in her wide lips. Through the thick glasses her eyes looked quite wild. David was her favorite. Me, she tolerated and bossed. "Rich—that's what she is," Fanny said. "Sneaky, too. Sneaky enough to get David." She turned me around. A small woman with wandering, big, dark eyes. She had brought me up and felt she knew all there was to know about me. "Mrs. Severn'll murder you for taking up with this Newlin Slatter, nice as he is. His mother's divorced."

"Now Fanny—" I took her by the shoulders. "Mama is not to know."

Fanny pulled away. "Don't keep after me!"

I leaned down, for she was a short woman, and kissed her. Affection made little difference to Fanny. Grumbling, she went out of the room.

Newly now started coming to see me during the week. We would go to the movies. An action-packed film was his favorite. "As a kid I couldn't tell William S. Hart from his horse," he said. He had an engaging chuckle. Mama and Papa tolerated him in their condescending manner. Newly either stood up to them, or disregarded them, or maybe did not see what happened. Mama admired his spirit, although the idea of liking or not liking him never entered her head. She rather enjoyed sparring with him.

"Tilden won again, I see," Mama said, one night when Newly was there for dinner. It amused her to pretend Newly's only subject was sports.

"And Little Poker Face," Newly said.

Mama raised her eyebrows, looking up from the pork chops. (When Ted Rickard came for dinner we had squabs.)

"Helen Wills," Newly said.

"Oh, yes."

That was the evening Newly decided to wrench Mama away from sports. He explained to me that with Mama there were only question-and-answer conversations. They needed a new subject.

"What is your opinion of *A Lost Lady*, Mrs. Severn?"

Mama turned her blue eyes on him rather critically. "I know nothing about it," she said and went back to the chop.

From his rather silent end of the table Papa said, "I liked *O Pioneers!*."

"Did you, sir?" Newly swung eagerly toward him, round eyes shining. Now what? I wondered. I could hardly believe Newly read Willa Cather. He was a non-reader. He astonished me, mentioning Cather's feeling for Nevada.

Papa put down his knife and fork in the exact center of his plate. "Cather interests me more than Virginia Woolf, a strange writer."

Newly had evidently shot his bolt, for after cocking his head on one side in a pleased manner he fell silent.

Robert came in and shuffled the plates onto a tray. Meals lasted forever and were a torment to poor Newly, but also a challenge. He tried a conversation about Prohibition, citing the way the law had been hustled through Congress and that bootleggers were selling some forty million dollars worth of liquor a year. But he verged on the subject of corruption and neither Papa nor Mama would permit such a discussion. It resembled politics. Papa said briefly that he felt the bootlegger and the speakeasy existed in a deliberate spirit of revolt and that he, for one, intended to obey the laws of his country. He was as good as his word—not even wine was served in the house, although I always suspected Fanny smuggled wine in to Mama, whose breath frequently smelt of liquor, in a mild way.

Newly did not mind Papa's rebuff, he still glowed from his Cather sortée.

"Went rather well, don't you think?" he said when we were alone in the parlor. Of course when Newly and Papa talked investments, Newly's big cheeks shone. And once at the table he was so intent on making a point that he actually moved a saltcellar.

Mama and Papa were not consciously unkind. Newly was someone they must acknowledge, but they were completely disinterested in him. He was "Not One Of Us." Jim Rickard held a very different position. His mother might not be invited to all the teas, but the Rickards went to the Assembly and were eighteenth-century Philadelphians. (Because my family did not come from Philadelphia I was barred from the Assembly, which Mama never ceased saying she so regretted.) Individuals were not regarded as people by Mama and Papa unless they were wholly familiar and their family line known in all its branches down to second cousins, Episcopalians everyone.

Nothing was recognizable about Newlin Slatter—a name best forgotten. They had approved of Tom Shiver. Tom's mother was a Biddle—from the wrong side of the river, it was true, but still the name counted. Mama thought his tender, solicitous air betokened the manners of a gentleman, and although if I had allowed him he would have seduced me, to Mama and Papa he was a thorough gentleman.

12   As Newlin Slatter and I tramped around Fairmount Park I knew he was seeing me under the most trying circumstances. My nose was red from the cold, spit curls blown out by the wind, and I wore my old school coat and galoshes. He did not seem to care but would give me a keen glance and ask me what I thought about Harding, or Coué, and when I was old enough to vote would I be a Republican as a matter of course? He was *interested* in me and believed in me, and I began to think even loved me as I was. David always wanted me to be "better" at something, dancing, my "line," even the violin. But Newly did not want me changed at all.

We discussed Couéism seriously and Newly confided, with evident embarrassment, that when a lump had appeared on his neck (I suppose he meant a boil) he had deliberately said out loud every night that the lump was getting better and better, and it had disappeared. Newly told me this with utter seriousness, almost solemnity. I was willing to go along with him if it bolstered his confidence. But I couldn't really believe in Dr. Coué. Life was too unexpected, with too many sharp corners for me to trust that chanting words would dispel the threat, or make my eyes big and glamorous.

Newly and I discussed politics seriously. I took to reading the newspapers. When we strode along the Schuylkill in the snow or climbed up to Strawberry Mansion or drank tea and danced

(Newly's arm pumping) in the parlor on a rainy Saturday, I felt protected, cared for, wonderfully appreciated. Although David still was close, whole days would pass when I scarcely gave him a thought.

I did not go to the Framelys as often as formerly, but I kept the Bride's Book up to date. Mrs. Framely must have noticed, for one day she said, "Eva, you are keeping Newlin Slatter all to yourself. How does that happen? Mr. Framely and I want to know him."

Dinner with the Framelys was a great success. Newly and Mr. Framely hit it off at once. Newly evidently had the right business outlook, even though Mr. Framely felt doubtful about his politics. (Newly told me Harding was a "hot-air artist" and had rotten friends.) Of course, Newly said, Harding had appointed Hughes and Herbert Hoover and Andrew Mellon to his cabinet. But was Mr. Framely all that fond of the Mellons?

"A fine family," Mr. Framely said, as he stood to carve the big rib roast. "There's a feeling in the country against these crackpots like Wilson who want to improve the world. We're doing all right as we are. I think Harding's going to reduce taxes."

Newly said that Harding was all for business but that he never gave a thought to the farmers. "Those fellows are having a tough time. They're bothered about a surplus." Newly took a quick drink of water, excited by the argument. "And you've got a tariff smacked on a whole lot of stuff." Anything political always made Newly go red in the face.

"You're against tariffs?" Mr. Framely stopped carving, stood, knife in hand. "You sound like a Democrat!" His little shiny eyes looked angrily at Newly.

But Newly seldom saw anyone's irritation. Now he laughed and said, "I'm one of the few Democrats in the Guaranty Trust."

Newly was so evidently unaware of tension, that after a moment Mr. Framely went back to his carving. "You won't find Harding upsetting the applecart," he said, bearing down on the knife. "It's business as usual. And that's what the country wants. That's why people voted for him. They don't want government messing up their lives."

The maid put a plate in front of Newly with a large slice of beef on it. Food at the Framely's was always marvelous and lots of it.

Newly said he'd like to know what Albert Fall was doing selling those oil reserves that weren't his to sell.

Mr. Framely, prepared to sit down, having helped everybody, picked up his napkin. "All this stuff in the newspapers about the Teapot Dome," he said, looking directly at Newly, "what does the average man know about such things? Or care? You're not going to find a man like Albert Fall doing anything shady. It just doesn't happen." Mr. Framely pulled in his chair. "These stories are largely made up by reporters to sell papers," he said, tucking his napkin right into his collar. "It won't come to anything."

Newly didn't answer. But I could tell the way his mouth set that he didn't agree.

Mrs. Framely remarked that Mama had told her the Stotesbury's bathroom fixtures were solid gold.

"It's all vulgar show," Mr. Framely said, quite crossly. "Like the Vanderbilts bringing those poor devils over from Japan to build their camp."

"But it was beautiful!" I said.

"And they didn't even have records for their victrola." Here Mr. Framely started to laugh, and then Mrs. Framely told the story of my walk through the woods. "Just imagine Eva going through those dark woods! Joyce should have been ashamed of herself!"

"If Joyce had come with me she wouldn't have danced with Bill Vanderbilt. And that's what counted!"

Then we all laughed, and nothing would do but Newly had to be told the whole story. This led Mrs. Framely into speaking of the low morals of today's boys and girls.

Newly said that he thought an awful lot of the people his age had a feeling of emptiness and futility. "I guess it's a rebound from the war."

Mr. Framely asked Newly "how he had served." And Newly without the least embarrassment said he had been turned down on account of his feet.

"Your feet?" I cried. "But you walk my feet off every weekend!" Newly laughed. "I came up against an extremely intelligent medical man when I was examined," he said. It was a relief to hear someone speak of being turned down without apologizing. Newly, I knew, had a poor opinion of war. And then I realized something quite astonishing. The Framelys evidently took the relationship between Newly and me for granted. Newly was my "beau." We were, in their minds, practically engaged. This attitude made Newly much at ease, evidently. He kept casting admiring looks at me, and smiling all the time as though he wanted the Framelys to know I was his girl. And I felt myself accepting the situation and liking it.

After that dinner with the Framelys Newly and I seemed to move miles deeper into our relationship. I felt I really knew him. His admiration, the naturalness with which he talked to both Mr. and Mrs. Framely, their pleasure in him, showed that the Framelys were Newly's type people. They were never this easy with David, who called Mr. Framely "Sir" all the time. Mr. Framely had even joked with Newly about the Guaranty. "You fellows buying your commercial paper from Goldman, Sachs. I go all the way to Lancaster and York to sell my paper." He and Newly laughed, and Newly blew out a big cloud of smoke from the cigar Mr. Framely had given him.

It was the following Saturday that Newly showed me a strange trick. (I know all of this has been told many times in the newspapers, but I want to tell it in my own words.) We were walking along the Schuylkill by the boathouses. I complained that my hands were freezing. Newly ripped off my gloves and put his bare hands around both of mine. He looked at me, very seriously. "Now you're getting warm," he said, holding tightly to me and squeezing my fingers. "Now you *are* warm!"

It was the oddest sensation, for I could feel warmth spread all over my body.

"It's wonderful!" I cried.

He dropped my hands and, I remember, he blushed and looked embarrassed, for some reason, and so sort of bumbly that suddenly—right there on the East River Drive—I threw both arms around him and gave him a great hug. Whenever I did this he usually laughed. But now he stood looking down at me. Then he said, "You know I'm in love with you, don't you?" He took hold of me, holding me by the waist, twisting me about so that I was facing him. "Don't you?" he repeated. I did not look at him, but beyond, at the blue, jumping waves of the river. He shook me gently. I looked back at him. "Yes, I know," I said. And I did. Quite suddenly the knowledge flushed through me, unimpeded. What a blessing! I thought, right off.

"I'm glad," I said.

"Are you?" he said. "Look at me, Eva!" I looked at him. "Are you?" he repeated.

"Indeed I am, Newly," I said.

He let go of me, quite content not to kiss me, which was nice, and a change. He held my hand and we walked on. He did not say much, but bounced along and then he suddenly said that he'd race me to the car, which was pulled onto the grass. This suited me exactly. "Let's go!" I yelled, and we were off. For a chunky man Newly was quite a sprinter. He outdistanced me in no time and when I came panting up to the car he took me in his arms, kissing me long and hard. And I let him and gave him back as good as he gave me.

Mama and Papa were out for dinner that night, and Newly persuaded me to have dinner with him. I was not supposed to go out unchaperoned for dinner. As a matter of fact, there was a dance that night, but again Newly persuaded me that I could skip it. His big face was so happy and he seemed so naturally affectionate that I did not have the heart or desire to say no. We went to a small restaurant on Eighteenth Street where I was not apt to be recognized. It was fun. Newly had his flask with him and gave me a drink. "You better kill the taste with ginger ale," he said. There was always liquor around. Tom Shiver drank heavily, and so had David at one time. But I never drank. The game I played, under David's tutelage, was always to be "peppy" and high-spirited. If I was seen taking a drink I could be accused of having "taken too much," which was considered "bad taste" and "fast" in a girl.

The combination of having dinner with a man, plus liquor, seemed enormously exciting. I enjoyed it all hugely, laughing a lot and eating every roll in the basket without giving a thought to my figure.

When we came home the house was empty, silent, and rather dark. Fanny was far off, asleep on the fourth floor. I think the whole evening had the end right along with it, for without speaking, we dropped our coats on the hall bench, walked down the living room to the long sofa. We lay clasping each other in the most natural and exciting fashion. Then Newly had my skirts up and his pants down and he was there in me and thrusting so that my "maidenhead" broke and, although I cried out, in a moment, when the pain was gone and he deeply within me, the sensation was so exquisite that I had an orgasm in quite a delirious and marvelous fashion. *So this was what it was all about*, I said to myself in high glee and happiness. We lay, with Newly breathing hard and utterly silent. His head was turned away. Then he withdrew from me.

"Oh my *God*. Did I hurt you? You're a virgin! I suppose I knew all the time." He suddenly knelt up, clasped his head in both hands, then turned and looked down at me. "Yet you came, didn't you?"

"Of course."

"There's no 'of course' about it. I hurt you."

"Yes. But not afterwards."

He flung on to me, putting both arms around me. He was looking right into my eyes. "You're so *wonderful*. I love you so *dreadfully*." Then, half sitting up again. "Now we'll be married," he said, immensely pleased with himself.

( 139

"You think so?" It was a question, but I smiled.

"You don't imagine I ravished you for any other reason, do you?" We laughed and laughed, rocking each other back and forth on the old hard sofa.

That night, after she came home, I told Mama. Because I had taken a long step away, I wanted her to know at once. She was in her room, putting the gray hairpins through the curls on her forehead. She then put on a net.

I waited until she had on her cap, for she did not like her ritual disturbed. Then I said very calmly and carefully that Newly had proposed to me and that I had accepted him. But of course I wanted her blessing and Papa's. I was bound not to use the word "consent" or "approval."

I saw her knobby hands grip the silver hairpin box. She faced me quite silently. What was she thinking? Her blue eyes shifted back and forth. Disappointment, annoyance, outrage? She so often looked irritatedly at me that I did not expect a fond glance.

"When did this happen?"

I smiled, realizing what she had unconsciously said.

"Tonight."

"You'll have to ask Papa."

I was not asking, but I did not draw attention to it.

"Yes, of course. But I wanted to tell you first."

Had she said all she wanted to say? I felt the old sour disappointment. What happened to me meant little to her. Perhaps she saw the look of disappointment on my face for she said, "Come here..." I stood beside her and she pulled my head down and kissed me on the cheek. "I'm glad for you, Eva. I hope you'll be happy." The ritual reply. But she meant more than that. As she had quietly withdrawn support from me, so she let me know that the decision was wholly mine. And I thought, looking back at her, that if this was all she would say, then so be it.

# Prelude

*Anna and Frederick are in Anna's bedroom. The room is colored and shaped by a beautiful Aubusson carpet, which flows beside the black marble hearth and sweeps under the large double bed, coming around to Anna's low bureau. At present she is seated on the bench. Frederick is by the fireplace, looking handsome in a dark maroon robe with a black, silk collar. The room is chilly, as are all the rooms in the house, cold being more healthful, according to Anna. Also chilliness will spur Fanny, Robert, and Mrs. Mertz to work all the harder in order to keep warm. No coal burns in the fireplace; the flue does not work properly. The mantle is white marble, pleasantly shaped.*

*Frederick continues their conversation:* "She told you tonight, then?"

"Yes, she came right out with it. No asking our permission. Slatter..." *she says the name quite viciously. But in spite of her anger her hand falls dispiritedly into her lap.* "Do you suppose we could possibly get him to change it to Slater—take out one 't'?" *She half turns to Frederick. Her face has no color and she seems listless. She knows her question is idle.*

"I do not," *Frederick says. He is at the moment rather taken up with arranging his moustache for the night, a ritual he performs with nice precision, twirling the ends.*

*Anna sits unmoving on the tapestried stool. In fact, although not really too hopeful, until tonight she has been seriously considering the Rickards for Eva. They loomed as large as St. Regis mountain compared to the Slatters. And what a joy to speak of Eva as Mrs. James Ulbeck Rickard (even though no one had ever heard of the Ulbecks).*

*Frederick, who has been watching her—sensing that she is perturbed—comes over and lays a hand on her shoulder. "There's no sense allowing yourself to be disappointed, my dear. Don't dream of a match with Jim Rickard. We should have to be seeing them, you know. The Rickards would have wanted to make a good thing out of the connection. The very thought of dining with the Rickards makes me unhappy." He squeezes her shoulder and actually gives her a little shake. "Come now, you couldn't have borne it any better than I—in fact, worse!" He laughs down at her. And as always she responds with a wide, quite charming smile. Even in the unbecoming cap she looks roguish.*

*"You're right. We shan't have to see Mrs. Slatter at all, except at the wedding. Fanny tells me Mrs. Slatter is divorced, although I shan't let on I know. I gave Fanny my old white lace mitts for the information."*

*Frederick, who never pays attention to Anna's practices, has gone back to the mantle and says, "We can't expect too much, after all."*

*"True. Although lately Eva has been looking better."*

*"Love!" Frederick cries. And suddenly raises both hands above his head, lifting his face. The gesture is youthful and unexpected, the thin, bearded face transformed with a satanic grin.*

*Anna chortles at him. "Oh, Frederick, you are so naughty. Imagine the poor girl in love." But at the words, the smile fades. She frowns and starts picking among the things on her bureau. "I suppose we're lucky someone is taking her. What would she have done after the trip to Japan?"*

*"I thought you rather liked Newlin."*

*"I never considered him one way or the other." Anna rests both clasped hands on the bureau, steadying herself. "Of course now I shall have to." Then she says, lowering her head and speaking quite brokenly, "Somehow this Slatter thing makes David's match all the worse."*

*Frederick moves beside her. "Now Anna, don't fret yourself about all that again, my dear. Don't attach one to the other—it's fatal."*

*Anna grips her hands tighter. "I have no intention of it, Frederick. There is the money. And David—" she pauses, perhaps to swallow, for she is bound not to choke, "seems to have made the adjustment with hardly a backward glance." She raises her head to Frederick. "This is hard on you, Frederick. You must have so looked forward to discussing your work together."*

*Frederick leaves her and walks to the end of the room, looking out at the darkened street. Large snow flakes drift languidly by the window, catching onto the black branches of the maple. He does not answer. They have had this conversation before, and although he appreciates her mentioning it, he would as soon she didn't. His disappointment in David has been so fierce it startled him. There had even been a moment when he wanted to say something quite violent and unforgettable to the boy. But in the end he made no comment at all, was simply silent. This, he knew, was the most cutting thing he could do. All the color left David's face. They had stared at each other. Then Frederick finally said, "I wish you good luck." The tone had rung with awful falseness. David turned and left the room. Was it the worst disappointment of a lifetime? Frederick wonders, standing looking out at the monotonous flakes forever falling. Or was not being made head of the anthropology department at Pennsylvania worse because he knew he could accomplish so much, and knew where he could lay hands on money. It was impossible to measure or compare disappointments. The latest always seemed the worst. But then David had never shown any real preference for the kind of life that he, Frederick, had craved. The moment upon coming to the Platte River when he had taken off all his clothes and entered the river, floating free down its shallows. The finding of a skull in a cave where he had been so frightened he had taken a bad fall. . . . But David? David liked to play tennis and golf. He really seemed to be engrossed in interest rates, and talked about meeting bank presidents as though shaking hands with Plato. And Joyce of the beautiful breasts, which she exhibited occasionally, once lighting Frederick's cigar, leaning far forward so he could look his fill. . . . What manner of girl was that? And oddly he thinks now of Eva, to whom David as a child and youth has been so passionately devoted. What will David think of this match of Eva's? From subconscious knowledge, Frederick is sure David will hate seeing Eva attached to Newlin Slatter.*

*Frederick hears himself say, "I hadn't realized Eva was serious about this fellow, had you?"*

"No." *Anna goes on tidying her bureau, straightening the silver mirror, her comb and brush, the hairpin box.* "But then I never gave Eva much thought, which is wrong of me. I knew she wouldn't have Jim Rickard. Certainly she is better marrying this Newlin—whatever—than trying to be a stenographer. And I did not particularly care for the way she cultivated the Framelys. She seemed willing to take anything from them, trips to Japan, clothes. However—" *Anna went on quickly as Frederick showed signs of being about to interrupt,* "I have never understood how she attracts men. She has had three beaux. That's not many, of course, but who would imagine she'd have one?"

*Frederick says,* "I should like Eva to be married from the house, Anna. Are you prepared for that?"

"Yes," *she says finally, having not much choice.*

13 Mama made it very clear that Newly and I were not to announce our engagement (considered a most important step) until after David and Joyce were married in April. I was on no account to confide in Jim Rickard, she said. Maybe she thought that in a month I might change my mind. I know she wanted David to be solo in the limelight. But an announcement in the paper that I was marrying Newlin Slatter would hardly shake the foundations of society. It was embarrassing not telling Jim, who still "rushed" me at parties and wanted to call and tried to kiss me. Of course I had deceived Mama many times, but this stipulation which she made—although ridiculous—nevertheless was the last condition she would ever make, and both Newly and I decided to abide by it. I minded terribly not being able to wear my engagement ring, which Newly produced with enormous satisfaction; a diamond set in gold prongs. It was old fashioned and I liked it. I'd never had a ring before. Newly came right out and told me it was his mother's engagement ring, given to her by the divorced husband.

Another reason for abiding by Mama's wishes, which of course were also Papa's; I was underage, and must have someone give permission for me to marry. I wanted everything to go as smoothly as possible and to walk down our stairway on Papa's arm, a granddaughter at last.

"You don't want to hurt the old folks," Mrs. Slatter said. "It wouldn't be right." Mrs. Slatter made a fuss over me. It never seemed to bother her that I was not a pretty, little pet, not the heiress that I'm sure she thought her son deserved. She explained Newly to me. "Won't wear warm enough clothes in winter. You notice? Doesn't care how he looks. Good digestion. No trouble there." Mrs. Slatter ("call me Edna, *do*") clattered her bracelets and flung her legs around. She longed to be much more intimate than I could manage. "We'll go on a real spree!" she'd cry, clasping be-ringed hands. "Lunch at the Bellevue and then a shopping binge with maybe a movie. The Arcadia's still playing *The Sheik*. I could stand seeing it again. What do you say?"

If I had been able to tell David about my engagement, perhaps his reaction might have been different. But Mama got to him that night and whatever he had to say, his first reaction was gone. Instead he came into my room hand outstretched, lips parted widely over his even teeth. "This is great, Evie! Simply great! Best news in the world. He's a lucky fellow." The performance was nauseating. Like Mama, he settled on the surface. Even Joyce had a more personal reaction.

"So you're tying the knot," she said. "How long have you known him?" She was asking more questions than Mama, digging at me, critical.

"About a month and a half."

"That's not long." Did she disapprove?

"Long enough. We went for walks in the Park."

"In the *Park*? In winter?"

"It was fun."

"I just hope he's the right man for you," she said.

I flushed, angry. What was she implying? I had not thought she took that much interest in me. Had she been enjoying a feeling of triumph that my engagement in some way spoiled?

"You make me wish I hadn't told you."

She was at once contrite. "Don't say that, Eva." Her big eyes smiled. "I'm honestly glad for you." She wore heavy scent that seemed to surround me. I was suddenly aware how seldom she touched me. For now she put her arm around my neck and kissed me on the cheek. I stood very still. I *must* not jerk away. Then her arm was down and she stood off. David would want Newly for an usher, she said. Poor Newly, he could do nothing but submit.

It was really with the Framelys that Newly and I celebrated. I knew Mrs. Framely was pleased. She looked at me, cocking her head. "So you won't be going to Japan with us," she said, and kissed me.

Tall, blond, smiling, David and Joyce, as Mama said, were a handsome couple. I saw them at parties, walking closely, arm in arm, whispering together with sly glances aside. Seeing them, sensing the bond, I told myself that the boy David I once had loved and to whom I belonged had been rooted out, flung off. Instead was this steadily preoccupied, smiling stranger. He patronized Newly, gave him advice, or tried to. Would Newly like to be put up for the Racquet Club? (What *was* all this about clubs? Newly asked me.) He also called him "Newl," as though he must make something ridiculous out of a pet name. Why couldn't he accept Newly on Newly's terms, much as I accepted Joyce, or tried to? Newly had walked me out of my predicament; David should be grateful. Had he known nothing of my situation, or had he purposely looked away? He was capable of doing either or both.

I did not compare what I had once felt for David (could I feel it again if called on?) and what I now felt for Newly. If I could not say I was "in love" with Newly, I nevertheless loved him and was dependent upon him. I clung to him in a way that might have distressed him if he had not partially realized David in some way had hurt me, and resented it. And also I must admit to being wild to try again what we had done before on the sofa so successfully. But Newly was adamant. He would not let our kisses get too "passionate." "Stop it! Just don't—" he'd jerk away, walk off down the room, or if we were in the Maxwell, he'd start the engine. "And don't try to trap me, either," he'd say, looking quite fierce. "You make it tough, you know? What happens if you get pregnant?"

I was silent. Then rather hesitantly I asked why he couldn't— uh—wear something?

If he was shocked, he did not show it. "Just lay off," he said. "We're not sleeping together until we're married. We're not going to drift into that sort of thing. I thought we agreed on it."

I took to barely kissing him on the cheek. He was good-natured about it all. I must say we walked more than ever.

It was while we were engaged that I discovered Newly's grandiloquent plans for the Guaranty Trust. He had designed a beehive of offices to be built in the beautiful rotunda of the bank. Nothing excited Newly more quickly than talk about his plan. He spent so many hours working on the details that I couldn't help encouraging him, even though it seemed sacrilege to mar the bank's rotunda with ugly offices. Newly had a friend, Dan Ruber, who was equally enthusiastic about the reorganization. I do not mean to make these offices overly important, but in view of Newly's Great Change, his plan is significant, for if the bank had only taken hold of his idea maybe Newly might have stayed as he was.

Naturally I recognized that Newly and I had different tastes. Newly considered Maxfield Parrish terrific and Norman Rockwell tops. He read *The Saturday Evening Post*, skipping Faulkner and Hemingway. Newly had no feeling for appearances, which I had been taught were of paramount importance. He wore ties that made me want to cry. His overcoat was too long; he looked uncomfortable in a tuxedo. Trying to change Newly proved impossible. He felt perfectly happy in his ties and overcoat.

He was incurably gregarious. The men in the office were "great guys," whom he wanted me to meet. He constantly fell in with strangers, talking to everyone. He also showed a stubborn side that I had not expected. For instance, with Mama and Papa, he insisted that if he just persevered, they would give in and treat him as a member of the family. So he pursued them, refusing to acknowledge they would never admit him, in fact barely recognized him. Fortunately his mother took a more realistic attitude. "The old folks want to be by themselves," she said, when Mama and Papa refused her invitation to tea.

David behaved in quite a poisonous way with Newly. "You're in the Research Department, aren't you, Newl? What's your next step, Investment Advisory?"

Newly would frown. "No, I don't think so. I'd have to go through the Trust Department."

"Who's head of Trusts now?"

"I don't know too many of the fellahs..." Then frowning, "You don't get ahead very quickly at Guaranty."

"In spite of Joe Simpson?"

Newly said quietly, "He's considered one of our top men."

David laughed. "And who wants to be vice-president?"

David's attitude sobered Newly and puzzled him. Although partially realizing the tension that existed between David and me, nevertheless Newly wanted to think of David as another "great guy," and David's subtle antagonism confused him.

Mama, I noted, apparently welcomed Joyce, an outsider—in Mama's terms. Joyce, Mama thought, could be manipulated. Mama was wrong, of course. But then she never really wanted to know why people acted as they did. Joyce's admiration of all Mama represented, the quickness with which she grasped the finer gradations of society and its customs, delighted Mama. She tolerated Joyce's sloppiness. I think she felt that in time she would change Joyce. Mama never conceived it possible that Joyce would slowly squeeze her out of David's life until she stood completely outside, not even permitted to look in.

Still weaving through all our lives were the parties. The scene seems so strange. The great Bellevue ballroom with the gold scrolled boxes and the big urns filled with American Beauty roses and Paul Whiteman in tails smiling at everyone. We were the elite, the favored. Excitement and fear—that swelling of the heart which I felt when I went to my first ball and heard the blast of the orchestra—were gone. If Mama had not insisted I still go to parties—I'd have stopped gladly. Now and again David would dance with me, pulling me over to a corner where he put me through all the steps he knew.

Or he would make me spin around the entire room, a show. He embarrassed me, which was the object, I suppose.

"You're still a good dancer," he said one night. "A pity you have to give it up. We might have done exhibition dancing, like the Castles."

"Irene Castle is beautiful, don't forget."

As always, any reference to my looks infuriated him. He told me to shut up and put my mind on my feet.

David spent the night before his wedding at home. He'd had a rather sedate ushers' party. (Newly said it was a frost.) Except for Newly, I had only a bare acquaintance with a few of the eight ushers. They were mostly men David had known at Yale.

I heard David come in the house and go to Mama's room. He stayed with her a long time. What could they be talking about and what was I doing waiting for him? I knew he must come in to see me. I heard him on the stairs. He appeared at the door.

"You still up? It's late," he said.

"I waited to see you."

He came over and sat on the foot of my bed. "Yes, sure."

He seemed exhausted, very pale, eyelids swollen, eyes bloodshot. He did not look drunk, he looked lost.

"It's so damned cold in here," he said.

I threw him the quilt. He wrapped it around himself. I don't know how long we sat there. We didn't speak. Then I felt the end of the bed lift. He dropped the quilt. He said nothing and did not look at me and went out the door.

After he left I lay quite still for a long time, letting wave after wave sweep over me. I just let it come, uncontrollable feeling, great rolls of it that went through me in a physical rising, then dwindling, then rising again. I had thought all that was dead, gone, but now feeling surged out of me unchanged.

The day of David's wedding was clear with an ice blue sky, no wind, cold. Behind the altar of the church masses of flowers hid the ugly wall. In a large, purple hat and violet dress with an armload of delphinium and baby's breath, I looked all nose and chin. David's ushers wore cutaways and spats. The organ warbled "O Promise Me." (Surely David or Mama could have seen to the music.) As I stood waiting to go down the aisle I thought that an air of richness overlaid the scene. How pleased Mr. Framely must be! "Our" side of the church was packed; the Framelys' side nicely filled with three Negro maids sitting at the back. Mama looked glorious in a pink toque, tiny veil, her diamonds, actually cleaned for the occasion. She gave my dress a tug as she passed and told me to hold my shoulders back. The bridal party looked like a musical comedy with an all-male chorus and me. David and Jeff Casper appeared. David insisted on having Jeff as best man, down from Providence and hadn't laid eyes on David in ten years. But they used to go fishing in Cherokee Creek and had been at camp together. Nothing would do but that "old Jeff" see David through the wedding. The organ squeezed out the wedding march. I started down the tilting aisle. This was the moment I dreaded. To be made conspicuous. But then I realized people were looking beyond me to Joyce and little ah's went around the church. At last I was by the altar, which was nothing but a shiny table with a big lectern behind it and Dr. Richcomb. David looked strangely flushed, and Jeff Casper appeared more piglike than ever, with his short neck bulging over the stiff collar and his bristling, blond hair. When I reached the table, I turned. Joyce wore Mama's real lace bridal veil shaped into a kind of crown—unbecoming, I thought. Her dress had the old, full skirt and a bodice to show off her bosom. She looked like a haus-frau, but was declared beautiful by everyone. She appeared quite demure, walking on her father's arm, but she shot me an amused glance as though the whole scene was a farce and only she and I knew it.

During the ceremony the organ kept up a soft tremolo, one sentimental piece after another. I did not dare look at Papa. He was by far the most distinguished person in the church. His beautiful cutaway fitted to perfection, he stood straight and slim and serious.

Beside him Mama was also stylish and proud with every curl beautifully turned. They shook my heart. They must have longed for a Cadwalader or even a Biddle, and what they had was a Framely.

The moment had come when I must hand Joyce back her bouquet. I had positively dreaded this instant, the symbolic gesture of proclaiming Joyce a married woman. But when I stepped forward it was only Joyce with her big fronts showing more than they should and only David kissing her rather primly. So we marched back. Newly managed to untangle himself from the other ushers and walk with me, holding my arm, for which I blessed him.

Being the only bridesmaid, of course I was made much of. After we had our pictures taken and stood in the receiving line, I took off my hat and drank quantities of champagne which the ushers kept bringing me. There was an orchestra and I remember doing a solo Charleston while five of the ushers cheered. Actually, it was fun.

David did not function in my life. We had sat in cold misery last night and said goodbye, or made an end. He was no longer—I was going to say, mine. But that's not right. He was *hers*. And that made the difference.

14 In the cellar of the DeLancey Place house Fanny found two small, upholstered chairs and a matching sofa all done in red velvet. Papa persuaded Mama to give them to us, and Newly refinished the woodwork. Mrs. Slatter cleaned the old velvet, red like the curtains Fanny discovered in a trunk and Mrs. Slatter hemmed to fit into our little bay window. I thought the whole effect dazzling.

At first sight our half of the double house we were renting on India Street was distressing. Streaked walls, scuffed floors, unworkable toilet and filthy stove, cracked linoleum. Newly said he'd have the place fixed in no time. We used my "nest egg" to buy our bedroom furniture. Newly found out that the money left me by my mother could have been used at any time (for instance, for college). But I was too taken up with marriage to feel angry or properly resentful. Mrs. Slatter gave us a round deal table and four chairs. Dr. Tilley, our next-door neighbor, the dentist, taught Newly how to refinish the table. Newly and I both worked on the furniture until it began to look like aged pine.

Our wedding had been a quiet affair, to our liking. I walked down the stairs of the DeLancey Place house on Papa's arm. Steve Waller was Newly's best man and Debbie O'Halloran my attendant. I wore a short blue dress that Mrs. Slatter had bought at Naomi Finch's sale, and a tulle circlet that went across my forehead. To everyone's relief David and Joyce were in Italy.

My reaction to marriage was the wildest elation. I kept reminding myself that everything in the house was ours, much of it actually mine! I felt set free and went around banging doors and singing. I could eat when I wanted and what I pleased; no more cream ladled out of a bottle; no more glances sliding off my face and the imperious "Eva!" called down the stairs. I did not even miss Fanny. I could read or play the fiddle when I pleased and not with Mr. Jaffrey.

India Street was only three blocks from Mount Pleasant Station. And although The Mount, as the inhabitants called it, was within Philadelphia limits, Cherokee Woods ran along the foot of the street with a greenish creek winding through a hemlock forest. At the head of the street stood the great India Oak with vast branches throwing shadows back and forth across pavements and lawns.

Newly was busy all the time—a carpenter at heart, he said. He planted tomatoes and string beans in the backyard. Down in the cellar he and his friend Dan Ruber, who lived three houses along the street, were constructing their office models, planned for the big rotunda of the Guaranty Trust. Newly still appeared confident the bank would embrace his plan. When I expressed doubt he became quite red in the face and as good as told me to mind my own business.

Newly had quite definite ideas about my role as his wife. I should not take a paid job, which I suggested, in one of the dress shops along Sedgwick Avenue. Or perhaps his mother would say a word to Naomi Finch. But Newly was adamant. In a way I think he wanted to feel I was a kind of luxury item, too delicate for the hurly-burly. He stood in awe of what he called my background, which was most fortunate, for when I said we were not going to hang his Maxfield Parrish and Norman Rockwell reproductions, he did not seem upset.

Newly took over the cooking, being quite experienced, his mother told me, and liking it. Newly was impervious to appearances, and was perfectly comfortable sitting down to dinner in his undershirt. He seldom talked about the Research Department at the Guaranty, although quick to tell me if "one of the fellows" had just married, or was in any kind of difficulty.

When I decided to let my hair grow and wear it drawn back into a low knot, Newly thought these changes admirable. "You mustn't look like a kid anymore. You're a married woman!" Although he laughed at the way I clattered around the house, he realized the great relief and joy I found in marriage. "You don't miss the parties?" he asked quite seriously. Newly had no idea of my ordeal and fright. And if it confused him to see me drop my party-girl role so suddenly, he did not ask the reason. Of course I should have told him. I kept far too much back, associating all of it with David. Nor did I ever confide in Newly that although I accepted David's feelings for Joyce, yet, like a child, I still felt I belonged to him. If I had only been able to talk about David objectively I might have seen our relationship in some kind of perspective that I could live with. Or if I had opened up my feelings about Joyce and let out my resentment, the situation surely would have been more tolerable.

Newly did not examine relationships; he had not that turn of mind. Instead he talked about Mrs. Alfred Berkley's new Lincoln, which she drove around The Mount and which was rumored to have cost $8,500, or Shipwreck Kelly and his flagpole sitting, or how good Penn's football team was this year.

I slowly became aware that Newly had an inwardness that did not include me. Even in those first months of marriage I felt a kind of concentration going on in him, not shared. I would see him standing quite still in the backyard, holding both hands at either side of his face, staring at the ground. When I asked what troubled him, he would give a start and then laugh or blush. "Nothing, nothing at all." I asked if he was worried about those offices for the Guaranty. "Oh, no. They're coming along nicely." Quite evidently he did not want to talk about whatever was on his mind. Having lived with people who regarded any confidence as a breach of taste, I did not press Newly. However, I found out soon enough. We were at the movies. The night had turned cold for that time of year, and as we stood in the ticket line a young girl started complaining to the boy beside her that she was "freezing," as she put it. Quickly Newly moved over to her. "Give me your hands," he said to the girl, a pale creature with straight blonde hair. "I can warm you. See if I don't." Newly spoke in a strange tone that I had never heard him use. "Don't be frightened," he said. "Just give me both hands." Obediently the girl held her hands out. "Now," Newly said, taking hold, and still in this peculiarly resonant (later called "stained glass") voice, "now you're starting to get warm. Aren't you? Aren't you warm?"

"Yes, yes, I am! I'm warm!" Newly dropped her hands and she danced around, making the other people in line feel her hands. Most fortunately the line started moving toward the ticket window and we were able to get inside without any further excitement. Newly had done for the girl what he once had done for me in Fairmount Park. But how could he suddenly pick out some silly child in public? ... If he did this to total strangers, would warming people turn into a parlor trick?

"Ordinarily," Newly said quietly to me after we had found seats inside the movie house, "I would not make such a display. But I had this strange feeling that I *must*...."

That night when we came home Dr. Tilley, our neighbor, was standing in his front yard and asked us about the movie. He was a fat little man, always ready to laugh. Some perversity got into me and I told him about Newly. I think at the time I was angry and also I felt Newly was being too solemn about his "trick," or whatever he called it and needed someone to laugh at him, or make him laugh. Dr. Tilley roared. Newley could make a fortune.

Newly finally laughed, too. (At first he just looked hurt.) But when we were inside our own house he said quite seriously that he did not like my joking with Dr. Tilley.

I said, "But I don't want you going around warming people in movie theaters! And the girl was such a ninny."

Newly was quite serious. "Don't you remember that day in the Park, Eva."

"Of course I remember. But it's all some sort of hypnotism, or mesmerism, isn't it?"

"No, I don't think so." Newly was quite earnest. "I felt as though I had real power over that girl at the movies. And if I have that kind of power—where does it come from?"

He looked rather irritatedly at me. I said flippantly, "From God. Like Aimee Semple McPherson." And I looked right back at him.

He ignored my crack about McPherson, for he'd always said she was a quack. "But I'm an agnostic!"

There was something repulsive as well as ludicrous in this conversation. I couldn't believe we were having it.

"What are we talking about, Newly? You're using hypnotism, and I think you ought to stop it."

At this, to my surprise he became angry. His mouth squeezed up and he looked almost mean. "Don't keep saying it's hypnotism, Eva, when I know damn well it's not! I am totally ignorant of the principles of hypnotism." He seemed amazingly upset. For the first time I realized he was serious.

Now it may not appear unusual to come upon someone who believes they have supernatural powers, but to come upon it in one's own husband is very upsetting. I suddenly realized that Newly's anger came from being scared. Although this sounds ridiculous and, as I said, repelled me, for I had a low opinion of all "healers," yet at least Newly was talking about his feelings and now I understood what must have been bothering him as he stood in our backyard.

Before I could say something reassuring, Newly said, "If I have this power, why couldn't I have other powers? Making people cold for instance?" He walked to the window, leaned his hands on the sill, looked through the screen at the night. "Or maybe doing people harm?" he said, his voice breaking.

At this I rushed over to him. I couldn't bear his distress. "Newly—I'm sure there's nothing evil in all this—whatever it is!" I cried. "There can't be. It wouldn't be you if there was anything awful connected with it. But you must stop brooding, Newly. Don't fool with whatever it is. Try and just forget it." I had grabbed both his hands. His face was still pale. "Just give the whole thing up. No more practicing."

He looked at me in an odd, rather blind way. "You really think so?" He drew off.

"I'm sure of it."

"Well, I told Dan Ruber, and he thought the whole thing was terrific, with a terrific potential. That's why I tried it on that girl in the movies."

"I thought you felt compelled?"

"Well, I did. And there was also the desire to try."

"You can't listen to Dan Ruber, Newly!"

Newly looked down. "Well, maybe not. But Dan thinks I might be able to cure people, and that I've been given this power for a reason."

The feeling came over me that we couldn't be *having* this conversation, seriously considering Dan Ruber's opinion about mystical powers. The scene outside the movie had been like a farce, with that girl yelling and people staring ... Dr. Tilley's reaction was quite right, and Dan Ruber's typically wrong. At that point I don't believe I thought of anything more than "wrong." I did not think "dangerous." In fact, I was more apt to think "ridiculous." Not that I wanted to hurt Newly's feelings, but all this—whatever it was— must be stopped. I did not really like Dan Ruber or his wife Cora, although we saw them frequently. It was typical of Dan to use words like "terrific potential." Newly would make a fool of himself. I could not bear to have people laugh at him. But how to go about convincing him? He looked so very solemn and also worried, even frightened. I could lay the blame on Dan for suggesting Newly might cure people, as though Newly was in the hands of a power greater than he realized. This would frighten anyone. What are the limits? Could he bring someone back from the dead? Newly himself had used the word "harm." Did "power" suggest Satanic acts?

"Newly," I said, "I am closer to you than anyone, isn't that so?" He nodded.

"But darling, I don't think you have any great secret power." I smiled, almost shyly, "I know your powers in bed and this is marvelous—but Newly—" and here I threw both arms around him, "don't mess up our lives with a whole, big problem that shouldn't and I'm sure *doesn't exist.*"

I think my reference to our sexual life brightened Newly. For now he smiled, and then in his turn he put his arms around me. "You're right, Evie. I'll just push it right out of my mind. That's the best way. Just forget. No more practicing," he said, and I felt his relief.

We went upstairs, arm in arm, and quickly to bed. Deliciously, the release and desire I had felt that first time Newly and I had sex together was constant, a delight to both of us. Being naive in our sex habits made every move fresh and exciting. We could not have enough of sex and slept together every night. And on this particular night we were closer together than ever before because I wanted

Newly to feel every part of me belonged to him and I gave myself as I never had before. In fact so wonderful was the effect that we had sex three times that night.

I did not see Dan Ruber until the following Saturday when I was walking along India. As I came to the Ruber's gate Dan stood up. He had been clipping the grass. I complimented him on the lawn, and he moved toward me.

"Looks pretty good," he said. Dan was a tall man, thin, with scant auburn hair parted in the middle. He had a long, handsome roguish face and was full of conceit. Dan's attitude toward me was embarrassingly deferential. Later, this manner completely changed and he accused me of all sorts of treachery. But in the beginning, Dan and his wife Cora took an overawed attitude, which made any relationship impossible. Dan thought Mama queenlike and no amount of telling him I was not a Severn made any impression.

"Dan, I'm bothered about this idea of Newly's that he may have some secret power—"

Dan broke in, "Oh, that. Yeah." The debonair pose of a second ago was gone. His little amber eyes narrowed.

I said, watching him, "In my opinion hypnotism is not to be experimented with."

Dan stepped closer. "In *my* opinion we may be in the presence of an important manifestation. I've been making my own survey. So far I have not come upon anyone who can make another person warm. They can put you to sleep, stop you from biting your nails, get you talking about your bitchy mother, but no warming."

I had to change tactics. I smiled at him. "What name do you give Newly's gift?" I asked.

"Healing Grace," Dan said. Standing on India Street, I first heard the words that were to become so nauseatingly familiar. Dan went on, "Of course we must find out how much Newly can do. Quietly, among ourselves."

"You're overlooking one angle," I said.

"Oh?"

"Newly wants to forget the whole thing. Right now he's fretting. I don't like to see him unhappy. I'm sure you don't either."

"Absolutely not!" Dan got out his cigarette case, put it back again.

"Then we're agreed." I managed to sound as condescending as Mama. I held my hand over the fence.

He returned a loose clasp. "You betcha! Every time!"

# Prelude

*Anna and Frederick Severn are dressing for dinner. They are having a family party, a rare event: David and Joyce, Eva and Newlin, Mr. and Mrs. Framely (whom they never call Paul and Helen). Anna has an important announcement to make. For the occasion she will appear in the costume she wore at David's wedding, and Frederick will wear his pinstripe suit.*

*"I imagine they'll be surprised," Frederick says. Looking at himself he gives a wry smile. He has trimmed off the ends of his moustache and is disappointed with the effect. He now appears so ordinary-looking he can hardly bear to glance in the mirror.*

"Surprised?" *Anna speaks over her shoulder. She is seated at her dressing table.* "Gracious, Frederick, they'll be flabbergasted! The Lowndes Silver—imagine receiving such a gift!"

*Frederick says it's too bad they have nothing for Eva, and that he doesn't quite understand why Eva and Newlin were asked.*

*At this Anna turns completely around to him.* "You can't seriously think any of our silver suitable for that grubby, little house! Eva and Newlin were asked because we did not want to have just the Framelys with David and Joyce." *Anna has much to forgive Eva. The last offense was coming down the stairs of the DeLancey Place house on Frederick's arm, a bride, preening herself.*

*Frederick says coolly,* "I think Eva's done rather well with her little place."

# Ugly Girl

"Thanks to our furniture and curtains!"

"We had to do something for her."

Silence. Frederick is busy with the knot of his tie. He is older looking, the lines at the side of his mouth are deeper. He seems thin. Time has not laid a hand on Anna. She looks rosy as ever. She has just been brushing her hair, leaning forward and tossing it over her head, quite a feat at her age. Now it stands out in a white mist. Only the curls on her forehead remain in place. She says rather tentatively, "Doesn't it seem strange that David never comes to see us?" As she speaks, a little of the color ebbs from her face.

The subject is almost too painful for Frederick, but he manages. "Yes, I wonder why not." He keeps his back to Anna as though the conversation were not taking place.

"Do you realize we have not seem him in three months? I mean, without her." Anna lays unconscious stress on the last word.

"Yes, I do."

"But why is that?" She has started and now stumbles along like someone trying new country.

"I haven't a notion."

"We know nothing of their plans. Or even if they enjoyed Italy."

"We hardly were told they had moved into that big place in Villa Nova."

"And when we go there for dinner it is always with the Framelys."

"Yes. And I am very tired of Paul Framely." Frederick seems easier with words now he has started speaking. "Framely will talk politics. He almost makes me wish I weren't a Republican."

Anna: "It's so odd Joyce and David haven't a child."

Frederick, rather coldly, "I cannot imagine Joyce in the role of mother."

Anna, regaining her spirits, and not being all that eager to be a great grandmother, says, "I imagine the Lowndes Silver will make a difference to them."

Frederick, with unusual irony: "Gratitude, you mean?"

Anna, irrepressibly, "No, but it's a reassertion of our kinship. It will touch David deeply, I'm sure. And even impress Joyce." Revived, she starts combing her curls carefully. "Not much does. I try to keep up contact by *phoning her. But really there's nothing to phone about...*"

*Frederick turns to his wife. He is in the process of putting his arms into his vest.* "There is no sense pretending, Anna. We both dislike her intensely. I distrust her."

*Anna, excited—with again a sense of new ground—for Frederick has never come out so directly, says,* "I've never trusted her, not from the first. . . . She's common, of course. Her manner to me is not what it should be."

*Frederick has steadfastly avoided this side of the subject and has no intention of taking it up now.* "Neither of the children made really good marriages. Newlin Slatter may be the soul of goodness, but no one could call him interesting."

*Anna is at once put out.* "How can you criticize, Frederick. She is lucky to have caught Newlin!" *Anna stops mid-air. Frederick looks expectantly at her, but she hustles on:* "Eva's a poor housekeeper and she can't cook. I wonder what Newlin sees in her."

*Frederick:* "What was it you heard, Anna? Something about a girl at the movies?"

*Anna impatiently:* "A girl outside a motion picture palace complained of being cold, and Newlin took hold of her hands and supposedly was able to make her warm. The entire thing sounds ridiculous."

*Frederick, turning agitatedly to her,* "Warmed the girl? How?"

*Anna crossly:* "Really Frederick, I've no idea!"

*Frederick leans against the bureau. He feels as though some sort of wave has gone over him. He gulps little gusts of air, his mouth hanging open.*

15 I noticed a change in Newly. He no longer stood in the backyard with his hands pressed against his face. His good humor restored, he cracked jokes and whistled. Dan Ruber and Newly still worked in the cellar on the offices, but the "awesome power," or "Healing Grace," was never mentioned as far as I knew.

We often had dinner with the Framelys; Mama and Papa came twice for Saturday lunch. In the year we had been married, David and Joyce had been to the house once. I sensed Newly's discomfort with David, who still called him "Newl." David now collected Impressionists and came home from Rome and Paris with a small Pissarro and a Cezanne drawing of a girl's head. David and Joyce were now in the "smart set," their dinner party guests listed in the society society columns. I saw Joyce frequently. She would drop by for a tomato and lettuce sandwich. Her boast, made on a clear day in the Adirondacks, she meant. She had sold five stories, two were in the *Saturday Evening Post*. Publishers queried her. I envied her to my soul for I, too, was trying to write. I sent stories out under the name of Penelope Wood, and had them returned. I learned to type on Newly's old machine. The idea that I was seriously writing embarrassed Newly, so we did not discuss it. Joyce and I talked about writing. Although Joyce was not a particularly literary person, we discussed plots, my weak spot. Joyce had started work on a book laid in the sixteenth century about which she knew nothing. She had hired a researcher. *The Lady of Bleeding House Yard*, the book was called, about Lady Hatton, wife of Edward Coke, Queen Elizabeth's Chief Attorney. Joyce asked me if I would read the manuscript and help her with it. In a fit of weakness, I said yes. One reason I could stand seeing so much of Joyce was because her relationship with David was so strange. She spoke of him without affection.

Mama phoned and with a kittenish air asked us to dinner. "There will be a surprise," she said, before hanging up.

The night of the dinner Mama laid on her best. The curtains were drawn in the dining room, the great candelabra lighted, the silver tureen filled with grapes, and a maid hired to help Robert, who shambled even more slowly around the table. Meissen plates shone from the thin lawn tablecloth. We had guinea hen, always a festive sign. Joyce sat on Papa's right, Mrs. Framely, handsome in black lace, on his left—a strange arrangement. I sat between Mr. Framely and David.

"What in God's name have you done to your hair?" David flipped open his napkin.

"You're getting fat," I said. Not that it was altogether true, but he was no longer skinny. Soft fat lay beneath his skin. He was tanned. He and Joyce had spent time on Nantucket last summer. I thought David seemed even more aggressive, or defensive.

Mr. Framely had hardly spread his napkin before he expressed pleasure in Coolidge's nomination. "He'll win hands down against that fellow Davis and that blow-hard William Jennings Bryan." I threw Newly a cautionary look and he winked back at me. He knew better than to talk politics at Mama's table.

Papa asked David if he had read Kopen's work *The Climates of Primeval Geologic Periods*. David's color deepened as he admitted he did not know the book. Papa subsided. "I see," he said gloomily.

Newly and Mr. Framely started talking about Notre Dame and Knute Rockne. Mrs. Framely asked Mama if the "beautiful tablecloth" had been in her family and Mama said yes, it was her mother's, bought in Florence.

Above the mantle Mad Anthony's coat seemed wonderfully blue; the long draperies, so shabby in the daytime, now swept elegantly upward. I thought how strange we all were, no relationships existing between couples, except ourselves and the Framelys. Joyce sat with her large lids lowered. There was Mama, silvery in her dress and with a coy air. She kept asking David what he'd done in Rome, as though knowing nothing about his trip. Mrs. Framely smiled nervously. Mr. Framely was not his usual positive self, his black eyes darted about and he asked me what kind of heat we had in the house, as though desperate for a subject. Papa had lapsed into an unhappy silence, eating almost nothing.

It was not until the door had closed on Robert that Mama made her announcement, leaning toward David and smiling roguishly.

"You're to have the Lowndes Silver, David. Papa and I have decided. You and Joyce." A quick smile toward Joyce, who looked stonily back.

David dropped his eyes as though shocked. Then swiftly, "This is most generous of you Mama. And you, Papa." He smiled uneasily, his expression watchful.

I could not look at Newly. He would not understand how such a handsome present was given in this fashion, particularly to one child and not the other. He still had moments of forgetting I was no relation.

"It would come to you eventually, David," Papa said, touching the ends of his moustache rather grandly. "We thought you'd like to use it now."

"Thank you very much," Joyce said. Her face showed nothing. The flaccid cheeks, the coiled hair.... Her bosom rose and fell visibly while her large pale eyes stayed steadily on Mama.

The gift was stupendous and a great sacrifice. Mama used the silver service every day for tea. She polished it with her own hands. What had made them decide on such a present? They were not accustomed to generous gestures. Had they hoped to force David's attention, be admitted? Then they had not reckoned with Joyce.

"I don't think we should accept," David said, having recovered something of his debonaire manner. "Of course Joyce and I very much appreciate your generosity."

In an instant Mama looked ready to weep. "Oh, David—you *have* to accept!" She was like a child, wheedling. She must often have experienced disappointment with him, for she so quickly fell into this infantile, despairing role.

David regarded her. Was he calculating that to refuse meant unnecessary cruelty? Why should he want the silver? But then how much did I know about David? Maybe he had got greedy. Joyce never served tea. Would the silver sit on the sideboard? Suddenly David smiled, the old, warm, merry look on his face. He rose to his feet, went over and kissed Mama's cheek. "Thank you very much," he said. Then moved to Papa, shook his hand. "Thank you very much, sir." Papa smiled, patted him awkwardly on the arm.

I did not give a hoot for the Lowndes Silver, nor had I the faintest right to it. But why was the gift paraded in front of me? I imagined even David felt uncomfortable for he shot me a look that I thought was rueful. I could see Newly's face set iron hard. He clattered down his spoon as though he would not eat another bite. I tried to smile over at him but he only stuck his lower lip out.

Joyce said rather coolly, "I wonder why you have decided on such a handsome gift now, Mrs. Severn."

"So you can have the pleasure of using it, Joyce."

"It's a large responsibility," Mrs. Framely said unhappily.

"Better look after the insurance." Mr. Framely gestured with his cigar in David's direction.

"I always enjoyed the silver," Mama said, quite imperturbably. "And you will, too, Joyce. I'll tell you about the polishing."

Joyce looked put out, and Mama smirked, then rose. The meal was over. As we filed through the door, Newly grabbed my arm and pulled me back into the dining room. "What a nerve!" he said.

"David's their grandson, why not?"

"But to do it in front of you, Eva!"

I reached up and kissed his cheek. "Don't fuss, Newly, I don't mind. I minded at first, but now I don't care."

"You're so big-hearted!" He looked ready to cry.

"I'm just used to Mama and Papa."

He took my arm and we walked out of the room.

In the parlor Joyce was talking to David. They might have been alone. "I went to New York today," she said. As I came in she looked up. "This will interest you, Eva. Ross and Exeter want me to expand Lady Hatton. They're definitely interested and are offering me a contract."

"Fine," David said. Was that all? His face showed nothing. Surely he must know how much this meant to Joyce.

"That's wonderful, Joyce," I said.

"Good girl, Joyce!" Mr. Framely clapped his stubby hands.

"It means more work for you, Eva." Joyce looked coolly at me. "Are you willing?"

"Yes, I am," I said, and meant it. For I knew that if Ross and Exeter were enthusiastic anything could happen. And even though I had not been successful with my own writing I had what Joyce called "literary taste," which she needed.

"Writing is a nice hobby for you, Joyce," Mama said, her glance frosty. She did not like the limelight shifted from her gift.

Joyce looked back with her bold stare. "I'm going to make a career out of writing, Mrs. Severn."

Mama lowered her eyes. "I never thought of my poetry as a career. It was something I loved doing." Readings in the barn with Mr. Jaffrey at the piano. Surely Joyce remembered. "A career," Mama said, moving carefully around the words, "rather depends upon your husband, doesn't it?"

"Oh, no," Joyce said, keeping her eyes on Mama. "We don't intend having children."

A slow red slid across Mama's face. Never in her life had anyone spoken more immodestly. And the news itself was shocking. As though taking leave of everything she counted on, Mama cried, "But the silver? Where will it go?"

Joyce gave back the words: "The silver will go to a museum, where it belongs. It's far too valuable to be lying about."

In Mama's house the Lowndes Silver was put into its special case every night.

Evidently enjoying herself, Joyce said: "The Philadelphia Museum has a nice collection of silver. I understand George Horace Lorimer has given some valuable pieces."

I avoided looking at David. He sat on the sofa with his legs crossed, but I could tell from the way he gulped his coffee that he was furiously angry. He would not forgive Joyce for speaking so openly and so cruelly to his grandmother.

Mama looked ready to cry. Papa's face was still.

"That is hardly a proper announcement, Joyce. I think you owe an apology to Mrs. Severn." Mrs. Framely sat stiffly in her chair, a spot of color in each cheek.

"Well, it's the truth." Under her mother's correction Joyce's bravado faded.

"I think we must go home." Mr. Framely was on his feet, shaking Mama's hand. He had dignity, and Joyce evidently offended him.

David walked over to the coffee table, put down his cup. "Thank you again, Mama." He clipped off the words. Mama smiled down at her hands, evidently unable to answer. A little, shriveled woman in a too-young pink dress, all sparkle gone.

I kissed Papa's cheek and thanked him. Newly shook his hand. With a flutter of silk Joyce made for the door. Her color had not changed except briefly at her mother's rebuke. Now she sailed out the door.

In the hall I let the others go first. I waited for David. I could not remember the last time I had spoken in private to him. But as soon as he appeared I said, "What's all this about, David?"

"Just what you heard."

"But you like children!"

"Not particularly."

He shocked me. He had gone from anger to defiance. He might object to Joyce's speaking out in front of Mama but Joyce had spoken for him, too. Now he was pretending not to care, amenable, tied round with gifts until he didn't know his own mind. In my whole life I had never felt sorry for David before. Now I reached out and touched his arm. Instantly I knew him, the curved waist, the long thighs, the pale skin.

He did not speak. We stood for a moment.

"David!" Joyce called.

David moved forward, held the door, and we passed through.

16     Newly and I never mentioned Joyce's announcement. Perhaps because I did not become pregnant. Every night when we slept together I told myself *"This time..."* I went to a gynecologist who told me there was no reason I could not have any number of children. Finally Newly was examined. ("I won't go through *that* again," he said.) The report came back that Newly had a low sperm count and that his ability to have a child was improbable. However, the doctor said, extraordinary things do happen and that if we tried a regime of waiting for my ovulation, fourteen days after I started menstruating, and did not have sex for a week before this, we might have a child. In other words Newly must try and build up sperm. Newly was devastated. Did I want to divorce him? Surely I had the right to have children. He used the word eunuch, and deeply shocked me. Evidently Newly felt his manhood challenged, and one night after we'd had sex he wept. It was terrible to feel his big body trembling and hear his sobs. I could not seem to give him any comfort. At the time I did not realize that one reason for his despair was a subconscious link to his belief that his power to warm held the possibility of other vaster powers. But if he could not rule his own body then what good was warming a

blond-haired girl at the movies? It was a strange linkage, but I'm sure Newly made it.

The night Newly cried, the solution came to me. I see no reason to keep what happened a secret. I carried out the solution and freely admit it. Nor am I excusing myself. Nor did I ever feel any guilt, except rarely. I would do it all over again—perhaps not in the same fashion—but hoping for the same result. Newly and I had been married for over a year. Now we had this report. Everything pointed toward Newly's not being able to have a child and toward the equal probability that David could. It was when I acknowledged this to myself that a plan formed.

There are people to whom the solution will seem very wrong, a sin, utterly incomprehensible, wicked, a crime against my husband. And what about Joyce? Toward Joyce I felt no responsibility whatever. Toward Newly—I hoped to do what I could for both of us. As for fearing God would punish me, that fear does not fit my character. And as I said, in some strange fated way, the plan seemed right.

At first, my plan turned out to be almost impossibly difficult because I could not reach David. He went "up-country" every week, not returning until Thursday. Every Friday he was in Framely & Brick's office. From his secretary I discovered that David ate baked beans at Horn and Hardart's on Fridays. The secretary confided this with a giggle. So in the basement of Horn and Hardart, among the thick, white china, the bang of trays being loaded, the clap of the little glass doors shutting, I found David. He was seated at a table with a fat, white-faced, jowly man and a small, thin woman in a bright pink straw hat. There was also a fat child holding a large naked Kewpie doll and spooning up vanilla ice cream.

I began a guarded conversation, whispering.

David paid no attention, kept on throwing beans into his mouth. I had surprised him in this place. He refused to understand what I was trying to tell him. It was not easy to tell. How could I begin with Newly? So I said, whispering, that Newly was going to New York. David threw another forkful of beans into his mouth.

The putty-faced child stared. David looked white and tense. No more handsome air. Usually pulled together, now he seemed rumpled. He had loosened his tie. Unthinkable. Even more astonishing was the derby hat which he wore and made no effort to remove. I had thought—although I did not know why—that he would grasp what I said right off, because the plan was so shockingly plain. But he didn't. He apparently either refused to listen or did not comprehend. I finally followed him out of the restaurant, and it was on the stairs, against the white tile, that I blurted out my plan. David leaned against the rail. David's glance did not know me. I felt the same way—now my purpose was out. A crazy, mad idea. Faced with David's all-seeing and not-seeing look I realized the impossibility of it and I wondered if my suggestion was not a provocative insult. And then from David's lips issued one word: "Where?"

In the back of David's maroon-colored Marmon, parked at the edge of a quarry not far from his house, I conceived. The moment that perhaps all my life I had waited for was painful and difficult and totally without affection. A clinical act. He took me, not caring, I suppose, if I was ready to be taken—which I wasn't—but forcing his way into me until I gradually lubricated. His orgasm came quickly and with a cry, rung out of him and ringing in the old quarry. At this, I held his head tightly in my arms to stifle the sound.

As I said, I was positive I would conceive by David, and so it turned out. That month I did not menstruate—and kept it from Newly, then told him the following month. Newly was enraptured, restored entirely. In fact when I told him (which was in bed) he leaped onto the floor and started jumping around the room crowing like a rooster. How much better this solution than adopting a child, which we considered. Now we knew precisely what we were getting and I would have the experience of pregnancy. I also felt that Newly shared in this, for although the actual performance might not have been possible for him, the result would be wholly to his liking.

It is also true, although I did not think about it at the time, that I was no stranger to labyrinthine ways, a gloss easily formed over my conscience. I did not *want* to deceive Newly, but was it not for his own good? And he would never know, of that I could be sure. The only person I felt quite desperately uncomfortable with was Mrs. Framely. I knew to my soul that she would regard my act as the basest deceit. Her uncomplicated honesty would believe I had taken advantage of Newly, to say nothing of her own daughter. I must put her out of mind, and I did. But she kept me close to hers, making a beautiful bassinet with a ruffle of dotted swiss. Blue, she said, although partial to girls. She and Newly shared in the preparations. Newly was completely awed at the tiny shirts, the flannel petticoat with Fanny's row of featherstitching around the bottom. Newly constantly bumped the bassinet down the stairs to show everyone, even the mailman.

There was the unforgettable night when we went to Joyce's for dinner. Entering that all-white house was like walking into an egg. Nervous, because I had not seen David, or Joyce either, in four months and was now "showing." I had one dress of blue cloth with lacings at the side that could be let out. Pregnancy did not become me. I looked all nose and was a bad color, but carefully not marcelled. I was so self-conscious that I missed the two steps into the living room and sprawled, belly down, on the white rug. Newly rushed forward, he and Joyce dragged me onto the sofa. My nerves that had stood by me, suddenly broke, and I started bawling in a dreadful way. If I had lost the child...

"For God's sake, David, don't just stand there," Joyce yelled, "Get her a drink!"

David had indeed just stood there, not touching me. Not helping drag me onto the sofa, but staying off. Even later, after we had called Dr. Brazzaro, who told me to go home and to bed, David was unable to lend a hand or help me to the car. Joyce must have noticed, for she told him for God's sake to hold open the front door. Newly said he guessed it just showed how badly David felt about not having children.

According to Mrs. Slatter, the child being born on the third of July, 1925, a month before expected, was due to the fall. Although Dr. Brazzaro assured her Ken was a nine-months-old baby, she could never be convinced. Ken weighed nine and a half pounds at birth, for I ate like a plowhand during pregnancy and Fanny sent out chocolate cake and doughnuts by Robert. "To keep your strength up," she said. My delivery was long and hard and best forgotten.

Fanny came home with me and the baby—a special dispensation from Mama. We named the boy Kenneth after a cousin of Newly's, recently dead. Fanny and I had the happiest days in the little house which just held us all. From the beginning Newly had great influence on the child. Ken was a fretful baby, but Newly could stop his crying. As the cries ceased Newly would smile at me over the baby's dark head.

17    *The Lady of Bleeding House Yard*, Joyce's fictionalized biography, came out in 1930 and was an instant success. There were six printings the first month and a total of 200,000 copies sold. The willful, half-mad Lady Hatton appealed to people; they even liked her irascible husband, Sir Edward Coke. The Depression seemed to have little effect on sales. Joyce told me her agent and Cecil B. DeMille's office were starting negotiations.

Joyce found writing the book harder work than she had imagined. Her tenacity and stubbornness, plus the ever-present desire to have her own way, made her a remarkably determined writer. What she lacked in style she made up for in narrative drive. She was quite conscienceless and would have made up any number of characters if I hadn't challenged her. Such practice is not unethical but can lead to difficulty when a writer is queried in public. Joyce had a real flair for sixteenth-century parlance and was an adept researcher, spotting not only needed facts but the lively story that brightens the page. Working with Joyce was a change in role. She had always seemed so much older and more experienced, I often feared her subtlety. But now I was the one to point out her weaknesses and to call for more and better performance. The recent reading I had done (and even my own unsuccessful writing) had given me respect and recognition of style and a positive hatred of the mawkish sentimentality into which Joyce occasionally fell.

I did not find her easy to work with. I may not have handled her skillfully, being new at editing. When I praised her she did not believe me, and when I criticized her she argued. At one point I resigned. The next day Joyce appeared on my porch. She spoke agitatedly through the screen, her little mouth twisted and her big eyes squinting as though in pain. She looked almost ugly.

"I can't do the book without you, Eva." It was an extraordinary admission.

"Of course you can." What did I know about the sixteenth century?

"I give you a hard time. I know that." She lowered her voice.

"Yes," I said, still speaking through the screen, not asking her in. "You take criticism personally, whereas I'm criticizing the work. You think it's a personal challenge. You argue. It's exhausting." Surely she knew David stood between us, a constant presence, there to cause friction and worse. I had taken on Joyce's book realizing this, but wanting the experience. I was tired of rejection slips for my own work. Joyce had a contract, which meant that whatever I did would receive recognition with the possibility of professional status. But unless the work lifted us above the existing situation, we were done for. When Joyce became defensive she became personal, and we fell into a dangerous area which was intolerable. Joyce might not be perceptive enough to put all this into words, but she sensed danger and realized she had jeopardized her book and our tenuous relationship.

"All right," I said through the screen. "We'll try again."

Having gone this far, I hated to give up. I found, to my surprise, that editing came naturally to me. The desire-to-please, which permeated so much of my life, made me know intuitively what the reader wanted and how much the reader would take. Working with Joyce, I did no rewriting, but rearranged sequences, made drastic cuts, called for new material, badgered Joyce to strengthen her sentences. The pages we worked on were black with marks. Joyce would sometimes write a chapter five times, but once she became convinced a chapter sagged, she tore into it again. I admired her stubbornness. I could feel the book growing as we struggled over the pages, working at my round dining room table in the mornings when Kenny was at school. At the end of nearly two years, Joyce handed me a check for one thousand dollars. I considered the sum munificent. I would have done the work for nothing.

Dan Ruber had become a fixture in our lives. He and Newly were rebuilding their model offices, working in the cellar. Although the Guaranty had turned the offices down, a bank in Seattle was interested.

Dan had not changed in the years we knew him. Tall, bony, with the same thin orange-colored hair, he had a smile that showed every tooth. A clown, folding effortlessly into a chair, but watchful, and in his way ambitious. Dan believed in chance, luck, a "break." Newly's seriousness amused him. "Old Newly with his nose to the grindstone." Cliches rattled out of Dan like pebbles.

> "Life is just a bowl of cherries.
> Don't make it serious.
> Life's too mysterious..."

Dan sang it every day. He knew a "safe" bootlegger and which night a shipment of liquor had been landed on the New Jersey shore. Some years earlier he had tried to persuade Newly to buy a lot in

Coral Gables. The first stock market crash wiped out whatever money Dan and Cora had, but although Radio Common had gone from 101 to 2½, now, in 1930, Dan still thought it was a great buy. Dan believed in "the country." The "plain, ordinary people" and good old Hoover would bring the Depression to a halt. I have since wondered if Dan did not have a long range plan for all of us because when the moment arrived, he moved in fast.

Dan told me in absolute seriousness that he looked forward to seeing Mama again because he was sure she must know his connection with Lloyd Paget. "That snob," Mrs. Slatter said, "who lives in the big, stone house and sleeps with the chambermaid."

Cora, Dan's wife, had the same orange-colored hair, only short and frizzy. Her self-regard was impenetrable; she never owned up to a mistake. She had a passion for artificial flowers, sprays of violently colored gladioli spouted from vases no matter what the season. Her former work in the bookkeeping department of J.E. Caldwell, the jewelers, and her memory of credit ratings, made her formidable. Newly set store in what he called her "common sense." Even Mrs. Slatter thought Dan a "card," urging him to tell stories about his war days in the Coast Guard. Dan was still "located" in the same posh haberdashery on Sedgwick Avenue.

When our son Kenny tied up the cat and it nearly strangled, it was Dan who talked to him. "The kid only wanted to keep the cat from crossing the street and maybe getting run over." Dan always had a new riddle for Kenny, who was almost seven, and somewhat small for his age.

He was an unusual little boy, not affectionate, but very spunky. He looked like me with dark hair and a pursey mouth, small eyes. On a boy his features did not seem so asymmetrical. I must admit we brought Kenny up permissively, a method recently introduced. Having had such a strict childhood, I could not bear to discipline Kenny. We never told him he must obey, he was cajoled. "Don't you want to see the lovely toy elephant up in your room, Kenny?" He would hide under the dining room table eyes glinting bright as a fox's. Newly idolized the child, and when Kenny sassed us back, grinning "fresh as paint," according to Cora Ruber, Newly and I would both laugh and often end by hugging him. Although Kenny was spoiled, I nevertheless tried to break him of the game he played. "Hiding," he called it. I found the game most distressing. I would miss Kenny and then sometimes hunt for half an hour before finding him in the bathroom closet, or behind the refrigerator, or next door in Dr. Tilley's catalpa tree. I could not persuade him to stop this game, which always petrified me, as I feared he might have wandered off, or been kidnapped, the latest scare.

Kenny did not understand when older boys picked on him at school and although he was not demonstrative, he would come home, his face all smeared with dirt and tears, butt his head into my side and let me put my arms around him. I admired his independence, I told myself. I had been a fighter, taught by David. Newly took Kenny for hikes in Cherokee Woods, and bought a Sears Roebuck tent (exactly like the one David had years ago in the Adirondacks), which they erected in the backyard. Newly was always patient with Kenny's scrapes. "He's only a little fellow," he'd say. "He doesn't mean any harm."

Kenny did not often bring friends home. Newly thought this strange. "Gee, at his age I had the house packed." Mrs. Slatter did her best to be a good grandmother, but it was plain she and Kenny did not hit it off, although Kenny liked her to read to him. He was a people-watcher and spent a large portion of his time either sitting on our porch steps or on the curb. Mrs. Paget complained he sneaked around her house and she caught him pulling the heads off her roses, a charge Kenny fiercely denied.

"She's a meany, Mom."

"Then stay away from her."

We were at breakfast with Newly about to leave for the train.

"Can I walk to the corner with you, Pop?"

"Sure." Newly grabbed his briefcase, kissed me. "And let Mrs. Paget's roses alone!"

"Lloydie, Lloydie." As they banged out the door Kenny mimicked Mrs. Paget calling her son, a grown man.

My great friend during the early years of my marriage was Flora Cruickshank, who lived four doors down on India Street. Flora was in her middle fifties, a strong spare woman with gray hair and a most aristocratic nose set between chippy blue eyes. Flora was the first literary person I had ever known. The simplicity and accuracy of her speech changed my Philadelphia drawl. I wanted to talk the way Flora talked. She played the cello and occasionally invited me to play second violin with her quartet. Flora had been married to an alcoholic whom she supported until he died, "mercifully," she said. She worked as an editor on *The Atlantic* and for Atlantic, Little Brown, the publishing house. She now taught a course in eighteenth-century literature at Bryn Mawr. Right at the start of our friendship she took my education and my reading in hand, talking to me about Veblen, who excited me, or William James. Flora would tell me I must read *The Meaning of Meanings* or *The Golden Bough*. Besides literature she discussed the Scopes trial. Flora was infuriated by the acquittal of Doheny in the Tea Pot Dome scandal. She talked excitedly about Ramsay MacDonald and the Labour Government, said Hoover was a jackass. She was a Socialist and had been a suffragette for years, now an ardent feminist. She didn't give a hoot for a federal deficit and said the government ought to be making a nationwide plan for the men out of work. "Under Republicans this Depression is going to last and get worse."

When I brought some of these ideas home to Newly he said although he admired Flora, and knew she was my friend, he could not go all the way with her beliefs. Dan Ruber dubbed her a Communist. "Without doubt," he said. All I knew was that in her house ideas seemed to spark. Flora was always excited over something. If it was not the farmers or the Dust Bowl, it was the unions. And then in between these frenzied periods she would lie back in her chair and listen to me read her *Persuasion*, or *Mansfield Park*, or one of my story ideas. She liked Newly and he liked her. They argued good-humoredly. I never dared introduce her to the Framelys. Mr. Framely would have wanted her jailed.

Flora, imitating G. B. Stern, loved to examine Jane Austen. "How long do you think Mr. Knightley had his eye on Emma?" she asked.

"Not from the beginning," I said. We were in Flora's sitting room with Flora lying back in a Victorian chair, a gardening glove dangled from her hand, her eyes were closed, a blissful smile lighted her handsome face. She adored *Emma*, and read it every year.

"Eva," she said, opening her eyes, "you are cultivating your taste and will soon be a literary snob. This is excellent. I wish you'd be more yourself in the stories you write. They don't *sound* like you. Beautiful ladies moving woodenly around uttering polite phrases. It's not real. It's a fantasy world. Why don't you write about being an orphan?"

"Or about a girl with my face?" It came out before I knew what I said.

Flora's eyes stayed steadily on me. "Well, all right. You're rather super-conscious of your looks, aren't you?"

No one ever talked to me like this. I shrugged. "Maybe."

Flora said matter-of-factly, as though hustling the situation together, "Write whatever you want, only make it something you *know*."

"Naturally I'm conscious of the way I look," I said rather sullenly.

"Eva!" she sat up agitatedly. "I'm not criticizing. You've got very smart-looking."

I found this gratifying. For I spent hours selecting a dress. Newly's salary (he was now in the Trust Department) of one hundred and fifty dollars a month, which was considered ample, left little money for clothes. I would far rather talk to Flora about what I wore than about my looks.

Flora sat back. "I've noticed," she said, "that people have to grow into their faces. It's a kind of self-acceptance. My family used to call me "Nosey," and told me my upper lip was so long it almost deformed my face. They feared I would be vain. It wasn't until I became eighteen that I realized I was quite handsome."

I laughed. Flora would be handsome in her eighties. She showed little curiosity about my childhood and no sympathy. She had never met Papa nor Mama. She thought David too good-looking. She did not like handsome men. Joyce she disliked. She considered the check for a thousand dollars measly. "I don't approve of fictionalized biography," she said, speaking of Joyce's book, "but this is a first-rate job. I can feel your hand in it. You ought to go see *Harper's*. They're always looking for rewriters."

"I don't want to rewrite."

"There's nothing to it."

I left shortly after this. I could feel Flora's disapproval; she wanted me to expand in some way. I meant to get ahead by my writing. I liked my life as it was. I had status, a married woman with a husband and child, a house. I relished my marriage and I never tired of the routine. For the first time in my life I did not have to fear what I thought of as the fall-of-an-axe. Released from the tight bind of Mama's requirement—how could I tire of my new life? I now wore my hair cut short again with small bangs hanging over my forehead. I no longer had to pretend to be someone I was not. And although I knew a sense of confusion over who and what I was, I believed in time I would find out. Right now I could feel myself changing. First my voice and speech. Reading and Flora had shown me a different world. I noticed the difference in the women who played in Flora's quartet. They were serious, witty, wasted no words, were critical. They expected the best from me and sensed my weaknesses.

"She's had no real training," Flora said, "but she's naturally musical. You can tell that by her phrasing."

The two women (one played viola, the other violin) looked at me. I remember thinking, *if I had only gone to college*. Even though I loved being married, yet there was this other life that I might never achieve. It seemed to me these women lived in rarified air with a different set of customs.

During this period, which went on from the time Kenny was about two until he was seven, I told Newly almost nothing of my aspiration. He knew I was still trying to write, and of course he knew I worked with Joyce. Occasionally he would look at the books lying about, but generally his interests lay elsewhere, in sports, investments, the new fellow who had just moved in at the top of the street, or Dr. Tilley, next door—"a prince," Newly called him. Small and fat with thick eyebrows and a waxed moustache, Dr. Tilley had a concentrated, positive manner. Mrs. Tilley worked in a dress shop on the Avenue. She was very tall and thin and had buck teeth and dull black hair. Mrs. Tilley struck the tone of our relationship the first week we were in our house. A perfect neighbor, she said, was never a borrower. "You know what I mean, Mrs. Slatter. Coming in for a quarter of butter or a lemon, that type." And she drew her thick lips back over her big teeth.

Newly preferred Dan and Cora Ruber to anyone else and would have happily asked them every night for dinner. I found evenings with the Rubers long, but then I discovered that no one thought me rude if I went up to bed. Although this was a relief, I did not realize that without me a peculiar intimacy was forming. I still regarded Dan as a clownish kind of man, innocuous, and not to be taken seriously.

In the winter Newly and I took walks, bringing Kenny with us. When he was little Newly would put him inside his coat; when he became older and complained of cold Newly would hold his hands and tell him he was getting warmer, reminding me of that afternoon by the Schuylkill River and later with the girl at the movies. Kenny was not a laughing child, but one of the times he giggled was when Newly made him warm. Newly claimed Kenny was quite a jolly little fellow. "Like me," Newly said, batting his eyes with pleasure.

Only when Newly drew parallels with himself did I feel a twinge of guilt, which could be quite sharp. I was relieved we saw so little of David. He still traveled every week and on weekends, I gathered from Joyce, they were socially "busy."

Kenny liked Flora to come along on our winter walks. We made a yearly pilgrimage to see a particular tulip poplar, scarred by fire. Flora told Kenny about Thoreau visiting certain trees every year. "We're going to see our tree just like Mister Toro," Kenny would tell her, holding her hand firmly. Flora taught us to look at the sprouting skunk cabbages, watching where the purple curl broke through the ice and snow, noting the sudden green of a new spike.

I remember once asking Flora if I could be a "twice-born," as William James said. "I would like to think so," I said. Her flinty eyes regarded me without sentiment. "Perhaps," she said. "You are waking, that's surely so." She patted my hand.

I set about acquiring a "library." Newly built shelves by the fireplace. At Leary's Book Store I bought an incomplete set of Thackeray, Dickens, Jane Austen in one volume, and Lamb's letters. I was also able to buy an edition of Henry James' letters, using small sums from our "nest egg." Flora told me to read Thoreau's diaries at night before going to sleep. "It will help your writing style," she said. Newly paid little attention to my acquisitions. *Beau Geste* was a better "read."

Newly talked more and more about The Mind, as he called it. Dan Ruber listened mesmerized. Newly knew stories of people who were able to communicate without speaking. Groups of people influencing other groups. I did not listen very carefully and am not sure if Newly used words like extrasensory perception or not.

Occasionally I would copy something from Thoreau's diary and take it in town to Papa as a little gift, just to see him smile. He so seldom smiled any more. Both he and Mama had aged since David's marriage. (I didn't count my departure because I knew they were relieved.) Mama still complained about Joyce. Robert had driven her and Papa out to Villa Nova one Sunday. Of course, Mama had phoned beforehand. Nothing, she said, was ruder than this new habit of "dropping in." Joyce had greeted them. David was out. No explanation, no excuse. Simply not there. They had been offered nothing to eat, although it was tea time. Finally after about twenty minutes they left.

Joyce was playing a mean game, I thought, and David was abetting her. When I tackled her, she just pooh-poohed what had happened. "I've really had enough of Mama, as you and David call her. She never comes into the house that she doesn't criticize. Once during tea, she reached over and straightened my cup. Imagine! Or she will refuse the cake and tell me where to get scones. She drew my attention to a run in the maid's stocking. She notices the ivy has started to die on one side of the house."

"I think she's lonely."

"Of course she's lonely! She's alienated everyone in Philadelphia. I'm sure you don't bring Kenny in very often to see her."

Bringing Kenny in was impossible with all the knickknacks in the parlor. Mama, I told myself, was not fond of children.

"I don't think Papa's happy," I said.

"Oh, Eva—he doesn't give a damn! He'll start writing another one of those unreadable books. He's hardly civil to David."

As time went on I had to admit that Kenny was not proving more amenable or easier to handle. There was no persuading him against his will or getting him to bed easily. Then one night he sneaked out of the house. The first we knew he had gone was when Mrs. Paget phoned. She had caught Kenny in their front hall looking through the portieres. "You better come get him," she said frigidly. She was a horrid woman with prominent, light brown eyes; large combs held up oily hair.

When I came into the house, looking for Kenny, the two Paget daughters stood in one corner of the living room, faces stiff with disapproval. To my horror Mrs. Paget walked down the hall to a closet door, turned the key. Kenny burst out. He ran screaming to me. I threw my arms around him, turned furiously on the woman. "How *could* you lock a little boy in a closet!" I shouted at her. Without another word I lifted Kenny in my arms, big as he was, and rushed out of the house.

Now we faced a dilemma. Flora, Newly, and I discussed it, sitting in Flora's parlor. This latest episode did not come under the heading of boyish prank. Kenny was a "people-watcher." He must not become a "Peeping Tom." Mrs. Tilley complained he peeked in her windows. What about psychiatry? Flora asked. In the 30s this was a serious move, particularly for a child. Newly was against it. He wanted to talk to the boy himself. If in two weeks Kenny showed no improvement, then we must consider a psychiatrist. Flora was silent, but I agreed, knowing Newly's closeness to the boy. Now that we realized the problem, surely we could help Kenny. Soon after this we left Flora's. We walked silently along India Street. A hot July day, the leaves on the catalpa hung motionless. Then Newly said, with no emphasis: "I really believe I can change Kenny."

Something in his tone made me suspicious. Surely we were not going to talk about Newly's "powers" again.

"I know how you feel, Newly. But we've gone way beyond that."

"No we haven't. I'm just beginning."

I remember feeling the sun strike my head. I had the oddest sensation of not being able to locate our house. I heard myself say I wanted something cool to drink. We turned in our path, mounted the porch steps. Once inside, Newly went to get some ginger ale. He reappeared with two tall glasses and we sat down at our round table. I did not want to think about what Newly had just said. I wanted to think why I was not able to manage my own child. Of course, I had been permissive. But surely without barriers a child could dance about, be free. Then I wondered, thinking solely of Kenny, maybe love is not allowed. By that I meant one is not allowed to love enough. I hungered for love from Kenny, for my love to be returned. But I had not been allowed to love David. Now I may not be allowed to love this child.... How do I love Newly?

These speculations were so awful I did not even realize Newly was talking and suddenly heard him say, "So Dan and I have built this kind of big chair on a platform in the cellar..."

The chair, it seemed, was for Newly.

"For you? Why?"

Newly spun the ice in his glass. He took a sip, put the glass down. Then he wiped his mouth, plainly upset. He looked right at me, almost malevolently. "You remember the power I have?"

I nodded. I dreaded what was coming.

"Well, I've been exercising this power in other ways, not just warming."

"Oh?"

He looked away and said in a rather far-off voice, "This power is pretty extensive. For instance, it stretches to Curly Matlack, who lives two houses down. You remember he had those awful warts?"

"Of course."

"I cured them."

"You cured them?"

"Yes. They're all gone."

I could only stare at him—in profile—for he kept looking toward the street.

Then Newly said: "The Kubie boy in the wheelchair, you know?"

I kept my eyes on his face.

"He's coming over tomorrow night."

I could not take in what he said. "But all this is in the *cellar?*" As I spoke I was suddenly overcome with a most awful weight, so heavy I thought my head would sink. I held my head with one hand. What was happening to us? We should be talking about Kenny.

"The cellar was Dan's idea. Get the whole—uh—process out of the way. We have that old buffalo robe your grandmother gave me draped over the back—"

"The back of what?"

"It's kind of like a—well—like a throne." He did not look at me but kept tinkling the ice in his glass.

I could not believe him. Was he saying that he and Dan were trying to perform some kind of ... miracle—*in our cellar? What had happened to Newly?* I had not watched, not seen. Newly had slipped—fallen—away from me. What was this thing he was engaged in? *Craziness?*

"I don't know how it will work on Cyd Kubie," Newly said, perfectly naturally. "I certainly want to see what I can do with Kenny."

I told myself I must be careful, very careful. I started again. "You now feel it's religious, this ... power?"

"No, I don't," Newly said, quite matter-of-factly. "It's just a kind of feeling I have. Not for everyone. And that's what I'm afraid of—that I won't have it for Kenny. But I feel the blood rush through my veins. At least that's what it seems like. And then I have this enormous sense of power, a kind of surging. I am flooded with it. I put my hands on people. The warts were all gone in the morning." And looking sidewise at me: "I think the Kubie boy will walk."

I said steadily, "I don't think you ought to try anything with Kenny." I managed to sound quite normal.

"No?"

"No. You'd frighten him."

"You think so?" He seemed perfectly unconscious of the effect all this was having on me. Cyd Kubie had been in a wheelchair for years. He must be eighteen by now. No one knew what was wrong with him. One day he just couldn't walk. He'd even been to the Mayo Clinic.

What in God's name was Newly doing? He must believe all sorts of strange things about himself. Or perhaps *feel* odd sensations. Why hadn't he told me?

"You never said anything."

"No. I didn't know how you'd take it."

"But surely this—this affects me, too."

"Yes, I guess it does." He appeared perfectly natural. He looked the same. The pallor had gone from his face. "I was going to tell you if I got Cyd Kubie up."

It was like some ghastly—well—game, mockery. Only real to my husband.

"Oh, Newly..." I pressed both my hands on his.

"Yes," he said perfectly calmly, "it *is* strange."

18    Although I heard what Newly said, I did not fully take it in. How could I? Suddenly to have one's husband say he had come upon supernatural powers was upsetting enough, but then to learn that he had plans, fomented in secret, with a throne and buffalo robe thrown in, and would attempt to make a crippled boy walk, was petrifying. I not only feared for Newly, but I had no understanding of him. I did not know him. Years ago we had had our discussion about his "powers," when he felt most concerned and was even frightened, wondering if such a thing as having an extra sense, or power, might not, if it worked for good, also work for evil, and therefore was to be shunned, forgotten. Certainly not experimented with. And I could remember Newly standing in the backyard with his hands pressed against his face, so troubled. He had deliberately put his "power" away, except very occasionally during one of our winter walks when he warmed Kenny. What had brought it out again? How could he and Dan have all these plans and Newly never mention them? He had seemed so assured when he announced that he was going to try and make Cyd Kubie walk.

*Ugly Girl*

I know there are people to whom my self-concern must seem unpardonably selfish, in view of "Healing Grace" and all the rest of it. But to be married to a man, and have that man take on a whole new life which cannot include you destroys the structure of your marriage. And I cared far more for my marriage than I did about Cyd Kubie—or warts, for that matter. There was also Newly's announcement that he meant to try some of his powers on Kenny. It was one thing to cure Curly Matlack of warts, or even attempt something with Cyd Kubie, but when it came to my child, then everything stopped.

In spite of my resentment (imagine a "throne" in my own cellar!) and fury, I knew from the way he looked and peculiar way he said "It *is* strange," that I must not fly at him. To persuade Newly and make him see the irresponsibility of what he was contemplating, I must be calm and loving. At the moment I felt neither.

The next train of events, as the "Healing Grace" pamphlets put it, happened that same night. As we were going to bed and Newly reached up to turn off the light, the picture of Frank Prescott, Newly's boss at the Guaranty, fell off the wall, glass splintered all over the rug. Intact and staring at us was the nail that held the frame. Newly scrambled out of bed, started to pick up the pieces of glass. I went down the hall to the linen closet, grabbed a whisk, and we both swept the glass onto a newspaper. We had no sooner got rid of the glass and hung the picture back on the wall (the wire was also intact) when the phone rang. It was Marie Prescott. Frank had shot and killed himself ten minutes ago.

Through all the horror following Frank's death Newly kept blaming himself for not noticing Frank Prescott's depression, as though he could have done something about it.

Finally life returned to normal. I never went down to the cellar and I never asked Newly about any of "that," as I started calling it. I knew he had put off seeing Cyd Kubie and I thought again that Frank's sudden and awful death would make Newly forget the whole thing. I seem to have a weakness for believing fearsome events

( *190*

will disappear. Now I did nothing. I might so easily have talked to Newly, but I did not speak.

Although I tried to head her off, Mrs. Tilley insisted on telling me exactly what happened with Curly Matlack's warts. "You never saw such warts as on that poor boy's hands. Studded with them, nasty black things. He's a big boy for his age, about fourteen, I guess, and curly-headed, which he hates. 'As though kinky hair isn't bad enough, now I've got warts,' he said, speaking over the privet hedge to your husband, who was standing with Kenny beside him. I saw the whole thing from my porch," Mrs. Tilley said, pulling her lips back in what I took to be an understanding smile. "Well, your husband was calm as a cucumber, Mrs. Slatter. He just reached across the gate and took both of Curly's big hands in his. He held onto them by the tips of the fingers, shaking them up and down, telling Curly to relax, just let go. Then your husband stopped the shaking, held Curly's wrists for a few seconds and then released his hands. 'I think that's done it,' your husband said, just like fixing a spark plug. 'They'll go away now. About tomorrow maybe.' Then he just turned. He and Kenny went into the house."

I hoped that would be all, but Mrs. Tilley, leaning one hand on the black iron fence that separated our yards, made ready to tell the rest. "Next morning, being Saturday, Newly was home. I happened to be out on the porch." Mrs. Tilley adjusted one heavy coil of hair with an evident sense of the importance of her words. "Curly Matlack came through your gate, walked along your path, up the steps and across the porch. Newly opened the screen to him. Curly didn't say a word, just held out his hands. They were perfectly clean, not a wart on them, just scars here and there. Well, I waited to see what would happen. Your husband smiled and told Curly he was real glad. Poor Curly never was one to get words out easily. So he just mumbled something. But I stopped him before he got to the gate. 'Curly,' I said, looking him right in the eye, 'did you use potato skins?' 'No, Ma'am,' he said and his blue eyes looked back at me. 'I didn't use anything at all.' Then your Kenny, who'd been standing on the path said, 'My Pa made you well, didn't he, Curly?' 'I guess that's right, Kenny,' Curly said, and he went on out the gate."

Newly and I had not slept together for a week. This in itself was very unusual. There had been Curly's warts, and then the bad time with Frank Prescott. And then Newly had a dream about the ring. I know I have said that I never owned a ring until Newly's engagement diamond, but that's not entirely accurate. My mother's brother, Uncle Carter Bigelow, whom I had never seen, and who seldom paid me any heed, for no understandable reason sent me a gold ring with an opal in it. Uncle Carter evidently thought I was still in rompers because the ring was baby-size. Mama said she would not have it enlarged as the stone had no value. But I treasured the ring. I used to let Kenny play with it occasionally, and he seemed to understand and sympathize with my feelings and always knew we were doing something special when he was allowed the ring. Then one day it disappeared. I kept looking in the little blue plush box, but it was neither there nor any place in my bureau. I questioned Kenny carefully, not wanting to make the child feel guilty. He cried, one of the few times when he put his head in my lap. He had loved the ring. The loss seemed to depress us all. Then Newly dreamed the ring was in the bathroom wedged between the wainscotting and the toilet bowl. And there it was! Kenny shouted and stood right on his head for the first time. Newly hugged me and then rushed into the kitchen and made us all hot cakes for breakfast. Of course we were pleased, but I never thought about it in a significant way.

After Frank Prescott's death Newly started going to church. He had switched from Methodist to Episcopalian but did not want to discuss it. Newly also had private meetings with Dr. Plummer, the minister. We now said grace at every meal, which Kenny loved, occasionally saying a few words himself, and always clasping his hands devoutly. I fully appreciated Newly's need for the church and envied him his faith. I kept hoping we would not be separated over this, because I found Dr. Plummer boring and the service too full of forgiveness of sins to be tolerated. I told myself that maybe it was best Newly and Ken were in this together. I knew Newly was talking to the boy because occasionally Kenny would ask me if I knew God was always with us. Whatever influence religion had seemed beneficial; Kenny stayed near home, but he no longer sat on the porch steps watching people, and there were no more complaints from the neighbors, particularly the Pagets.

Of course Newly and I had had differences and fights in our married life, but now I not only felt cut off from Newly, but repelled. I asked myself again how any grown man, particularly one whom I knew so closely, could be building some kind of throne in our cellar and curing warts? What made him *do* it? It was madness! Where would it lead? He and Dan Ruber were again talking about getting Cyd Kubie to walk.

When I spoke to Flora about Newly, she drew away. It was odd, but she seemed at a distance. As though this manifestation by Newly made the difference between us all the more pronounced. She would not talk about it. I no longer read Jane Austen to her. She put me off. We'd have to start on someone new, she said. But we did not read any more. She said she imagined I was too busy to do much writing. . . . I didn't answer. I was not "busy," but disheartened. Ideas did not come. Was I not being separated from my husband? What would bring us together again? Failure? But what would that do to Newly?

And how about poor Cyd Kubie? Raising that boy's hopes was sinful! How could Newly be party to such cruelty? Newly was the kindest man in the world. He had mesmerized himself into this craziness. . . . When I thought of craziness, I paused. I had used the word before. Yes, and "madness." Was Newly having some kind of fit? Breakdown, it was called. But Dan believed in him. Even Mrs. Tilley appeared awed. When I spoke to Newly's mother she clapped her hands and cried, "Isn't he the real McCoy?" It all seemed a lark to her. Well, the warts *were* gone from Curly's hands. . . . Thousands flocked to hear Amy Semple McPherson....Newly had no other strange and unusual symptoms. He seemed more himself than ever. He did chores around the house much as usual. I could not honestly believe him mentally disturbed.

Newly's mental state did not concern me nearly as much as our apartness. And I do not mean just sex, which was bad enough. He was deliberately involved in a consuming interest that might change his life and could not possibly include me. By apartness I mean that evidently this "power," as he called it, had been building up in Newly. Why had he not shared it with me? Why Dan Ruber? Had he and Dan and Cora talked all this over on the nights I went upstairs and left them?

It was as though some awful spreading blight had entered our lives, deadly serious because Newly took it seriously. Here was a side of Newly I had not dreamed existed. A fallibility, naiveté that I had never seen. He had seemed the most sensible man imaginable. Dan Ruber was the unstable one, going on about the stock market and Coral Gables....But *Newly*? He worked in a bank and paid our bills, he made shelves for my books, emptied the trash, and clipped the hedge when needed. Just like other married men. How could he suddenly believe this of himself? How could he *play* with it? For wasn't that what the throne in the cellar was all about? Games. When I thought this, the paralysis that had gripped me dropped away and I rushed right out the back door to where Newly was hosing the trash cans. When he saw me he stopped hosing. "What's up?" He knew I was perturbed.

"Newly!" I cried, grabbing hold of his bare arm, "you can't do this to Cyd Kubie!"

A deep red flooded Newly's neck and face.

I shook his arm.

"You might do him harm, Newly. Don't you remember when you were afraid if you made that girl at the movies warm why couldn't you also make someone cold? You said then you weren't going to fool around with any of this...this hypnotism. Because that's what you're doing—hypnotizing people."

Newly jerked his arm away. He looked hotly at me, slitting his eyes in some new fashion with his mouth all pulled down.

"No!" he cried. Just as he had years ago. "There's no hypnotism about it!"

"Then what is it?"

"I don't know what the power is exactly. But I know now there is no harm in it—and it's real. You better believe it!" Now he was close to me in a manner I had never seen before. I felt his breath on my face. For an instant I thought he might strike me. I stood back, squeezed with fear. He had never looked so—so hatefully at me, never. What was happening to us? I could have wailed, wrung my hands. But instead I rushed for the door and into the house, away from him.

I went at once to the telephone. I looked up Dr. Plummer in the phone book and called the rectory. Fortunately he answered the phone. I plunged right in. I told him I was frightened and upset and could not make out what Newly was liable to do next and that he intended seeing Cyd Kubie tonight. I started to cry and had trouble speaking. He'd be right over, Dr. Plummer said.

I felt no calmer. I had no real confidence in Dr. Plummer. I phoned him because he seemed the only person who had influence with Newly, and someone must stop him.

Dr. Plummer arrived in five minutes. As soon as he came in the room I knew he wouldn't do any good. He was too immaculate, untouched, too well-bred. I knew the type. He'd spent a year at Oxford and sometimes managed to sound English. He could not possibly understand the situation.

"My dear Mrs. Slatter! I'm so sorry about all this." He hurried across the room, put both hands on my shoulders. Even on a hot day there wasn't a crease in his gabardine coat.

"I've been frightened," I said, mopping my eyes, wishing I wouldn't cry but not being able to stop.

"Frightened?" Dr. Plummer dropped his hands, actually smiling. He has a rather small face with a moustache and very red lips, hair turning gray, light brown eyes, very neat, precise. To him, being frightened was sloppy, ill-mannered. One must be in control at all times.

"Yes, it's frightening," I said, putting away my handkerchief.

"Mrs. Slatter—Newlin will get over all this. He's just sort of experimenting..." He smiled.

"Experimenting—with poor Cyd Kubie?"

Dr. Plummer's face fell. He looked rather startled. "Well, no. I don't like that."

The back door slammed and suddenly Newly was in the room. He spoke right up.

"What don't you like, Dr. Plummer?"

Dr. Plummer smiled. "Hello there, Slatter! Your good wife just called me. She seems rather worried about you. We don't want her worried, now do we? What is all this about Cyd Kubie? Aren't things getting rather out of hand?"

"No. I don't think so." Newly had an old rag in his hand and he wiped his hands off and then stuffed the rag in his back pocket.

Dr. Plummer's smile faded. Silence. Finally Dr. Plummer said, "You still don't feel this is a religious power?"

"Well, no, I don't." Newly hooked both hands in his belt. "It's something I've always had, I guess. Only now the feeling's stronger." He said quite simply, "I can't *not* use it."

Dr. Plummer apparently thought this over. "You don't think it's some kind of mental influence you exert?"

"Nope."

"What do you think it is?"

"I'm a healer. I have been given force in my body, in myself. I can destroy disease in another person. It's nothing strange. There are healers all over the world."

"But why have you suddenly discovered all this power, Newlin?"

I had sat down, but now got up. I wasn't angry nor frightened.

Seeing Newly against the ordinariness of our living room reassured me. There was the dining room table and four chairs, the screen by the fire that Newly meant to paint. Newly was not going to destroy our marriage, or go off by himself, or do something crazy and hurt Cyd Kubie, or cut me off. He was just trying out what he called his power. He'd find it wouldn't work and we'd forget it. When Dr. Plummer brought God into it I saw how impossible and improbable the whole situation was. I had not thought Newly would be so weak and foolish, but after all was I in a position to judge?

Newly had let go his belt. Now he rubbed his eyes the way he does when he is thinking particularly hard. He meant to answer Dr. Plummer. "Well," he said, "it's just that I've been feeling some kind of force lately."

Dr. Plummer said, "Couldn't that go as quickly as it came?"

"Yes. But it won't."

"Well look, old man," Dr. Plummer came forward. He was shorter than Newly by quite a bit and tipped his head to look at him. "It would be wonderful if you could really cure people. But you and I know that only God does that. That's your faith, Newlin. That's what you believe. You profess this belief every Sunday."

"Yes, I know I do." Newly dropped his hand, put it in his pocket. He was staring down at the rug. Then he looked up and smiled at little Dr. Plummer. "That's the only thing that bothers me. I can't have it both ways. And that means the church has got to go."

Dr. Plummer stood very still. "We all have moments of doubt, Newlin," he said in a kind of rasping voice.

"It's not that," Newly said. "It's simply that everything has changed for me."

"You mean there isn't room for God?"

"That's about it," Newly said, quite cheerfully. "I've been try-ing religion. You and I have had a lot of talks. But none of it touches this feeling I have now. There is nothing *wrong* with the feeling. Don't get that idea." Newly looked hard at Dr. Plummer. "If I have to say this power comes from God or it doesn't exist, then I split from the church."

The fear that I had felt outside in our yard, crept back.

"Newly!" I cried.

"No, no, Eva!" he looked seriously at me. "It'll be all right. Don't be frightened." He stood where he was and smiled.

"But it's all mad!"

He didn't even hear. "I must go ahead," he went on, really pompously and with horrid superiority.

"Just tell me who you're committed to!" I was almost yelling at him and didn't care.

"Well, I don't know, quite." He spoke seriously. "It's myself, mostly."

The rationality of his tone was awful. I was so frightened, yet all the time had such a feeling of unreality, as though now the shape of the furniture kept fading in and out. Stability and reality were wiped away by Newlin's hideous, unpiercable confidence. Then, squirming sluglike into my mind, came the awful question of Newly's sanity. I watched him. He had some new quality about him, breeziness. I'd never seen Newly like this. Had he developed it in the night? He had seemed doubtful, wondering. But now he was full-blown—oh, God!—committed?

"Newly!" I cried, "don't you see what you're doing?"

He paused, as though at a new thought. And then he fixed me with a hard look.

"I'm doing what I must," he said.

*"You're making it all up,"* I cried.

Then stopped short. Kenny had come into the room. He looked fearfully at me. I went over, tried to take his hand, but he held it behind him. Newly waited a moment, then spoke: "I wish you hadn't said that."

"Yes, Mom!" Kenny started jumping up and down. "Don't say that to Pop!"

Dr. Plummer took his leave.

When Cyd Kubie arrived I saw him from the window of our bedroom. He was pushed by tall, thin, mournful Mr. Kubie, his father, and by Kenny. They managed getting through the gate. "Better come round back. Too hard getting up these steps," Newly's voice said. Mrs. Tilley appeared. I heard Kenny say loudly, "My Pop is going to cure you, Cyd." I left the window, sat on the bed. How could Newly let Kenny be with him?

Cyd Kubie has been an invalid for as long as we've lived on India Street. Polio, everyone says. Mr. Kubie insists the whole business is a mystery to the Mayo Clinic. Occasionally Cyd can stand, will suddenly get to his feet. He says there's no reason for it, just an urge. Poor Cyd is not a very likeable type, although everyone tries. But he's not very bright; in fact, retarded might be closer. His head is rather V-shaped with thick, blond hair at the top, and he has large violet-colored eyes, watchful, and a surprisingly small mouth. He is long in body like his father, and as thin.

How were they to get Cyd down the cellar stairs? Silence below, long dreadful silence. The Ruber's terrier barked. A car passed, hitting the pothole. I got to my feet. Whatever repugnance I felt I must conquer. I must not only see what Newly was doing but try and get Kenny away. I walked slowly down the stairs.

They were in the living room. I stood at the door. No one noticed. They had moved the sofa and the armchairs. Cyd and the wheelchair were in the center of the room. Cyd's smile was lopsided. Newly started walking slowly toward him. "You got the wheels steady, Ken?"

"Yes, sir." Kenny never says "sir" to his father. And there was Mrs. Tilley by the window. Mr. Kubie had sunk onto a chair, evidently done in.

"Cyd," Newly was saying, and already his voice had changed. There was a hot breathiness to it. "I want you to get on your feet. Right up. We'll help."

"Don't need help," Cyd said in his high, cracking voice.

"All right," Newly said. And then hoarse and loud: "STAND!"
Cyd stood. There he was, hands dangling, still with a smile, only a little forced.

"Go ahead, Mr. Slatter," Mr. Kubie said, taunting.

"Quiet!" Newly was walking towards Cyd, carefully, step by step. Now he was close. He held his chin down as though he were going to lift a heavy weight. His knees were slightly bent. I was sure he did not see the sneer on Cyd's face. He had his head turned a little, seemed to be looking past Mrs. Tilley and through the window to the privet, perhaps. Then he reached over, placed a hand on Cyd's shoulder and in a huge voice shouted: "WALK!"

And Cyd Kubie, raising one foot and then the other, without fumbling, or tipping the chair but circumventing it as though he knew all the right steps, walked. Over to the door, across the porch, down the path and through the gate, then onto the pavement—and on down India Street.

19   When I saw Cyd Kubie walk down India Street I rushed over to Flora's, burst into her living room. "Cyd walked!" I cried.

She jumped up from the sofa, book in hand. "Phone Mr. Framely!" she ordered and threw one arm out wildly.

"What for?" I stood stupidly.

"He'll know what to do. Cyd's walk may be on radio."

Radio . . . the bottom of my stomach seemed to drop away. Were we suddenly to be confronted—with what?

Framely & Brink. I looked up the telephone number, spoke to the operator, and reached Mr. Framely. He grasped the situation at once and started giving directions at full voice, just like Flora.

"Don't talk to anyone! That's vital. Keep Kenny in the house. Get Newlin upstairs. Don't answer the phone. I'll be there in thirty minutes and I'll bring David."

His directions shook me. What did he mean? Not answer the telephone? Newly *upstairs* ... did he expect crowds? I sat down on the chair with the broken leg and nearly tipped onto the floor. This seemed typical of the day. "Take another chair!" Flora cried. I moved. Why was everyone shouting? I had never seen Flora so flustered. Her little flinty eyes had the wild look of a bird.

Why was Mr. Framely bringing David? Surely unnecessary and awkward. It suddenly occurred to me that David hadn't seen Kenny in two years. Now was not the time for my mind to wander, I told myself.

"What's come over Newly, Flora?" I, too, threw my arm out, directionless as Flora. "What *is* all this? You should have seen Cyd get right out of that wheelchair, spry as anyone. No help. Not a word. Just walked down the street..."

"Well, God knows." Flora now stood by the window, her hat pulled well over her eyes. Suddenly she strode to the sofa, sat down. "Newlin hasn't had an attack, or anything? Flu, gallbladder?"

"What difference would it make?"

"Well, none, really." She leaned back resignedly.

"Newly is just the same, Flora," I said. Then, after thinking: "Well, not quite, I suppose. Since that damned picture fell off the wall and poor Frank shot himself."

"Shock." Flora evidently was not paying attention. She hated having her reading time interrupted, which I had done. And she did not like being involved in other people's troubles. Messes, she called them.

"No, it wasn't shock, Flora. It was after the picture and finding my ring that Newly started going to church."

"Dr. Plummer." Flora blew her nose on a crumpled Kleenex.

"Yes. Before that warts and then grace at the table." I kept thinking of Newly and the voice he used to Cyd Kubie. I said, remembering, "Newly seems swollen in some way."

"Fat?" She had taken to monosyllables.

"No. Larger, expansive. He's very confident. And then sort of—well—sort of *winning*." I didn't know how to express it.

"Magnetic personality." Flora examined the backs of her hands.

"Well, yes."

"All of a piece."

"He seems much older," I said, with sudden comprehension. Being with Flora made me see Newly. "He sighs all the time. And he's rather silent. I've tried to talk him out of all this. I minded frightfully about Cyd. I told Newly not to try. And now what? I mean what's *happened*?"

Flora said, looking aside, "What's to happen now is the question."

"Why is Mr. Framely so steamed up?" I kept my eyes on her. For although Flora refused to be involved emotionally in my life, yet she could be ruthless and this was what I needed. With Flora I would not have to wade through the possibility that a Stronger Being had hold of Newly. Or that I must take the Wife's Position: Supportive. How could I support such pretense? Hypnotism, plain and simple. Why couldn't Newly at least admit the possibility? It was on this point that Newly and I could not meet. For in my mind I accused him of lacking honesty. He refused to consider the possibility that maybe the warts were ripe and fell off, and maybe Cyd Kubie had been walking secretly. How could Newly believe that his power cured the warts and made Cyd walk? Or that Frank's picture falling off the wall had any meaning? I even tried to imagine what it would be like to hold someone's hands and feel them grow warm all over and know you were doing it. Maybe one thing led to another and you experimented. But when it came down to gripping some poor cripple and bellowing "WALK!" ... Well, you couldn't. You daren't. Newly profoundly shocked me. I felt it in my stomach.

Sitting on Flora's hard chair I asked myself: Was this the other side of Newly? The humorless, very tough, ambitious side? In the years we had been married I noted determination and a certain stubbornness, but not a very marked ambition. A hard worker but not aiming at the bank presidency. Very tender in bed. Loving. Kind and honest. Level-headed, so it seemed. Now was I faced with an entirely different character—growing, as it were, in the dark? Certainly away from me.

What would "all-this" (as I now called it) do to his position at the bank? What would be the customer reaction? And I thought in a panic that the bank must not know. Although later it was said that I failed to appreciate the implication of what had happened, this was not quite true. I just did not want the news to get out. But of course that was naive of me—and much too late.

Flora spoke: "I gather from your conversation with Mr. Framely that he expects reporters?"

"Oh, I hope not. I don't know what he meant." And then, "Dan Ruber and Newly have built some kind of throne in the cellar."

Flora glared at me. "What else? You better tell me."

There was no sense trying to explain to Flora what was happening to my marriage and what Newly was deliberately doing to it. We did not confide personal difficulties. I said, "I've tried to talk to him, but it's no good. I think he feels under some awful obligation. I don't know what's going to happen," I said, looking at the wall.

Flora removed her hat, held it loosely in her hands. Her bare head with its dome of sleek, gray hair made her look old and vulnerable, storklike. She said rather casually, "You may have to prepare for a whole new life."

"Like what?"

"Crowds, laying-on-of-hands, whoop-de-doop..."

The words were so unlike Flora that I could not answer. Then, rather stiffly, "Newly would never allow things to go that far." I believed it.

She was silent. How much confidence did she place in Newly? She always told me I was lucky to have a husband who would let me write. Most husbands minded. But Newly himself? I don't think he

interested her. But I had no time for these speculations. I must rely
on Mr. Framely. (I simply could not imagine David's role.) Mr.
Framely surely would do his best to persuade Newly to give this
whole business up. I could imagine Mr. Framely speaking to the
Guaranty and reassuring them. And I saw that I should have to
stand firm and be against Newly and that this might be exceedingly
difficult and painful. I had tried only the other day, with no success.
Perhaps Newly could continue his "work" in some minor way in the
cellar.

"Well," Flora said, clapping her hat on her knee, "it can't be
helped now." As though she'd forgotten to return a library book.
"Newlin believes it himself. You're lucky he does not believe his
power comes from God, or positive thinking..."

"Or Coué," I said.

"That old fart."

From Flora, this shocked me. Now she stood up. She had on
her denim skirt with the pink pockets made from bits of an old sofa
cover. All her movements were impatient. Necromancy, she'd think.
Rubbish! I thought so, too—only I was living with it. And also, not
quite rubbish for I had seen my husband touch Cyd's shoulder.

Flora said, "You watch Dan Ruber, Eva. He'll want to make a
big thing of this. You know Dan's weakness for easy money. What
you don't realize is there may be money made on Newlin." She
turned, walked to the screen door, opened it. "You better be getting
back." She gave me a wicked smile. "And isn't it nice David's
coming?"

When I walked into our living room, to my surprise, Newlin
and Kenny were sitting on the sofa. Kenny had brought down all his
train tracks and they lay in a mass at their feet.

"Did you see anyone as you came in, Mom?" Kenny jumped up.
I said no and then sent him into the kitchen for some orange juice.

Faced with Newly I couldn't think what to say. We had no
connection. How could I tell him Mr. Framely suggested he go to

his room? Who was I to order around a man who could make people walk, or worse? The skin on Newly's face looked stiff, his big cheeks hard. He stared at the floor and I had the feeling he did not really know I was there.

Mr. Framely banged open the front door, bustled in, followed by David carrying a large carton, as immaculate and detached as Dr. Plummer. Behind David came Johnson, the chauffeur, with another carton. Mr. Framely closed and locked the front door. He was smoking a cigar. "Get the back door, David. You and Johnson put that gin under the table."

David, I thought, would now see Kenny.

Newly got slowly to his feet. "What's going on? What *is* this?"

Mr. Framely went over to him, laid a hand on his arm.

"Newlin," he said solemnly, removing his cigar, "you've got to be protected."

"Come on!..." Newly moved away from Mr. Framely. I could tell he didn't like what was happening, and I could hardly blame him. A man does not want someone else locking his front door.

"Let me tell you, Newlin." Mr. Framely sat calmly down in Newly's chair, moved an ash tray closer, crossed his short legs. "You're going to have every newspaper in the city out here. Right on your porch. And unless you play this whole business carefully, you'll be nation-wide on radio. You foretold a friend's suicide. You've cured warts." He ticked each item off on his fingers. "Now you've made a paralytic walk."

"Nobody knew for sure he was a paralytic," Newly said, suddenly red in the face. He drew his mouth in the way he does when displeased. He went back to the couch, sat heavily down.

"Being in a wheelchair's enough." Mr. Framely flicked an ash. "If this thing is not handled—and I mean handled—you'll be mobbed. And that's not pleasant. You won't like it one bit."

"Why would the newspapers know anything?" Newly said. I kept trying to see some further difference in him. But he looked just the way he always did on Saturday morning, dressed in old clothes and no tie. Both Mr. Framely and David wore ties, having been in town.

"One of your neighbors phoned in," Mr. Framely said.

Mrs. Tilley.

Kenny had come in from the kitchen, orange juice glass in hand, followed by David and then Johnson. Kenny sat down by Newly. David moved in cloer to the couch, regarded Kenny, who was looking at him through the orange juice glass. David said: "That's a lot of track," he pointed to the pile on the floor. "Any of your trains run?"

Kenny fired up at once. "They *all* run. They're just a little mixed up." He cocked his head on one side, a manner I particularly disliked.

David said, "Can I help you fix them?"

Kenny sucked on the glass, then said, "Have you got a quarter on you?"

Lately Kenny asked everyone for money. We couldn't seem to stop him. David was certainly seeing his worst side.

But I had forgotten David's short attention span. He didn't even answer, walked over to Mr. Framely. "How about my going to see this Cyd—what's his last name?"

"Kubie!" Kenny shouted, bouncing up and down on the sofa. Then beside himself, he cried, "I helped bring him over in the wheelchair. Cyd didn't want to come. But I made him." Now he jumped to his feet and ran over to Mr. Framely, who promptly handed him a quarter. I was too tense and distracted to take issue and I don't think Newly noticed.

"Kubie will talk," David said.

"No, he won't," Kenny said. He was staggering around the room trying to balance the quarter on his chin. I had never seen him so brash and unattractive. Even Newly looked annoyed. Kenny went on in a singsong voice, "He won't talk because he's sitting out on the roof and he doesn't want to see anyone. He went right up there after Pop cured him. He's always wanted to sit on the roof, he says. He's not talking to anyone until he makes up his mind whether he wants to stay cured or not."

Dumb silence from all of us.

"What are you saying, Kenny?" Newly spoke patiently.

"Wouldn't you like to know!" Kenny pocketed the quarter, went over and started clattering with the train tracks.

"Get that kid upstairs, can't you, Eva?" Mr. Framely looked put out.

"I'll take him up," Johnson the chauffeur offered. He leaned close to Kenny, uniform rippling. "Pick up that mess of tracks and beat it. I'm following."

After they had disappeared, Mr. Framely said, "I think Eva's the one to go over and try to knock some sense into this Kubie fellow. Whether he decides to walk or not, we want him to keep quiet." All eyes focused on me. I had on the lavender-striped dress that even Flora said was unfortunate.

"Good idea," David said.

"I really don't know Cyd very well." It sounded weak.

"You'll manage," David said. "Come on." He went toward the kitchen to let me out the back door. I thought as I followed him that he had bugged me into situations since I was Kenny's age.

I walked across Flora's lawn and from there could see Cyd sitting on the flat, red roof with his legs stretched out. In the center of the Kubie's roof is a square structure with four windows decorated with white wooden scrollwork. Cyd had evidently crawled out on the roof from one of the windows.

"Hi, Cyd," I called up to him when I got closer. It's great you can walk again. Mr. Slatter's awfully pleased."

Cyd's large violet eyes rolled. But he didn't speak. I walked around the house to the front, knocked on the screen. Mr. Kubie let me in, loomed above me in the dark hall. Mr. Kubie had an extraordinarily deep voice.

"Don't ask me what's wrong," he said.

"May I speak to him?"

"Go ahead. Much good it'll do you."

I climbed the stairs. As far as I could tell all the rooms were empty. Maybe Mr. Kubie slept downstairs in order to take care of Cyd. From the third floor a ladder led to the cupola, or whatever it was called. I climbed the ladder, then crawled out the window. The roof was hot. Tin, painted red, flat. I stood up.

"It's pretty hot out here," Cyd said. "I thought maybe this whole thing'd wear off in the sun."

"Oh, I don't think so, Cyd. I think you're meant to walk."

I tried to keep my voice down because I didn't want Cora Ruber next door to hear. Dan I knew was working at the store.

"Well, I'm not so sure..."

"But Cyd—don't you want to be well? You used to get so tired lying around. You told me so."

"Well, it was better'n this darned hot roof."

"Come on inside, then."

"That's just it," he said, gazing at his long legs. "I'm not too darned sure my legs will make it. That ladder is something!" He looked wildly at me, throwing back his head. He was, I saw, close to tears.

"I'll help you," I said, making toward the window. Perhaps Cyd really liked being an invalid and had withdrawn into it, only to be rudely jerked out. Aside from whatever Newly had done, it was so terribly important that Cyd walk, that he believe he could. He'd start living again—and *that* would be the miracle!

"Give me your hand, Cyd."

"Have you got power, too, Mrs. Slatter?"

"Of course not! Just give me your hand and we'll get you through the window."

"But I'm afraid to stand up!" Tears started to run down his long face.

"Of course you're afraid, Cyd. But you'll get the hang of it. So just grab hold of my hand, get up on your knees, and crawl toward the window. I'll hold onto your belt."

And that was how we did it. Cyd sobbing all the way. I went through the window first, Cyd knelt outside. Fortunately the ladder was not long.

"You've got to believe in yourself, Cyd."

"Well, I do. Only I'm inexperienced."

Suddenly Cyd said, "Well, OK then. Here goes." And with a smile of positive beneficence, he stood. I could have cried. Instead I hugged his legs, which I could just reach from the ladder.

Back at the house, when I got there, David and Mr. Framely were arranging glasses on the dining room table.

Mr. Framely came right up to me. "Is he all right? Can he walk?"

"Yes, he's all right," I said. Mr. Framely and David seemed to have taken over our house and our lives, too. "I certainly don't think he's going to talk to reporters. He's a little reluctant to accept the cure."

Newly said, "I was afraid of that."

The doorbell rang.

Mr. Framely hurried across to Newly. "Wouldn't you be happier upstairs, Newly? Then you won't have to answer a lot of questions." Since Newly had turned into whatever he had turned into Mr. Framely treated him like a child.

"Good idea." Newly made for the stairs, then stopped. "What about Eva. I don't want her bothered." He was thinking of me. I flushed with relief.

"Don't worry about Eva," David said. "We're right here to take care of her." Newly disappeared. David turned to me. "You'll have to watch that tongue of yours," he said in his old, bossy way. "Don't try to be funny. This is serious."

"Eva knows it's serious, David," Mr. Framely said. "Don't talk like that. You'll scare the poor girl." He came over and patted my shoulder. I could see how nervous they both were.

The doorbell rang, louder this time.

"You'll have to lie," David said. "How good are you at that?"

"First rate," I said, looking right at him.

From outside came voices. A man's voice saying that there must be someone inside for he'd just seen a woman go in the back door. The voice sounded like Lloyd Paget. What could he possibly be doing on our front porch?

David said, "They're going to be more interested in you than anyone, Eva. Just remember you don't know anything and haven't seen anything. And remember we're all in this together. It's not just you and Newly."

"That's right, son," Mr. Framely said. Under grave stress did he always call David "son"? "Don't mind having your picture taken, Eva. Can you push a comb through your hair? Or maybe it's better the way it is. You're supposed to be a homekeeper."

David handed me a comb. "Wearing bangs, aren't you?"

Even in the confusion and the pounding on the door, I managed to say quite calmly that since I'd been pregnant my hair had changed texture.

Mr. Framely now opened the door wide. "Come in!" he cried. A short fat gray-haired man stood in the doorway. "I'm from the *Record*," he said. "Understand someone's been walking on water around here."

Mr. Framely gave a loud laugh. "Can I get you a drink?"

"Never refuse," the reporter said. Then catching sight of me. "Mrs. Slatter? You're the Frederick Severn's granddaughter, aren't you?"

I said not really, and smiled directly at him.

"What's all this about your husband?"

"He's not here," I said.

"I understand this Kubie kid is sulking up on a roof somewhere."

By now we had been joined by Lloyd Paget who held a straw hat in his hand and was dressed in white flannels.

"I was coming to see Mr. Slatter myself," Lloyd said. I'd never seen him this close. He was tall with big hips and almond-shaped, almost yellow eyes. I remembered him at parties.

"You got warts?" the reporter asked him. Mr. Framely put a glass in his hand. He sipped cautiously. Lloyd Paget gave him a scathing glance and moved off.

"Where's Slatter?" the reporter asked.

"He's in Harrisburg," David said, to my surprise.

"Governor send for him?" the reporter asked sharply.

"He's there on bank business."

The reporter was silent. Then with his small gray eyes looking directly at me, and in between sips, he asked, "What's it like to be the wife of a miracle-worker, Mrs. Slatter?"

20    News of Cyd Kubie's walk must have been broadcast over the radio because people crowded into our living room. For instance, the Deerings, who live next to the Pagets and barely speak to us, now came right into the house. And old Mrs. Marburg, very deaf, who lives alone in a big place with a heated swimming pool was there. Strange faces wandered back and forth. A group formed around the sofa, using our ash trays freely. Mr. Framely was busy at the bar, set up on the dining room table with a block of ice in a bucket. David was serving as a kind of waiter, moving from group to group and asking who wanted a drink. Cora Ruber, who had arrived soon after Lloyd Paget, stuck beside me, and answered many of the questions, particularly the one about Newly being in Harrisburg. I didn't seem able to sound convincing when I knew he was right upstairs. People regarded what had happened either as equivalent to having won the Sweepstakes or contracting a terminal illness. Some asked about symptoms. Others

wanted to know if Newly was going to set up in business. I knew I was on display and hated being seen in my old striped dress with my hair not properly fixed. I saw Dan talking earnestly to Bernard Cranby, the newspaper man. Then, to everyone's amazement, in walked Mrs. Alfred Berkley, white gloves, white felt hat turned up on one side with a pheasant's feather, white suit. I made my way to her. "Well, my dear," she said in her high-pitched Philadelphia drawl, offering her cheek, "you seemed to have whipped up quite a bit of excitement." Her little raisin eyes missed nothing, trim and elegantly tiny, she surveyed the scene, nodding to the Deerings and old Mrs. Marburg. She moved regally on. A flash, and her picture was taken. "You better ask for police protection, Eva. My car could hardly get along India Street." She seemed highly amused. "Wait 'til your grandmother hears about all this." She waved her gloved hand. "What was it your husband did? Brought someone back from the dead?"

"Cyd Kubie, who has been in a wheelchair most of his life, walked."

"Your husband got him up?"

"Yes."

"You don't seem very interested."

"She's dazed, poor thing," Cora Ruber put in.

Mrs. Berkley ignored her. "It's extraordinary, Eva. As though your husband had suddenly turned into Houdini."

"Yes—it is." How odd that this self-centered woman should be the only person who gave my feelings a thought.

She went on: "I'm not all that crazy about healers myself. But Alfred is mad for them. Went all the way down to some poor old hermit who lives in the New Jersey Pineys. The man didn't do him a bit of good. But Alfred's sure Newlin can fix him up. What else has he done besides the wheelchair?"

There was no reason why I should gratify Mrs. Berkley's curiosity. To my embarrassment a crowd had formed around us waiting for me to speak. It was no longer a question of speaking but of shouting, since the noise level had increased, aided by free gin. "Newlin has done nothing that you'd be particularly interested in, Mrs. Berkley. Mrs. Ruber can probably give you more details than I can."

With surprising strength Mrs. Berkley pulled at my arm until I leaned near her. "That's the wrong attitude, Eva. In public you should support him, no matter what you think." She had a wicked, teasing smile and her little eyes, peering at me under her white hat, delighted in my dilemma. Fortunately, David came up and she turned to him. "I was wondering if you'd forgotten me," she said, bridling.

"Of course not!" David said, with just the right smile. "Isn't it the most extraordinary crowd of people? We don't know half of them. But Mr. Framely and I thought that if we made it seem like a cocktail party, people would forget what they came for."

"How *very* clever!" she laid her hand on his arm. "So you think Mr. Slatter is liable to perform again?"

"Who knows?" David bent over her. Handsome, laughing at her, not a blond hair out of place, he could make any woman feel attractive. I had not seen this charm in many years.

David and Mrs. Berkley turned away. Mrs. Berkley said she must be going. "I'll see you to your car." David actually offered his arm.

I had not noticed Bernard Cranby's approach until he suddenly spoke. "I'd like to get your side of this picture, Mrs. Slatter. Is there any place we can talk privately? Upstairs, maybe?"

I said with all Mrs. Berkley's aplomb: "My son is upstairs, Mr. Cranby. I do not want him disturbed."

Cranby had light gray eyes, a fleshy face, wide mouth, a deceptively passive manner. He held his hat awkwardly under his arm, a cigarette in one hand, highball in the other. "How about the kitchen?"

As we entered, Mr. Framely was chipping ice from the remains of a block in the refrigerator. He hurried out.

Mr. Cranby sat down at the table.

"You're going to have to answer a lot of questions from a lot of people, Mrs. Slatter. You might as well get used to it."

His manner was not so much threatening, as watchful. I had the feeling that he would read his own meaning into anything I said. I sat down opposite him. In spite of all the excitement, Newly had turned the gas off from the stew we were having that night. This homey sight brought our life back again, and made those people in the next room unreal and unimportant to me. I even started to feel differently about Mr. Cranby. Monday morning Newly would catch the 8:05 as usual and go in to the Guaranty. All this noise and craziness would be over.

Mr. Cranby said, with what he must fancy was a winning smile, "Let's begin with my original question. What's it like to be the wife of a miracle worker?"

"I haven't been one very long, Mr. Cranby."

"Long enough to know what lies ahead."

"I wouldn't say so. My husband and I lead very quiet lives. I expect no change."

"You surprise me. I hear big plans for some kind of revival in St. Mark's Church and a young girl who's never walked in her life being brought down from Wilkes-Barre."

He was trying to trap me. "I'm sure you're mistaken. I know nothing about it."

"What's your reaction?"

"I can't have a reaction to something I don't believe." What was he talking about? Dan Ruber had filled him full of lies. It would be like Dan to dream up something so impossible. But on the other hand, where had the idea of Wilkes-Barre come from? It seemed quite definite and specific. I began to feel the yawning-pit sensation again, an awful uncertainty. Was this all a *plan?*...

Cranby appeared unmoved. "If he made the Kubie boy walk today you've got some idea whether he can work the same thing with this Wilkes-Barre girl."

"Why should she?" David had come into the kitchen. He held a highball glass in his hand and walked up to the table. "Mrs. Slatter is not ready to talk to reporters."

Mr. Cranby looked him over, apparently not at all put off. "You're David Severn, aren't you?" He took out his fountain pen, made some notes on a piece of paper. "While you're up, Severn, how about getting me a refill?"

"Sorry. We've run out."

Cranby's light eyes dropped from David's face. I did not need David's high-and-mighty tone. I could handle Cranby.

Ignoring David, Cranby turned directly to me. "When did you first notice anything unusual in your husband's behavior, Mrs. Slatter?"

Before David could answer I said quickly that I really hadn't noticed anything unusual at all.

"Come on now, Mrs. Slatter," Cranby gave his froglike smile, "you must have seen something. First the warts, then the picture falls off the wall and there's a suicide. Now Kubie walks. You can't tell me all this doesn't change a guy."

David said sharply, "There is no difference in Newlin Slatter. You can take my word for it."

Cranby looked up at David. "I'd like to talk to Mrs. Slatter alone. I think you make her uneasy."

David replied, sounding unbearably pompous: "She is not giving interviews."

I did not see the point in making Cranby mad, and said quickly, "I really know very little, Mr. Cranby."

"Is your husband excitable—moody?" Cranby said.

Again David broke in: "Mr. Slatter works in the Trust Department at the Guaranty. A highly responsible position. He is hardly one to give way to fits."

"Who said fits?"

"Moods, then."

"That's a long way from fits," Cranby turned to me. "You notice any fits?"

"There is no difference at all in my husband."

"Just suddenly able to make cripples walk, but the same nice guy."

"That's it," David said.

Cranby looked up at David, who seemed to loom very large in the kitchen. Cranby said, "I'd appreciate it if you'd just move along and leave me with Mrs. Slatter."

"You're not getting any information out of Mrs. Slatter, Cranby. She doesn't know anything and she's not saying anything."

"What's all this to you, Severn? You taking a personal interest?"

There was something more than insulting in the way he spoke. It was sly. Before I could move or speak, David grabbed Cranby by the collar of his coat, yanked him to his feet. David's arm swung out and then thudded against Cranby's body. He must have aimed at his shoulder and got him in the ribs. Cranby spun round, his chair crashed to the ground and he toppled over it. At this moment Mr. Framely rushed through the door and took hold of David. I leaned over and tried to help Mr. Cranby.

"What in hell were you doing, David?" Mr. Framely shouted.

Cranby was on his feet, holding his side, breathing hard.

"Assault and battery. I'll sue!" Cranby now leaned over the table. Mr. Framely let go of David. The last I saw of Cranby he was being led out the door by Mr. Framely who was offering him a drink.

David stood in the center of the kitchen. He stared at me, eyes wide. He didn't seem to know where he was. A kind of wild flush lighted up his fair skin. He ran his hand through his hair, pushing it back, then jerked at his tie, straightening it.

"What's got into you, David? You can't go around hitting people like Cranby. I was doing just fine until you butted in."

David walked aimlessly to the sink, turned. "I hate that fellow Cranby..." He still looked dazed. Then more positively: "He's a real bastard. He had no business going after you like that." He heaved a great sigh. The flush receded from his face. There was something different about David. Not just additional weight; in spite of this latest violent episode, he no longer seemed as belligerent, as edgy, toward me, anyway. Ordinarily I would have expected him to light into me, telling me I handled Cranby badly, or that I should have refused to talk to Cranby. But now he seemed to be considering the situation, not only from my angle, but as a problem. It had been a long time since I was alone with David. Maybe his experiences up-country had altered him in some way, for there was a kind of stillness about him, almost resembling patience. Could marriage to Joyce have done that?

I said, "The last time I saw you hit someone was Bobby Frazer in Rittenhouse Square and I was ten years old."

"I couldn't stand Cranby's fat face." David suddenly smiled with all the old sweetness as though remembering that day in the Square. Then sobering: "What's Newlin *doing*, Eva? Did he really get this fellow Kubie to walk? What's he fooling around with that kind of stuff for?"

"I don't know!" His query plunged me into the whole mess again, and all the questions I was asking myself.

"Has he turned religious?"

I shook my head. "He feels he's got some kind of power..." I'd given this answer innumerable times today. And remembering this brought back the crowds of people, the shouts from the street.

David said, "There's going to be some sort of rally. I heard Dan Ruber telling Cranby. Newlin's supposed to make a paralyzed girl walk."

"I don't believe it!" I glared at him. Bringer of bad news!

"You better. They've got the whole thing set up." He looked at me as though I were a curious specimen. (I had a sudden desire to ask him how he liked my hair.) He went on: "I don't understand what's come over Newlin. What makes him go in for this kind of thing?"

"Bad taste, you mean? Cheap? Not done?" I fired right up. As usual David's disapproval made me defensive.

"Well, no. It's confusing to have someone you know turn into a

( *217*

kind of miracle worker."

I said nothing. Then, "I thought Newly had forgotten all about his power—as he calls it. But now it's worse than ever. Oh, I hate it!..." I suddenly sat down at the table, put my hands over my face.

I heard David move across the floor, came over near me. He would tell me to brace up, as usual. But instead he said in a remarkably gentle voice, "You better think about it, Eva. You've got to make up your mind what to do."

I dropped my hands, looked at him. His face was quite calm, his eyes serious. It was so strange not to have him challenge me. Would it be possible to confide in David? I was wary of it.

"I don't want anything to do with—with all of this!" I banged my fist down on the table.

"That'll be pretty difficult."

"I don't want to see my husband being made a fool of!"

"Maybe he'll flub a few and the whole thing will die down."

"That won't stop him!" I twisted toward David. For a second he looked down at me, then abruptly swung away. He put both hands in his pockets and stood by the sink, his back toward me. Silence. Then, in a tight voice, "How does Kenny take it?"

"He gets much too excited. I mind it more for him than anyone." Now I was nearly crying again at the thought of Kenny. I had believed our life would go back to normal. But in fact I knew that nothing was to be the same. I could not imagine what was going to happen, or how I would manage. I only felt a kind of awful apprehension and held my breath and then let it out, and then held it again. David did not speak, as though silence would help me find my bearings. I knew he watched me.

After a little I got to my feet. There was Newly to face, and all the dirty glasses.

No more noise came from the living room. People must have left. Mr. Framely pushed open the door. "There's only one person here and he's drunk," he said. It was Lloyd Paget. He had lost his hat, his tie dangled, his big almond-shaped eyes wandered foolishly.

He probably had never drunk gin in his life. He finally disappeared down the front steps after I'd promised Newly would see him next week. Johnson came into the room with Kenny. Newlin stayed upstairs. Mr. Framely had brought a big hamper to cart away the dirty glasses and the bottles. I tried to make him tell me what we owed for the gin and the ginger ale, but he brushed me aside. "I think having this kind of neighborhood party took the curse off it," he said. "If you understand me. We didn't want a riot, or have to call the police out. Mrs. Berkley's appearance helped greatly" As he followed David through the sceen door, he turned and said in an undertone to me, "You dont think Newly's going to make a habit of this, do you?"

"I hope not."

"Bad for the kid," he said. "Bad for you."

I smiled at him, grateful for the sympathy. David, too, had shown a certain understanding, and if it had not been for that abrupt turning away, we might have really discussed the problem.

The furniture in the room was awry and I went about pushing chairs into place and emptying ash trays.

# Prelude

*Anna and Frederick Severn are sitting on the dock of their Adirondack camp, facing the shoreline and thereby avoiding the little breeze that has sprung up, ruffling St. Regis Lake. A sailboat race is taking place in the distance, of passionate interest to the campers, but warranting scarcely more than an occasional glance from either of the old people. Sitting on a camp stool before them is a plump smiling man, Bernard Cranby, whose gray hair occasionally lifts in the breeze. He has a rather froglike smile, at present he is being excessively agreeable. He has even listened to Anna recite a few stanzas from her latest poem, "The Breath of Daffodils."*

*Anna and Frederick in their turn are quite impressed with Mr. Cranby. This is their first encounter with the Press, particularly* The Record, *which is read in their kitchen but is never seen in the front of the house. Mr. Cranby has driven over from Lake Placid, setting up an appointment well in advance. The* Carafa *with Gordon at the helm was sent to The Landing. Mr. Cranby has said his interest and sole reason for this trip is the Shawnee tribe. Information he has read speaks of the tribe having been in northern Pennsylvania and he wants verification of time and place from Frederick. He has also been looking into the background of Britisher Alexander McKee, loyal friend to the Shawnee. Frederick is enormously gratified and flattered by this (to him) young man's interest and the effort he has taken to seek out such an inaccessible, purposely isolated spot, simply to check facts which a glance into Catlin's* Indians In North America *would have confirmed. However, it also seems that Mr. Cranby wants particularly to meet Frederick, "our greatest living Indian scholar," he says. He holds the firm belief that the present book, upon which Frederick is now engaged, will be what Mr. Cranby calls "a best seller." The thought of one of his books selling more than a few copies to libraries and colleges is stupefying to Frederick. Mr. Cranby is talking in terms of third and fourth printings. Frederick's book will coincide with the recent revival of interest in the Indian. Mr. Cranby rattles off various Indian organizations, "Equal Rights for Indians," "Protect the Cherokee Tribe," among a string of names Frederick has never heard of. He is full of helpful suggestions, ways to get in touch with certain important people in what he calls "The Indian Movement." Frederick is almost fluttery with anticipation. Mr. Cranby asks if he has had a photograph taken recently, and when Frederick says no, produces a camera, posing Frederick against the pines. When he asks permission to take the main cabin and the breakfast cabin, Anna and Frederick are enchanted. As they resume their seats on the dock, Mr. Cranby mentions the peculiar happenings on India Street and hastens to add that he hopes they have not been annoyed by the publicity. Anna says the whole business is distasteful and most undignified, but now fortunately over, she understands. Well, no, Mr. Cranby gently disagrees. There is to be a church meeting. Oh that, Anna says, glad to have the jump on him for once. "The girl they're using is mentally retarded and paralyzed. There'll be no miracle at St. Mark's." Mr. Cranby, to Anna's surprise, replaces his camera with a notebook, saying, in as prim a tone as Anna's, how distressing all this must be to them.*

*"We hope it does not jeopardize Newlin's position at the bank," Anna says. "It's all so ridiculous. When I phoned Eva's house a woman's voice answered saying, 'Healing Grace.' When I heard it I hung up. I wrote Eva I would not telephone again."*

*"Eva Slatter, your granddaughter?"*

*"She's really no relation. You see . . ." and Anna modestly sets forth their generosity to the poor child, Eva Colby. She describes her arrival, her sad appearance, their decision to keep her. The difficulties. Private school. Eva's stubborn nature.*

*"She had her debut," Anna says. "We gave a tea."*

*"I'm sure she was grateful," Mr. Cranby smiles widely.*

*"No, I wouldn't say so."*

*"Now, my dear," Frederick breaks in, "you underrate her."*

*Cranby says to Anna: "She cut quite a swathe."*

*"I'm afraid I do not know what you mean."*

*"She was quite a hit."*

*"Well, frankly, I always thought she made herself conspicuous."*

*"The cigarette holder, the haircut, you mean?" Mr. Cranby fills in*
*eagerly.*

*"I don't know anything about a cigarette holder."*

*"A silly rumor, Mrs. Severn. I'm sure any girl brought up in your*
*household would be a model of decorum."*

*Anna smiles, runs her fingers along the pleat of her dress. For the first*
*time Frederick looks suspiciously at Cranby. He has paid little attention, nor*
*did he attempt to stop the conversation when it turned to the Slatters and*
*Newlin. "A perfectly ordinary young man," Anna says, when Mr. Cranby*
*mentions Newlin.*

*"With an interest in Willa Cather," Frederick says.*

*This observation dies. David and Joyce are touched on. Joyce's beauty*
*eulogized by Mr. Cranby, until he notices the displeased expression on Anna's*
*face and quickly says what a pity she is overweight.*

*When it comes time for Cranby to leave he stands up in a very manly*
*fashion and tells Frederick that he wishes him good health and spirits for the*
*task of finishing his great work. "So important, but in your hands we are*
*assured of more than competency." It softens Frederick, who for a moment has*
*suspected Cranby, but now believes him quite earnest and, one could almost*
*say, dedicated. The last words they hear from Cranby as the* Carafa *pulls*
*down St. Regis Lake, are that he will be in touch with the Indian Equal*
*Rights Association and hopes to bring good news when they meet again.*

21 For a week Newly's "miracle" made headlines in the Philadelphia papers and the inside pages of *The New York Times*. The first pictures showed both of us standing on the porch steps (looking like fugitives from the Dust Bowl, particularly me), and one of Newly with his hand holding Cyd's, who stood on the other side of the gate. Newly was billed as a simple guy upon whom this momentous power had been bestowed. "NOT FROM GOD," one headline announced. This rather took down the interest. My line: "We lead quiet lives," was the key to Cranby's article in *The Record*. He made me out an insensitive type, too dazed to speak intelligibly. No mention of David. The meeting to be held at St. Mark's was vaguely referred to. Dan Ruber kept complaining, "We need another Cyd Kubie. Let's hope my Wilkes-Barre cousin works out."

Newly seemed preoccupied. The Maxwell was dirty; the screen door bolt kept sticking, the grass would soon need a scythe. Newly did none of his usual chores, although he went to the bank every day. He smiled all the time, a soft uncomprehending grin.

People stopped in front of our house or stood in the yard. It was during those early days that our hedge started to lose its shape. It would be stripped down to bare twigs eventually, when pieces of privet were taken as souvenirs. (In time our iron gate and fence disappeared.) At night people came right up on the porch and looked in the windows. We kept the shades down. The first week after Cyd walked, distressingly crippled men and women came to see Newly, hoping for miraculous cures; also a blind boy and a man with only one leg. Newly spoke to the crippled, but he angered them with his talk about believing they could cure themselves. Ogden, the blind boy, came back. He and Kenny were about the same age and sat on the porch talking.

A bus drove by every day, the announcer calling out that this was the famous healer's modest home. Cyd Kubie would hear the bus turn off Sedgwick Avenue and made it a point to be discovered walking down our path.

The first time I shopped on the Avenue a group of women standing on the corner by the bank pointed me out. "That's her! That's the healer's wife! I saw her picture in the paper!" I darted into Gallons Hardware, and fortunately they did not follow. When I gave my name as a charge the salesgirl asked if I was any relation to the healer. I took to ordering food over the phone, not caring if I spent more money. I stayed off the Avenue.

In less than a week our living room had been turned into an office. Mrs. Slatter and Cora Ruber were part of the office force. Two desks and a file cabinet held "Healing Grace." The furniture was all moved while I was in town at the dentist's. I came home to find the sofa and chairs shoved against the wall. The red velvet curtains had been removed. When I told Dan Ruber he must bring my furniture right back and get rid of those desks, he said quite sharply that I better ask Newly. "It's not forever, Eva, just temporary, until the St. Mark's meeting is set." As Cora, plus Mrs. Slatter were listening, I asked where they had put the velvet curtains and walked out of the room into the kitchen.

Mrs. Slatter followed me. I faced her. "You let them move the furniture! How *could* you? Whose house is this?"

"Your husband pays the rent."

"The furniture is mine," I said, like a child. I couldn't help it. To come home and find my house now an office and realize Newly had agreed to it was terrible.

Having Mrs. Slatter go against me seemed particularly cruel. The day after Cyd Kubie walked I had been going over to see her; I wanted to ask her advice and appeal to her for help. But she had suddenly appeared on the front porch, sailed through the screen door, barely spoken to me but greeted Cora graciously. From that moment on she started to work, consulting Dan, contacting people, answering the phone. "'Healing Grace,'" she'd say. "May I help you?" She came to work every day and had ignored me up until now.

I cried: "How can you be part of all this when you know what it's doing to Newly—and to me—and to Kenny?" She was standing on the other side of the stove and I glared at her across the burners.

"It's been the making of Kenny," she said, and smirked, as though she'd won a point. "He obeys his father, does everything he should. I never saw such a change in a little boy."

I was silent. There had indeed been a change in Kenny. I did not care for it. He seemed tense and excited. He spent too much time with Cyd Kubie. The little blind boy no longer came.

"What Newly's doing is wrong. Surely you know that?"

"Wrong?" Her voice cracked. "How can you speak so wickedly? Yes—wicked!" She now was shouting at me. Cora in the next room would be listening avidly. "How dare you say it's wrong to make Cyd Kubie walk?"

"I'm afraid the cure won't last. Cyd may decide he just doesn't want to walk."

"That's a terrible thing to say about poor Cyd Kubie! What's got into you?" I saw her grip the big match box on the stove and I knew she would like to hurl it at me. Surprisingly, she wore no make-up. Without mascara her eyes had a naked stare. I hated having her so angry with me. We had been friends. Now she turned on me, quick as a snake. It was not only outrage for her son that I saw. I felt her lack of certainty; she had defended Newly too violently. She did not really believe in Newly's "powers." She was a realist. Never a woman to be taken in by anything she couldn't put a name to or her hand on. Even unbelieving, did she see fame for her son? And therefore quite naturally despise the wife who stood in his way?

"I don't want Newly shown up—" I began.

"Don't worry!" she broke in. "He won't be. His father had

much the same power. Not as great. He couldn't cure people. But he saw into the future." She was triumphant, tossing her head. "You ought to be ashamed of yourself not supporting your husband. What will people say? How will Newly look standing before crowds of people without his wife?" Her face flushed. The strange, naked eyes stayed on my face.

"If I mean that much to him he better not go!"

"That's the most selfish statement I ever heard!"

Now I leaned across the stove toward her. All the disgust I felt boiled over. "Can't you see how I hate all this—this fakery! Newlin Slatter can't cure people. There's no such thing. What he's doing is hypnotism, and that's deceiving people, and it's terrible! How can you be a party to such fakery—and encourage him? You shock me!" But she had already turned and walked out the kitchen door.

I spent most of my time in Flora's house. The days when she taught at Bryn Mawr she gave me the key. Occasionally Joyce stopped by. She regarded Newly's cures and "Healing Grace" as a kind of monstrous joke.

"If this Wilkes-Barre caper comes off, how do you fit in? Willing helper? Proud wife?"

"I can't go along with any of it." I was tired of always making the same reply.

"I read in the paper that Newly is planning a big meeting in Atlanta. If you're not careful you'll find yourself riding the bus to Georgia dressed in white."

In a way it was a relief to joke. Joyce never showed interest in relationships or my marriage or even Kenny. She knew that David had hit Cranby. "So stupid. David goes absolutely wild at times." It was one of the few personal remarks she ever made about him.

Joyce took the success of her book coolly. Or perhaps she had been confident all along. She appeared twice on the Martha Dean Show. Her picture and an article came out in *Time*. She now had a lecture agent. The publishers gave a large, dull party for her. Although she seemed unaffected, I had the feeling that if the publicity department slipped up she would bring them back into line. Underneath her placid exterior a little adding machine ticked away.

Mama wrote from the Adirondacks saying that she and Papa had been having a most interesting time with a man named Cranby. "He's talking to Papa about his new book on the Shawnees. Papa says he had no idea there was so much general interest in the subject. He takes quite an interest in you, Eva, and we joke about Newlin's 'Miracles.' Mr. Cranby has come twice to camp and is charming with the servants and has quite won Fanny's heart by bringing her chocolates."

I wrote Mama that Cranby was dangerous and simply pumping her. "He may seem shy," I said angrily, "but he was so persistent with me that David had to knock him down." Mama wrote back that David had coarsened with marriage and she would apologize for David's unseemly behavior that very afternoon when Mr. Cranby came for tea.

I gave up. By now Cranby had all the material he wanted. I couldn't figure what he was after. But I hated his raising poor Papa's hopes.

Even though I detached myself from "Healing Grace," I could see the entire organization building up. There were now fliers around; the phone rang constantly; Cora banged away at the typewriter. Mrs. Slatter talked on the phone. I overheard Dan Ruber talking to Newly about getting a publicity woman named Ida George over from New York. The meeting in St. Marks was scheduled for August 15th. Newly pretended not to notice the commercialism that now pervaded "Healing Grace."

I saw little of Newly. In the evening he usually was busy with his "patients." Kenny and I would eat alone in the kitchen, the living room now being an office. I had not spoken to Newly about this awful shift; my darling little couch and red chairs ranged against the wall. (I had covered the furniture with a sheet.) Somehow the deliberate changing of the house, our living place, put such a barrier between us I literally could not speak. When Mrs. Slatter had said Newly paid the rent, a gate banged shut. Newly was doing more than "experimenting," as he called it, with Cyd Kubie. He was setting himself up as a healer. He may even have felt he was called. And if so there would be no thought that he was sacrificing his marriage; he would feel I must join with him, even believing a new relationship would grow up around his "powers." That I denied this, refused to believe in him, he regarded as willful, nasty stubborness. Newly had never delved deeply into relationships; his gregariousness was unexamining; he embraced the world. Our differences had never bothered Newly as they bothered me. He had never fully realized the change in me, or showed particular interest. He knew little about my efforts to educate myself. His relationship with Flora was superficial; he enjoyed sparring with her. But he did not see her as my teacher, a person who had turned me in a new direction. He would not realize or care that she enlarged my technique on the violin, introducing me to chamber music. None of this Newly shared. But having embraced, and to some extent won, an intellectual life, I was even further removed from the emotion that motivated Newly's "power."

We still slept in the same bed, lying side by side, quite still. One night Newly stood at the foot of the bed in his pajamas and gave me a short lecture on Ghandi, who tested himself by sleeping alongside his young cousin and never touching her, announcing that he, Newly, should be doing the same thing, only that with me it was worse. And here he choked up and got red in the face and was unable to go on, but just stood there with his mouth open and a huge erection jutting from his pajamas. Then he dashed for the bathroom, hurled off his clothes and jumped into a cold shower. I must say I enjoyed thi꞊ Let him suffer. He was not the only one. But on the other hand, although I wanted badly to sleep with Newly, something strange was happening to my feeling about his body. In losing my respect, he also lost some attraction, although, to be honest, the latter feeling came and went.

I seemed so often to be raking through our relationship, looking for the traits I used to love in Newly, his humor and kindness. I kept thinking of our walks in Fairmount Park, trying to picture the snow outlining the great trees, the fanlight at Lemon Hill, the look of the dark gray Schuylkill, the fuzzy haze of a blizzard, Newly reading from the guide book. But this was hard to imagine in July.

Even with our differences, even with the change in me, I had thought our marriage worked wonderfully well. We'd had good sex. There was much we did not have in common, but we had the will to make our marriage work. I must admit that part of the reason for the success of our relationship was Newly's acceptance of my looks, that I was "cute as a button," and my smile "adorable."

It had been a long time since we had talked at all. Newly expected me to rejoice in his new discovery of his "powers." Would he soon ignore what he was doing to our marriage?

Perhaps I should have talked to Mrs. Framely, but I was unused to confiding in anyone. She seemed puzzled and hurt. She was a simple, devout woman. For her to watch a man, whom she knew and admired, claiming to be some kind of Messiah must offend her deeply. I explained to her that though I was unsympathetic to all this, Newly was definitely not identifying with faith and God. Mrs. Framely just looked sadly back at me, holding my hand and shaking her head. "I'm so sorry, Eva," she said. I nearly broke down. But I couldn't burden her with a problem that was so outlandish, that had a touch of craziness in it. I felt her affection but I had never really confided in her. Mr. Framely was rather cool. "Like a carnival sort of thing," he said. "That fellow Cranby has a lot to say, hasn't he?" Then, seeing my distress, he changed the subject and told me that David had made quite a name for himself around Lancaster and York. "Made a lot of friends in the banks up-country. Got interested in antiques—a new craze, he says. He bought a table the other day and a pine cupboard, the kind we used to have in the kitchen. A fellow named Dr. Barnes is up-country buying antiques. Got a collection of paintings, according to David." Mrs. Framely said she didn't think Joyce was much interested in antiques. Then we all smiled at each other and everything was easy again.

As time went on our sleeping arrangements became ever more difficult. Newly simply could not get into bed with me. Evidently the temptation was too great, and yet he wanted to "save" his powers and used Ghandi as a constant example. So he took to sleeping in the living room on the sofa. One night Kenny surprised him there. "What you doin', Pop?" The boy put on a desk light and stared at his father. I heard voices and ran down the stairs.

"Your father has a cold," I said, which was partially true.

"He doesn't look it. When I get a cold my eyes and nose run."

But Newly wasn't satisfied with not having the boy know the truth. "I am hoarding my powers, Kenny," he said, perfectly serious.

"But why can't you hoard them sleeping in bed with Mom?"

"I have to be alone," Newly said, managing to put some dignity into his position, although his hair stood on end and the bed clothes were falling on the floor. He was too long for the sofa and had to sleep in a half-sitting position.

"You sure don't look very comfortable," Kenny said, and headed back up the stairs.

One Sunday when Kenny was away on a picnic, I spoke to Newly. I could not hold in any longer. "All this is like a bad dream, Newly."

"Oh, no it's not, Eva! It's going to save us!" We were standing by the back door and per usual Newly was fixing the trash cans.

I said straight out: "What relation do you think I have to 'Healing Grace?' "

"If you'd join us—you'd be the star!"

"Oh, Newly...you can't honestly believe all this. You can't believe I could be part of it."

I expected him to stiffen and be angry. But I failed again to notice Newly's growing confidence. He had taken on additional stature. His stubborness had increased. As he stood beside the trash can he did not lack dignity and he certainly showed no doubt.

"When you see what can happen, Eva. I believe you will change."

"Newly," I said, and heard my voice break, "if you brought in loaves and fishes my attitude would not change. Why do you think it will?"

"But it must. It's our life. It's to be our life together."

"Did it ever occur to you I might be consulted?"

"How could I? Everything just happened."

"Because you wanted it to."

"Yes. I suppose so. But it's bigger than I am, Eva. You must see that."

"Well, no, I don't." How could I tell him again that I did not believe in him? I said: "You know how I feel. I also think this plan of yours can have the opposite effect and make people turn against you." Anger overcame caution, for he stood there smiling with his head raised high and a look of such condescension I could hardly bear it. "Suppose this poor girl you're dragging down from Wilkes-Barre simply does not get up. How can she? Don't you know what polio does to people?"

"It's not polio."

I stared at him. "It's not?"

"No. She was threatened with spinal meningitis when quite young. She has never been mentally alert. She lies in bed most of the time in the fetal position. She's a cousin of Dan's."

"Then it's fake!"

"Not at all." He regarded me coldly. "The doctors doubt she could walk if she wanted to."

"Oh, Newly—how did you get mixed up in this? Some poor, retarded girl...and the build up..." I was crying now, turning my face away. He made no move toward me, which was so strange and frightening. He always comforted me.

He said in a peculiar resonant voice I had only heard once before: "Our marriage is going to be a better marriage than you ever dreamed. The ties that bind us will be stronger. We may even have another child!" He had lately taken to wearing heavily rimmed glasses. These he removed and lifted his face. Could this be the same man who exuberantly threw his arms around me by the Schuylkill River? Who so tenderly broke through my maidenhead on Mama's old sofa? Who had shown me nothing but kindness and understanding? I wanted our old life back. I could have been content with it forever. Perhaps the poor girl from Wilkes-Barre would be a failure and we'd go back to normal. But why should we? I had thought the commercialism would sicken Newly, but he looked aside. Whatever had happened to Newly took a deep hold. Newly might fail—only to believe that *next time*...would he draw crowds like Billy Sunday? I was in the presence of someone frighteningly strange. Heavy-faced, rubbery cheeks, merry smile, thinning hair...I did not know him at all! There should be a clue. All I had was his stubbornness. Yet someplace in his character lurked this—this *vanity.* I could think of no other word.

"Newly," I said, drying my eyes with the back of my hand, "you are wholly committed to a way of life in which I can have no part. We no longer sleep together. Have you considered what that means to me?"

"Indeed I have, Eva. But you know it is only temporary."

"That's not the point. I can have nothing to do with this—this 'Healing.' We'll be separated, because you are wholly involved. Do you want that, Newly?"

"Don't say such a thing, Eva! Separation is impossible. I must have you with me. I know you'll come. 'Healing Grace' has been asked to Houston, Texas, and to Atlanta, Georgia."

I could not speak. It was hot under the shed roof. The cicadas burred. From Texas to where? India and Ghandi?

I put my hands together in a prayerful gesture. "Newly, I ask you to give up this meeting at St. Mark's. I want you to tell your mother to go home and send Cora away. Get rid of the files and desks. This whole venture must end. It's disastrous."

"You can't ask me, Eva." He no longer looked confident. He was glaring at me, deeply offended. Yet I thought some part of him pled with me.

"I do ask it," I said. And I stood straight and pushed my hands down at my sides as I had done once before in discipline.

22 "There is a Power—not God—but close and available to everyone. It is a kind of trust in ourselves. Each of us can feel it. We will feel the Power if we have the Trust. It's an emptying of self. It's the will to receive..."

Newly was speaking over the radio. I listened in despair and awful fascination. Then shut if off and walked upstairs to Kenny's room. It was late, the boy slept. I had formed the habit of sitting in his room on nights when Newly was out. There was comfort in being near the child. For by now the insecurity and change, the constant movement of the new life had fully enveloped me. I had pled with Newly, told him he must stop, made a kind of ultimatum. It affected him not at all. He did not believe me. He kept right on, fed constantly by the people around him: Ida George, brought over from New York, squat, orange-haired, beady-eyed.

Friday morning I had come into the house to find Newly addressing the "staff." "You'll want to hear this, Eva," he said, quite casually as I entered. "Today I resigned my position at the Guaranty. When I left, Mr. Franklin, the President, shook my hand."

I stood in the doorway staring at him. He could make this announcement in an offhand manner? He had not considered the shock to me; the ignominy of being told such a decision in front of these other women. "But what about your salary?" I blurted out.

Cora Ruber spoke up: "Contributions are coming into the office every day, Eva. Surely you are aware of that."

Mrs. Slatter weighed in. "A wise decision, Newlin. One you will not regret."

I turned and left the room.

Newly without a job? Money from strangers? What sort of a life were we to lead? The Guaranty was Newly's solid grip on real life. Newly working in a bank made him no different than other husbands. Now he declared himself a full-time Healer.

I went straight to Flora.

"Newly has given up his job at the Guaranty." I stood. She rose.

"When?"

"Today. Just now. He just told me."

Silence. Flora shoved her hands into those ridiculous pockets. She said slowly, "He didn't talk to you about giving up his job?"

"No. Not a word."

Silence. Flora said slowly, "Eva, you don't think he's psychotic, do you?"

I had asked myself the same question. I said, "No, no I don't. He really seems perfectly normal—except for this feeling he has some exceptional power."

Flora turned toward the fireplace. "I think he's losing some perspective, Eva. Giving up his job without talking to you...all this adulation must affect him."

"What can I do?"

"You're planning to wait it out, aren't you?"

Hate rose like bile in my throat—I was *The Healer's wife*. How much self-control could I count on? Able to ignore the "throne" in the cellar, the new black Amish-type robe Newly wore, the memento-seekers, my mother-in-law, the effect on Kenny, the worst of all. A husband spouting worn out phrases over the radio. A husband propped most nights on a couch downstairs saving his potency?

I could not answer. Flora waited, then said: "Newlin Slatter is God's most gullible man. He's not an examiner or questioner. I tried to interest him in some of the experiments that were carried out in the eighteenth and late nineteenth century. Mesmerism was in great vogue then. In fact a doctor whose name I've forgotten was able actually to perform operations on the Indians of Bengali, cut right into them while they were in a trance. Then I mentioned to Newlin the very interesting experiments being carried out by Dr. Joseph Banks Rhine of Duke University to confirm or debunk the legitimacy of parapsychology. Dr. Rhine has his subjects try to use supposed paranormal powers to "see" the designs on special cards concealed from them. The experiments being carried out are new and exciting. I'm sure Dr. Rhine would be interested in Newlin's ability to change temperatures. I urged Newlin to get in touch with Duke University, but he told me flat out that he wasn't interested. He felt, he said, that his power had been bestowed upon him to help people. He said he did not have the time or the inclination to—as he said—mess around with experiments in a laboratory, or be a guinea pig."

"You never told me about this, Flora."

"I knew it wouldn't do any good. You're understandably emotionally involved, with too much at stake. Have you ever thought of Mr. Framely? Newly would listen to Mr. Framely."

"Listen about what?"

"Being told he's jeopardizing his family life. Being asked how much he expects of you. And just exactly what *is* this organization 'Healing Grace'? Newly needs someone sensible and knowledgeable like Mr. Framely to question him and try and make him see where he's going, and at what price. And that if Newly wants an outlet for his "powers," as he calls them, at least he should be willing to experiment on a scientific level."

"Oh, Flora, he's too involved!" I heard my voice wail. "I've pled with him. I made an ultimatum that he must give up St. Marks,'

'Healing Grace,' all of it. His answer was to resign from the bank."

Flora came right over and faced me. I could see where perspiration gathered on her forehead. She was more distraught than I ever remembered.

"Eva, I beg you to talk to Mr. Framely. I think it's essential he see Newly before this St. Mark's business. Someone has got to show Newly that other people's lives are at stake here. What does he expect from you? What is to happen to Kenny? Try, Eva." Her flinty eyes stayed right on my face. "Don't you know you can always get help if you cry 'help' loud enough? Why do you hesitate?"

"I'll call him from here," I said.

The offices of Framely & Brink occupied a whole floor and were more elaborate than I'd expected. The receptionist sat at a switchboard. A pink African violet bloomed beside her. Was she the woman I had talked to seven years ago trying to reach David?

Mr. Framely came toward me, hands outstretched. "Come in! Come in!"

He took me into his office, closed the door. A large room. The windows looked out on City Hall. "Eva, you want to talk about Newlin, don't you? Mrs. Framely and I have been very puzzled."

I explained about the power Newly felt, about his sense of dedication. I told Mr. Framely quite steadily about my pleas to Newly and what I felt this constant excitement was doing to Kenny. Then I told him that Newly had given up his job.

This shook him. He kept biting at his moustache and frowning. "I don't like that, Eva. Not a bit."

"That's one reason why I came to you, Mr. Framely. I wondered if you'd talk to Newly?"

"Talk to him?" Mr. Framely's dark, very round eyes opened wide. He gave a strange grimace and his moustache stuck out. "Well, of course I *could*. But I don't know's I'd do much good."

"He respects you enormously."

"I'd have to think over what to say."

I seemed to be dragging Mr. Framely up hill. I had imagined he would plunge in with suggestions, understand immediately what his function was. "There's also this organization called 'Healing Grace—'"

"I know about that," Mr. Framely said quickly. "We got an appeal in the mail. Mrs. Framely tried to reach you by phone but she kept getting the 'Healing Grace' people."

"I'm over at Flora Cruickshank's most of the time."

Mr. Framely was silent. Then leaning across his desk he said, "Eva, I'd like to get David in on this. He's in the office today and although he had an unfortunate encounter with that reporter Cranby, still I think his advice right now would be valuable."

David. Of course. It was Friday. David would make an entirely different situation. I could not very well refuse. "Whatever you say, Mr. Framely." He appeared quite relieved, spoke to the operator and in a few moments David was in the room. To my surprise he was in shirt sleeves. Mr. Framely had on a light gray suit. An electric fan in the corner threw hot air around. David and I shook hands, our usual greeting.

"Eva's been telling me about Newlin," Mr. Framely said.

"He's certainly in the news," David said seriously. He looked well, healthy, the out-of-doors type. He was also big, just as I remembered him in my kitchen that day he hit Cranby. He certainly was relaxed with Mr. Framely, sitting with an ankle crossed over his knee. "A friend of mine on *The Saturday Evening Post* says that if Newly makes this Wilkes-Barre girl walk he'll be on the cover of *Time*, and the *Post* will do an article on him."

"He's given up his job at the Guaranty," I said.

David looked at me sharply. "He has? Why would he do that?"

How I hated to say it, especially to David. Mr. Framely saved me, breaking in. "He's giving full time to this healing thing. 'Healing Grace,' it's called."

We were all silent. Finally I said: "I think if Mr. Framely talked to Newlin he might make him see that he was going too far. Talk to him objectively. Or maybe look into the 'Healing Grace' organization. I didn't know they were appealing for funds." It was all shameful, outrageous. And outrageous that I should be sitting here taking up these two men's time because of my husband.

David put his foot down, straightening in his chair. "I think this thing has gone too far. You won't get any place talking to Newlin. Isn't that your feeling, Mr. Framely?"

"Well, yes, it is. I wouldn't know what to say, but I don't want to let Eva down, either." He looked seriously over at me.

I said, "Flora Cruickshank tried to persuade Newly to join experiments in parapsychology that are going on at Duke University. This would have been wonderful if Newly had cooperated. He'd be on a different level."

"Got no place?" David asked.

"Newlin wouldn't consider it."

"I don't think he'll listen to talk," Mr. Framely said, "but I'll see him if that's what Eva wants."

David said, "Those Duke experiments were the best idea. Get him away from all this excitement and all those hangers-on. And 'Healing Grace.' What a God-awful name!" Then as though he realized my intense discomfort and embarrassment, he looked over at me, his eyes suddenly sad. "This is hard on you, Eva. And—uh—Kenny."

"Yes. You told me I better think what to do. But nothing I do has any effect."

Mr. Framely suddenly spoke out. "I've got an idea. I think it's good. I think it might work. It came to me when David said something about getting Newly away from all this excitement." Mr. Framely put both arms on the desk. He seemed tense, biting his moustache, waiting for the right words. "My brother Jim is head of the Allegheny Trust in Pittsburgh. I was talking to him yesterday. They're having one of their shakedown periods, switching people around in jobs. He was saying he couldn't find just the right man to head their trust department. Now why couldn't that person be Newly?

I gaped at him. David banged his fist on his knee and said: "You've got it! That's just the ticket."

"But do you think he'd do it?" I hated to say it, they were so enthusiastic.

"Would you? Would you be willing to leave India Street, The Mount?"

"Of course, any time," I said.

David stood up. "The whole thing fits. Newly's got real ability. I've heard the men in his department talk about him. He'd be able to handle the Trust Department."

"He's good with people," Mr. Framely said. By now his face was quite red and he kept biting his moustache.

"The trick will be to get him out of town before the meeting at St. Mark's."

"That's next Saturday."

David addressed Mr. Framely: "Do you think your brother would see Newly in Pittsburgh on Monday; then if all goes well he could tell Newlin he's got to start work on Wednesday. No sense going home. Eva can take out his clothes and they can start looking for a house."

Mr. Framely said, "Jim owes me a favor. I gave his brother-in-law a job in our bond department and the fellow is only good for opening mail." He laughed. "I'll tell Jim the newspapers have been making too much of Newlin as a healer. I'll phone Jim this afternoon. Then I'll get hold of Newly and say I want to see him tomorrow morning. It's Saturday. I don't know whether you ought to be there or not, Eva."

"I think not," David said.

"She might come in after I've had a chance to explain the proposition; let him get used to it. I don't think he's going to eat this right up."

I sat in a daze. I couldn't speak. I kept smiling at Mr. Framely and finally said, "Thank you."

"Don't count those chickens too soon, Eva," Mr. Framely said as he opened the door.

In the hall David's expression was suddenly serious; his wide forehead creased in a frown. "We aren't there, yet, Eva. I don't think you can relax until you're on the train bound for Pittsburgh."

"But Newly can't refuse a really top-notch job, David! He's always cared about his work, and been proud, too."

"This healer racket is heady."

"It's games."

"A lot of people stand to gain through Newly. They'll want him to keep on."

It did not seem strange to be having this conversation with David, and in front of the receptionist, or to be relying on David.

Some of the relief I had felt in Mr. Framely's office receded. David must have seen this in my face.

"Don't misunderstand me, Eva. I think you've got a good chance."

We shook hands. I did not know what to say. I intended to rely on Mr. Framely. Once Newly heard the offer of such a big job he would realize he couldn't waste time fooling around with some poor soul from Wilkes-Barre.

As I walked through the hot streets to Broad Street Station, I smiled and smiled.

When I arrived home I walked into our one-time living room. Dan Ruber and Ida George were waiting for me. Dan held out what looked like an invitation, very fancy stationery. It was an invitation to the White House. For lunch. President Hoover wanted to meet Newly.

This was just the sort of thing Mr. Framely and David were warning me about. The invitation to the White House was for next Wednesday, the day Newly was supposedly seeing Mr. Jim Framely at the Allegheny Trust Co. in Pittsburgh.

I handed the invitation back to Dan without saying anything and left the room. Did being recognized by the President of the United States acknowledge your claims as a healer, even obligate you for the future? Were there many who would turn down an invitation to the White House?

I went to Flora. I told her about Mr. Framely's plan. She banged her hat on her knee and cried "Bully! That's bully!" Then I told her about the invitation. She sat down quickly on the couch, put her head back. "Oh, damn!"

"Yes." I leaned against the mantle. But Mr. Framely was a powerful, persuasive man. He'd just have to try harder.

"After all, Flora, it's only an invitation."

"And recognition."

"I'd thought of that."

"It will make him all the more sure he's on the right path."

"But when you think how chancey the whole thing is, Flora! Whereas this job ... why it's our whole future."

"You're right, of course. But Newly—if you'll excuse me—is being such a fool."

I still felt sure. Here was a job he'd always wanted. He might have been terribly foolish, but when it came to plain reality then the common sense I had often seen in him would come forward.

Somewhat to my dismay Newly took the invitation to the White House rather calmly. As his due? I couldn't tell. I had not realized how far he'd turned until he said to me, "I don't suppose you'll want to go."

"No. I don't think so." I was not all that eager to shake President Hoover's hand, but I certainly did not want to shake it as the wife who believed in her husband's mystical power.

We were in the kitchen eating supper. Kenny jumped up from the table, his dark face twisted with excitement. He clung to his father's arm. "May I go then, Pop? May I?"

Newly, whose manner had suddenly become almost regal, said,

"I don't see why not, son. We'll have to write, or perhaps telephone and say you are taking your mother's place." There was reproof in his tone.

That Friday, about two in the morning, I went downstairs. Newly was sleeping hunched up on the couch. I touched him on the shoulder. He woke, sat up. "What is it?" Light from the street shone on the foot of the couch.

"I have something I want to ask you."

"It's awfully late, isn't it?" He was only half awake. I had counted on that. I stood near the couch.

"Do you love me, Newly?" He scrambled forward, reaching out his arms for me.

"Eva, you know I love you."

"How can you? How can you have both?"

"But of course I can!" He was gripping me against him.

"I don't see how."

"But we'll always be together, Eva. Don't you know that?"

"No."

His arms dropped. "How can you say no?"

"We never sleep together—"

"Eva, that's only temporary."

"Why? There'll be other times."

He was silent.

"Won't there?"

He said nothing.

"Have you no tenderness for me that you can do this to me?"

"I love you with all my heart."

"No. You have this other," I said. "You are crueler to me than I would have thought anyone could ever be."

"Eva!"

"It's true. I believe it. *I live it*."

"Oh, my God..."

"What did you think would happen? Have you consulted me, or

really considered me?"

"I—I thought you'd be proud."

"But I told you I did not believe in what you were doing. That it was wrong. I pled with you."

"I thought you'd change. I was sure of it." He loosened his hold on me.

I said: "You have done nothing to make a change. You have gone away from me. Every day further away. You are wrapped in yourself—like a cocoon, layers and layers of *you*. ... Now you have even given up your job."

I doubt he heard, for he said, "Wait 'til this St. Mark's meeting is over. Then we can solve everything."

"You think you can be two people?"

"No," he said quite calmly. "I feel no split."

We were back in the same place. I had not moved him an inch. Yes, he cared for me; he cared what happened to me. But the fact that he was making me desperately unhappy, desperately concerned for our marriage—he could not recognize. He rationalized; he would deal with me later. He seemed so positive I could not imagine the Allegheny bank offer moving him. Nor that Mr. Framely himself could affect what now seemed to be Newly's perfect faith in what he was doing and would do in the future.

I think he was telling himself—because he must have been aware of my attitude—that after St. Mark's he would go on to Atlanta or Houston, believing that with exercise his powers would grow. He knew he could not ask me to go along. But then, his mother would do, and Dan Ruber. When it was all over Kenny and I would be here to come back to.

In the dark I could just make Newly out, propped on one elbow. He had the side window open, and the smell of fresh damp earth blew into the room.

"I can't live this way, Newly."

"Yes, you can. I know you can!" He was now off the couch.

Suddenly I wanted him so badly, so engrossingly, I ripped off my nightgown and went to him, pressed myself against him, untying his pajamas, forcing them down. And then we were on the floor, and there was nothing else that mattered.

## 23

"It's certainly changed." Mr. Framely walked slowly into the living room. He shook hands with Newly. Fortunately Newly was not in the Amish gown, but wore his old work pants and shirt. He seemed a little uneasy with Mr. Framely, not knowing why he had come. There were only office chairs to sit on. (Every morning Newly put a sheet over the red couch and pushed it back against the wall.)

"We're moving into larger offices," Newly said. "Everything happened very suddenly and we're not squared away." He smiled broadly in a pleased manner.

Mr. Framely appeared momentarily lost, holding onto his straw hat and coming forward in slow steps. I had phoned him from Flora's, telling him about the White House invitation. Perhaps this had rattled him.

I now excused myself. I was taking Kenny to a friend's house.

"But you don't have to go now, Eva. It's early."

I explained that Kenny must change his clothes. I could see Newly felt something odd was happening.

As I went upstairs I heard Mr. Framely say forcefully and in the friendliest voice, "Newlin, I've got some *wonderful* news for you!"

I closed Kenny's door. Kenny's complicated system of tracks made moving around difficult, but he finally managed a clean suit and submitted to having his hair brushed. He kept wanting to go downstairs and see Mr. Framely, but I told him his father and Mr.

Framely were discussing business and could not be disturbed, and that he must not ask Mr. Framely for money, anyway. Kenny looked at me, and then burst out laughing. His laugh was so merry and he looked so spruce in his clean shirt, and I felt such a relief from the strain of the past hours, that I laughed with him.

"Can I wear my checked shirt to the White House, Mom? Can I?" I said yes and gave him a hug, which he permitted. We went quietly down the stairs and out to the car. I dropped Kenny off and drove back to the house. A full half hour had gone by. I must now find out what had happened. My feelings were confused. After last night I was both fulfilled, certainly softened, but also shut off, denied. Because after Newly and I had sex, he went back to his sofa. I remember how slowly I put on my nightgown. Seeing him sit down on the sofa struck me so sharply. I had thought he would come upstairs to our bed. My emotions had been so full, my orgasm so deep, I was bound to him. I could summon up no other feeling. In the dark I groped my way by the desk and chair. I could not speak. I slowly walked upstairs. I did not get inside the covers of the bed. I lay outside as though I were not in bed at all.

If he could do this to me then his feeling for me had changed. I could not look away from that. There was a quality in his treatment that went deeper than denial. True, I had seduced him and I probably had that in mind from the beginning. Now I was to be shown that sex was at his pleasure, when he was "ready" and his "powers" were not jeopardized. He knew I would not soon come down to him again if I must go back alone. There had been something stubborn and stolid in his remaining on the couch, hunched over. The hopes I had, my vision of the Pittsburgh house (a screened porch and short, concrete driveway) shriveled and blew away, gone in that moment when I pulled on my nightgown in the dark living room when I should have been naked and held close to him.

Mr. Framely was sitting at one desk, Newly at another. They were not speaking and looked up as I came in. The forceful positive-ness of Mr. Framely seemed oddly altered. He not only looked tired but confused. Newly, on the other hand, seemed jubilant. "Come in, Eva! Something so very nice has happened." I had not expected this approach and glanced at Mr. Framely who continued to stare at the floor. "The Allegheny Trust has asked me to head up their Trust Department. I know I have our good friend Mr. Framely to thank for this fine offer." His false, hearty manner was nauseating. Mr. Framely, elbows on knees, continued to stare at the floor. Never a large man, he now seemed even smaller; all his bounce gone.

"I haven't been able to persuade him, Eva," he said.

I turned to Newly. His confident flamboyant manner was infuriating. "What are you thinking of, Newly!" I cried. "It's the position you've waited for! Don't tell me you're not going to take it!"

His tone when he answered was conversational. He crossed his legs. He seemed completely outside the reach of Mr. Framely's dismay and my anger.

"Well, that's true," he said quite reasonably. "I liked my work at the Guaranty and this could be even more interesting." There was a nasty chattiness about his speech that froze me.

I said, "How many offers are you going to get like this, Newly? Who knows what it might lead to. Is there a man in your department at the Guaranty who wouldn't jump at the chance?"

Newly looked over at Mr. Framely, smiled. Had he heard me?

I went on in a louder voice: "Can't you imagine what this would mean to Kenny and me? We could go back to our old life, live normally. We can't go on living the way things are now. Constant excitement. Don't you realize Kenny will have to be sent away to school? Is that what you want?"

Newly raised his eyebrows and said in a detached voice, "There's no cause for any of this."

"You mean if I will be a healer's wife, be with you when you try your powers?"

"That's your place."

"And Kenny?"

"He can stay with the Rubers or Mother."

"Oh, Newly…" A despairing wail. "None of this would work. I've told you over and over how I feel about what you're doing. I said it again last night."

Newly jumped to his feet, his face fiery red. He came close to me, speaking in a kind of loud whisper he'd taken up lately: "But your actions bely your words." He said this in a most disagreeable manner, poking his red face close to mine.

I wrenched away toward Mr. Framely. How could Newly use our sex as an argument? I felt so torn and desolate, as though some inner part of me tumbled away. Newly believed that our sex last night meant that I had capitulated. Or maybe he felt that my complete involvement could only mean that I eventually would. So maybe he had sat on the couch and let me go upstairs to show me his command. And instead I knew that I could never go to him again.

Newlin now leaned on one of the files. "I don't see how you can forget my invitation to the White House and what this recognition means."

Perhaps it had indeed been President Hoover who changed Newly. The queer whisper, the flaring temper, an enormous sense of excitement blew from him. I even thought he had grown larger, but it may only have been the commanding way he stood. He turned.

"I'll write your brother, Mr. Framely, and thank him myself."

Mr. Framely picked up his hat. "I'm sorry Eva. He had his mind made up from the first."

"It was so good of you." I bent and kissed his cheek.

"Not at all. I've just got time to catch the train."

I went no further than the door. He and I had nothing to say that would make either of us feel any better.

As I turned from the door Newly said, "So you two have been plotting."

"For your own good," I said.

He folded his thick arms across his chest. I had always thought his brown eyes very shiny, laughing, merry. Now they seemed

lighted with some kind of wildness. Refusing Mr. Framely's offer
had exalted Newly. The sacrifice: a declaration of belief. He also felt
he had shown me my place. His voice bounded across the room.
"Save our marriage? 'Healing Grace' will do that." I turned away not
wanting to see or hear him and did not know he had left the room
until the kitchen screen slammed.

Although last night I had had a premonition that I would never
see Pittsburgh, the reality and Newly's bloated ego were worse than
I could have imagined. Had I thought to soften him last night? We
had moved even further apart. Impossible any longer to think about
Mr. Framely, or David, or The Allegheny Trust Company. I would
go upstairs, get out my fiddle and practice the last movement of
Beethoven's Opus 95. Flora's quartet was playing it Thursday. Practicing would take all my concentration.

Strange people can rescue you, if you're ready. Maybe Mr.
Framely sent Joyce, but anyway around noon that day she appeared
at the door. "I've got a picnic in the car," she called. "Come on, Eva!
You always loved picnics." Maybe my nature is mercurial, but I
wanted to get out of the house and away. Beethoven had helped.
Without so much as combing my hair, I walked through the door
and off.

A man stood alongside Joyce's car; Eric Hartly, editor-in-chief
at Ross and Exeter, Joyce's publishers. He was tall, bushy-haired, a
man about my age with a long intelligent face, very elegant looking.
He held out his hand, said he had wanted to meet me and that Joyce
had spoken so often of my work on her book. "She calls you 'Old
Poison,' so you must have done a good job." He laughed and I found
myself laughing with him.

We went to a farm of Mr. Framely's beyond Bryn Mawr. There
was a natural pond, a stream, and water spilling over a small dam.
We sat on the bank under willows. It was all like a miracle. Joyce had
brought cucumber sandwiches and thin ham, pears for dessert, iced
coffee. By agreement, so I imagined, Newly was never mentioned.
Joyce and Eric talked about a booksellers' meeting in Richmond

where Joyce was to speak. Eric talked about Joyce's book, mentioning Queen Elizabeth and the scene of her dying.

"The best scene in the book," he said. He leaned against a tree, sandwich in hand. The sun shining through the tiny willow leaves made speckles on his long face. He was the first editor I had ever met, and like Flora he seemed to come from another world, peopled by writers. He was intelligent and quick, listening carefully.

"Would you consider doing freelance work?" he asked.

"I don't know what you mean," I said.

"We sometimes need work done on a manuscript outside the house, rewriting, tidying up. We might have a book for you."

This was work Flora had suggested. I took a swallow of coffee. "All right," I said. Something solid among all the floating debris. Grab at it.

"Can you learn copy-editing?" He ate the last of his sandwich.

Flora knew how to copy-edit. She would teach me. "Yes," I said.

"Good."

Joyce said, "I suppose now you'll be too busy to work on my new book."

I laughed. I felt euphoric. "Well, hardly," I said. She had undone her hair, wound it into a thick yellow plait. On our picnics in the Adirondacks I used to scan her face, noting the clarity of her skin, the blush of color. She was still beautiful, with her great eyes, the lovely molded nose, a certain stillness of expression and a little sullenness around her mouth. In the Adirondacks I had shrivelled under her beauty, poor thin mousey child. To some measure I must have grown into my face. (Eric Hartly paid my looks no heed.) Whatever my appearance, it had nothing to do with Joyce's, I thought. Not that I had conquered envy, but I could live with it.

A loud splash. Eric Hartly, clad only in his underpants, was swimming across the pond while Joyce stood on the bank laughing. I jumped to my feet, parting the willow fronds to see him. The churned water caught the sun in a dazzle. Yellow leaves swept against the bank, rising in a small wave. In the midst of being distraught and wretched, how extraordinary that there could be this surcease and uprushing happiness.

Joyce drove Eric to North Philadelphia station where he could catch a train for New York. "You'll be hearing from me," he said. "Good." I did not quite know how to answer, not wanting to seem over-eager, but wanting him to know my interest.

Joyce insisted on driving me home. It wasn't until we were riding along Wissahickon Avenue that she spoke of Newly. "So you're not going to the White House. Isn't Newly wild?"

"I don't think he cares. He's taking Kenny."

"When is it?"

"Next Wednesday."

"That soon?"

"Yes. The meeting at St. Mark's is on Saturday."

"What about the meeting. Will you go?"

"I don't want Kenny to be there without me. I don't want him to go at all."

"Pop told me about Newly's turning down the Allegheny offer. You'd like living in Pittsburgh."

"I'd like living anywhere, just so the place didn't have 'Healing Grace.'"

Joyce said, "I don't see how Newly could turn the job down."

"He had no trouble at all."

"He's really more involved than you thought, isn't he?"

"Yes, in a way. It's as though every time I come up against Newly the healer I get a fresh shock. After all, how can I accept what's happened, or believe it? And now some poor, retarded girl is being hauled into St. Mark's..." I was back in it all again. I said slowly, "I kept hoping he'd change. But now I know he won't. Kenny will have to be sent away to school." Joyce did not speak. Hot air blew in the car window.

Joyce said, as though curious rather than concerned, "But what kind of life will you have, Eva? He's supposed to be going all around the country. Will you go with him as the healer's wife?"

Maybe it was her lack of personal involvement that made me detached, too. "No, I couldn't do that."

Again, quite impersonally, she asked, "Won't you leave him?"

A shocking, far too intimate question. I'd been evading it since Cyd Kubie walked. The same way I had never allowed myself to realize how many times I had pled with Newly, or said he must stop, and as a final gesture, slept with him. It had added up to being told 'Healing Grace' would save my marriage...

I could not, would never, leave Kenny. He was already fearful, insecure. He had cried because he felt I did not believe in his father. He must be given the reassurance of a family. He must know that although his father might go off on some evangelist— "rally" (the only word I could think of), he would come back to the India Street house and we would be together. (At that point I could not envision the Billy Sunday crowds or Dan Ruber riding around in a white Cadillac.) No matter how fervent Newly became I believed he would still be objective about the boy. Wanting Kenny at St. Mark's was all part of the local scene, but he would not subject him to a tent in Atlanta. And wasn't there always the possibility that Newly's present excitement might wane? ("Maybe he'll fumble a few," David had said.)

I turned to Joyce and with all the assurance that I was able to muster said, "No, I shall not leave Newly, Joyce."

She did not say anything, did not look at me, just kept driving. Now we were on McCallum Street approaching Mount Pleasant. Fixed to the poles along the street were posters: "Healing Grace" and a picture of Newly.

The visit to the White House received full coverage, certainly in Philadelphia, where pictures of Newly holding Kenny's hand as he walked up the steps were a favorite. The radio carried Kenny's speech: "It's mighty nice of you to ask my Dad and me to your house for lunch, Mr. President."

Kenny had managed to bring back six matchboxes, with the White House name in gold. He seemed to have very little feeling about the trip, or maybe he was disappointed. Mrs. Hoover was a lovely lady, and asked him if he didn't want to go to the toilet, which he did. President Hoover had not said much and wiped his mouth a lot. "He told Pop one of the secretaries had warts. Pop was pretty upset by this and said right out that he wasn't at all sure he could do anything for her. Pop explained that his powers came in waves and that right now he was in a kind of ebb. It was pretty embarrassing, our eating their lunch and all. But nothing would do President Hoover but Pop try. So I went down with one of the guards to look at the gymnasium. It had everything. A rowing machine and rings that the guard let down so I could do some of my stuff. He was pretty impressed and said that President Hoover wouldn't dare stand on his head the way I did. So then I climbed the bars while the guard did some rowing.

"Then we went back upstairs. Pop was apologizing to the President, saying he was afraid he had not done the secretary any good. Pop was red in the face. But President Hoover just shook his hand and then hurried off someplace. Mrs. Hoover came to the door. We got into this classy limousine with tassles and lace covers and drove to the station. On the way home Pop said he never would have gone if he'd known about the secretary's warts. But I had a good time."

Cyd Kubie turned out to be a reluctant walker. In spite of our emotional scene on the roof when I had thrown my arms around his legs, he did not care for his cure. "No Cure For Kubie." The newspapers quoted him. Cyd occasionally sank back into his wheelchair.

When I spoke to Newly about Kenny, saying I wanted him kept away from whatever proceedings were going to take place about Cyd Kubie, Newly interrupted.

"Proceedings? What proceedings?"

"I just want Kenny out of the excitement. I think he sees too much of Cyd Kubie."

"Keep him home then."

"He says he's seeing Cyd for you. He says he's helping with the cure."

"And that, of course, offends you."

"I think Kenny is unnaturally excited. He is hard to manage."

"You've never been able to manage him."

We were doing the dishes and I simply walked out of the kitchen, leaving the dishes in the dirty water, where I found them the next morning. Newly had walked out, too.

24 Now a strange lull took place, action suspended. Only three days remained until the meeting at St. Mark's. Ida George left for New York, promising to be back. Mrs. Slatter went home. Not many calls came over the phone. Cora Ruber answered in the morning, and in the afternoon I let it ring. The bus no longer stopped by; the curious people who once stood in our yard had disappeared.

Dr. Plummer, the rector from St. Mark's, was in and out of the house at all hours. The church was receiving very strange questions concerning the meeting on August 15th. Dr. Plummer regretted having agreed to the meeting now that he realized Newly's "healing" was not God-sent.

During the lull Dan told me he was "softening up" Mrs. Alfred Berkley with an eye to her husband, crippled from a broken hip. Mrs. Berkley liked to do her own marketing, Dan said, with Philo, the chauffeur-butler, carrying the packages. She always wore a large-brimmed hat and white gloves. Dan made it a point to be in Ziegler's

Market and would politely give way over a box of strawberries or a spear of asparagus. Mrs. Berkley, being a sociable soul, although a great snob, entered into conversation with Dan, which he carefully opened by speaking of his friend Newlin Slatter and his remarkable cures. Even when Mrs. Berkley referred to Cyd Kubie's relapse, Dan hinted a temporary set-back. "I'm not betting on the wheelchair!" Dan said, with his easy laugh.

I was therefore not as surprised as I might have been when Philo rang our doorbell on Thursday afternoon and said Mr. Berkley would like to see Newly. I said he was out but would be back later. "It'd be a favor if you come speak to Mr. Berkley, Miss Eva. He sitting in the car, mighty impatient." Philo overdid the black-retainer's act. He reminded me of Robert only not as tall. I followed him out to the car.

Mr. Berkley sat in his big, gray Cadillac, canes beside him. I stepped down from the pavement to the car window.

"Nice to see you, my dear." He leaned forward, removing his Panama. "This blasted hip makes getting out of a car difficult. You'll have to forgive me." He was a short stout man with a chubby reddish face, a tan mustache and a petulant manner. His full lips made his smile seem to stretch forever. "I saw your grandmother the other night, looking remarkably fit."

I smiled, not correcting him. Mama and Papa were unexpectedly in Philadelphia. The dining room roof at camp had suddenly collapsed. Mama couldn't stand the workmen's constant hammering, so they were back in town just when it would have been most convenient to have them safely isolated in the woods. I wondered if Cranby continued his calls, but did not ask.

"My wife's been telling me about your husband." Mr. Berkley scrabbled forward on the seat. "I understand he's doing some pretty fancy experimenting."

Newly and I might be painfully separated because of his "powers," but I was not going to stand by and have him made a fool of.

"No, I don't think so, Mr. Berkley. Newly was not experimenting at Cyd Kubie's expense. He is completely serious. He wants to help people. You may doubt what he is attempting but you have to accept his intention." I sounded like Ida George. I had never stood up for Newly in this fashion. Mr. Berkley's snide attitude was intolerable. I went on hotly: "My husband feels he has been given the power to make people believe they are cured."

"You don't say." His little eyes darted about.

"My experience with Newlin's so-called power was when he took my hands on a very cold day and told me I was getting warm. And my whole body glowed with heat."

"Did he, by George!" Mr. Berkley's face became scarlet.

Philo broke in. "That's what I told you, Mr. Berkley. You goin to get cured."

I stood beside the huge car and thought how I *hated* it all. Putting distance between us, I stepped onto the pavement. Mr. Berkley managed to stick his head out of the window. "Tell your husband I'll be over tonight," he called.

"I don't think he's seeing people, Mr. Berkley."

"He'll see me." Mr. Berkley sat back, put on his Panama. An autocrat. Used to getting his own way. Around his famous trophy room hung heads of extinct animals he had shot. He and Mrs. Berkley ran a "home" for unwed mothers, dubbed "Waywards." The "Wayward" roof was reputed to leak; few toilets worked and there was no fire escape.

Philo stepped onto the pavement beside me, said softly, "That Mr. Ruber is counting on making a pile of money out of your husband. He'll charge Mr. Berkley plenty."

I faced him directly. "My husband does not charge the people he sees, Philo!"

"You don't know Mr. Ruber stands out on the street?"

"That's not so!" I stared into his black face. Without another word he turned to the car. In a moment they were gone.

Later that afternoon, when I came back from Flora's, Newly was playing "jacks" with Kenny on the front porch. I had been studying proofreader's symbols in Flora's big Webster's Dictionary. "Mr. Berkley wants to come over tonight," I said.

Newly looked down at the jacks. "I've been feeling strange all day."

"It's your powers coming back, Pop!" Kenny yelled, and started prancing around the porch.

"If you want to make that kind of noise do it in the back-yard, Kenny," Newly said. Kenny obediently disappeared around the house.

I stood looking at Newly. He had a sedentary quality that was new. He had always been bouncy and active. I could not imagine him running through the snow in Fairmount Park, chasing me along the Schuylkill River. He seemed years older; his face, with its heavy cheeks, had settled. I had an instant's fantasy of his appearance in five years, his nose more fleshy and prominent, eyebrows shaggy, cheeks veined, and the stubborn look, that now only appeared occasionally, I saw drawing down his face, setting his jaw. In a flash of memory I rode again in the old Maxwell along Montgomery Avenue and heard Newly's voice: "You've got to *believe* you're a designer and then *be* one." I remembered how his hand banged down on the steering wheel. The "believe-and-be;" Newly was living it.

Long ago he had sought to change the face of the Guaranty Trust by building model offices, and ended fashioning a throne. None of this pointed the way or warned me; I had been blind to it all.

I had made up my mind to be a healer's wife. I told Joyce the day of the picnic. But this afternoon I quailed, and Philo was the last straw.

"Mrs. Berkley's butler told me Dan Ruber is taking money from the people you see in the evening."

Newly started gathering up the jacks. "That's simply not true."

"It's a rumor going around. Why should Philo lie?"

"I can't help rumors. There'll be lots of them."

"Who paid for the desks, all those posters?" We had fallen into a way of challenging each other.

"Mother." He did not look at me.

"What about Ida George?"

"We are charging a modest fee at St. Mark's."

"Newly—money is being solicited through the mail, right from this house."

"That's not my affair."

"Whose is it then?"

"It's the staff."

He was deceiving himself all around. Once you went down the trail...I looked at him. Where had he got to? Or where was he? Skipping around in some kind of garden? I mounted the steps, walking by him into the house.

Right after supper that night Dan came over. He and Newly went down to the cellar. I was sure the place needed cleaning. The idea of Mr. Berkley going into our cellar was almost more than I could stand.

At eight-thirty the bell rang. Mr. Berkley stumped along the porch on his canes. Philo had brought him and was holding the screen. "Mr. Alfred Berkley," he said, in his most formal tone. Newly and Mr. Berkley shook hands. I went upstairs with Kenny to try and quiet him by reading. I could hear Mr. Berkley slowly making his way into the cellar. I simply must shut my mind to it. Kenny did not want the *Just So Stories*, but one more reading of *Treasure Island*.

I finally got Kenny settled. He actually put one arm around my neck when we said goodnight. "Don't be worried, Mom. Pop's going to pull this one off. I'm sure of it. He said he'd been feeling queer all day. Didn't you hear him?"

"Yes, I did." I smoothed back the boy's hair. Then I leaned forward and kissed him again.

"You ought to have more faith in Pop," he said.

I smiled at him. "I'll try," I said.

"Flora doesn't believe in Pop either. And that's not good. What he needs is people who have real faith, like Dan and Curly Matlack. Curly got one of his warts back and Pop just took hold of his hand and the next day the wart was gone."

"I didn't know that, Ken."

"There, you see! You've got to make Pop think you believe in him all the time."

"I'll do the best I can, Kenny."

"That's what you should do, Mom. It's important."

"You go to sleep now." I turned out the light and closed the door.

But there was not to be sleep for Kenny that evening because all of a sudden there was a crash in the cellar and Mr. Berkley came charging up the stairs. "It worked! I can walk! Look at me. No canes!" He walked steadily, if slowly, to the door. "Philo, you black bastard, come see what's happened to me!"

So then Dan Ruber appeared and Mrs. Tilley and Cora with Kenny running around in his pajamas.

Mr. Berkley held up his hand. "I want you to take notice of the faith I have in our healer, Newlin Slatter. I intend to donate five hundred dollars to 'Healing Grace.' Newlin Slatter performs miracles. And I'm a living example of cure!" He walked to the door, shook off Philo's hand, and marched down our front steps with never a cane near him.

# Prelude

*Anna has taken to her bed, lying against faintly yellowed, linen pillowcases. She wears a blue lace jacket, and all five curls are accurately placed on her forehead. A newspaper lies on the bed with a large photograph of Frederick enlivening the front page.*

*"Your picture in the paper!" Anna cries, twisting her head aside as though she might weep. "And on the front page!" To be conspicuous, Anna knows, is considered ill-bred. Perfectly permissible to be included in a group, taken perhaps at the Devon Horse Show, a charitable affair. But to have your picture spread on the front page is equivalent to being caught at the scene of an accident. And in the* Record, *called a scandal sheet by Anna.*

*"The photograph was taken at camp against the pines," Frederick says sadly. He is sitting slumped on the end of Anna's bed. He does not seem himself; even his moustache droops, uncombed.*

*Anna says, "Fortunately no one we know is in town. At least we're not publicly humiliated." Then, pressing a handkerchief to her lips, she utters a little cry. "Oh, if we were only at camp!"*

*"Soon you will be." Frederick reaches over and absently pats her feet. "The roof is nearly finished." Then in an entirely changed manner, "That fellow Cranby ought to be whipped."*

*Anna stares at him.*

*Frederick goes on. "The Equal Rights For Indians has no connection with publishing. It's a money-raising organization. I was very embarrassed to have written them. They answered suggesting I send funds or become a life member."*

*Frederick's publishing problems hold little interest for Anna. Now she says fretfully, "Cranby is doing a whole series of articles. He seems to be concentrating on Eva. That means our name is going to be in the paper again. It's too dreadful! Imagine what he must have pried out of Fanny, she's such a jackass!"*

*Frederick says sadly, "He got plenty out of us."*

*"But we trusted him!"*

*"More fools we."*

*Anna, as always, refuses to shoulder the blame. "At least, so far, his tone is properly respectful."*

*"I find that particularly nauseating." Frederick stares at the carpet.*

*Anna cries, "Cranby keeps saying Eva is our grandchild when he knows that's not true. We told him the whole story. He implies we adopted her. You know, legally. And that's another lie. Don't you think we might sue for libel?" She looks eagerly at Frederick.*

*"And see ourselves spread all over the papers again. No, I don't." Frederick lets his clasped hands fall between his knees. Seldom has he seemed so disheartened. He had envisaged a dazzling future with his books eulogized in* The Saturday Review, *praised on the front page of* The New York Times Book Review. *He had been positively fluttery with hope, ridiculously expectant. Nothing had ever happened to his other three volumes; why should there be interest in his fourth, which even he felt dragged a bit? But Cranby had been so positive! Hooking him easily and now cooking him in the* Record. *How well his picture had turned out, backed by the magnificent pines!*

*"When you see what's happened," Anna is saying with infinite bitterness, "I wish we'd never taken Eva."*

*"The poor girl isn't responsible, Anna!"*

*"Why not? He's her husband, isn't he?"*

*"That has nothing to do with it. He's concerned with his own power. I've watched medicine men in the Hopi tribe. If a medicine man invades the spirit of one of the tribe that Indian dies."*

*"I don't believe it." Anna fiddles with her jacket.*

*Frederick shrugs. "I sensed trouble when Newlin made that girl at the movies warm."*

*Anna says sharply, "Frederick, that was years ago!"*

*"But Newlin hasn't forgotten. Who knows, he may have been practicing all this time. It takes years of practice to become a medicine man."*

*"I do wish you'd forget those Indians!"*

*Frederick does not answer. Anna lies back against her pillows. They are waiting for Eva.*

25 Mama phoned Friday. "What on earth is your husband doing with Alfred Berkley? Surely Papa and I deserve an explanation."

I would see them that afternoon, I said. Although what to say I could not imagine, or how to reassure them—on the contrary, wouldn't the situation worsen? Various other "cures" had already taken place; people again gathered on India Street in front of our house, sometimes coming right into the yard. The hedge once more dwindled; the gate was gone. Besides the drama of Mr. Berkley, a woman with a lump on her breast, said to be cancer, had been treated by Newly and the lump declared non-malignant. In Manayunk a totally blind woman reported that after an interview with Newly she was now able to discern the furniture in her room. Cyd Kubie's father, suffering from stomach ulcers, said that he had three conferences in Newly's cellar and the pain left him.

The bus came by again. "This is the healer's humble home," the announcer shouted. The telephone rang constantly; a special truck delivered the mail, and Mrs. Slatter and Cora looked increasingly harried. Only one day before the St. Mark's meeting. Newly stayed upstairs in our so-called bedroom. "Healer Readying For Miracle Test." Newly's picture showed him in his long black Amish robe, which he now wore all day. Mrs. Tilly reported Kenny was doing a brisk trade on India Street selling stones he said "came right from the place where my Dad stood when he cured Curly Matlack's warts." I did not try and stop him; I would deal with Kenny later. While Newly sat upstairs, I sat in Flora's living room. She and I were trying to find a not too expensive boarding school some place out west that took young boys. I told myself that Newly would see the wisdom of sending Kenny west, and wrote to three schools.

Joyce was in Richmond addressing the Booksellers' Convention. I could not imagine confiding in Joyce. If I described the life Newly and I now led she would just ask the same question. Was I going to stay with him? I needed counsel, not challenge.

David? I had not confided in David since I was a child and sat on the foot of his bed and cried. In Mr. Framely's office he had told me this healer business was heady. The day Cyd Kubie walked, David leaned over a chair in the kitchen, closer than we had been in years. "You better think about it, Eva. You've got to think what to do."

On Friday afternoon Mrs. Ida George waited for me at the foot of the stairs. I was on my way to see Mama and Papa. Short, big-bosomed, with hair as frizzy as Cora Ruber's, Ida George's manner was decisive. She had clever eyes, framed by black-rimmed glasses. As I reached the bottom step she smiled, lips curving agreeably. I looked back at her carefully, being more used to my mother-in-law's sharp attacks.

"You know Cyd Kubie is walking again. He manages to be on view when the bus stops." She smiled more widely. "Then Mrs. Carlton Maltis' cancer of the breast has now been diagnosed as a cyst." Pause. Bright eyes on my face.

"So I heard." She would get no more from me.

"Mr. Lloyd Paget is almost a nightly visitor and seems helped by Mr. Slatter, although the nature of his ailment is not known." Her pleasant expression did not change. "There is no doubt Mr. Slatter's powers have increased." She said this unemotionally but with conviction. I did not reply. She went on: "There is a woman from Los Angeles whose eyes did not focus properly due to an automobile accident. Mr. Slatter gave a date when the woman's eyes hopefully were to be cured. But the date has passed and her eyes remain the same. It's one of his few failures."

"I see." I knew I sounded stiff. Ida George apparently did not expect enthusiasm from me, for she continued in the same agreeable and, to some extent, confidential tone.

"Mrs. Slatter, I understand that if possible you want to be inconspicuous. You realize that as Mr. Slatter continues there will be additional public exposure." Again the smile. "I wanted to tell you that we will do everything we can to protect you."

"Thank you."

"Saturday night should not be difficult. The church is small."

"My husband wants Kenny at the church."

"He seems to depend on Kenny."

"Yes."

"The boy seems quite stable emotionally."

A compliment. I smiled back. "I think he's selling those stones because he wants to be part of the show."

She laughed. A surprisingly hearty sound. I liked her. It was a relief to be talking to someone in terms of the problem instead of wading through the aura of awe that permeated "The Staff."

Ida George said, "I'm sure Bernard Cranby's articles are upsetting, Mrs. Slatter. There is another picture of Mr. Severn in The *Record* this morning, and one of you. Does Cranby have a grudge against you for some reason?"

"David, my stepbrother, didn't like the questions Cranby was asking me and knocked him down."

"That's unfortunate."

"It's worse for Mama and Papa."

"Didn't Cranby interview them in the Adirondacks?"

"Yes. He lied about his purpose and they believed him."

"That lets you off the hook, doesn't it?"

"Not really."

She studied me. "A pity," she said, and with a nod went back to the office. I let myself out the side door.

I drove slowly by the Wissahickon Creek on my way in town. Brown water, swollen by recent rains, flowed sluggishly. Two mallards clattered into the air. If Kenny had been along he'd laugh at the ducks. Would he have come with me or given his usual excuse: "I want to see what Pop's doing?" It was true that Newly increasingly depended on Kenny; I could see this happening. (Not until years later did it occur to me that Kenny was taking my place.) Ida George might feel he showed emotional stability but I knew how tense he was. I tried to persuade him to play Parcheesi or jacks or go to the zoo. But he always wanted to be with his father or Cyd Kubie. Of course, any little boy would be entranced by a father who turned into a kind of magician. Hadn't Mrs. Berkley mentioned Houdini? Kenny was being swept along in an excitement he could not understand and which I felt should not be prolonged. I did not intend to dwell on it, but after Saturday night I meant to speak to Newly about boarding school.

I parked the car on DeLancey Place in front of the house. Then a prolonged wait on the stoop in the heat, and finally Robert opened the door.

"Don't you got a key?"

"No. I saw a friend of yours recently."

"Philo. He says your husband got old man Berkley dancing. It's a big relief not having to haul him 'round, Philo say."

"Keep your fingers crossed."

"You mean it won't *last?*" He started off down the hall. "It's just like you to be so sour." He disappeared.

The quiet of the house seeped around me. Cool. Nothing changed; the blueness of the living room hovered like a mist; blue rug, heavy blue portieres drawn against the summer sun; little tables studded with Mama's Staffordshire figurines; the grand piano like a brown pool. As a child I would burst in the front door and then fall silent in the silent house. Upstairs Mama was resting and the stairs squeaked unless carefully trod on. David used to say if you walked by the wall you'd get by. He and I would slide along late at night after a party. (It had been leaning against these stairs that I heard Mrs. Framely's voice from the living room: "David wanted to be

an anthropologist." And Papa: "There never was anything definite about it. Evidently David wants to marry your daughter..."
I remember climbing the stairs and then going to lie full length on my bed.)

Mama wasted no time. "All this dreadful publicity!" she cried, when I came into the bedroom. "Our name in the paper!" Her blue eyes flew open. "Being conspicuous in this horrid way has made me ill." She turned her head sidewise against the pillows as though she could not bear the sight of me.

"It's disagreeable, I know, Mama." I had been written up as a spoiled, rich parasite. "Eva Colby knew the feel of silk, the taste of champagne..." Cranby had a fanciful mind.

"But what is Newlin doing in the *cellar*, Eva?" Mama's voice whined.

"He and Dan Ruber have built a—uh—chair in the cellar," I said.

"It looked more like a throne to me. There was some sort of extension out in front."

Mrs. Slatters red sateen canopy.

"Well, yes," I said.

"Wasn't that my old buffalo robe thrown over the back?"

"I think so, yes."

Mama propped herself up on one elbow. "I hope you're not part of all this—" she waved her free hand, "this folderol."

"No, I'm not."

"Then why don't you stop Newlin? He's your husband!" She flopped back against the pillows.

"I told you Newlin believes he's helping people, Mama. And in a way, he is. He helped Mr. Berkley."

"But there wasn't anything physically wrong with Alfred! According to Ella he was afraid to put weight on his hip."

I seemed to be defending Newly, yet I must speak of his intention. Nothing justified the means. We were all aware of that. I had not expected comfort from Mama; that would have been ridiculous.

Nor could I, as Newly's wife, accept sympathy without seeming to disapprove of him. I would like to have told Mama how much I regretted having them brought into what they must consider a disgraceful public show.

"Your picture is always in the paper! Papa's picture was in today!"

"Some things I can't help, Mama."

"I hardly recognized Newlin," Papa said. He stood by the window, barely part of the scene.

"I cannot understand what Carter Plummer is doing." Mama pulled at the sheet. "Imagine allowing St. Mark's to be used for such an exhibition!"

Dr. Plummer was being maligned. But to exonerate him required a complicated explanation.

Mama had not finished with me. "Bernard Cranby turned out to be a fraud. He knew nothing about 'The Equal Rights For Indians.' They are not interested in Papa's books. The whole affair was most embarrassing."

"Mama, I warned you about Cranby."

She turned her head away. "Oh, pooh!"

"You were too late, Eva." Papa walked away from the window, leaned against the mantel.

"But Papa, you saw him twice!"

He disregarded this and said with sudden animation, "I've decided to attend Newlin's experiment at St. Mark's tomorrow."

"Frederick!" Mama sat up in bed.

"Yes. I'm going. My mind's quite made up. After all, I've witnessed remarkable exhibitions by medicine men—not the warming of humans; I think this is Eastern. However, I'm quite familiar with driving out demons, which was no doubt Alfred Berkley's case. So, although I regret this dreadful publicity, I shall nevertheless watch Newlin's experiment."

Interrupting this extraordinary statement came Fanny's knock on the door. She entered carrying a glass of lemonade on a salver. We all greeted her in silence. As she went by me she tugged at my dress. "You've a pin in that hem. Come up to my room and I'll mend it." "You better go now, Eva," Mama said, taking the lemonade. "I doubt I can stand much more."

I kissed Papa and left. It had always been peaceful in Fanny's room. She sat on the old rocker sewing my hem, and I sat on the floor in my slip. The bulb still hung by a cord from the ceiling; the plaster replica of Jesus in a blue loincloth tilted on the bureau. Fanny herself wore much the same black dress with white collar and cuffs. Thick glasses magnified her dark eyes.

"It's God's doing." Fanny referred to Newly. "He always was a grand fellow. I remember when he sent you the white roses."

Sad, white buds. I smiled at her.

"He's famous now." Fanny drew out a long thread. "He'll cure that girl from Bethlehem, you'll see."

"Wilkes-Barre," I said.

"Whatever." She bit off her thread. "Mr. Cranby, that reporter, gave me candy when he came to camp. Lovely chocolates they were."

"And you talked to him, Fanny?"

"He only wanted to know about you. What was the harm?"

When I arrived home Newly was on the porch addressing a group of people. His manner, I must admit, had changed. He no longer pontificated as he had on radio. He appeared quite easy, relaxed. He leaned against the railing. People stood on the porch and in the yard. "I'm a plain man, just like anyone else. The difference being that I have been given a kind of force. Often I can communicate intimately with ill people. And sometimes I can't. But I'm trying to build up that pulse and help people. I'm afraid I cannot be much help to those of you who have been crippled a long time. I have only partially been able to help one sightless person. But there are other ailments that can benefit. I suppose the great thing with me is that I *believe*. And it's also a kind of understanding, as though I entered into *your* problem. So in preparation, before you come and see me, try and relax, try and think about what it is you want cured. I'd like to see all of you, but I have only limited time. And to those of you whom I don't see, I suggest you come to the meeting that is being held tomorrow evening, August 15th, at St. Mark's Church."

I suppose Newly, in a way, was teaching a kind of yoga, control of the body. Maybe that is stretching it a little far, although now there are people who say that Newly's belief in the other person's strength to cure himself is almost like biofeedback.

At the end of his talk Newly turned and thanked me for attending. He might have been speaking to a stranger. It was the same manner he used when he accidentally bumped against me in the hall on the way to the bathroom in the morning.

At nine-thirty that night the woman from Los Angeles phoned, screaming that her eyes were in focus. Newly charged up from the cellar, took the phone from me. Kenny dashed downstairs in his pajamas. The woman was yelling so loudly Newly couldn't hear what she said and finally hung up. Kenny started out the door. Newly grabbed him.

Kenny cried, "I want to go tell Cyd about the lady's eyes being in focus just like you said!"

"It's nearly two weeks late, Kenny." Newly paused. "I don't understand. The date came so clearly to me."

"She's lucky her eyes are all right," I said.

"Not lucky, Mom! My Dad cured her!"

Kenny's dark face was tense.

"The woman's all right," I said placatingly, "and that's wonderful."

"But you won't say Pop did it!" His dark eyes squinted angrily at me.

"I'm sure your father helped her through a difficult time."

But Kenny was not pacified. Excitement had built up in him and suddenly I was the focus. "Pop cured her!" Kenny cried.

Newly put his arm on the boy's shoulders. "Now, son," he said, "your mother has a right to her beliefs and you to yours."

"I believe in your father's goodness," I said, and I looked right into Newly's face. His eyes met mine, wide open, guileless. For weeks we had not looked at each other. I thought in another moment he would take me in his arms.

But instead Kenny started to scream, "No, you don't! You don't at all, Mom."

Newly dropped into a chair and took Kenny on his lap, pressing him close. He knew how overwrought the child was, for Kenny started to cry. He seldom cried and I ran to him, knelt beside him, kissing his cheek. He did not resist. The boy was exhausted. Maybe part of him hated all this excitement. It was too much for him.

We sat there, the three of us, I don't know for how long, Kenny quietly crying, while I held his hand, now and again wiping his cheek. But there wasn't any comfort for us. We weren't together any more.

26  St. Mark's church is small and dark with thick, stone arches that reach to the roof and seem to lower heavily over the heads of the people jammed into the pews this particular evening in August. The crowd is dense and some must sit sidewise. The night is hot and in the church the heat is so intense it seems an actual presence. Men mop their faces. All through the crowd white leaflets (distributed at the entrance) flutter like gulls' wings as the women fan back and forth. On the side of each big stone pillar small red and blue lights twinkle, at Ida George's request. She wants a mysterious murky effect, and therefore the regular lights which usually flood the church have not been turned on.

A large crowd stands outside the church, waiting on the grass. Frederick Severn and Robert have arrived too late and cannot force their way into the church or even reach the door in spite of Mr. Severn's call to "Let me by, please. I am a friend of Newlin Slatter. A serious student. I must see this experiment." No one budges. Robert says, "Better give up, Mr. Severn. No one is going to let you in. Us seeing the ambulance is all." As they start back someone yells at Robert, "Get that old man off the road!"

The crowd is careful to leave the gravel driveway free, and only occasionally does anyone dart across the road. At any moment the ambulance is expected. Already the meeting is half an hour late starting. A rear tire blowout has delayed the ambulance near Allentown. However, they are now close by, with the girl, Sarah Winkler, prone inside. She has made no fuss about coming, cooperating fully, Dan Ruber says. Three of The Mount's most prominent doctors have publicly stated that she probably will enjoy the ride, not getting out often. They reassert their belief in her paralysis (sight unseen and unexamined), as she has been threatened with spinal meningitis, and also suffered the effects of lying constantly in bed. In their opinion the entire affair at St. Mark's is bound to fail, a cheap show.

But the crowd is mad with hope of a real miracle! Some are rumored to have come from Eagle Butte, South Dakota, bringing with them a boy who cannot speak. And there is a group from Sault Ste. Marie with two blind girls. They are seated on the front row. Scattered throughout the crowd are people from the Pineys in New Jersey who are heard to boast loudly of their own healer. However, they are soon quieted when told that Newlin Slatter, the Master of Healing Grace, got Cyd Kubie, who never took a step before, walking. The Master has cured cancer. But, more importantly, the rich man who went to the Pineys was *not* helped by the Piney healer; however, after seeing Newlin Slatter only once, he has thrown away his crutches and is now playing golf! The general expectation of success is high for Sarah Winkler.

Many in the church have arrived early and brought sandwiches, hot dogs, cold drinks. Papers and bottles lie about the aisles. The church's two toilets have long since ceased functioning.

Waiting in the vestry of the church I have viewed the crowd through the glass-topped door, and come away sensing an awesome pressure, a held-back force that could burst through and overrun us all. I hold tightly to Kenny's hand. He does not pull away but walks close beside me. Pretty, blond high school girls run in and out of the vestry. Wide yellow ribbons stretch across their bosoms: HEALING GRACE printed in green. "We've got those two blind girls in the front pew," Mrs. Ida George says. The heat has made her short dyed orange curls sag, revealing the smallness of her head. She is all glasses and mouth. Dan Ruber, as Newlin's assistant, is wearing a borrowed, long black gown. He will be part of the procession into the church. Dan announces to Mrs. George that the photographers are in the front pew and have been given spiked orangeade. Kenny cries, "I want some orangeade, Ma."

"This heat is something terrible," Mrs. Slatter addresses me for the first time in days. Perspiration dots her long, upper lip. The usual sleekness of her pompadour has disintegrated, the part in her hair shows gray.

"It will be even hotter in the church," I say. "Why can't Kenny and I just stay here."

"*No, No!*" Kenny starts to scream, trying to wrench his hand from mine.

"Surely you intend to make an appearance, Eva." Mrs. Slatter's black eyes, that once were kindly, show real hatred. She has made enough of an overture toward me and turns away. Mrs. George asks two of the yellow-haired young girls if they've managed to get rid of all the leaflets. Everyone is hot and tired; the delay of the ambulance affects us all.

Newly appears in the vestry and Kenny pulls his hand from mine, running to Newly crying, "Hello, Pop. How are you, Pop?"

"I'm fine, son, just fine." Newly's face has expanded. There seems to be more face than I remember, as though his hair has receded. His eyes bulge nervously. He looks around but apparently sees nothing, not even Kenny, and passes by without noticing me. He uses an authoritative tone of voice with which he seems perfectly comfortable.

Mrs. George, sweating heavily under the arms, speaks to the radio announcer, a tall thin man standing in the corner. She reminds him that because of the people waiting for "The Message" outside the church, he must be sure and describe everything that happens. "You'll be in the chancel, hooked up alongside the lectern, so you can see what's going on."

"Isn't Mr. Slatter speaking?"

"The Master," Mrs. George corrects him, "does not expect to speak, certainly not loud enough to be heard inside the church, small though it is, let alone outside." She scrapes her upper lip with a sodden handkerchief.

Now a special group of men and women are coming through the side door. They all seem old, and give a rich appearance. The women carry expensive-looking handbags and one elderly woman has a lace fan. Mrs. Berkley is not with them. Newly shakes every hand, smiling in his usual genial fashion, but lingering over his handshakes in a way that nauseates me. Occasionally, when Newly does not remember a name, Dan Ruber makes the introduction. These special people are to be seated in the vestry. "At least it will be cooler," one tubby, white-haired woman says. She gives a catlike smile. "We'll be close to the miracle." She makes it sound like a circus act.

For some reason the tubby lady's speech or smile register with Newly; he suddenly twists away; I see his cheeks sag, his lips part, and catch a look of real terror on his face. He stares, eyes wide. All this takes only an instant, and I'm sure no one else sees. For he quickly adjusts, pulling briefly at his black collar as though it bound his neck, then turning with a smile to greet a large gray-haired man in a checked coat. The genial manner falls over him again, smoothly as his Amish garb. He moves from person to person with an air of confidence, pressing hands, clapping men on the back. As I watch him I wonder if I have not witnessed his last instant of self-doubt and if Newly is not really propelled by a power which he cannot resist, and even feels he must cultivate. Newly, it seems, is finding himself.

The knowledge is so startling that I feel my knees weaken, and deliberately go to a chair and sit down. I take Kenny on my lap in spite of his protests and tell him to sit quietly if he wants to see Sarah Winkler.

A loud murmur comes from the crowd inside the church. Once a raucous voice shouts, *"Let's go."* But no other voice is raised. Through the open windows of the vestry the sound of voices from the people standing outside is plain, and now and again there is a shout and once a woman shrieks. Far in the distance a ukulele is being played.

The whole scene is quite real. I am indeed sitting in the vestry of St. Mark's with a squirming child on my lap waiting for my husband to "cure" a girl from Wilkes-Barre, a relation of Dan Ruber's. About the proceedings there is a kind of low-grade commercialism projected by the blond girls with their broad yellow ribbons spelling out "Healing Grace."

A siren sounds. Shouts come from all over. The ambulance has arrived! At once there is a scurry at the vestry doors; both are thrown wide. The side of the ambulance comes into view and stops. Two men in white arrive simultaneously in the vestry, receive orders from Ida George, go back to the ambulance. Dr. Plummer appears, fortunately not gowned. He seems completely detached, even cool, in a gray suit. "It must be time to go into the church," he says. "As you know," he addresses Mrs. George from a distance, "I am giving a prayer. It is against Newlin's wishes, but this is God's house and we shall pray."

Mrs. George does not even look at him. "The ambulance men

don't want to get Sarah out until you are ready to have her go right into the church. So will you please move along." Turning to me: "You and Kenny and Mrs. Slatter are all seated in the choir stalls. And be careful, don't tip on the wires. They're for the loudspeakers and the radio."

Am I going to be able wo walk into the church, parading along with "Healing Grace," and with Kenny?...*Just walk into it. There have been other fakes in your life...*

"Isn't Pop going to pray, Mom?" Kenny asks. He has on his best white suit. His hair has fallen over his eyes. On impulse I lean forward and kiss the top of his head. He seems the only innocent person in all the crowd.

"Will you please move right along," Mrs. George has taken Mrs. Slatter by the arm. "The ambulance men are anxious to get Sarah Winkler out of the cab."

We all walk slowly toward the side door. First Dr. Plummer, then Mrs. Slatter, Dan Ruber, Kenny and I. Now we are through and into the main body of the church. The heat and crowd overwhelms, smell of sweating people. Faces of all colors stare back. Rows and rows of heads dimly seen, and over all the flutter of white leaflets fanning. The heavy stone pillars, the arches, the darkened windows....A spotlight glows suddenly on the chancel steps. Then the door opens again, and Sarah Winkler is wheeled in on a stretcher by the ambulance attendants. People in the audience get to their feet. There are calls, shouts. Some woman near the front cries, "God be praised!" Then comes Newly, and the whole church rises. People shout unintelligibly. Pressed close in the front pew alongside the photographers are two women, Indians, who stare forward. There are three cripples. One girl has no legs; one man is wholly deformed ...I put my hand on Kenny's shoulder. We must keep walking.

We mount the chancel steps, file into the stalls. Now I see Sarah Winkler. She has blond, rather stringy hair, a skull-like face, and enormous eyes. Protuberant eyes that are almost a deformity. They are brown and they move, although her head remains still. She lies curled in the fetal position. Her cheeks are sunken; her nose a shaft, the skin about her mouth wasted. There is nothing young about her. She seems barely alive. A monsterish girl. She has a fixed animal-like stubbornness. She seems totally part of the stretcher. There is a sheet draped over her, but you can still see the position of her body, on its side with the knees curled. She starts turning her head to look at the people.

Dr. Plummer comes down the chancel steps and in a full voice cries: "Let us pray!" He waits for the noise in the church to subside and then says, "Oh Heavenly Father, bless this Thy House and all that are here tonight. Bless this sick child, Sarah Winkler, who has come to Thy House in love and trust. Make her well if it be Thy will, Lord. For it is only Thee who can perform this cure. For Christ's sake, Amen."

He seems to hurry the end, knowing Newly's natural reaction. "It's Pop who's going to make her walk, isn't it, Ma?" Kenny whispers to me, raising his face. I squeeze his hand, but do not answer. I realize he is holding my hand quite unresistingly, even clinging to me. Kenny has changed, too. I sense he is glad of my presence, standing against the crowd, and that he may be frightened.

Newly comes down the chancel step where he has been standing during the prayer.

("Now The Master is going toward poor Sarah Winkler..." the announcer is whispering into the microphone...)

Newly reaches the stretcher. To my shocked surprise he does not pause, but without a word scrambles onto the stretcher beside the girl. There are cries in the church. A woman moans in front and falls on her knees. Newly simply lies beside Sarah Winkler. I see him reach down and straighten her legs. He manages to get one arm under her and the other around her so he holds her close to him. Then he starts talking to her. I cannot hear what he is saying. She keeps her enormous eyes turned toward him. I hear him tell her she can and must walk. Newly's face is now beet red, his eyes bloodshot. He only whispers a second to her. For suddenly he cries at the top of his voice: "RISE UP!" He makes a kind of backward leap from the stretcher to his feet. "RISE UP!" he cries again. And in an instant, so it seems, the girl is standing beside him. She has literally sprung out of bed. And then without so much as a look at anyone, she starts to walk, walking quite steadily toward the side door and out. A shout goes up. The two Indians in front kneel. People are sobbing. There is a huge roar. Shouts sound again and again: "Praise the Lord! Praise The Master!"

Newly stands on the chancel steps smiling, raising his hands. Light bulbs flash. He stays on the steps while people push and crowd around him, wanting to touch him. His face has a childlike, innocent look of pleasure, and he is very pale.

As the crowd presses forward Kenny suddenly pulls his hand from mine and darts among the people in the church. I try to run after him, but the press of bodies is too dense. I call and call again, finally give up hope of following him, and dash around to the side door. But here people are coming from outside. I call his name but my voice is lost in the shouts of the crowd.

I never knew precisely where Kenny went, but people told me he was crying "Sarah, Sarah!" as he squirmed through the crowd. By this time Sarah Winkler was sitting in the front of the ambulance with the two drivers. She could not possibly have heard him. Evidently Kenny squirmed through the side door of the church, meeting the crush of people, but managing to push through without harm. The ambulance stood high and although people tried to make way for it, the men finally set off the siren and people scattered, knocking each other aside. I will never know whether the crowd knocked Kenny into the path of the oncoming ambulance, or if he ran across, but two of the ambulance's wheels passed directly over his body. He was killed instantly. I was told he was dead when they picked him up from the roadway.

# Prelude

*Anna and Frederick Severn are sitting silently in the breakfast room. Out-side rain pelts down, dark clouds hang over St. Regis mountain as they have for days, making the camp cold and gloomy. Frederick considers ordering Gordon to light the fire, at least carry logs. But Anna has set rules. One simply ignores the cold; "roughing it," a slight discomfort. Her only indul-gence is having Fanny put hot water bottles in their beds at night, the tent being unbearably damp and quite cold. Now, as the rain falls unceasingly, Frederick watches drops splash into a puddle rimmed with pine needles that has formed outside the door. Again he is longing to be at work; all his old enthusiasm has returned. The battle for the Ohio Valley has gone exceedingly well, and Frederick finds he has a flair for delineation of character and has made Alexander McKee, the Britisher, quite a hero. Unfortunately, when he and Anna were in the DeLancey Place house earlier in the summer there were so many interruptions that his work suffered. They endured the awful upset over that poor child's death, and all the publicity...a terrible picture of Eva kneeling on the road beside the body....Then the dreadful funeral with an unbelievable white coffin, the crowds of people. Afterwards reporters were constantly phoning, even coming to the house. And now Newlin was masquerading around the country as a healer, appearing in tents, curing odd diseases, and making people walk, supposedly. A far cry from the real medi-cine men.*

*Most unfortunately, whenever the papers mention Eva she is accused of* "deserting" her husband, a favorite topic of that traitorous Cranby, who constantly refers to Eva's "connection" with the "aristocratic Severns." The whole affair is disgusting. Yes, and tragic, of course, with the boy's death. Eva seems to have vanished.

"But where is Eva?" Frederick asks, staring out at the rain. When it rains this heavily in the Adirondacks it is liable to keep on for days. He is going to have Gordon light a fire in the studio and let Anna make what she will of it.

"How forgetful you've become, Frederick! She's in Nantucket visiting David and Joyce."

"But the papers speak of desertion. Now they are talking of divorce." He looks angrily at her. "One does not tell an historian he is forgetful, Anna!"

Anna ignores his irritation. "It's all Eva's bad management. When asked if she was going with Newlin to the meeting in Atlanta, she said no— she was leaving!" Anna sucks her lower lip in displeasure. "And when that awful Cranby asked if she meant divorce, she refused to answer. So of course there is all this stir and publicity." Anna puts down her sewing, accidently pricking her finger, which further annoys her. "At least Eva had the wit not to mention Nantucket. Probably no one asked her." Pause. Anna, too, looks out at the rain. "I do wonder about my sofa and those nice chairs. I don't give a fig for the red curtains; they were mildewed, anyway. But the furniture is very different. I suppose Eva thought it was a gift. I can only hope she has everything properly covered. Of course she'll come back to the house. Where else has she to go? And why didn't she give a straight answer to Cranby?" Anna resumes her sewing. "I'm certainly not going to ask Newlin Slatter about that furniture."

Frederick says sharply, "I thought we gave Eva the furniture as a present. It just sat in the cellar."

Anna straightens. "I regarded those chairs and the sofa as a loan." She smooths out the work with her thumb. She is on her third doily for the cream bottle, the first being admired years ago by Mr. Jaffrey. This change of thought quickly improves her temper, for Mr. Jaffrey is at the moment in the music room, composing the accompaniment for Anna's long poem, "Hector and Agamemnon: An Epic."

*Ugly Girl*

*She will give a recital the second Saturday in September. A little show of spirit that will extricate them from this latest, unfortunate occurrence. Of course they must express sorrow for the boy, so senselessly killed. But steadily deny any connection with Newlin Slatter. The other night when she and Frederick dined at the Denby camp, Newlin's name was mentioned. Frederick took an amused, scoffing attitude and spoke of the public's gullibility. It had all gone off rather well until someone asked Anna directly about the girl from Wilkes-Barre—was she still walking? Anna replied that she had no idea. "Nor any interest," she added in a cool voice. Then she deliberately changed the subject. Anna has many talents: one of them is putting people in their proper place.*

*Frederick, unaware of Anna's change of mood, now returns to Eva. "I really wish Eva had not gone to Nantucket, Anna. I'd hate David to be mixed up in this nasty business. Robert told me Cranby had written very insinuatingly about David and Eva. Cranby is evidently doing a whole series on Eva's childhood. 'Social Butterfly,' the last one was called. David's close relationship with Eva was mentioned." Frederick shakes his head. "I did my best to separate them, but you would have their rooms on the same floor."*

*"Really Frederick! You can be so tiresome. David has always thought of Eva as his sister. It's vulgar of you to keep making these innuendos. You're not yourself." She quickly folds the doily, puts it in her work bag.*

*Ordinarily Frederick would rather enjoy her anger, her heightened color. But now he does not even notice. Their relationship has altered, unacknowledged by either of them, except occasionally in a nagging way. The sparks and fire that used to blaze up between them have simply died out. They are more easily irritated by each other, less interested, and they complain more. There is little evidence of fondness between them. At night in their tent Frederick no longer notices Anna's nightgown or the enveloping net over her hair or wish she would not pin the five curls on her forehead so meticulously. He does not go to the door of the tent to look at the stars. There is no Eva scrambling down the steps, slipping into the cold lake. Frederick is more thankful for the hot water bottle that waits in his bed than for any star in the heavens.*

27 The steamer slowed for the breakwater. Two cormorants flew off the beacon. Gulls swooped above the boat, wings fluttering like leaflets. I went quickly below deck to my rented car. I would discover the "charm" of Nantucket in my own way. Seeing the golden spire and cluster of gray roofs had satisfied me from a distance. The wind was a little chilly and I hoped I had brought enough warm clothes. Joyce said September on the island could be cold.

Cars were lined up on two sides of the hold; mammoth trucks occupied the center space and would be first off. I squeezed into my car. The steamer came into the dock with a great churning of water; the gangplank banged into place and the trucks rattled off. Then the cars started to move and suddenly I was in sunlight. People stood waving from the dock. I saw David. Then he was running alongside the car. "My jeep is parked ahead on the street. It's green. You can follow me out of town." Children, dogs, and bicycles milled about. I concentrated on driving. Yet someplace I felt the shock of seeing David.

The air had a sea smell. Cobblestones, a red wooden house, then gray shingled houses. I did not try and take in the scene, simply followed David's green jeep.

The night Kenny was killed David phoned from Nantucket, but we barely spoke. He said Papa had called him. Later he wrote me a short note saying he would not be there for the funeral. He said he hoped I would come to Nantucket. I could live in their guest house and be completely private, which I wanted, and yet I would not be entirely alone, which I feared.

Now we were driving along an open road; moors stretched on both sides, varied greens, handsome junipers. Poison ivy, I noted. In Paradise?

That morning when I awoke in the Buzzard's Bay Tourist Court I saw again that my bed had a curious unwrinkled neatness. I must have been sleeping curled up tightly, gripping myself, because in the morning my arms sometimes ached from the tight hold.

They had not let me see Kenny. The two ambulance men held me back when I tried to pull the cover off the stretcher. Now I could not remember Kenny's face, how he looked. I remembered his straight black hair and his thin body, but not his face. I had a snapshot of him in my suitcase but it brought back nothing. Lately I developed a weak defenseless way of crying, the tears slipping out of my eyes as though I did not know I was crying. The night it happened I had sobbed in a violent wrenching way with Flora's arms tight and brittle around me. But this violence only happened once. When Mama and Papa came (I lived at Flora's), Mama said Kenny had been a handsome boy. She had kissed me. They seemed removed, awfully old, shocked and speechless, leaving soon. Mrs. Framely sat holding both my hands, and again the tears fell down my face although I was scarcely aware of crying.

The funeral was held in the house. I insisted. India Street had been blocked off. People stood in the street, in the yard, came up on the porch. Ida George had the ceremony broadcast. I did not know this or I'd have forbidden it. Newlin agreed to have Dr. Cousins from Holy Trinity. Certainly not Dr. Plummer. Dan Ruber arranged a way to bring people around the crowds and into the house through the side door. Debbie O'Halloran came, the Framelys, Mama and Papa and Robert, Fanny. Perhaps Newly had chosen the dreadful white coffin. The chairs had the funeral parlor's name on the backs. None of this mattered. Flora stood beside me, stiff as I was. On the other side Newlin wept. He did this with strange gulps, wiping the tears off his face again and again. There was some dreadful tremulous feeling behind this weeping. I thought it guilt. Was he saying to himself that but for this "healing" Kenny would be alive? Of course he was guilty. And when I thought of it all I hated him. And not afraid to say it. He was like a weak child blubbering. Sorry? *What good now?*

And *now* he was—Dan told me—rededicating himself to "Healing Grace." I could not think about it. It was as though I might lose consciousness. Was he not going to give the whole dreadful idea up—with Kenny dead? What manner of man was he? Dan said that after the funeral Newlin was holding an open meeting at the Veteran's Hall. "Don't tell me about it," I said, and left the house.

During the funeral I did not want to stand beside Newly. I might accidently touch him, and held myself stiff, unmoving.

"Lord let me know mine end, and the number of my days: that I may be certified how long I have to live... Hear my prayer, Lord, and with thine eyes consider my calling: hold not thy peace at my tears:

For I am a stranger with thee, and a sojourner; as all my fathers were.

O spare me a little, that I may recover my strength: before I go hence and am no more seen."

Dr. Cousins had a plain voice and therefore the words kept their own meaning.

There was the house to be emptied. Kenny's games I gave to Cyd; his books to Curly. For some reason I kept his slingshot, which I had objected to at the time. Newly gave his tent away.

I know my attitude toward Newlin was unrelenting. He must have grieved terribly over Kenny. Kenny's love for his father had been strong. I knew I must not blame Newlin. I knew I could not live with blame and that it would fester and that in time I must somehow reconcile my feeling.

( 287

From the night Kenny died I never expected to grieve with
Newlin, never looked for it. That seems queer in view of the past.
But now we were completely separated. I was the one who went to
the hospital. Newlin had been surrounded by people. He may not
even have known what happened. The same ambulance that brought
Sarah Winkler took Kenny to the hospital. There was no other way
to do it. Sarah rode in front with the drivers. I suppose she had
no choice. Dan Ruber took me in his car; he made the arrangements. It was not until we were about to leave the hospital that
Newlin appeared, running in the door, gown billowing, not even
noticing me.

I knew I was allowing bitterness to take a strong hold. Better
than self-pity, although a certain similarity exists.

I had seen Newlin two days ago in Kenny's room. I was packing
a suitcase. Since the funeral we had had almost no contact. Now he
stood in his robe by the doorway. His face had always been rather
stiff and ruddy; now he was an odd grayish color and his skin fell in
spongy folds. His eyes were bloodshot. His manner impatient, carefully checked, but as though a stream of fierce irritation ran through
him. He spoke from the doorway.

"Is it true you are packing? You can't have stored the furniture?"

I looked across the bed at him. (Not Kenny's bed, an old cot of
Flora's.) "Yes, the sofa and two chairs. A trunk with my clothes,
some of my pictures. Only things that I felt were mine. I left the
dining room table, chairs, china, kitchen things."

"Eva—I can't believe you would leave—after what happened to
Kenny! You can't go. It's not possible." He spoke in a queer loud
whisper, maybe fearful Cora Ruber would hear. She was still working in the living room.

What crossed his mind? Where was he? Had our whole separation passed him by? It might be that he was so taken up with
"sharing" his grief publicly that he—what?—did not miss our grieving together? Possibly he had become so concentrated on himself,

on expressing himself, that he had not realized the ordinary way of grief?

I tried to imagine him in his old corduroy pants and shirt, but the picture wouldn't stick. The black robe was too engrossing, brought with it the crowds, heat, waving leaflets, shouts, and I saw again the white side of the ambulance slide by.

I lifted the suitcase off the bed to the floor, glad of action. "You know my feeling, Newlin. I don't want to go into it again." I smoothed the counterpane on the bed. "I cannot live the life you are leading. I explained that. Why does my leaving surprise you?"

I doubt he even heard me. "But now there is even more reason for our being together!" he said, in the same hoarse voice, head up. I could not bear this new pose. Noble. It was sickening. Falseness had taken hold of him.

"The grieving parents hand in hand."

This time he heard. "That's a terrible thing to say!"

"Yes."

"I don't know what's happening to you, Eva." A stranger asking questions. He took a few steps into the room. "Where do you think you are going?" He kept staring at me with his strange, lax expression.

"If you don't know it will be easier, Newlin. When reporters ask you it is simpler to tell the truth. You have no reason to want to reach me."

"But the plan, Eva. What's the plan?" His thick lids opened, he glared at me from red eyes.

"I don't know. It's too soon to talk." It was terrible to be having this conversation. By the window was the chair I used to sit on when Newlin spoke over the radio, while Kenny slept. I said, "It's easier if I just finish my packing."

But he stepped further into the room. He no longer looked lost or unsure. He was furious. "You'll put yourself right out of my life, Eva, if you're not careful. You refuse to comfort me, to take part in 'Healing Grace'—just when I most need support. What are you doing living over there with Flora? You're *impossible*." He flung around at me. "Even your face has changed!"

"Leave my face out of it!" I shouted, maddened now.

As I heard the sound of my own voice, my anger fled. I stood shaking. The boy was gone. No matter how. Or if that was what broke my heart, I must somehow live it out. I could not focus on Newlin. My grief was my own. And so was his, in his way. He had this "healing" to save him. I had sorrow, and sorrow would bring weeping. And for that little boy I had nothing but tears.

It was a relief to be driving through a placid landscape. I was observing, far less rigid. And even rolled down the window and started breathing in the incredibly fresh air.

We turned down a dirt road. A few bends and I saw blue water ahead. David went in a driveway, motioned me to stop. I was in front of a small shingled house with big blue hydrangeas blooming by the door.

David walked over from the Jeep. "I'll take your stuff in." He looked at me but did not smile. His manner was neutral and a relief.

Shallow wooden steps, a small open porch. "You'll like the house," David said. "Joyce wants you to come over whenever you're ready. It's just across the road." He was holding my two bags; for the first time he smiled. "Hey! you didn't bring your fiddle."

"It's in the trunk," I told him, and went into the house. The living room was small with a fireplace and a sofa alongside. There were comfortable chairs, and a pleasant dining area. The kitchen was more elaborately appointed than the one on India Street. I followed David up the steep stairs to the second story. There was a long bedroom with deep eaves, a window at each end. I saw water again.

"It's all lovely," I said, turning toward him.

"Good." He put his hand briefly on my shoulder, not looking at me. Then he ran down the stairs. I walked quickly to an end window and looked out. I could see the town, the brown curving shore.

As I watched, a gull hovered in the blue air, and let drop a shell on the stones below, cracking it open.

I walked across the road through a small grove of strangely twisted pines to the main house, gray shingled, a modest size. Stone steps led to a rounded grass terrace edged by a vast stretch of water; in the distance I could see a narrow spit of sand. Far to the left was the town; to the right a headland and waterway. I could not ever remember being so conscious of the sky.

Joyce called to come in. She was sitting on a sofa with one foot propped on a chair. "I've broken a toe. Isn't it silly? I'm sorry not to meet your boat."

I walked toward her, bent and kissed her cheek. I saw the gold hair, the faintly tanned skin, the huge, gray eyes. Her beauty no longer gave that sinking feeling of inadequacy.

The room was dominated by big windows and a large fireplace. Joyce, most fortunately, had let the room alone. It was attractive and simple, with rattan furniture, a rocker, and a small sofa.

"David says you brought your violin."

"Yes. But I promise only to play when you're out. You don't seem to have many neighbors."

"You won't disturb anyone."

Joyce never had any real understanding of people. She was curious. She knew her own feelings without being able to define them. She insisted she was the realist and I the romantic. In her book she had trouble with the many-sided, sly, Sir Francis Bacon, but no trouble at all with Queen Elizabeth. Now I expected detached kindness from her and that would be enough.

Every time I saw David I hoped to become more reconciled to the change in him. Physically, he seemed enlarged, having filled out. Also he had new lines by his mouth and across his forehead. He might have been in his forties, although actually he was not yet thirty. A very contained manner; a kindly spectator. For so long I had put thoughts of David away from me. Now I did not know quite how to live with them. I was acutely aware that the hand that pressed my shoulder a few moments ago was Kenny's father's hand...

In an instant I turned, walked out the door, and stood on the bank above the water. No tears. I felt a tearing sensation. Seven years of denying. Now the realization was here. I mean, *with me*. Yes, part of me, of Kenny. I had thought of David's grief, and then put it aside. But now it was to be faced, calmly, *freely*. I suddenly realized this and my heart lightened. I breathed in. Freely, I thought again, with the first sense of hope.

I was only gone a few moments and when I went inside the house David was standing by the fireplace. I smiled, and the tenseness went out of his face.

"How bad is your foot, Joyce?" I moved toward her, picking up my drink. There was a detachment about both David and Joyce that made being with them easy. My sudden departure a moment ago had not affected them. Joyce said her foot was really not painful, but she could not walk far.

"Don't waste sympathy, Eva," David said. "Joyce has a show coming off at the library. They're exhibiting chapters of her book and giving a tea."

"Fame!"

Joyce smiled. "I'm pleased because the library has never done anything like this for an author, and we have plenty of writers on the island."

"But Joyce, isn't the copy in very messy shape?" I sat down in the rocking chair and sipped my drink. The feeling came over me that this was the first time I had really sat down in weeks. I was actually conscious of the chair itself and of resting.

"The copy is all right," Joyce said casually. Then with more attention, "Wouldn't you like to have dinner by yourself tonight, Eva? You must be tired. Moira, the cook, can bring it over to you."

"Yes," I said, "that's exactly what I'd like."

The next morning I looked down on the same, strange, smooth

bed. Again my arms were stiff. I heard geese honking and ran to the end window as seven big-winged birds flew over the water.

David was having breakfast. Joyce, he told me was working. Moira, tall, rather stiff-faced, hiding a warm heart, for she was kind last night, took my order for an egg and toast, coffee.

David was in dark blue bathing trunks, with some kind of undershirt for a top. "Would you like to walk up the beach?"

"Yes. I'd like that." We must talk sometime.

I had on a linen skirt, long-sleeved waist, and sneakers. David made no particular effort to talk and we walked easily. When I lived with Flora she, too, often was blissfully quiet.

"We can walk to Polpis Harbor. You can swim, if you like."

"Tomorrow, maybe."

The tide was out; we walked over rocks. From the bank a horse looked down at us. "There should be Ruddy Turnstones and a few Black-Bellied Plovers and Curlews," David said. He had always known birds. We walked slowly. It was the first exercise I'd had in a long while. And although I did not really take in the scene, yet I was conscious of the wind and the waves. David pointed out two Plovers. He led the way further back on the beach to the foot of a dune.

"Sit down, Eva. Let's talk."

"Yes," I said. He sat with his arms clasped around his knees. "I don't want to take you through all of it," he said. Then: "Did he die instantly?"

"Yes. I'm sure of it. The doctor at the hospital told me." I waited. Then I cried in full voice—"*I never saw the body...*" The words tore out of me.

David gripped my hand. His hand was firm, gritty. I held onto it, then haltingly: "I bought a plot of ground at Oak Hill Cemetery and I made a will to be buried there, too. I didn't want him with Mama and Papa, and I didn't think you would, either."

"No, I wouldn't." He dropped my hand. Neither of us spoke. David watched the Plovers. Then turned to me.

"He seemed a happy boy."

"Yes, he was, in his own way. All this business about Newlin made a big impression. Kenny believed absolutely that Newlin was a healer. It was all far too much for a boy of his age. He was too excited."

"He was seven, going on eight," David said, not looking at me.

"I thought Kenny must get away. Flora and I were looking up schools. Someplace in the west where he could have a horse. You see, Newlin was making money. It came through the mails, just as Mr. Framely said in his office that day. So I didn't have to worry. Kenny would have liked riding, I know he would." The picture of Kenny on a horse broke through to me. I moved forward, spread out on the sand, my head in my arms. I simply could not talk about my darling son, not this way. I raised my head. David's face was strangely blotched. He was looking out over the water.

"Go on," he said, "I want to know, Eva."

I sat up. "I cry like this but I don't think it means anything."

"No. Go on."

"Well, you see, there was this terrible split in the house, in our lives. And Kenny felt it. He accused me of not believing in his father. And this upset him terribly. He sensed that Newly and I were divided, and he was frightened. For of course I didn't believe in Newlin's 'powers.' I thought what he was doing dreadful, and wrong. And I thought Kenny being with Newlin all the time was a great mistake. But I was helpless because Newlin wanted Kenny there. I'm telling you this to try and explain to you why Kenny was at St. Mark's—that night."

David didn't speak.

I said: "I stood out against Newlin. I told him how dangerous and wrong I felt he was and that he was hypnotizing people. He became very angry. He took to sleeping downstairs. We soon had no relationship. Then there was all the publicity which was so awful— and the crowds. Kenny became frightfully excited. I felt that if I could just get him through whatever happened at St. Mark's, then I could get him away. Because even Newlin realized how bad the excitement was for the boy. I couldn't go up to Sedgwick Avenue, people would recognize and point at me. It was so dreadful."

David was pouring sand from one hand to the other. I could not look at him. It was all I could do to keep talking. And yet I felt he must know the exact situation, that he must know everything so he completely understood not only what had happened but why.

"Mama and Papa told this reporter, Cranby, everything. He was the man you knocked down in the kitchen."

"I remember him."

"Cranby wanted to find out about me and about you. Of course he's trying to get back at you. He even talked to Fanny. He makes snide innuendos. And it's awful."

"Don't bother about it, Eva. I don't care. Joyce thinks it's amusing."

This shocked me. "It's not at all amusing."

"No, it isn't." He looked clearly at me.

We sat not speaking. A Black-backed gull waddled nearby and flew into the air. I said again, because I repeated it so much to myself: "I suppose I should have just taken Kenny away someplace. But he was a willful child. He wanted to be with his father." And then suddenly the constant repetition of this was too much for me and I heard myself cry out, "The child is dead! My Kenny is dead!" and I flung myself forward on the sand.

I don't know how much longer I wept. David kept his hand on my shoulder. At last I sat up, then rose, went to the water, and bathed my face. I stood in front of David. His face was drawn with heavy lines. Whatever he suffered—he spared me, and I was grateful to him.

I said: "Newlin was devoted to Kenny. I want you to be sure of that. We had...we had a good marriage. If it hadn't been for Newlin's healing ideas Kenny would have had a good life. I mean Newlin and I would have been truly loving parents."

"Yes, I'm sure of it." David's eyes were very clear and wide and terribly sad.

I didn't know how to speak to him. "This is so hard on you, David." I sat down.

He looked away. "It's better in some ways now you're here. We can speak of it."

"Yes. It's awful not being able to talk. I haven't been able to talk to anyone but Flora. And somehow that didn't seem fair. She felt so broken by it all."

David said, "But you had Newlin."

"No, David. You have not understood. We had no communication at all. He really turned from me, once he knew I didn't believe in him. See, he made our house his office. He moved in files and desks. His mother came over to work and the Rubers and a woman from New York."

"But you had no part in it?"

"No."

"When Kenny died why weren't you and Newlin together?"

"Newlin had all these followers and he wanted all of them to know how he felt. It was a kind of madness. Expiation of guilt. That was when I went to Flora's. And then I cleared out the whole house."

"You cleared out the house?" He was sitting again with his hands clasped tightly around his knees.

"Yes."

"But he let you go?" David seemed miles away. He kept staring at me."

"I couldn't stay. What was there to keep me, David? You don't understand. Newlin is now a professional healer. He is going to Atlanta, Houston, someplace in California. It's his life work. How could I be a healer's wife?"

I found to my surprise that I wasn't crying any more. David was looking right at me. And suddenly he gave his sweet smile. "No, I don't think you could," he said. "You've always had a rough tongue."

He got to his feet, held out his hand. "A swim would do you

good. We'll go back to the house."

I swam around near the shore. But David swam far, far out until I could not see his head in the pale blue water.

For the next few days it became routine for David and me to walk on the beach. For some reason my tears had stopped. I do not mean that I never cried, but that awful soundless crying stopped. I tried to tell David everything about Kenny. I admitted we spoiled the boy, but that he no longer spied on people. I told David about my reading program and my effort to educate myself. And then I went even further back to before my marriage and told him about discovering that Mama and Papa were not including me any more in their lives. And suddenly we were at the beginning, at Joyce.

"How do you mean, they didn't include you?"

"I wasn't going to the Adirondacks. As a child I had come with you. Now you were being married."

"But—my God—why didn't you tell me?"

"What would you have done?"

He was silent.

"Yes," I said. And then without a break in my voice I said: "From the night you took me in your arms, to your walk in the snow to Joyce, to your marriage and the Lowndes Silver night where Joyce said you were not having children, to the night in the car by the quarry, to now on this beach—it's all of a piece."

The warmth and consideration had gone out of both of us at my recital. I saw his face go hard and still. For some reason he reminded me of the night we had dinner alone in the DeLancey Place house. That was one of the last times I saw David. A thin, intent anthropologist chewing on a chicken bone and saying he was going to have money some day.

I said quite plainly: "I'd always been going to marry you. And you knew it."

"Yes. I suppose so. But I had to pretend."

"A cold-water third-floor walkup would not have suited."

He said nothing. Then got to his feet, walked to the water's edge. A big man and strange against the scene. Maybe this was the way he kept to himself, never quite fitting in, always keeping something back. Perhaps the background belonged too much to the Framelys. Now he turned and stood above me.

"I wish he had lived," he said.

There it was.

I got to my feet and walked away from him down the shore.

28   A large rock rose from the water near shore with a ledge half way up that made it possible to clamber to the top. There I sat almost every day, surveying the harbor. The departure of the steamer, white as a swan, sitting high in the water, far off. A yawl sailing majestically into port. At the base of the rock, smooth sand lay in a hollow of wonderfully clear water. As I had first begun to breathe the air of the island, so now I took in my surroundings.

That first week I was left much alone. Joyce had started another book and was being secretive about it, not realizing or perhaps not caring that I had neither the will nor the mind to work with her. Although we had for years managed a wary friendship, now David's presence stood between us in a way difficult to describe. I think she felt it more than I did because, although it had been a relief to confide in David, yet it wasn't like sharing grief, nor did I particularly feel or want or could bear his sympathy. His manner was remote. He played golf or tennis every day. His attitude toward Joyce was wary, respectful, friendly. I would not have said affectionate. There was about their relationship a kind of ultra-civility, as though they were self-conscious with each other, as though they added up points. I had never thought of Joyce as particularly mature; now she was worldly instead. They were asked out to dinner often, and they also entertained. I excused myself from their parties. David said quite positively who they were to invite. He was a Severn, he seemed to be telling Joyce. I wondered at what point he cultivated this attitude. Not that their guests were necessarily "socially acceptable," as Mama would say, but they must have an interesting profession or be unusual in themselves. David was a spectator, liking to be amused, except in business and sports in which he participated with great seriousness. Apparently, he no longer went up-country as frequently and evidently was active in Mr. Framely's New York office.

One night at dinner Joyce was talking about *Babbit*, telling David he ought to read it. "Sinclair Lewis won the Nobel Prize," she said.

"I hardly ever read fiction," David said.

Joyce turned to me. "I'm sure he hasn't read my book."

David broke off a claw of the lobster he was eating with a loud snap. "Of course I've read it."

Joyce's gray gaze fastened on him. "But you never said anything!"

"You never asked."

David then changed the subject and suggested we go to see *All Quiet on the Western Front*, which was playing at the local movie. It was a surprising incident and typical. Neither of them seemed upset. How strange that Joyce did not question him about her book. Didn't she care what he thought? Was he casual because he saw how little his opinion meant to her?

There seldom was talk about politics, which bored Joyce. David said the French had started building the Maginot line, but Joyce changed the subject. When David mentioned the migrant farmers and the conditions in the Dust Bowl, Joyce sulked. David read the stock market reports and told me privately that Mr. Framely had lost heavily in the crash. Nantucket might be suffering from the Depression, but in the life we led I saw no sign of it.

Joyce attended meticulously to my needs, making sure I had a large towel for the beach, sweaters, and a rain coat. I knew she would be utterly unable to imagine my state of mind, and I said nothing to her. I led a simple, healing life. I walked the beach, or occasionally took the jeep and explored the island. In the afternoon I lay in a chair at the rear of my little house reading mysteries. Somehow I did not feel in the mood for my violin and left it in the case.

The life I lived was strangely isolated, but I do not think I could have stood seeing people, or anyone's touching me, or making demands. I knew David watched me, but in kindness.

I no longer slept in that awful, still way with my arms wrapped around myself. Now the bedclothes were tossed wildly. I dreamed of people, a crowd standing looking at me. I was in the churchyard outside St. Mark's. There was the gravel road. Ambulances raced along streets. I would wake with a scream. These terrible dreams lasted four nights. I was afraid I would break down. There were days when my depression was so severe I could only live hour by hour. Then, miraculously, the dreams changed, the worst of my depression lifted.

David realized something of my distress for he made a point of going with me during the worst days, walking beside me along the beach. He said little, but pointed out birds, or showed me a place where Terns nested. He would walk to my usual place near the dunes and then go off, swim the inlet and disappear around the point. In this way we seemed to divide sorrow and in some way share the grief.

Baking sun would press the bitterness out of me. I wore a bathing suit and sneakers most of the day. When I first started my walks by the shore I saw Kenny everywhere. He ran along the sand, raced after a gull, or I saw him standing at the curve of the shore watching me. Slowly I came to see his face again, dark, and with his hair dangling. He had a smile as sweet as David's. Watching him brought the queer, silent tears. Then one day the image disappeared. The shore was the shore; the gulls waddled and swooped. It was about then that my dreams changed and I felt I would not lose my mind or break down. Grief became a lump that shifted from my chest to my throat to my stomach. I was learning to accept, to know I would live.

During this time I hardly ever thought of Newlin. I deliberately put out of mind scenes when the three of us were together; the winter walks when we would visit the great scarred tulip poplar and Kenny said, "Just like Mr. Toro." But Newlin, who had raced me along the Schuylkill, and slept with me night after night with such pleasure—what had happened to him? I still could be drawn rigid by the memory of our sex and the way Newly entered me. Our sex was enough to drive me back to him. How could all that simply disappear? And then I'd remember how he slept on the couch, the icy feel of my nightgown slipping over my back that last night I had gone to him, the stairs under my bare feet as I climbed to bed. Does one survive losing a son and a husband at once? And then I asked myself what there was to miss in The Master? He had made a deliberate choice, and the choice had nothing to do with the person I was or the life I wanted. We had not shared our grief, and this was terrible. I had never felt his arms holding me tightly to him, comforting me for the child I had borne, for the child we had idolized. Instead Newlin exhibited his grief, spoke of what he called "his loss" in public. We had been so estranged that even on the night Kenny was killed Newlin slept downstairs on the couch. I did not want to remember the hot August days when I cleared out the house, as though I broke up our life with every step. Newlin was so busy expanding "Healing Grace" that he had not even realized I was emptying the house.

David occasionally showed me an article in the paper about Newlin. The big meeting in California had been a failure. Newlin had not "cured" a paralytic. Dan Ruber was quoted as saying The Master's recent "loss" had taken its toll. And also that the forced absence of The Master's wife left him comfortless. She was returning shortly, Dan Ruber said.

Flora forwarded a letter from Newlin. Even his handwriting had enlarged and slanted authoritatively.

September 6, 1930<br>Pacific Grove

My dearest wife:

I have just come from a terrible experience, a humiliation which I know you would not want me to endure. Since our boy died I have felt a certain withdrawal of my powers. This, I suppose, is to be expected. He was so much with me, and I see that I relied on his complete belief in me more than I realized. It was an inspiration to me. And now I lack this inspiration. I write to tell you that as my wife I believe it is your duty to be with me. I know then my powers will again be strong. This power is greater than either of us. Therefore, whatever differences existed between us must be put aside. They do not matter, not in view of this greater gift that is mine. I need you. Your place is here. You cannot deny the closeness we have felt. And now particularly when our darling boy is gone...do not wreck our lives—and his memory.

I send you all my love,

Newlin

My answer was brief and tough. "Don't expect me to believe all that twaddle about my duty. I have no duty to you." I told him not to write, his letters would not be forwarded. And I sent Flora my letter to post.

In spite of my revulsion I told David about the letter. It was on a morning walk. A wind blew, and the tide was really too high for walking. We finally stopped and sat down.

"He's got something on his side, Eva," David said.

"What?"

"He's made a new life for himself, a very successful one. And he's not an insensitive man."

"No."

"Why shouldn't he try and get you back?"

"But the letter was so snide. It made me remember all the bitterness. I know I shouldn't blame him. But how can I help it?"

"If you blame him you'll never accept what happened."

"I've been afraid of going mad."

"Yes, I'm sure. But the trouble with you is you don't reach out. I never know what you think. I never know whether to move in or stay off. You've been like that all your life."

"You were not an easy person to confide in."

David went right on: "The point is that if you allow yourself to blame Newlin you will also sour the memory of the child. It would be like a blight." David had a clam shell in his hand and dug a hole, round and round. What he said was true. I had thought it myself. But how do you arrange memory? Or stop speculation? For instance, I could be wrung with regret because I had not removed Kenny, simply got him away so he never went near St. Mark's. I could accuse myself and try and live with the bitterness. No, terrible as the scene was, there must also be tenderness around it. So that one saw a small, agitated boy...and an accident no one could have foretold, nor place blame for. Then the child was at peace. And so— in whatever manner it could be arranged—must we be. Strangely, David and I.

"Yes," I said, "I know you're right."

David laid aside the shell, started pushing sand into the hole.

"Can you think what you're going to do?"

"Not much."

"Well, do you want to talk about it?"

"Yes, no, both..."

"Do you want to live in Philadelphia?"

"No, I don't think so. What would I do? After all this publicity. I'd be in a goldfish bowl. As to that, I'll change my name. I'm going back to Eva Colby."

"That's a start." He was patting the sand.

"Eric Harley, Joyce's editor at Ross and Exeter, said he might have some freelance editing for me. But I never heard from him..." The wind was whipping in, blowing seaweed. I looked at the side of David's withdrawn face. "I thought of asking him for a job, maybe as a reader."

"You wouldn't make enough to live on." David had always been matter-of-fact.

"I will be getting money from Newlin."

"Women don't go very far in the publishing business."

I suddenly remembered Eric Harley's mad plunge into the pond that day of the picnic. "I think Eric Harley might give me a job. I did first-rate work on Joyce's book. I feel pretty confident about it. I think Eric read some of Joyce's chapters before she and I had worked on them. Not many, but enough to see the difference."

David said, "Have you been to New York much?"

"No."

"Do you have friends there?"

"No. The first violin and the violist in Flora Cruikshank's quartet live in New York."

David was silent. "I'm over there quite a lot. We've opened a new office."

"I don't want to depend on you, David."

He said nothing, staring out at the water, now dotted with white caps.

I was pleased at my toughness. So much of my life had been pretense and now I was surprised at my readiness. God knows, I had lived for years with the undermining conviction that I had been abandoned. A train wreck had made me an orphan. I had lived through an unloved and neglected childhood; danced my way through a relentlessly cruel social scene; I had loved and been rejected; I had married and had my husband turn into a kind of freak. My child had been killed...I survived. There was a lot to be said for survival.

Fog was coming in, blotting out the far shore. I heard myself say, "You know, I've never really formed a relationship."

"Come on, Eva! What about me?"

"That's what I mean. You always had this brother-sister dream that you clung to. You made me your sister every day. All fresh. To protect you."

"I suppose I did."

"And when the break came—because I saw you suddenly as a man and you realized how I saw you, then all those defenses broke down. What you hadn't counted on and refused to consider was that my childish adoration of you had changed. And it formed a split which you couldn't manage."

Silence. He continued pouring sand. A Ruddy Turnstone flew in, all dazzling black and white. "I fled from it, I guess," he said.

"Yes. Even more than a cold-water flat. Which I doubt you ever considered."

"No." He turned to look at me. "Don't leave out ambition."

"Life on a platter?"

His mouth tightened. He flashed another hard look at me.

"I work for it."

I got to my feet, standing in wet seaweed. It was cold and I didn't want to sit with him any more. David had once saved me. But now he was at a loss. He might even doubt I could live in New York.

I said to him: "I've been a face all my life, David."

"You shouldn't be."

"That's what bothers you. You can't see me making my way."

He stood up. "I know how tough New York is."

There was a quality in his attitude that brought back Mama and Papa and, for some reason, that night in David's room when I had clung to the bureau and told him I couldn't come out, that I couldn't. He had been just as coolly aware then. Of course I was to do the accepted thing. I was his "sister." Mama and Papa expected me to make my debut even though Ida Shanker had killed herself.

"You know something, David? I'm going to wear my hair slicked back and plenty of lipstick. I'll just let my face *be* there. I'll either make out or I won't. But I'm sick of thinking how I look all the time."

"Try it," he said. "See how it works."

He walked up on the beach; I did not stop to see him go.

Saturday the Nantucket Atheneum Library was exhibiting Joyce's manuscript. She had said little about it, although I had again asked her if there were enough pages not too marked up, and she had said yes. I failed to understand why Joyce was excited about this little party, but she put on a pale blue dress, warm for the day, but handsome, setting off her great eyes, the coiled, yellow hair. Her broken toe miraculously was cured. I was eager to see which pages she had chosen of the manuscript because nearly all of them had comments, particularly the one where I said, "Should I read on?" Either Joyce or I crossed out paragraphs, sometimes whole pages. "Put this at 'A'" was a favorite. Perhaps all the comments would be fascinating to other writers. There were quite a few on the island, Joyce said. I was pleased that she chose to exhibit the work and wished that Eric Harley could see the manuscript.

The day of the exhibit Joyce went to town early; David and I followed in the jeep. We drove along, if not in companionable silence, at least in acquiescence. I understood him as well as anyone would ever understand David. His stoicism did not shut me out. We could never say "our son"; that was unthinkable. Each must stand alone. Yet David had fathered a son whom he could never recognize and now could never claim. This must be a bitter realization. It seemed as though Kenny's death would in some way affect David's marriage. For although he had supposedly given in to Joyce about having no children, yet when I faced him on the stairs of Horn and Hardart he had not questioned me but only asked "Where?" He had indeed wanted to father a child; it was a passionate need. And he trusted me.

There was no possible way I could speak of this to David. He had locked himself in with it. Though my own grief had been so overwhelming, yet he knew he shared it. For it had been to him I cried out. In those hours on the beach, although physically so distant, we had been brought together by grief. That was done, now. One did not retrace such steps. I think in many ways knowing David's suffering, watching his stoicism, was a help to me, pulling me upright.

Now in the jeep we turned out of the Polpis Road toward town. "This is a good time for you to practice calling me Eva Colby," I said, as we parked the jeep.

"You're quite right," David said. We started toward the library. "There are bound to be reporters. Mrs. Colby will mean nothing to them. Newlin has been in the news again. He seems to have got his 'powers' back." As we sarted up the steps of the library David introduced me to two women. Eva Colby came easily to him. The women showed nothing except vague interest.

The manuscript was being exhibited in a long, glass case at the end of a large room. Quite a crowd had gathered; tea was being served. People walked up to the case, moving slowly down it. Joyce stood at one side talking to a group of women. I went straight to the case, stood looking down. I stared at the copy. Chapter I. Not a mark on the page. I moved to the next chapter, then to another page. The copy was beautifully typed, the pages completely unmarked. One after another of these fair pages stared up at me. Joyce was exhibiting a carbon copy of the manuscript after it had been corrected, retyped, and sent to the publishers. I remembered asking her once to let me keep a chapter we had marked up because the changes were so interesting. But she always insisted she needed the pages.

I turned from the case and walked out of the building. David was sitting on the steps. He looked up as I sat beside him. "I didn't know whether to tell you or not."

"It's typical," I said. I did not care what I said. "She means no one to see my work. It's unbelievable. She wants the whole book to appear automatically perfect. Any writer looking at those pages will realize they are far from being work sheets. She knew I expected the exhibition to show the changes; she and I discussed it. It would be bad enough to see those unmarked pages at any time but right now it's unbearable."

"Eva, this whole thing was planned months ago."

"So what? She's probably destroyed the entire work copy."

"Probably."

"Let's get away from here," I said, rising. As we walked down the steps I spoke again. "Will you do me a favor, David? I think I'll leave by the early boat tomorrow. I was going in a few days, anyway. Can you get me a reservation? I'd like to pick it up on our way out of town."

David made no comment. He simply swung by the steamship office, disappeared, and came back with a ticket. We didn't speak on the ride back to the cottage. He dropped me off and then went on around the drive.

Before packing I thought I'd like one more walk and I'd swim across the inlet. I changed into my suit, brought cigarettes (I now smoked constantly), and walked across the road. David was in his bathing suit, waiting on the lawn. He smiled. "You always were a classy shape, even though you never knew it!"

"I know it now," I said. Suddenly I realized I was leaving. And that I was wonderfully relieved to be going. Joyce and I were through. The sharing I did with David was over. Neither he nor I wanted to dwell on it.

We walked down the beach and along the shore.

"In spite of everything, it's done you good, Eva," David looked across the harbor.

"Yes," I said. There was so much to throw away, to force myself to get rid of. I thought of those days when in imagination, fantasy, Kenny ran ahead of me on the beach. I said: "What can you bear and how much do you need and must remember? I am closer to knowing. And that is progress."

David stopped walking, turned, held out his hand. We had a quick handclasp. Unexpectedly, he leaned down and lightly kissed me on the cheek.

When we got back to the house Joyce was waiting at the door. She said in a rather tight voice: "I understand you're leaving tomorrow." How did she know?

I went right to her. "That was quite a show you put on at the library. I didn't recognize the manuscript."

"There wasn't anything left of the pages you and I worked on, Eva. They'd all been destroyed." She regarded me calmly. "If you keep too many copies around it becomes confusing."

"No record, then?"

"I suppose not."

What was there to say worth saying? Hadn't I always known Joyce had no moral sense? It was as simple as that.

She said, "Before you go I'd like to show you my work room, Eva. You've never seen it."

There seemed no easy way to refuse. I followed her into the house and up the stairs. We stood on the upper landing, looking out a bank of windows. Below was Polpis Harbor. In plain sight the dune where I sat and the spot where David and I had recently stopped. Had she brought me here to show me?

"Surely you're not disturbed by a brotherly kiss on the cheek?"

"Or those long, long talks by the dunes?" she said. "I've known about your relationship with David from the beginning, Eva. I've realized how you felt."

"Then you know more than I do," I said, and gave quite a brassy laugh. "It's a fine view, Joyce—and I wish you joy of it." She hadn't walked over me. Not this time. Let her think what she pleased.

As I went down the stairs her voice came clearly to me. "I don't think David is really interested in sex, do you? Of course I've had lovers. After all, David was away all the time. And we've never hit it off sexually."

"You could have spared me the details, Joyce." I faced her on the landing. "You've always been a bitch."

I felt dirtied and in some way stripped. And then suddenly knew she was lying. She had to tell me, make it up. Did she think she was getting even? Nothing could do that. And it would never occur to her that I minded her destruction of my work on the manuscript far more than any lie she could possibly invent.

I did not say goodbye or thank her. I walked over to the guest house and started packing.

The cormorants were on two posts this time as the steamer passed; gulls swooped and called. A tall, elderly man with a white moustache got up slowly from his deck chair. He addressed me. "Come throw a penny into the water at Brant's Point," he said. He wore a pince-nez and a Panama hat.

"Oh?" I said. "Should I?"

"Throw a penny in so you'll be sure and return to the island," he said, tipping a little as the steamer rounded the point.

"But I'm not going back," I said, and smiled up at him.

# Coda

*Mr. and Mrs. Frederick Severn are stepping out of the Carafa onto the dock at The Landing. They are now quite feeble and must be helped from the boat by Fanny and Mrs. Mertz, also Gordon and Robert. It is a fine clear day with little gusts of wind occasionally ruffling the lake. Although neither mentions it, they both wonder if another summer will see them in their beloved camp. The motor trip from Philadelphia and back seems longer and more tiring each year. The beautiful white tent, made especially for them by Abercrombie and Fitch, can no longer be used; they feel the cold and damp severely and now sleep in the bedrooms once occupied by Mr. Jaffrey and Eva. There have been no recitals in the barn for at least two years. Anna misses Mr. Jaffrey, although Papa is profoundly grateful there are no more Epics. He is still blissfully engaged with his Indians, outlining Volume V, which will take in the War of 1812.*

*Gordon, Mrs. Mertz, and Fanny, who wears a rather squashed, dark blue hat with a ragged feather but seems quite cheerful and much as usual, disappear with the luggage and to fetch the car. Gordon returns and hands Frederick the mail. There is only one letter to Anna and it is from Eva. "I'll just skim through it," Anna says. "She's still working." This is said as though pointing out a defect.*

*"Ross and Exeter," Frederick says.*

*"She's had a raise of some kind and is working with an author I never heard of. She's moved!" Here Anna speaks with more interest. "She has an*

*apartment she calls a 'walk-up' on East 48th Street. Oh, really...."*

"*East 48th Street is Turtle Bay. Rather a good section,*" Frederick *says.*

"*But imagine, no doorman! I wonder David doesn't speak to her.*"

"*I doubt David has much to do with it. His last letter said he hadn't seen her for two months.*"

"*I think Eva bores him.*" Anna *folds the letter.* "*And since she's taken to wearing her hair pulled back! . . . When she came to see us in that purple coat I felt she was close to being conspicuous.*"

*They stand in silence. Which is often the case. Frederick will not be drawn into an argument with her. Mention of David brings the boy into mind and he thinks again how extraordinarily life has worked out. For although David and Joyce have separated, David still works for Mr. Framely. It may be because David realized his grandfather did not like Joyce that a new relationship has formed between them. A great pleasure to Frederick. Although the boy lives in New York, he comes to see his grandfather at least once a month. Often David takes Frederick to lunch at a restaurant, a great treat! Occasionally Frederick insists they eat at the Philadelphia Club, where he introduces his grandson with great pride.*

*It was last winter as they were walking across Rittenhouse Square that David told Frederick about the boy Kenny being his son.*

*Frederick was deeply moved and for an instant must sit down on a bench and actually wipe tears from his eyes, dreadful though it was to be seen crying in Rittenhouse Square. Finally control was established and Frederick said, surprising himself,* "*Really, in a way, David, I suppose I've known it all along. Or if not actually about the boy, that some bond—an extraordinary one—existed between you and Eva.*"

"*Perhaps you have, Papa.*" David *had removed his hat. The new moustache made David very handsome, Frederick thought. Looking at him Frederick realized what tragedy the poor boy had been through!*

"*I should think Eva would be a comfort to you, David. I'm surprised you don't see her more often.*"

"*No.*" David *turned his hat in his hands. He appeared to be looking at the snow which lay in patches on the scrubby grass.* "*Eva is anxious to make her own way. She's got in with a group of musicians whom I don't know.*

*And as for what happened. . . there is something untouchable about it. I mean one does not touch it."*

*"I quite understand you, my boy. And I admire Eva. I thought she seemed very distinguished the last time I saw her."*

*"She'll be pleased. I'll tell her." David got to his feet. "You mustn't get cold, Papa. I'm sorry I upset you."*

*"No, no, dear boy. I am honored by your confidence, which of course I shall never divulge to anyone, as you know." Slowly he rises to his feet. He is still distinguished-looking, his beard once more quite long. Apparently he now speaks to himself, for he shakes his head and says, "On the same floor. . . I never could get Anna to listen. . ."*

*They walk across the Square silently, arm in arm.*